I hate mirrors.

Glass is dangerous.

Water is dangerous.

Anything

that reflects

me

back at myself

is a threat.

Books by Melissa de la Cruz
available from Harlequin TEEN and Inkyard Press

Something in Between
Someone to Love
29 Dates

someone to love

#1 *NEW YORK TIMES* BESTSELLING AUTHOR

Melissa de la Cruz

HARLEQUIN®TEEN

Recycling programs
for this product may
not exist in your area.

ISBN-13: 978-1-335-13974-0

Someone to Love

Printed in U.S.A.

someone
to love

part one

I never paint dreams or nightmares.

I paint my own reality.

—FRIDA KAHLO

one

"It's not that I'm rebelling. It's that I'm just

trying to find another way."

—EDIE SEDGWICK

The stall door won't shut all the way.

What the hell kind of bathroom does our school have?

The kind with crooked doors that don't always latch. The kind you don't want to get caught in. Not with your head above the toilet. Not when you're kneeling on the floor, puking your guts out. Not with a fifth of vodka—which I desperately need right now.

Shouldn't the stalls all lock?

Doesn't matter anyway. I'm done.

I wipe my mouth and take a stick of gum from my purse and unwrap the shiny paper. It makes me think of Andy Warhol's famous art factory, all wrapped in silvery aluminum foil and pulsing with artists and conversation. I can see Edie Sedgwick's haunting face. Her platinum pixie. Smoky circles around her eyes. Dangling earrings. That megawatt smile. She may have been one of Andy Warhol's superstars—those grimy, glamorous muses—but Edie was his angel too. An angel wearing a leotard and fur coat, hiding in the backs of limousines and dingy clubs. Skinny as hell.

I'd rather be in New York. Studying art. Living in my own art factory. Get out of this sunshiny, swimming pool state. I crumple the paper into a ball, toss it into the wastebasket near the door and head for the sinks. I turn on the faucet. Pump soap onto my hands. *Scrub. Scrub. Stare at the water slipping down the drain. Don't look up.*

I hate mirrors. Glass is dangerous. Water is dangerous. Windows are dangerous. Anything that reflects myself back at me is a threat. A punishment.

Welcome to my Monday morning. It's Eastlake Prep's yearbook photo day. Yeah. *That* Eastlake Prep—the one with the five-figure tuition and super-fancy alumni. Famous people have gone here, and famous people send their kids here.

It's the end of September—we're already a month into school—but I can't seem to get into the swing of school. And I also can't show up at photo day with frizzy hair and a pimple on my chin. As much as I hate taking them, I know the power of a class photo. Thirty years from now, when everyone has moved away and no one is following each other on social media anymore, people are going to pull out their yearbook and look at you. That's what you'll be to them forever.

Do you want to be the girl with the greasy forehead? Or the bad bangs?

No. I didn't think so.

The spotless surface reflects my double. I smooth my hands over my long dirty-blond hair and examine my skin, slightly jaundiced under the bathroom's unflattering fluorescent light. The problem with mirrors is that they show me only what's already there. It's I who has to see the potential, who has to see how much more there is to lose. How much smaller I can be. How much closer to perfection.

Speaking of perfection: Zach Park.

He's gorgeous. Thick dark hair tousled like he's been lounging on the beach all day. Wide green eyes with teardrop curves that seriously make me want to stop everything and get lost in them for an eternity. I've had a low-key crush on him since the end of freshman year when he transferred here from a Korean private school.

I had only one class with him—the last semester of first-year English—but I doubt he remembers me. I mostly drew pictures of other people in the class on my notes to avoid looking at him too much, even though I was always listening to him. He was so well-spoken and mature. So *different* from the other teenage boys who seemed to be interested only in playing video games or whatever party they were planning for the weekend.

Zach actually liked talking about ideas. Whenever the teacher called on him, he would say something insightful that I'd never thought about before, and I loved when he volunteered to act out scenes from the books the class was discussing, because Zach would bring them to life. It was like whatever character he was playing had stepped off the page into the classroom and was standing in front of you.

Not that I ever really talked to him.

Today's the day. *Maybe.*

I just have to pull it together for the camera, in front of all the other junior and senior girls with their immaculate hair and carefully coordinated outfits, in front of Zach and his perfect jawline and forearms. Even *thinking* about all of them staring at me, wondering who the loser is who wandered into their perfect midst, is enough to make me want to skip school and never come back.

I screwed things up enough my freshman year. I was dating this guy—Ollie Barrios—who was a really popular junior basketball player. I'd just lost a lot of weight and he was my first boyfriend. It felt amazing to be noticed. To be wanted—no, *desired*—by someone. I should have seen the red flags though. Ollie was always telling me what I should wear or who should be my friends. He'd even choose my food at restaurants.

I ended up gaining some of the weight back during the first few months of school, and Ollie dumped me. We were leaving from my house to go to the homecoming dance. Ollie stopped me before I could get in the car. "We're not going," he said.

"What do you mean?" I asked, thinking maybe Ollie made other plans.

"That dress makes you look like a stuffed sausage."

"I—I can go change," I stammered.

God. I was so stupid. That would have just been putting lipstick on a pig.

"How much weight have you gained? Ten? Fifteen pounds?"

"I don't know," I said.

My skin was crawling. I wanted to escape my body.

"Don't you keep track? Most girls weigh themselves every day."

"I'll start eating better. Exercising," I pleaded with him.

"Whatever, Liv. You obviously don't care about yourself."

He left me crying on the doorstep.

Ollie spread his version of the story around the entire school. He said our relationship wasn't working out because he was an athlete and I wasn't "disciplined" enough, which was obviously code for eating too much and not exercising enough. Everyone looked at me like I was the biggest loser. But Ollie was right. I was a fat cow. I immediately went on a revenge diet. I started fasting for days at a time, but then I would get so hungry that I'd binge and eat way more than any normal person should—pasta, burritos, ice cream, whatever was available—and feel so guilty about bingeing that I'd puke everything up.

I'll never let myself gain weight again.

I'm a yo-yo girl. What goes down must come back up.

I've been keeping myself from bingeing pretty well the past couple of months, but I still have to purge. I hate the feeling of being full. It makes me nauseous.

I smash the gum between my teeth, partly to cover the acrid

smell, but mostly to give my mouth something to do. *Chomp. Chomp. Chomp.* I try to push away the thoughts. I'm stronger than my hunger. I take a cleansing breath to clear my head.

One.

Food is disgusting. It never made you happy.

I exhale slowly. My breath is my mantra. My focus.

You are not a slave to your hunger.

Two.

I'm finally ready to take on this torturous rite of passage.

I leave the bathroom and am walking around the corner of Decker Hall when a guy staring down at his phone runs into me, nearly knocking me over.

"What the hell?!" I say, then I realize I know him, a smile forming on my lips.

It's Sam. We've been best friends since elementary school.

"Sorry," he says. "I was looking for you… You left class early."

"Obviously." I roll my eyes and make a sarcastic face at him. "I had to prep. Don't wanna turn out wretched in my yearbook photo." I look down at my simple, sleeveless black dress. The color suddenly seems so wrong. "What was I thinking? I look like a vampire. And not even the cool kind."

"Oh please," Sam says, laughing as he puts his arm around my shoulder. "You look great."

"Greatly *appalling*," I say. "Do we have to do this?"

I twist around to look into his deep blue eyes, trying to plead with him to cut class with me, but Sam doesn't cut class. He actually *likes* school. He's really smart—I'm sure he's going to be a genius-level scientist someday—and handsome in that geeky, still-needs-to-fill-out kind of way, but there's no *way* I'm ever going to tell him that.

"Why even bother asking?" Sam says.

"Fine," I say, moving his arm off my shoulder. "You can at

least walk me over to the shark tank. And button your shirt." I don't even wait for him. I start doing it myself.

Just like when we were kids. They don't go anymore, but Sam's parents used to take me sailing with him and his older brother, James, on the weekends. I remember standing on the deck, the boat going full speed, the wind whipping my hair back and forth across my face, feeling weightless and completely free from the prison of my own body. Sam may not be the best at dressing up for yearbook photos, but he seemed so confident on those sailing trips. The way he handled the ropes so deftly, how he steered the boat with ease. I envied him, because Sam was the master of his own destiny on the water.

I miss those days.

"They're yearbook photos. Who cares? We're all just going to stuff them in our closets anyway," Sam says.

"Wrong," I say. "Yearbook photos are like diamonds. They're *forever.*"

"Actually *you're* wrong," he says. "The whole *concept* of a yearbook is obsolete. Everyone blasts their lives on social media now, so what's the motivation to rummage through some old book?"

He takes over buttoning his shirt when I get up to his neck.

"Have you not seen the awful yearbook photos of celebrities on the internet? Just because they're not on social media to start with doesn't mean they won't end up there."

A tie hangs limply from his pocket. "Do you know how to tie that?" I ask.

"I watched a tutorial," Sam says. "It can't be *that* hard."

I laugh.

We must look like a couple, but everyone knows we aren't together. I love Sam. We always sit next to each other in classes because our names are so close. Sam Bailey. Olivia Blakely. He's super smart and will probably do something exceptional someday, like work on a giant particle accelerator. He's also the most loyal guy I know.

He's had a crush on a few girls over the years, but neither of us has been that lucky in love.

"We better get going," I say, continuing on my way. "I want to be early."

I start thinking about Zach. Again.

If only he knew that I exist. And that I'm totally in love with him.

He's always off and on with Cristina Rossi. God. That girl. Model gorgeous. And, since this is Los Angeles, she actually *is* a model. She even appeared half-naked for a Calvin Klein underwear campaign on a billboard next to the Chateau Marmont this summer. They both look like works of art. Ms. Day, my studio art teacher, might call them "aesthetically pleasing." Well-proportioned. Shapely. *Statuesque.*

Sam pulls the tie out of his pocket. He tries to tie it as he walks. It's as defiant as his unruly hair. He can't manage a Windsor knot to save his life.

"How 'bout just ditch the tie?" I say.

"Help me out, Liv. You've known how to tie these since the fourth grade."

Out of the corner of my eye I see a guy with brown, slicked-back hair and a gray suit striding across the quad like he owns the school. Jackson Conti. He's a mass of muscle and has the confidence to match. We sat near each other in biology sophomore year, but I haven't hung out with him outside of school or talked to him much since then. I hear he's planning an event with Zach, who happens to be his best friend, in Marina del Rey on a 148-foot yacht that belongs to Sean Clark, an up-and-coming action movie star.

Did I mention that Zach is also an actor?

He played a minor part in one of Sean's recent movies. Sean's letting him borrow the yacht to throw a killer party for his friends and cast members while Sean's out of town. It's not

15

the actors I'm interested in though—except Zach, of course. I overheard Cristina's best friend, Felicity, whose father is a big art dealer, telling someone that Geoff LeFeber, a major contemporary artist, is supposed to be visiting from New York and might be going to the party. I guess one of the executive producers of the TV show Zach stars on knows him. It seems like a long shot that he'll attend, but anything's possible in Los Angeles. It's a smaller place than people think.

I have to be there. LeFeber's my favorite living artist. He puts together these insane installations that completely alter your perception of reality. I've never been to one in person, but I watched a YouTube video the Museum of Modern Art put out that took you through this massive open room filled with tunnels of tape attached to the beams of the roof and pillars. It looked like you were caught in a giant spider's web from the perspective of the fly. Besides looking otherworldly, the installation was supposed to illustrate the dangerous intoxication of curiosity and wonder. I love how LeFeber can make simple shapes and materials seem dreamlike and surreal. I may be a painter instead of an installation artist, but I'd die to talk to someone like LeFeber.

My parents are well connected, but they're not that interested in art. They've taken me—or have let me take myself—to a lot of museums, but never to gallery openings or lectures where the artist is actually present. There are so many questions I would ask him. How do you come up with your ideas? Did anyone believe in your work when you were young? When did you really know you were an artist?

I'm determined to get an invitation to the party.

A girl can hope.

I glance behind me. Sam has finally managed to finish tying his tie on his own. I'm glad I ran into him before photos. Being around him usually makes me less nervous.

Now that I know Sam looks put together, I have to drum up the courage to see what I can find out about that boat party.

"I'll be right back. There's someone I gotta talk to," I say, leaving him so I can catch up to Jackson.

It's not like people don't know me. Dad's position as the Speaker of the House is high profile, but his job also means that I've spent a lot of time on both coasts and helping out my parents with their projects—mostly Mom's literacy campaign and whatever hot topic Dad happens to be dealing with at the moment—which means less time for making friends in LA.

After the Ollie incident, I've mostly been a loner the past couple of years. It's not like I don't have *any* friends, but I don't put myself out there that much.

"Hey… Jackson," I stutter.

My stomach instantly hurts.

"Olivia." He smiles. Jackson's all teeth and eyebrows. He talks to people like a salesman. Like they'll all be potential clients someday. I'm not interested in him, but he's the one hosting the party so I pretend to flirt. I *have* to be there.

"Is…that a new suit?" I ask. "You look great."

God. I'm an idiot. What a suck-up.

"You do too," he says. "That color is hot on you."

Did he really just say that? I try to stifle a laugh, but this ugly, garbled half chuckle, half groan comes out of my mouth. Who takes *sexy* yearbook photos?

I can feel Sam following behind, so I grab Jackson by the elbow to get away. I haven't told Sam about my plan yet. He would think I'm being stupid. Or shallow.

"Going inside?" I ask, propelling him forward. "I hate school photos but really love our photographer, don't you?"

I don't even know what I'm saying. I do this thing when I get nervous and start talking about anything to avoid an awkward silence.

"She's all right," he says without much enthusiasm. "Made my teeth look big."

"No!" I say to Jackson. "I mean, not too big. Plus, big teeth are in these days. Don't you watch *Silver Lake*?" The *entire* reality cast has giant teeth, like they're a bunch of big-toothed piranhas about to attack the cameras and each other in every scene.

"No..." he says. "Should I?"

"They all have them," I say. "That big teeth thing."

He stops, runs his tongue across his top teeth. "They do?"

I turn around. The hall is filling up. Here comes Sam. And Zach. And Felicity Pace. She's basically a teenage socialite, with her bouncy blond hair, which she swings back and forth as she walks down the hallway, linking arms with Cristina Rossi.

A massive crowd of students begins to descend on us like a horde of gorgeous, perfectly groomed, well-dressed zombies. *No. No. No.* I need to talk to Jackson alone. It's the only way I'm going to get invited to that party. Maybe I'll never have a chance with Zach, but I might still have one with LeFeber. I *have* to talk to him.

I grab his arm again. We head into the photo studio and join the queue.

"So that boat party," I squeak. "The one in Marina del Rey?"

"What about it?" Jackson asks.

"Dad mentioned..."

I don't want to tell him I overheard Felicity. Embarrassing.

"Yeah?" he says. "Aren't he and Sean pals?"

I nod. Ever since Sean Clark campaigned for my dad for the House, they're *tight*. Dad totally went Hollywood.

My family is nearly perfect—at least to the public. There's Mr. and Mrs. Blakely, the charming political power couple, Mason, who turned his life around after rehab and now works in venture capital in Silicon Valley, and Royce, who has already had an article published in the *New York Times* while in college.

Then there's Olivia Blakely.

I'm just trying to survive my junior year of high school.

"That's cool," he says. He seems like he's about to say something else, but he looks over my shoulder. I whip around to see Zach and his entourage walking toward us.

Cristina. Felicity, her best friend. Thin. Tan. Fashionable.

"Do you need us to bring anything Friday?" Felicity asks. "My parents bought a case of St. Germain. It's delicious with champagne."

"You lovely ladies just bring yourselves," Jackson says. "Zach and I will take care of the rest. And don't worry, we'll make sure the girly drinks are there."

My feet feel heavy. My purse feels like it's hiding an entire system of gravity and slings toward the floor. I barely catch it. The girls are laughing at something Zach says.

It's like they're all talking in slow motion.

So charming. So at ease with themselves.

I can't outwardly hate them. They haven't actually done anything mean to me other than to *be*.

But they don't have to weigh every single piece of food they put in their tiny bodies like I do. They don't have to count ounces and measure milliliters. Their brains don't constantly tell them that they're ugly and fat and should give up on their diets because they're never going to meet their goals anyway. They probably drink to have fun with their friends. Not to numb the hunger long enough to fall asleep.

Jackson turns away from me to talk to Zach.

I don't even register on his radar.

There goes my stomach again. It feels full. Gorged. I wish I hadn't eaten at all this morning. I'll be bloated for the pictures.

Then I really start to feel it. The invisibility. The cloak. Like an atmosphere, it surrounds the real me. The fullness is totally noticeable now. My stomach is bursting. My brain burns with shame. I'm fat. Everybody can see how huge I am right now. From my cheeks to my fingers. My waist. My hips. My thighs.

I just want to be perfect. I want to be worth noticing.

Is that too much to ask?

I ate half a grapefruit for breakfast.

I drank two cups of green tea.

Took two pulls of the vodka hidden in my closet.

Just to take off the edge.

I feel every pound I weigh, and every ounce, like my life, is too much. Even though I already threw up at the end of class, I feel like I have to get it all out again. I excuse myself and run back to the bathroom and start heaving in the empty stall.

Something has to come out.

Something. Anything.

two

"Creativity takes courage."

—HENRI MATISSE

"Can anyone figure out the origin of this painting?" Ms. Day asks, fluffing her afro with one hand. Her gold hoop earrings glint under the light of the projector.

My mind wanders from the class, thinking about how the photo I took the last period turned out. The photographer took the picture before I was ready, and I'm almost certain I had a deer-in-the-headlights kind of look, but they only take one shot before they shuffle you off and move on to the next person in line.

"Look at the subject," Ms. Day adds, patiently waiting for the class to respond.

The painting on the screen behind her shows a young woman wearing a pale pink dress being pushed on a swing above an admiring young man. The two figures aren't touching each other, but the artist painted their movements so dynamically that they seem like they're about to leap across the painting to embrace each other. A lush garden surrounds the lovers. Every leaf and flower has been painted with an incredible amount of detail and attention to light and shadow.

A girl at the front—Emma—raises her hand.

"The fashion definitely looks English or French," she says.

Ms. Day nods. She's not giving any hints.

I have her for two classes. AP art history and studio art. She's the only teacher I feel like I can actually talk to honestly about my future goals. Not because I like her subject the most—though that's true—but because she never mentions my parents. Or my brothers. Not that they would have ever dreamed of taking an art class.

"I'd say French," Emma's friend sitting next to her adds. "Even though she's wearing stockings, the way her legs are exposed is too scandalous to be English."

"Forget her legs." Nate, a boy who sits in the back, snickers. "He's looking up her dress. Bet he's totally going to get him some."

"Our very own connoisseur of the romantic arts speaks," Ms. Day says. "Tell us more, Casanova!" The other boys snicker, but Nate's too embarrassed to say anything else. I love how salty she can be with her students. She's my favorite teacher.

Ms. Day turns away from the painting and gives him some serious side-eye. She puts her hands on her hips and sighs. "It *is* French. French Rococo, to be exact. The painting's *official* name is *The Swing*. It was painted right before the Revolution by an artist named Jean-Honore Fragonard. The painting was commissioned by the notorious French libertine Baron de St. Julien as a portrait of his mistress. That's all I'll say for now. What do you think this painting is *about*? What's the context?"

The class is silent again. "History is important to understanding art," Ms. Day continues, asking us for our analysis of the piece before she gives us her interpretation. "But becoming a truly great artist means keeping your soul trained on the future. What will someone hundreds of years from now think or feel when they view your painting? What speaks across time and culture? Think about what truly moves you as a viewer."

Emma raises her hand again. "It's kinda playful."

"That's right." Ms. Day paces across the front of the room. "Many of the painting's critics called it *frivolous*. Why do you think they might have used that word?"

"Well," I say, leaning forward in my seat to see the painting better. "It's not like the subject is an important religious or historical person or event or anything. And the painting's focal point is clearly her pink dress."

"You think there's more to the painting than that…" Ms. Day walks up the aisle and pauses by my desk, gesturing toward the painting. "Don't you, Olivia?"

"She *always* has something to say," Nate groans.

I ignore him. This is pretty much the only class in which I feel in my element.

"That playfulness that Emma mentioned? I think she's right. I also think the painting is about seduction. Except the moment doesn't seem so planned out. It's like their desire is spontaneous." I wonder whether someone will ever feel that way about me. Why do so many things have to come together perfectly for people to fall in love?

"The French would call that *joie de vivre*," Ms. Day adds. "That translates to a cheerful enjoyment of life. An exultation of the spirit. Of the soul. Everything one does becomes filled with joy. Conversation. Work. Play. Eating."

I *wish* I could feel joy when I eat. The only thing I feel is dread.

"Why do you think the painting is about seduction?" Ms. Day asks.

"Besides the fact that the man on the ground is pretty much looking up her dress?" I pause for a moment. The boys in the back laugh. "They know they're being provocative. She's letting her shoe fly off her foot like she's Cinderella. He's her

Prince Charming. They're gazing directly into each other's eyes. Maybe they're in love."

"Or *lust*," Ms. Day says. The class murmurs like they're scandalized.

I trail off, thinking about Zach's eyes and what I might feel if he ever looked back at mine that way. I'd probably melt into a puddle on the floor.

While I've been thinking about Zach, Ms. Day has moved on to analyzing other parts of the painting. "What details do you notice? Look at the background."

The class goes silent. We're stumped.

"See this statue of a cherub on the left?" Ms. Day walks up to the screen and touches the left side of the painting. "Can you see what he's doing?"

"Oh my god," Emma squeals. "I totally see it."

Everybody squints and leans forward. We're still all confused.

"The little cherub? He's holding his index finger in front of his lips. He's trying to keep everything a secret."

Ms. Day smiles and draws circles around the other statues in the garden with her finger. "What about the other sets of cherubs? The ones below the humans looking up?"

A few students respond to her question.

"They look concerned."

"More like afraid for her."

"I think they're scowling."

"Yes. This is obviously an *illicit* love affair," Ms. Day says. "Yet the painter casts off the moral concerns of the day to illustrate a moment of lighthearted pleasure. It *is* frivolous. Free. In fact, the painting's alternate title is *The Happy Accidents of the Swing*."

"They're definitely, like, living life to its fullest or whatever," Emma says.

"YOLO," Nate adds.

"Exactly." Ms. Day laughs. "Homework for tonight is to research…"

I lose myself in my thoughts while she gives us tonight's assignment.

I can barely remember the last time I felt truly *happy* like the woman on the swing. When I was younger, tapping into that feeling of freedom seemed so much easier. I could ride my scooter fast down the street. I could get on a swing and pump my legs until I was soaring high over the playground. What happened to that girl? Did I lose her?

Am I living my best life? Am I even *trying* to?

The bell rings for lunch and all the students start piling out the door. I slowly put my notes and my textbook in my backpack while Ms. Day turns off the projector.

"Olivia," she says. "I wanted to tell you something in studio art this morning, but you were out the door too fast. Do you have time to stick around for a few minutes?"

Of course I have time. It's not like I actually eat lunch anyway.

I have only one rule about eating at school. I don't do it.

"Yeah," I say. "What's up?"

"There's an opportunity that would be great for you." She walks to her desk and grabs a neon-yellow flyer. "One of my old friends from grad school is part of the staff at an art gallery that wants to feature young artists from the area."

My pulse quickens. This could be huge. "Which gallery?" I ask.

"It's called the Wynn. It's fairly small, but they have a great schedule of contemporary artists lined up for this year. It would be a huge deal when you're applying to art schools to say you've shown your work there already."

"Sounds…great," I say, unsure.

I've heard of the Wynn before. It's an up-and-coming gallery that mostly features artists early in their careers, but I'm not sure I'm good enough. I sketch and paint constantly, but I don't like showing my work to people. I come up with these concepts in my mind, but I can never seem to execute them exactly the right way. Sometimes I feel as if my skill will never match up with my vision.

"It's a ways off—the show won't be until near the end of the school year—but you have to submit a portfolio to be considered. They're going to take only two or three artists total."

How can I pull off a full show in eight months?

I'm a perfectionist. I take forever to put together a painting.

"That sounds pretty intense," I say. "I don't know what I would paint."

Ms. Day puts down the flyer and looks at me. "Olivia. You need to start believing in your work. Really. It's time for you to push yourself. Find your voice. You've been experimenting with figure drawing lately. Why don't you try painting live models?"

I want to ask Ms. Day what she means by finding my voice, and exactly how I should go about doing that, when the fire alarm goes off.

"Really?" Ms. Day shakes her head. "We've had three of these damn things this week already. Wish I could catch whatever little delinquent is responsible for this."

Lights flash on and off as the alarm buzzes. The school installed these alarms with strobe lights that practically blind you. It's most likely a false alarm, but they're so annoying they make you *want* to leave the room.

She heads for the door. "You don't have to decide now," she says, holding the flyer out to me. "You're the only student I am recommending for this, so please promise to think about it."

"Yeah," I say, taking the flyer, my stomach tightening with nerves. "I promise."

three

I'm sitting with Mom and Dad at a table at Musso & Frank Grill on Hollywood Boulevard, dining under the chandeliers in the ambience of mahogany decor and literary ghosts. Faulkner. Hemingway. Fitzgerald. Steinbeck. Parker. You name the writer—they ate here. The restaurant is old Hollywood classy. Waiters wear red jackets and black ties. Mom and Dad love this kind of stuff. A sense of history appeals to them.

I had to go home after school to change just so I could go out to dinner with my parents, even though I have absolutely no interest in eating.

It's Thursday. Today was supposed to be a fast day.

I'm trying to break a plateau. My goal is to get down to 100 pounds, and I'm not going to get there by eating ham steak or a rack of lamb or whatever.

When the waiter delivers my salad, Dad starts doing this thing he always does at these dinners, as if his life suddenly revolves around *my* eating habits.

"A house salad?" Dad asks. "That's it?"

I get irritated with them at dinners because they're always

commenting on what and how much I put on my plate, making me feel guilty for whatever I do or don't eat.

Believe me. I already judge myself enough for my own eating habits. Like those two Rice Krispies treats Mom made that I binged on yesterday? They made me feel terrible.

Words slip out before I have a chance to process. "Why do you care?"

Sometimes I want to stand on the table and inform the congressman: *Sir, my life isn't about shoving millions of calories of dead cow into my body.*

They were the ones who encouraged me to lose weight in the first place. When I came home crying about how fat I was after Ollie dumped me freshman year, Mom was the first to help me go on a diet. She bought me weight loss guidebooks, exercise tapes and a food scale. I would give her a special list of what to pick up at the grocery store.

I counted every calorie. Weighed every ounce. Recorded every mile. It was healthy at first. I started to lose weight. Fast. I really did need to ditch some of the weight, but I couldn't stop even after I lost all the weight I had gained.

And everyone, I mean *everyone*, was nicer to me. Even my parents. But I don't want their attention anymore. They're more controlling with me than they were with either Mason or Royce. Dad claims I'm more prone to extremes. Mom says I'm too hard on myself. I fail to see either. I'm pretty average.

Devastatingly average.

"Give me the benefit of the doubt," he says. "I'm just saying that you don't *have* to order the salad. Eat whatever you want. You used to like the Manhattan steak."

I refuse to react. I take a small bite of lettuce, the smallest leaf I can find.

I chew thirty times, counting each one like a bead on a rosary. *30…29…28…27…*

It's way harder to come up with excuses for not eating at a

restaurant, and I can't go to the bathroom after dinner either. Too obvious. So I order light and chew my food for so long that when they're ready to go, I end up leaving half my food on the plate.

I may be a fairly average teenage girl, but I'm strong-willed. Probably more so than any of those girls who hang around with Zach. I can put up a good fight.

I smile at Mom as if to say, *Please keep the congressman behind the imaginary fence.* She looks at me and shrugs. I guess I'll have to fight this battle on my own.

So I feign deafness, take a sip of water and stare at the wood paneled walls, thinking about my conversation with Ms. Day right before lunch. Having my work shown at a real gallery would be an amazing experience. It would mean that I actually have the talent to be a professional artist someday. Just being good at art in your high school classes isn't enough. I have to test myself outside of school too.

I want to put together a portfolio, but I don't know where to begin. My mind goes blank every time I try to think of a concept or theme for the show. I need to find my inspiration. If only I could talk to LeFeber…

"You might consider returning to Earth once in a while, Ms. Space Cadet," Dad says. His mouth is moving, but his words are white noise. "Ground control to Olivia."

I'm a disappointment to him. Not only am I not interested in his job, I don't get as high grades as Royce and I'll never be as popular as Mason was in high school.

He taps his fork on my plate, clanging the tines against the glass to get my attention. I stare at him, hoping my smoldering irises are enough to laser some more gray streaks into his hair. "I hope the rabbits across America aren't starving…"

I scrunch up my forehead. *What the hell is he talking about?*

"You eat so much lettuce you must have tanked their food economy," he says.

"Congressman Blakely," I say, stabbing my fork into a leaf covered in sesame seeds, "I like salads, the rabbits will be just fine and, besides, I'm just not super hungry, okay?"

I started calling him Congressman Blakely about a year ago. I don't know why, other than I thought it was funny. *Maybe* I was being a little mean. It's a way for me to passively fight back in my own house. My own private revolution, for no reason other than that I'm a teenager. It's practically my *duty* to get under my parents' skin.

"Can you not be like this? I'd love to have a peaceful dinner." Mom wipes a touch of water from her lips, then folds up her napkin into a perfect rectangle. She's perfect. Intelligent. Tactful. Nothing—not one stray hair or wrinkled shirt—ever out of place.

I reach for my own napkin and realize it has fallen on the floor. Compared to my mother, I'm a hot mess. I'm not diplomatic in social situations, and I can barely manage to find a clean pair of jeans in the mornings. I don't know how I ended up so different from my parents. I would be the worst politician ever.

Dad has just opened his mouth to argue again when Martin Barrios—Ollie's father—approaches the table. Just seeing him makes me want to slink down in my chair and hide under the table. He's wearing a black toupee slicked tight against his head and a blue suit that's slightly wrinkled and damp from sweat. He's fresh from the bar, face red, and too happy—way too happy for me anyway. He winks at Dad as if he knows some big secret. Not only is Mr. Barrios Ollie's father, which is mortifying enough, he's also worked with Dad on a big downtown renovation project, so there's no getting away.

"Colin Blakely?" He squints at Dad and spills a few drops of his martini on the carpet. "Whoa! Don't want to lose that," he adds. "This is a Musso martini!"

Dad laughs. "I hope you brought that for me."

"Why? Is this a celebration? I mean, I hope it is." He looks at Mom. "You look lovely as always, Debra."

"How's Oliver doing at..." Dad pauses. "Where does he go to school again? Princeton? Or Dartmouth?"

"He's a Princeton man. Double major in economics and Near Eastern studies."

"That's good to hear," Mom says politely.

How can she keep smiling at him? I never told her exactly what Ollie's comment was when he broke up with me, but she knows he said something horrible to me.

Then Mr. Barrios turns toward me, training his bloodshot eyes on my face.

"Olivia?" he says in faux surprise.

It's so fake I want to laugh.

"I'm her doppelgänger," I deadpan. "The real Olivia has been claimed by the robotics industry and is now being mass manufactured."

I imagine a hundred little replicas of myself and shudder. I can barely stand seeing myself doubled in a mirror, let alone a never-ending assembly line of Olivia Blakely dolls.

Mom shoots me a death stare. She doesn't like when I'm sarcastic around adults. It's a liability. I say they could stand to loosen up. Why take everything so seriously?

"Is she?" He laughs like a factory-produced automaton. "You're all grown up," he says. "You'll be a marvelous woman. You have two great brothers. And mother..."

Gag. That's when I stop listening. I shut him off completely. I've heard this speech before from a hundred different politicians. He's lost interest within seconds anyway, because I'm not important to these kinds of people other than that I'm merely something to turn into a compliment for my parents.

I check my phone. There's a text from Sam. I answer as surreptitiously as I can. Mom and Dad don't like when I text at the dinner table, but I can't help myself.

SAM: Feeling better?

LIV: Yep ☺

SAM: Thinking about doing a bonfire at the beach. You down?

LIV: I wish. Dinner with my parents ☹

SAM: Bummer. Hang out tomorrow?

LIV: Totally. I'm down.

SAM: I have a surprise for you.

LIV: OoOoO. What is it?

SAM: It's a surprise...

"Liv? Could you put your phone down, please?" Mom asks. She places her napkin on the table like she's about to make a serious announcement.

"Yeah. One sec," I say, rapidly texting Sam back.

LIV: Gotta go. Txt later ☺

I was supposed to hang out with him after taking yearbook photos yesterday, but I just felt like locking myself in my bedroom after the disaster with Jackson, so I gave him an excuse about not feeling well. I'm a terrible friend. I need to make it up to him.

Mr. Barrios has waded his way back to the bar. I *really* wish I could join him. Maybe he could buy me one of those famous Musso martinis. I could use one.

Or three.

The buzz would help deaden the anxiety whirling in my stomach. I think about my conversation with Jackson—rehashing every tiny word and action over and over in my mind—until I convince myself that Jackson and all his friends, especially Zach, think I'm a freak who just wants to party with the popular people.

I'm feeling more nauseous by the second.

I'm just getting up to go to the bathroom when I realize Dad's been trying to get my attention.

"Honeybee," he says. He's been calling me that since I stepped on a bee at my friend's birthday at Griffith Park nearly ten years ago. "Don't go just yet. I have something to tell the both of you."

"Ugh," I say and sit back down. "I have to pee. What is it?"

Mom puts a hand on his arm. The news is something she's been anticipating. I've always been able to read her. And Dad? He's an open book. He'll tell anyone whatever he's thinking at any given moment. No secrets there. I guess that's something people admire about him, but I don't understand. *Everyone* needs a secret to call their own.

"There's a reason we went out on a school night," he says.

"What is it?" I ask absentmindedly, thinking about how much homework I have to get done tonight. I have at least two hours' worth. It's going to be a late night.

Dad jolts me back into reality.

"I'm running for governor of California," he says.

My stomach drops.

"We've been waiting to tell you," Mom says, her face full of joy. I'm pretty sure the expression on my face is communicating the otherworldliness of this announcement.

"Really?" I ask. "Are you serious?"

"Couldn't be more serious," he says.

I should be happy for him, happy for his achievements, but this is terrible news. This means even more attention on the family and more stress during my junior year, which everyone knows is the hardest school year ever, especially since I have to start studying for the SAT, working on my portfolio and thinking about art school—or at least how I'm going to convince my parents to let me go there instead of a regular university.

All eyes are going to be on us. That means I have to be more perfect than ever. Stronger. Nothing should be able to take me down. Not food. Not school. Not this election.

I push the lettuce around on my plate and crush the croutons with my fork while Mom and Dad talk like old high school lovers, excited about this new opportunity.

"This is *exactly* what we need. Imagine not having to fly to Washington all the time." I can tell that, in her mind, Mom is already decorating and ordering furniture for a new house. "We'll live in the governor's mansion. Sacramento is so lovely, and I miss having seasons."

The timing couldn't be worse.

My entire junior year is going to be taken up by this campaign. Probably part of my senior year too. Everything will be about him. Like always. Not to mention I may have to live in Sacramento for half of my senior year.

Sacramento? I mean, seriously, what's in Sacramento? A river?

Let me say it again: There's. No. Way.

Might as well join the Mars Colony. They're taking hip young up-and-coming artists ostracized from their power-hungry families, aren't they? Sign me up.

A campaign for governor changes everything. Forget making any friends, let alone hooking up with Zach Park. Dad winning the governorship would ruin all that. And Dad's scarily good at winning elections.

Fine. I'm just going to say it. Not out loud, but I'm going to say it in my head because it's all I can think. *I hope he loses. I hope his campaign completely tanks.* There. Said it. I just need to get on the ball and focus on getting invited to Zach's boat party.

That's my only chance to get on his radar and to ask for LeFeber's advice. I have to start living my best life. Stop constantly overthinking things and doubting myself.

No more being a wallflower.

No more being known only as the congressman's daughter.

Or Mason and Royce's little sister.
I have to make a name for myself. For my art.
Everyone needs to know who Liv Blakely really is.

four

It's Friday afternoon and I still haven't been invited to the party.

Do I have *loser* stamped on my forehead?

I've tried talking to Jackson three times. Three times!

This is what I'm thinking about as I walk to the front of campus *by myself.*

I cut across the parking lot from Ms. Day's room, where I was working late to put together an inspiration board for my portfolio. I'm starting with Frida Kahlo's work. She's always been inspiring to me. I even have a print of one of her paintings hanging above my bed called *What the Water Gave Me*. It's this strange picture of her feet peeking out of a tub of bathwater, except floating in the water are all these surreal images from her consciousness: a sailboat, a wrinkled dress, a conch shell, native plants from her homeland, a skyscraper rising from a volcano, a miniature figure of herself drowning in the middle of the scene.

I head to the front of the school, waiting for Mom to pick me up like the total nerd I am. Great Friday, right?

At least I have plans to go to the movies with Sam. We haven't had much time to get together since school started, and his text asking me to hang out tonight made me smile and helped take my mind off my complete failure to get invited to the boat party. Sam doesn't notice—or maybe he doesn't care—what a loser I am. He doesn't even mind picking me up *again*.

This is what happens when you're already sixteen and you can't drive. It's a movie called *Mommy and Daddy Are Always Too Busy to Teach Me How to Drive*. Starring me. I play the depressed Goth-girl artist. I don't even really wear *that* much black—I just consider sarcasm a never-leave-home-without kind of accessory. In the movie version of my life, I'm on the brink of insanity and draw images of sad carless girls on every wall I can get away with scribbling on. At the end of the film, I finally get to drive around the block. Big deal.

Mason and Royce could do pretty much anything they wanted in high school, which was partly because they each had a car to go along with their driver's licenses. Dad keeps promising me a car. Not that I even have my license yet. Before the end of the school year, that's what he told me. So I'm sitting on a low brick wall, waiting for Mom to show up, kissing away any hope of meeting LeFeber, when guess who walks up to the strikeout queen?

"Liv, Liv... Look at you sitting out here."

"Jackson! Hey!"

He looks at me funny.

I guess I sound a little overenthusiastic. I mean, it is the day of the boat party and all. I don't know what to say to Jackson and I start to panic a little. This is my last chance to get on the same boat as LeFeber and Zach. I consider just asking him for an invite, but then realize that would either be too tacky or would seem completely desperate.

"You're by yourself," I say stupidly.

"Yeah. Weird, huh?" Jackson laughs. "I had to see Mr. Richie about a test. Dude's holding back points again."

He knows, I think. He really knows it's weird that girls aren't

37

trailing him like a comet's tail. I wish I could be that confi-dent, but I never seem to be able to shake the names that are always underneath my other thoughts.

Fatso. Blimp. Heifer.

It sounds kind of crazy, but I call it my *other voice*. It used to sound like Ollie was stuck in my head—every bad thing I thought about myself was in his voice—but eventually it changed, and now the other voice's words are all mine.

"What are your plans this weekend?" Jackson asks, inch-ing closer to me. He's so close that I can smell his cologne. He smells like a cool breeze, like a pool of sparkling water. He puts his hand up to my hair and twists a strand around his finger.

Hold on. What's going on right now? The situation just got unpredictable. Is he flirting with me? This isn't supposed to happen. It may turn out to be a total fantasy, but if it's not, I'm interested in Zach. Not Jackson.

But I can't brush him off. This is my last chance to land an invitation.

"I don't know," I say. "Nothing much. Just like…"

"Seriously," he says. "I want to know what's going on. You can't be doing *nothing*. A girl like you doesn't do nothing…"

What girl like me? Are there girls like me? I want to know them. I also want to know why Jackson's flirting with me.

Before I can say anything, I sense disaster in the form of a car pulling up. Another ruined encounter. Mom has the worst timing.

Wait a minute. That's not Mom's car. It's a yellow Land Rover pulling up in front of us with a certain Dominican girl at the wheel, pumping salsa music out her windows.

I immediately squeal, "Antonia!"

I try not to scare Jackson off, but I totally was not expect-ing her to show up at school on a Friday afternoon. She's been visiting family in the Dominican Republic all summer and is arriving late for the school year. I didn't think I was going to see her until the beginning of October. She's almost a month early. And she didn't tell me she was back.

She rolls down the window. Her long, curly hair is swept into a high, messy ponytail, showing off her milk-chocolate eyes accented by thick black liner. "Baby, look at you," is all she says through pouty lips before letting out a wolf whistle.

I'm smiling ear to ear. She's the most no-nonsense, fun-loving human being I've ever known. I might be a perfectionist about a lot of things, but Antonia and I complement each other perfectly. She's all breezy and carefree while I can't go to sleep at night without obsessing over every little thing I've said or done the day before.

"I wanted to surprise you," she says. "I figured you would be here so I called your mom to tell her I was going to pick you up. Come to my house, we have tons to catch up on."

I grab my bag and look at Jackson, trying to decide what to do. I want to go to the boat party so badly, but I also want to hang out with Antonia. I've missed her like crazy.

"I should go," he says.

I don't know what to say. I've probably already ruined my chances. Why can't I just ask for what I want? Why can't I spit it out? "Yeah, I guess so," I say.

"Hold on," Antonia says, probably picking up on my disappointment. "What's going on, Jackson? What are you doing here after school on a *Friday* talking to my main girl? You're not being a bad influence on Livvy, are you?"

I sigh. Antonia *knows* how people work. She's so easy around them. She tries to coach me to not psych myself out, but I can't help it. It's just how I am.

Antonia starts sweet-talking him, grinning the way she does when she knows she's being *seen*. "You're the man of the moment, I hear. What's happening this weekend? I'm just back to town, all grown up as you can tell, and I want to see *everyone*."

"He's got a boat party out in the marina tonight," I say. "Well, I mean Zach does…"

"That's right," Jackson says, leaning in Antonia's window like some famous sculptor carved him right there on the spot. It's almost funny how full of himself he is.

Antonia smirks at him. "And?"

"And what?" Jackson asks.

Now he's flirting with her *too*.

"Are we invited?"

Jackson shrugs. "I just assumed you'd be there."

"Whatever!" Antonia slaps his muscular shoulder. It's obvious Jackson is obsessed with working out. He's pretty ripped. "You weren't even going to tell me. And neither were you, Liv."

I look at her. I can't believe she's taken about thirty seconds to get us invited, and I've been trying for *three days*. Even for her that must be some kind of personal record.

"You didn't tell her?" Jackson asks me. "Were you gonna ditch us?"

"Ditch?" I hesitate. "I didn't realize I was invited."

"Uh…of course you were."

"I was?" I ask, then attempt the clumsiest backtrack of all time, wishing I could appear at least slightly more confident. "I mean, yeah, I knew that."

five

"There is nothing I would not do for those who are really my friends.

I have no notion of loving people by halves, it is not my nature."

—JANE AUSTEN

Antonia pulls up to her house and parks the Land Rover in her driveway. In the car, she told me that both of her parents are back at work after their long summer vacation so we don't have to worry about being loud as we enter the house.

Going to Antonia's house feels like traveling to another country. The colors of their drapery and furniture are vibrant and deep and the hallways are filled with Antonia's mother's framed vinyl album covers—she's a famous singer from the Dominican Republic—and pictures of her with other famous singers and musicians. There's one photograph of her mother hanging in the entryway that's always been my favorite. She's very young—just barely twenty, maybe—and wearing a tight, sparkly sequin dress that fits her like she was poured into it. Antonia looks almost exactly like her mother, but with a darker complexion.

It's wild how much they look alike. Even though my mom is part Latina, no one ever guesses that I'm Mexican. It's the last name, I suppose. Blakely. Not to mention my skin is ghostly white. I spent most of the summer running around conference rooms and fund-raisers, helping Mom with her campaign to increase childhood literacy. I'm basically her intern and help with everything from setting up events to data entry. Sometimes I get to read to little kids at her events, which is my favorite part, but mostly I have to hang out with adults who think I have everything together but don't really know who I am.

Summers are hard for me. Without school to focus on, I'm always obsessing about my weight and how hungry I am. I binge more. This year, with Antonia visiting the Dominican Republic and Sam away working as a counselor at a surf camp, I got really lonely. I started eating a lot and feeling crappy about myself. I got to a point where I started vomiting after every meal. It was so bad that I couldn't stop myself from purging after a fund-raising luncheon, even though I knew Mom was in the stall next to me.

I told her I was sick.

I'm hoping Antonia being back will make things better.

"I'm grabbing a snack and then we gotta get ready," Antonia says, walking through the entryway toward the kitchen. "You want anything?"

"That's okay," I say. "I'm not hungry. I'll meet you upstairs."

Leaving her in the kitchen, I walk up the stairs to her bedroom and plop down on Antonia's bed, trying to figure out a plan to talk to Zach tonight without seeming awkward and obvious. Her bedroom is super bohemian. The shelves are filled with knickknacks from her mother's tours around the world. The room is also cluttered with different musical instruments—guitars, conga drums, a balalaika—that she plays. Multicolored batik rugs cover the ground, which is nearly impossible to see because Antonia's clothes are everywhere.

I daydream about the possibility of meeting LeFeber. It's not only his art that I admire. It's his life. His mother was an alcoholic who abandoned the family when he was a baby, and when he was sixteen, his father disowned him for being openly gay.

The article said that when he lived in New York during the '80s, LeFeber was practically homeless, trying to scrounge up enough money for materials and find places that would host his installations. I want to ask him how he found so much courage to pursue his dream. I want to ask him how he found so much courage to believe in himself for so long.

When she returns, Antonia shoves a plate of reheated black beans and red rice at me. Even though she's trying to be nice, I give her some side-eye.

Right away, I feel like a total jerk—why can't I just be normal about food for once? Why can I barely stand to eat in front of my *best friend*?

"Seriously not trying to be a nag," she says, "but you should eat *something*. Especially since we're gonna be drinking."

She's right. I can handle a few bites.

"Fine," I say, taking the plate and a fork from her.

I pick at the rice and beans, eating a few bites to make her happy, while Antonia digs through her closet, looking for something for us to wear to the boat party.

I'm glad she's going with me. I would have been nervous going alone. I don't even know how I would have gotten there.

My phone buzzes.

"Oh *crap*," I say, not even realizing I'm thinking aloud. I totally forgot that I'd made plans with Sam to go see a movie tonight. We're supposed to be there in an hour.

"What's up, BB?" Antonia asks, throwing a random pink shirt over her shoulder onto a pile of clothes and shoes behind her.

"Sam's going to *kill* me."

My phone buzzes again and I pick it up.

Yep. Just like I thought. He's already texted two or three times.

"I promised him I'd hang out tonight," I say. "He's supposed to be picking me up from my house soon."

"Okay, so? Invite him over," she says. "It's not like they'll mind one more person at the boat party. Everyone'll probably be so trashed that they won't remember anyway."

"I don't think it's going to be that kind of party…"

I really do love Sam as a friend, but hanging out with all three of us means that there's a totally different dynamic. I can be open with him about my feelings for the most part, but I don't want him to think I'm shallow for wanting to hang with Zach's crowd.

Antonia finally settles on a yellow dress, which she begins to pull on over her lean, muscular shoulders. "Of course it is. Why wouldn't it be?"

"I thought it might be classy. Since it's on a yacht?"

"Why are you being weird? Do you not want him to go or something?" Antonia asks.

Before I can answer, she slaps herself on the forehead. "Oh. I get it. *Duh*. You want to hook up with someone, and you don't want Sam around being all big-brotherly."

"Shut up," I say, feeling my cheeks flush. "I just want to hang out with you!"

Antonia smirks to show me she knows I'm bluffing.

She's right. Sort of. Sam and I have been close enough at times during our friendship to be mistaken for siblings, but that feeling has been shifting this last year. It's like we're almost becoming more mysterious to each other as each of us gets older. I don't know *what* I feel about Sam.

She throws a tiny piece of black fabric at me. "Try that on." The dress looks way too small, but I'm not about to argue with her. Handing the mostly full plate of beans and rice to Antonia, I get up and walk toward her bathroom. I can't change in front of other people. Not even her.

"You're so modest!" Antonia complains. "It's just me!"

"What should I tell Sam?" I ask.

"You *could* be honest," Antonia says, shoveling the food into her mouth with my fork. "Or you could just tell him that you want to hang out with me. Tell him you didn't know I'd be back. That's not lying."

I pull on the strapless dress. It *barely* covers the necessary parts. I keep fidgeting with the top, pulling it up to make sure my chest won't pop out from just breathing. The dress squeezes my ribs like a corset, punishing me for not being small enough.

"I don't know..." I say, not knowing whether I'm talking about the dress or how I'm going to back out of my plans with Sam. Even though Jackson didn't invite him to the party, I *could* invite Sam anyway. Except I definitely don't want Sam anywhere near when I'm trying to talk to Zach. I can't entertain him when I'm looking for LeFeber either. I need to step out on my own. And I really do want some girls-only time with Antonia too.

"Come on out," Antonia says, pushing the bathroom door open. She lets out a deep whistle. "When did my lil homie become a *grown ass* woman? Jackson is gonna be so into this."

I blush. It's hard for me to see why Antonia thinks I'm so beautiful, especially compared to her, but I'm flattered anyway. She *does* have pretty good taste, after all.

"I'm not going for him," I try to explain. "Not exactly."

Antonia squeezes by and starts rummaging through her bathroom drawers for makeup. "No? Then who...? It's Zach, isn't it?"

Am I really that obvious?

"It's more than that," I say, only partially bluffing.

"Right," she says, raising an eyebrow while twisting open her mascara. "Like I don't know you've been in love with him for the past two years?"

"Actually, I'll have you know that an artist I really admire is supposed to be there."

"Going for the older men now?" Antonia asks.

I laugh. "Yeah, right. I guess one of the producers of Zach's show invited him. He's supposed to be in town doing a gallery show. I really want to meet him."

My phone buzzes again. And again.

"You better answer him," Antonia says. "He'll start thinking something's wrong."

"Do you think Sam knows?" I ask. "About Zach?"

My skin flushes with warmth thinking about the possibility of his fingers intertwined with mine. I lean on the counter, waiting for her to tell me what I don't want to hear. One thing about Antonia is that you can always count on her to give it to you straight.

"Honestly…" Antonia stares at herself close-up in the mirror as she applies mascara to her eyelashes. "I don't think he wants to see it. But I think he also knows more than he lets on too."

"Meaning…?" I ask, pulling up the texts on my phone.

"How long have you and Sam known each other?" Antonia asks.

I try to count the years in my head. They all blend together.

"During elementary school. I don't remember which grade."

"And you don't think that this whole time, he hasn't had at least *one* thought about you guys getting together?"

I look at his texts, remembering how we used to be inseparable. How we used to walk around at the marina and pretend that someday we'd sail away on our own boat and travel the world.

It's different now. We're older. We're still friends, of course, but not *best* friends. Not friends who can tell each other *everything*.

It would be so weird to talk to him about liking another guy.

Hoping Sam will understand, I start to type out an apology.

SAM: Pick u up?

LIV: Antonia's back. She says hi ☺

"What did he say?" Antonia asks.

"He hasn't answered yet. He's probably trying to make me sweat."

"Just put the blame on me. He knows I don't take no for an answer. He can handle us having a little girl time without him anyway. He's a big boy. He's got his own life."

SAM: Does she wanna come?

LIV: Don't hate me...

SAM: But?

LIV: She wants me to go to a party. Girls only. You know how she is ☺

I can't bring myself to tell him the specifics—or that he's technically not invited and that I don't want him to crash the party either. When Sam doesn't answer, my stomach sinks. How do I always somehow feel like I'm disappointing him?

"Life's so different in the Dominican Republic," Antonia says, talking about where she spent all summer. "Besides, like, having family around *all* the time, there's practically a party every single night. Everyone's invited. Grandparents, little kids, the weird guy who lives down the street. People are so helpful too. I was driving in Santo Domingo and I ran out of gas in the middle of the highway. Some guy just went and got gas *for* me, then another guy stopped to siphon the gas from the jug with his mouth. I'm pretty sure he inhaled some toxic fumes just to help me."

"That's crazy," I say. "If that happened here, someone would probably just try to run you off the road."

Finishing her eyeliner, Antonia continues her story without skipping a beat. "And I met this old guy who started teaching me the accordion so I can play merengue. I know that's an instrument only nerds play, but I'm obsessed. Mama made a deal with me that she'll buy me one if I start writing my own music."

"Your mom's so cool," I say. "My parents insist painting is a hobby I'll grow out of." I might not share their love for politics, but I still respect their passions. I wish they could understand that painting isn't some kind of craft for me. It's my lifeline.

"Then you'll have to prove them wrong!" Antonia snaps her makeup case shut.

"Well, actually, I talked to Ms. Day earlier this week and she recommended I submit a portfolio for this gallery showing. It's supposed to be pretty prestigious…"

My phone vibrates again.

SAM: K. Surfing early tmrw morning. Night.
LIV: Sry. Wanna get together later this weekend?

There's no answer. I think about asking him, but I don't want to find out yet.

He's probably pissed at me. Maybe he doesn't actually care. Who knows? Boys are so hard to interpret over text. Why am I so worried about what he thinks about what I do with my life? We're not *together*. Tonight's about having fun. Letting loose.

That's who I am now. Right?

Liv Blakely.

Fun girl. *Life* of the *party*. Girl of the century.

six

"This is insane," says Antonia. "It's so..."

"Expensive," I say, finishing her sentence.

Antonia and I are scoping out the main open area of the upper deck of the *Royal Elizabeth*. It's decorated with gorgeous displays of white flowers everywhere, and lighting glows around the edges of the boat, making the atmosphere seem heavenly. In the center of the floor, where people are gathering and chatting, there's an open bar stacked high with pyramids of champagne flutes. A DJ plays low-key electronic music while guests lounge on chic white sofas or wander outside to lean against the railing, looking out at the water.

"*This* is why I love LA. You never know where you might get invited. I've been to a few parties, but I mean, this is ridiculous. Can you imagine if my parents let me throw a party like this? Or, like, if we had the *money* to throw a party like this?"

Antonia has become a complete chatterbox. She gets like this in social situations—all giddy and energetic. Her hair is down. Tight golden-brown curls fall over the spaghetti straps of her yellow dress.

I wish I were as gorgeous as her. It barely takes her any effort—or makeup—to look like a total superstar.

I'm her opposite, wearing the black dress she loaned me. It's my color lately. The dress still feels too tight though. The fabric constricts around my rib cage like a python. My stomach cramps as anxious thoughts bubble up behind my eyes. I'm too pale, practically a phantom, especially compared to all of the confident women strutting and giggling around the room. Half of them are probably actresses Zach knows from work.

Both Zach and Jackson are nowhere to be seen—not that I would have the courage right now to walk up and start a conversation with them anyway.

That's probably going to take some liquid courage.

"Look at those," Antonia says, watching a caterer walk by with a platter full of delicious-looking crostini. "Thank God, I'm starving."

Even though she ate at her house, Antonia makes a beeline for the hors d'oeuvres. I swear that girl can eat anything and not gain an ounce. I know I shouldn't eat and that I'll feel guilty later, but the appetizers look delicious. I'm thinking about whether I should approach the table when Antonia turns around with a plate in her hand. "You need to eat, Liv. Get something in your stomach before we start drinking."

"I don't know…" I hesitate. "This dress…"

"Stop. You look great. Don't you want to drink?"

I sigh. "Yeah. I guess."

Antonia puts a hand on my shoulder. "Girl. You have nothing to worry about," she says, nodding at a young woman walking across the deck with a scowl on her face. "Look at her. She obviously hasn't eaten all day. She looks completely miserable."

"All right," I say. It's impossible to not give in to her eventually. "I'll eat. But then you have to promise to go get us some drinks."

"Deal," Antonia says, turning back to the appetizers.

We load our tiny plates with spinach and goat cheese tart-lets, scallops and clams, and toasted bread topped with thyme-roasted tomatoes, then head over to a secluded cocktail table at one side of the deck. Both of us pig out on the appetizers like neither of us has never eaten before. The food tastes heavenly. I try not to think about the calories.

"I'll get us some bubbly," Antonia says, polishing off her last tartlet and setting down her plate on a table. "I'll bring you something strong."

I think about joining Antonia, but I figure this is a good time to gather my thoughts and to check whether LeFeber has shown up yet. And to figure out what I want to say to Zach when I finally see him.

As Antonia disappears to the other end of the room, I note the yacht's classy decor. The room is lined with white-cloth tables strung with lights. Along the outer tables are double rows of windows strung with sparkling lights too. The view of the harbor is magnificent. The ships are soaked in a lavender blanket of descending night. A few yachts are cutting slowly through the water like graceful swans. It's perfect.

Looking at the harbor reminds me of Sam, which makes me feel a little pang of guilt for ditching him tonight. As a kid, I always used to come here with him and his older brother, James, to go sailing. When James passed away last year, Sam asked to meet by our special bench just across the marina, where we still go to talk alone.

I held him while he cried. We kissed. Only once.

It scared me. I didn't want to have feelings for my best friend. And Sam never talked about it afterward. So I kind of just assumed that he wasn't really interested after all. It was just part of his grief from losing his brother at such a young age.

I look around and slowly start to recognize some faces even though I don't really know them personally. The yacht is swarming with teenage and twentysomething Hollywood actors and several small groups of adults. Crew members. Producers. Agents. Many of them are from the show *Sisters & Mothers*, about two women who fall in love and move in together. Each of the mothers on the show has a teenage daughter. Hilarity ensues when they all move in with each other. Zach plays one of the daughters' love interests, which is why I lock myself in my bedroom and watch every Thursday night. It's pretty good. He's not in every episode, but I watch the show weekly anyway. A couple of times, Zach has played guitar. He can sing really well too, which I *love*.

There's something so intriguing about creative men.

I expected more students from school to be here, but there's only a small group of Zach and Jackson's close circle of friends who have never given me the time of day. They probably don't even recognize me. It's pretty dark. Some people are dancing, and just about everyone is drinking. Antonia hasn't come back, and I think about going to find some champagne, but I want to feel empty. In control. This is where I wanted to be all week.

This is my last night to let loose before the cameras start rolling.

Though Dad's upcoming campaign announcement keeps nagging at me with all the attention that's going to be on our family soon, I'm not going to let that ruin my night. I mean, yeah, he's still the Speaker of the House for a little bit longer, but that's old news. No one's going to be paying attention to me until after the announcement. Right?

I wait for ten minutes, pretending to check my phone, before I accept that Antonia has ghosted me. I should have known. She's always been that way. It's not that she's trying to ditch me. She'll just get caught up in a conversation, meet some new people and disappear for an hour.

If she's gone, I figure I might as well look around for LeFeber. Except there's one problem. LeFeber is notoriously protective of his image. There are only a couple of pictures of him

online. They're pretty old, from his time in New York during the '80s. All I know, then, is that LeFeber must be at least
middle-aged and his hair's sort of red. *If* he hasn't dyed it. It's
not a lot to go on, but I figure I'll try anyway.

I nonchalantly wander around the deck, looking for someone who might be LeFeber, and for Felicity, who might have
seen him recently. I don't see her or anyone who fits LeFeber's
description. He might not even be here for all I know. It seems
kind of silly for a world-class artist to attend a teen actor's boat
party, even if it's an action star's boat.

As I'm about to head down to the lower deck, one of Zach's
friends waves me over to a group with bottles in their hands. It's
Morgan Dunn, one of the stars from *Sisters & Mothers*. She plays
the dark-haired sister, Abby, whom I connect with because she's
the one always pointing out the unfairness in every situation.

When I walk over, Morgan grabs my hand. "Who are you?"
she asks, smiling. "I just love your dress, everything about you."

"I'm Liv," I say, trying not to sound too shy. Even though
she's being nice, I feel uncomfortable. I really wish I hadn't
eaten those appetizers. "I know Zach."

"From his school?"

"God, I hated school," says the guy next to her. "Never got
the point."

I recognize Frederico Fontes right away. He's on *Style Wars*.
And since it's a reality show that makes a ton of money for the
networks, he's always traveling with the cast around the world
to major fashion events. I can't imagine him going to school,
or wanting to. I want to talk to him about my love of art and
how I want to go to one of the big art schools, but he's already
walking away from the conversation.

"Ignore him," Morgan says. "He's always a jerk when he's in
town." She leans in to me so close that she drunkenly brushes
my shoulder. "I think he hates traveling all the time, and I
mean, I don't blame him—it *does* get old."

"Oh," I say, "I'm sure." But I have no idea what I'm talking about. I've gone from here to DC many times, but that doesn't really count. It's not for *my* job.

"Don't get me wrong. I love my job. But you never get to stay in one place long enough to get to know someone, ya know? Never long enough to fall in love."

How could anyone not fall for Morgan? She's funny, talented and beautiful. Even *famous*. I'm about to say so when a woman across the room wearing a cherry-red dress and strappy heels gets her attention by waving a napkin in our direction.

"Excuse me," Morgan says. "That's my agent and my signal. There's a director I wanna talk to. Steven Weir. You know him, right? Wish me luck!"

Just like that, Morgan is caught in another whirlwind of people. I float away from the small crowd, wishing I could find Antonia, and end up running into a guy I recognize as Zach's sidekick on the show. Michael Louis-Kroll. He's always doing something goofy in contrast with Zach's character.

"I like your character on *Sisters & Mothers*," I say.

He lets out a sort of snort, like someone poked him in the stomach. "You mean, you like how I'm constantly getting steamrolled and taking it like a champ?"

"I didn't mean it like that. Seriously."

"Of course you did." He's giving me a smug squint.

He must be totally drunk.

"Aren't you playing the character that way on purpose?" I ask.

He thinks. Swirls his drink. "What's your name?"

"Liv," I say, realizing I don't even need to ask for his and he knows it. Even though my father is third in line for the presidency, a lot of people don't know his name. My family is important. They have prestige. But we're not exactly *famous*.

"Okay, Liv. You're the director. It's your show. How would you have me portrayed? Would you be sort of shallow, catering to the whims of mass television by giving the show a requisite punching bag? Or would you do something different?"

The guy standing next to him thinks his buddy is getting out of line. "Michael," his friend says. "Take it easy. She was just trying to compliment your work."

This time I interrupt. If he wants to test me, I'll rise to the challenge. There's nothing more that I hate than when a guy talks to a girl like she's ridiculous for having an opinion. I hold up a hand to Michael's friend. I don't need his chivalry. "No, no. I got this," I say, feeling a burst of confidence as I examine Michael. He's grinning like he's testing me, like he wants to see what I'm made of. "I think if I were the director, I'd want an actor to challenge my thinking. I'd be open-minded to new ideas, fresh takes on characters."

He rolls his eyes. "Right."

"No, really," I say, wanting to drive my point home and to show Zach's friends that I can hold my own. "I'd want actors who can explore character. Shake up the show. Shake the audience. Pull in the viewers by showing a range of emotions. A character might start out like yours, just a throwaway punch line, but I'd imagine a greater arc over the course of the show, with the character becoming more serious and complex in the end."

Michael's buddy starts cracking up. "She got you, fam."

I don't know where the surge of confidence came from—maybe I'm not as socially awkward as I thought. Maybe I *can* think on my feet.

Before Michael can say anything and turn the conversation into awkward silence, I follow Morgan's lead and excuse myself. "Sorry, boys, but I have to run. It was nice meeting you."

"That girl can hang," Michael says as I walk away. "Who is she?"

I'm laughing to myself, weaving through the people, when I feel the familiar buzz of a text through my clutch. I look at my phone. At first I think the text is going to be Sam telling me off, but then I see my brother's name flash across the screen. It's Royce. The phone buzzes again. Two texts? Royce never texts me this late at night.

I'm afraid to look. Something bad might have happened.

ROYCE: Don't ever fall in love.
ROYCE: It's not worth it.
LIV: Are you and Jas fighting?

He doesn't answer. Or doesn't *want* to answer the question.

I can barely remember what life was like before her. I *do* remember that being the only girl in the family was definitely no fun. I love Jasmine. He'd be stupid to do anything to lose her. I've always looked up to her, ever since Royce started dating her during their senior year of high school. She's practically my older sister, with the benefit of not having the same parents.

She's always encouraging me to pursue art even when my parents tell me they would rather I become a lawyer. "If your parents don't love your career choice now," she says, "that doesn't mean they won't later. Believe me. My parents haven't always agreed with my decisions, but they support me. Keep being yourself. Keep dreaming."

I don't even know why he's texting me about this. What do I know about love? It's not like I've been in a long-term relationship—a years-long relationship—like him and Jasmine. I don't really talk to either of them about their relationship. My heart sinks. I'm finally realizing that maybe that was because they never needed to until now.

Royce still hasn't answered.

I text Jas, trying to say something that won't make her think Royce is talking to me about their relationship problems. That would be pretty weird.

LIV: What's up? We haven't talked in forever!

JAS: Just studying. Gotta get into med school ☺

LIV: Always so responsible ☺

JAS: What's going on? You need something?

LIV: Just your presence! When are we going to hang out?

JAS: Idk. Maybe Christmas?

LIV: That's so far away!

JAS: It's my only big break. Can you come up here?

LIV: I'll ask <3 xoxox

I can't tell what's going on. She doesn't seem any different from normal. If they're fighting, that's none of my business anyway. Though the fact that they might be fighting is *totally scandalous*. They *are* the perfect couple. Not kidding.

I glance at my phone again for a text from Royce.

Nothing.

Now I'm really starting to worry. What if he's rallying the troops? Is he going to turn this into a *family emergency*?

Then I have a worse thought. Maybe Royce came home to talk to our parents—and they're trying to get him to figure out where I am.

They would *kill* me if they found out that I was at a high-profile party without permission. I'm trying hard enough to please them with good grades and this whole responsibility act to get them off my back so I have at least a *teensy* chance of getting them to let me apply to art school instead of a regular university.

I think about texting Antonia to ask her to take me home. I can't breathe. I mean, seriously, everything is just not right. My hair is pulled back too tight. My dress is uncomfortable.

I'm starting to feel bloated. Fat. Ugly.

Then I see Zach.

He's wearing a shiny navy suit with a crisp white shirt and

thin black tie and talking to a middle-aged gentleman with hip Coke-bottle glasses drinking a highball. Cristina is standing right next to him as she chats with Felicity. Is that Geoff LeFeber?

Goose pimples spread up my arms from excitement. If that's really him, I can't believe my luck. I have to find a way to talk to him without seeming weird—and without drawing the attention of Cristina and Felicity. But then I have to figure out how to not be awkward around Zach either. How will I figure out whether that's him or not? Should I walk right up to them? What should I say? Even though I kind of am one, I don't want to come off like an obsessive fangirl right away.

I don't even realize I'm staring until Zach looks over and smiles.

Not just in my general direction. At *me*.

Part of me wants to scream from excitement. The other part of me wants to climb into a deep, dark hole to never be seen again. *Keep it together, Liv. You got this.*

Trying not to blush, I return his gaze before he looks away to talk to the man again. Wishing Antonia would come back so I can look busy, I watch Zach *and* try to figure out whether they're talking to LeFeber or not. Each time I glance at Zach, Cristina, with her dark hair and doe-like eyes, is hanging on to him. More people are starting to dance around them, and I can't hear what they're saying. I'm feeling suffocated, staring at my phone then glancing up, trying not to let Cristina notice. Zach's still glancing back at me, eyes lingering a little too long for it to be chance.

I pretend to be a little embarrassed even though I really feel like I'm going to explode. I want to go up and talk to them, especially to find out whether that's LeFeber, but I can't bring myself to approach Zach when he's standing next to Cristina. She's started staring me down whenever Zach glances away to talk to someone else.

Cristina says something to the man with the glasses, then he looks at me and laughs. I'm mortified. What are they saying? Is LeFeber laughing at me?

Cristina's not dumb. She knows Zach's turned his head my way too many times to be a coincidence. I'm excited—more than I have been in years about any boy—but I'm also nervous. God, where's Antonia? Or that drink she was supposed to bring?

I could use a rescue right about now.

I shouldn't have eaten that food with her. I need a release. A burning sensation is creeping up my throat. My insides are trapped, swirling in a storm that I can't control.

Not now. Not now. Not now.

My plea to my insides isn't working.

I hold my purse to my stomach to make it feel like there's a wall between stomach, skin and dress, and I start searching for a staircase, hoping to find an empty bathroom. My stomach cramps become nearly unbearable. I can't ride out the pain. I need to find a bathroom on this boat. *Now.*

I finally find the staircase and walk into what feels like a living room. There's a fireplace, big orange chairs, a couch, doors leading to hallways.

There are people all over down here and they stare at me, thinking I'm drunk, but I don't care. I just say, "Bathroom?" to the nearest girl.

She points to the left. "That way, honey. You gonna make it?"

The whole ship is caught in a whirlpool, spiraling downward into a tiny hole. Whatever is in me has become a spinning mass that desperately needs out.

I enter one of the stalls, lock the door and dry heave over the toilet. I stick my finger in my throat and gag to make myself throw up. The food comes up easily. A wave of relief washes over me.

When I'm done, I realize someone else has come into the bathroom. I think about waiting her out, but I've already flushed and that would just be awkward.

As I open the stall door, I'm mortified to see Cristina. She slips something into her purse and looks into the mirror, wiping her nose. Her gaze flits over to me.

I can't keep staring like some kind of creep.

I definitely can't hide back in the stall.

As I exit the stall, Cristina gives me one of those fake smiles, the kind that means *I know what you're doing and you know what I'm doing.* Then she pushes past me and leaves the bathroom before I can wash my hands or completely catch my breath.

I might not be able to catch my breath.

This might be one of those moments where I completely lose control over my stomach. It's not about to heave again, but the swirling down there hasn't stopped. It's as if my anxiety has turned into a ball that's slowly growing and spinning. I'm hoping Cristina thought I was puking from drinking, but I suspect otherwise—that look on her face said everything. Though she's probably skipped a meal or two herself.

I need to get off this boat.

I decide to explore the deck, looking for the man that might be LeFeber, but I can't seem to find him again. How many places could he be? I start down a hallway, then enter another room with music blaring and people dancing. I'm making my way through the crowd when I literally bump into Zach, almost knocking over the drink he's holding. How does he manage to be everywhere at once?

"Liv," he says as if I'd been missing for a year.

"Zach!" My voice involuntarily squeaks. So embarrassing. "Have you seen Antonia?" I stammer. My nerves are on fire. I wish I could touch him again.

"Yeah, she's right over there." He points.

I'm an idiot. She's in the middle of the dance floor owning

it. Should've known. I want to run to her but stop myself because of who's next to me, and also who's not here.

No Cristina in sight. I think about mentioning what I saw her doing, but really it's none of my business and I'd die if she told him I was just puking in the bathroom.

Zach turns to me from watching the dance floor. "Want to dance?" he asks.

"I'd rather talk," I say. "I need fresh air."

He smiles. "I wanted to talk to you earlier but it was kind of awkward with Cristina following me."

"Oh. Yeah," I say, hiding the welling knot in my gut, suddenly acting like I have everything together because the last thing I want to do is screw things up with him.

I smile into his eyes. They're green and soft even in the dark. He's so handsome. No wonder he was cast on *Sisters & Mothers* as a love interest. He could be on posters around America. *Wanted man. Love interest at large.*

"Must be nice to be around so many people from your show," I say, thinking it's a stupid thing to say even as the words leave my mouth. Though I've said worse. "They seem really nice."

"Eh," he says. "The only real friend I have here is Jackson. The rest are just coworkers. It's different. You always feel like you're competing with each other."

"Really?" I say. "I didn't realize..."

"Honestly I'm getting pretty bored with that show. I know Michael is too."

"I kind of talked to him about that," I admit.

"It's hard when you get on one of these shows. There are all these expectations and once you act a certain way, people not only think that's really you, but they expect you to behave just like your character in real life." He rolls his eyes. "It's crazy to think people are that oblivious, but it's true."

"That must be kind of..." I begin, but he speaks over me.

"I don't even know why my father wanted me to throw this party in the first place. It's a stupid way to get the attention of a director."

"I can imagine this part of your life is pretty lonely," I say, trying again. "Being in the spotlight and all. But at least *you've* made a name for yourself."

"You've always seemed pretty cool." He nudges my arm with the hand holding his drink. "Artsy."

"How'd you know that I like art?" I ask.

I didn't think Zach knew anything about me except my name.

"I saw your painting hanging in a show at the library last year. The self-portrait you did? The one where you're staring at yourself in a shattered mirror."

"Oh yeah," I say, trying to downplay myself. "That was my majorly emo stage."

"No way. It was amazing how you could see all these tiny reflections of your face in the glass. Felt like I got to know you just by looking at the painting."

Zach has this look on his face like he's probably said too much and should just shut up. "I'm craving sugar," he says. "I can't eat any while we're filming, but the season just ended and Cristina's *nonna* made some amazing Italian desserts for the party. Want some?"

I shake my head and ask for a drink instead.

"I can do that," he says. "Anything else?"

"Actually..." I pause. "That guy with the glasses you were talking to earlier? With Felicity? Did that happen to be Geoff LeFeber?"

"Who's that?" Zach seems confused.

"He's an artist whose work I admire. I overheard Felicity saying he might be here..."

"*Oh,*" Zach says, gently pushing my arm. "*LeFeber.* Yeah. She was talking him up earlier this week saying that one of our producers invited him, but I don't think he's coming. She would have already been trying to become best friends with him."

Part of me feels relief, knowing that the man laughing at me wasn't LeFeber, but the other part feels pretty disappointed. I really wanted to talk to him about his art.

"I'll go get those drinks then."

He's about to enter the crowd when I grab his arm to stop him. There's something I have to know. "Zach?" I hesitate. He turns around and lingers next to me. He's so close that I can smell his cologne. "This is kind of an awkward question, but I have to ask."

You're strong. You can do this. This is easy.

He looks down at me through his long eyelashes as I stare up at his prominent Adam's apple. I wish I could reach up and touch his neck, pulling him closer to me.

"Are you and Cristina dating?" I finally ask.

Suddenly, I don't want to know the answer. I've waited so long for this moment. To be this physically close to him. To practically feel his breath on my hair.

"It's..." He looks away at the boats gliding across the harbor for a moment. "Cristina and I have history together, but... We're not *together*. It looks that way sometimes. I know. We were really close. I still try to be a good friend. The breakup was hard on her."

"I didn't mean to bring up bad feelings," I say, feeling stupid for asking the question in the first place. I just don't want to be played.

"It's cool. I like being up-front with you," Zach says. "I'll get a couple drinks. Then can we keep talking?"

I nod, my heart pounding in my chest. *Being up-front with me?* I can barely believe that, of all the people on this boat, he wants to spend his time talking to me.

I'm watching him walk across the room when I see Cristina come out of nowhere and latch on to him like a crab. Guess I better kiss that drink away. After he's done ordering at the bar, Cristina takes the second drink—my drink—from his hand, and I'm forgotten like an ugly stray. *Don't even kick a bowl of milk my way.*

I head upstairs and grab a drink from the bar on my own.

I just want to drink. I've lost Antonia. I can't seem to find LeFeber—*if* that's even him. Cristina not only totally caught me purging, she's practically claimed Zach for the night. And I can't manage to work up the social skills to mingle with anyone either.

Two champagnes and a vodka tonic later, I find myself in a corner of the aft deck with Jackson. He starts twirling my hair like he did this afternoon at the front of the school. "I didn't know you showed up," he said. "I saw your friend, but every time I went to ask her about you, she was dancing with someone else. Who dances that much?"

"She does," I say. "She's on the dance team. She's got endless dance in her."

"Do you have endless dance in you? Judging by those legs and that ass, I'd say you probably do your fair share of dancing," Jackson says.

I don't like the way he says that. I'm not his sleaze toy.

"Didn't you come here with someone?" I ask. He shakes his head.

"Naw, I was hoping to hook up," he says.

"Hook up," I echo.

"You know, meet someone. Meet you. See if you want to hang out."

"Hang out?"

I'm feeling light-headed from the champagne. It's not helping my stomach, so it's not the kind of buzz I was hoping for. And now that Jackson is half drooling on my dress, I just want to leave. I *could* like him. But not like this. Not when I have this tiny chance with Zach. Not when Jackson's being a creeper. I just can't. Why are boys so complicated? Why do they all expect so much from you?

"Do you want a ride to my house?" Jackson laughs. "I mean, home?" He slips an arm to the wall behind me, as if I need his hulky body over mine. He really thinks he's funny. Jackson might have the muscles of a superhero, but he obviously has none of Zach's gentlemanly charm. "I have to be honest," he continues. "You look way different from freshman year. You got super hot, Liv. I never would have guessed."

"Have you thought about mouthwash?" I say and duck under his arm.

"My breath doesn't stink," he says.

"Something does," I say just as Antonia returns.

"What did I miss?" she asks, eyeballing the situation.

We instantly communicate telepathically, and I don't know whether that's a good idea or not, because she walks up to Jackson.

"Hey..." Jackson says, trying to remember her name.

"Jackson Conti," she says. "You don't remember my name."

"I do," he says, thinking.

"I'm taking her home," she says and grabs my arm. We leave Jackson deep in drunken thought.

"I didn't even have to say anything to make an ass out of him," she says. "He just stood there like an idiot."

As she leads me off the boat, I catch Cristina's eye. She's standing close to Zach like a fierce cheetah protecting her young. We each share a secret now.

I just hope she forgets by tomorrow.

seven

"How hollow to have no secrets left;

you shake yourself and nothing rattles."

—ANDREW SEAN GREER

"If people behaved like the particles inside an atom," Sam says, drawing a picture of an atom on his notebook, "then most of the time you wouldn't know where they were." He brushes his wavy blond surfer hair out of his face. It's still bleached from him spending so much time outside this summer working as a counselor at a surf camp.

Those are the two things Sam talks about all the time. Science, and the water. Sam spends most of his time outside of school either surfing or sailing, though I don't really go with him anymore. He's needed more time to himself since James died and I'm so busy between schoolwork and helping my parents that I never seem to have the time. Sam's a good student too, which frustrates me sometimes because he barely has to study.

"What's that supposed to mean?" Antonia asks. She closes her chemistry book, tosses it in the middle of my kitchen table. We're at my house studying for our first test of the year. "It didn't say that anywhere in the chapter. God. Staying in San Domingo for a month put me so far behind."

I see what he's doing right away. He's talking about when I ditched him to hang out with Antonia last week. He wants me to stop being an unpredictable particle, to be a better friend. It's been a few days since I ditched him to go with Antonia to Zach's party.

I get the hint, but I don't want to let him make me feel guilty. I don't have to tell Sam about *everything*. He may be one of my best friends, but can't I have a life outside of my friendship with him? Antonia has other friends besides us. Why not me?

"He's talking about quantum mechanics." I give Sam that *I-know-what-you're-talking-about* look. He obviously didn't like my ditching him for the boat party. Sam can be a little overprotective at times. It's something I like about him—that loyalty and willingness to care. It's also something that frustrates me. He *isn't* my big brother.

"But we're not learning that stuff," Antonia says, still confused, getting frustrated. Her telepathy isn't picking up this hidden conversation between us. "Does that have to do with atomic laws?"

"I've been reading this book about quantum entanglement by a Swiss physicist," he says. "Yeah. Whatever. Call me a nerd, but it's actually super interesting."

Antonia thinks that's hilarious. "Interesting? Sounds pretty worthless."

"It's not worthless at all," Sam says. "It means teleportation could be possible one day. Wouldn't you want to go to London for lunch just for the hell of it?"

"I would *love* to go to London," Antonia says. "Doesn't mean I want to *teleport*."

"There's already been successful teleportation of entangled atoms."

"You're just showing off now."

I laugh. I love listening to Antonia and Sam debate each

other. Sam's a really philosophical person. He reads a ton and is easy to have deep conversations with, while Antonia's funny and quick on her feet. It's great when they get so salty with each other.

"Do you know the creepiest part?" Sam asks. "If you teleport, you die."

Antonia appears disgusted at the thought. "That's the *dumbest* way of traveling I've ever heard. How's that even possible?"

"Because you're reborn," Sam says. "Not cloned per se. Just transferred."

"I don't want to die, and I definitely don't want to be a baby if I'm going to London for lunch," she says. "You going to be there to push me around in a stroller when I'm reborn?"

"The idea has already been tested with photons over dozens of miles," he says. "The theory is that one day you will step into some kind of particle tube that will scan your trillions of atomic particles and send all the data to another particle chamber in London. It'll create a new you, as you are now, no different. Same you. Same thoughts. Same everything. Only the old you will disappear into a blur of particles. *Poof.*"

Antonia leans away from Sam in disbelief. "So you mean that in the movies whenever someone is beamed somewhere they die every single time?"

Sam laughs. "I guess so. Something like that anyway."

"Whatever," Antonia says. "I'll just have lunch here."

"You can teleport me to New York," I say.

"Didn't you hear what he said about teleporting?" Antonia pretends to be serious. "You have to die to do it. Not cool."

"But it's the same *you*," Sam argues. "Nothing would be different."

"Hell no," Antonia says. "Isn't that immoral? Killing people to teleport them? Nope. I won't support any technology that makes you die to use it."

"I don't think it's immoral at all if you're just as you were," he says. "It's not like you'd see anything gross. Your old particles would just be gone. Replaced with new ones."

"Immoral," Antonia says. She's obviously joking, but I can tell she's pushing his buttons. He's looking down at the kitchen tile. Something's definitely bugging him. I try to think of the situation from his perspective and start to feel guilty.

He probably wouldn't have liked going to the party anyway—Sam's not a big party kind of person—but now I feel like a jerk for at least not inviting him.

"Want to watch something?" I ask. "I need a break from all this studying."

"It's hard to rationalize immoral," Sam says, "when you two were hitting some swanky boat party last weekend. I'm sure there were lots of important people."

"You *told* him?" I snap at Antonia.

"You were probably drinking too much to remember," Sam whispers so Mom doesn't hear from the living room, "but *you* told me you were going to a party. It wasn't that hard to figure out which one. The whole school had been talking about it."

"Who said anyone was drinking?" Antonia says, feigning shock. "That's *your* assumption. I'll have you know I was queen of the dance floor." She points at me. "I can't speak for *lover-girl* though."

"Me?" I say defensively. "I didn't do anything. You rescued me anyway."

"From who?" Sam asks, alarmed. "You okay?"

"It doesn't matter," I say. "You don't need to protect me."

He looks down at his lap. I automatically feel bad for snapping at him, but I don't want him to know about Jackson. It would make the whole situation worse. Sam has never liked Jackson. He's too flashy, too full of himself. I think Sam is jealous.

"Don't worry, Sam," Antonia says to him. "She handled herself… Once I walked up, anyway."

"It wasn't anything like that," I say. "I was ready to go."

"Uh-huh," Antonia says.

"I hope you weren't too drunk," Sam snaps.

I start to feel even guiltier. Not because of the drinking, but because Sam must really be hurt that I didn't invite him. He never talks like that. But I'm not backing down.

"I can handle myself," I say back. "You don't have to fight my battles for me."

"You two need to find your chill." Antonia stands up, looking for something around the room. "Speaking of drinking. You don't have anything in your bedroom we can...do you?"

"Are you serious?" Sam asks, leaning back in his chair and looking down the hallway to the living room to see if Mom is near. "Right now?"

Antonia's eyes are wide, matter-of-fact. "Of course I'm serious. Never been more serious. Maybe you should lighten up."

"I'm chill," he says.

"I might have something." I give them both a mischievous grin, thankful that Antonia derailed the conversation. I really don't want to fight with Sam. "Let's go look."

Sam holds up his textbook. "What about the chemistry test?"

Antonia is the first to get up. "Like you're even talking chemistry, quantum leap boy."

I nod my head. "I think I've had all the chemistry I can handle for tonight."

"I guess you're right," Sam says.

He follows us up the stairs to my room. I push open the door, wait for them to come in, then shut and lock it. "You never know," I say.

"Better safe than sorry," Antonia agrees. "Wow, your room hasn't changed one bit," she adds. "It's still so *dark*."

She's always teased me about how little sunlight I let inside my room. The walls are painted navy, but I'm not a total vampire. There are twinkle lights under a white canopy over my bed that gives the room this dreamy atmosphere. It helps me sleep.

Besides the framed Frida print, there's a giant chalkboard leaning on the wall next to my bed where I doodle and write my favorite quotes. The bookshelves are stuffed with diaries, art books and old records. A pale green chair sits next to my easel. Art supplies are scattered on the floor around it. Drawing tools mostly. Some paints. And a big stack of art pads of all sizes.

"Same place?" Sam asks.

I nod. The familiarity of our friendship makes me feel better. Our fights have never lasted long. It feels good to be reunited with both of them. All three of us haven't hung out together since the beginning of summer. Antonia was traveling. Sam was working. I was helping Mom with her literacy campaign. Though Sam and I have known each other since elementary school, we formed our trifecta with Antonia at the beginning of high school in world history when the three of us were assigned a research project on the Middle Ages. I never thought any of us would have been friends with each other, but I guess we can thank Vlad the Impaler for bringing us together.

As Sam walks into my closet and reaches behind one of my shoeboxes, I notice how tan and muscular he's gotten over the summer. Maybe he doesn't need to fill out as much as I thought. He brings out the vodka, twists off the cap and offers the bottle to me.

It's almost empty.

"Damn, Liv," Sam says. "How much have you been drinking this summer?"

"Shut up. Just give me the bottle."

I take the first pull. The alcohol burns its way down.

"I have a confession to make." Antonia grabs the bottle. "Better give me a drink first."

"Confession?" I ask. "What's this about?"

Sam takes a double shot. After all his talk about *immorality* and *swanky boat parties*. "Maybe she's willing to teleport after all," he says.

I look at Antonia. She looks like she's about to burst with secrets. Is there something she hasn't told me about what happened during summer vacation?

"Nothing like that," she says. "It's this girl."

"Girl?" Sam and I say at the same time.

"Yes, a girl. I've been talking to this girl from the track team." Antonia fidgets with her front pocket. "I'm pretty sure we want to hook up with each other."

"Are you serious?" I ask. "Why didn't you tell me?"

We've talked about guys before, but Antonia always turned the subject back to me. Though she has a flirtatious personality, I guess I just thought she wasn't interested in dating people in general. She seemed to always be able to have fun on her own.

"I wanted to make sure I really knew before I told you," Antonia says.

I hug Antonia tight. "I'm so glad you said something."

"You guys are the first people I've told," Antonia says, smiling as I let go of the hug. "Except for her, of course. I'll eventually tell my family, but they're open-minded. I'm not worried."

"*Dude.* From the track team?" Sam says. "You've got some serious game."

"There's a problem," Antonia says. "Better give me another drink."

She takes the bottle from me and sends another shot down her throat.

"What is it?" I ask as she wipes her mouth.

"I think she's scared," Antonia says. "She doesn't want to be *labeled*. You know? Her parents are pretty old-fashioned. She said her father won't even watch a TV show with a gay character. At least that's what she tells me about him. Real loser."

"Screw that guy," Sam says, taking the bottle from her. "Do what makes you happy. You should definitely go for it."

"Yeah," I say. "I'm so here for this. For you."

"Thanks, Sam." Antonia squeezes his bicep and winks at me. "So now that I've made my confession…you guys can't leave me hanging. We've barely seen each other in like three months. There must be some new deep dark secret you're dying to tell us."

"I don't know," Sam says, looking down at my carpet.

"You must have hooked up with some hot surfer chicks over the summer." I take another swig from the bottle. It's finally starting to make me feel like the warmth is radiating from my bones. "Come on. You know you want to tell."

As soon as I say those words, I regret asking about other girls. If there are any or have been any over the summer, I don't want to know. Thinking of him with other girls creates knots in my stomach. Even though I don't want Sam to be overprotective, I suddenly feel protective over him. Everything about our relationship feels like a paradox.

"Yeah. Right," Sam mumbles. He looks up at Antonia. "Let's talk about something else, please?"

"Come on." I swing my arm around Sam, leaning my head onto his shoulder. "You can tell us. We always talk about *everything*."

"Yeah." Antonia shakes her index finger. "No secrets."

"It's really stupid, but I keep having these dreams about my brother," Sam says. He absentmindedly tucks his hair behind his ear. "We'll be surfing, joking around, racing each other to catch a wave, but then he disappears under the water. I can never save him."

"Sam," I say, hugging him, remembering how he cried into my chest the day he found out his older brother, James, had died. It broke my heart. It still does. "You okay?"

James died last year from a drug overdose at their house. It was completely unexpected. He was a super nice guy who would stop anything he was doing to help someone else. James had been visiting home from the University of Chicago, where he was on the crew team. We didn't know until later, but a doctor had prescribed heavy painkillers for a back injury that happened during a rowing competition, which I guess led to James getting involved in doing harder drugs.

I was shocked when I found out. He'd only been back three days for Christmas break when he overdosed. Sam found his body. We've only talked about what happened once or twice, but Sam doesn't say much. It doesn't seem like the kind of thing I can help him with. I can't take away his pain or erase what happened. Whenever I think about what Sam must have had to go through, I get a lump in my throat. I feel helpless.

My problems seem so trivial compared to Sam's loss. What right do I have to fall apart when there are other people who've been dealt a hand much worse than mine?

"Yeah." Sam pulls away. "It's just a really weird feeling. I wake up and the only person I want to talk to about James's death is...James." We all go silent for a moment until Sam takes the bottle from me. "Anyway. I took my turn. Fair's fair. Liv?"

"Oh man," I say nervously. It's my turn to do some talking about my personal issues. I think about how depressed I was this summer and how much I wanted to tell them that I felt like a ghost haunting the real world, but I couldn't, because they were living their best lives and I didn't want to be selfish and ruin their happiness.

Because Sam and Antonia were both gone, I started spending a lot of time online. I started looking up tips about purging and I stumbled onto a pro-bulimia forum. Then I found myself making an account so I could talk to other users of the site. My thoughts about food started getting more obsessive the more I read the posts. One night, I saw a thread where the original poster asked for photos of other people's binge foods.

I scrolled through and examined the dozens of food photographs. The one that got to me was all of this half-eaten food spread across a table with all the wrappers—leftovers of a take-out chicken shawarma, a slab of meat lasagna, cookie batter, a chocolate milkshake. I couldn't stop thinking about how good a nice big binge would feel. Just looking at the food made me feel excited to eat, so I went downstairs and raided the pantry. I took everything that was either leftover or premade: bacon and cheddar potato skins, three microwave burritos, a can of sweet corn, three hot dogs, a container of cake frosting, a quarter of an apple pie, carrots and hummus, a small bag of pita bread and half a jar of peanut better.

Looking at the pictures while eating made me feel so much less alone. It's not like I can talk to Antonia or Sam about my bulimia. What would I say? That I've started wearing ponytails because my hair has thinned out so much? That puking actually feels like a relief? I wouldn't wish this on anyone. It's uncomfortable and disgusting. But knowing other girls are bingeing too is so cathartic. It's the easiest thing to eat.

So simple. So animalistic.

The sensory experience of chewing and tasting was euphoric. Finishing off one thing made me immediately want to start on the next. I couldn't do anything to stop it. I had to give in to it until I was so full I literally couldn't stuff anything down my disgusting throat. Then I vomited and vomited until there was nothing left.

I'm almost certain Antonia suspects something's going on with my eating habits after I kept hesitating every time she asked whether I wanted to eat with her. She knows me too well. I need to throw her off that trail, because she can be relentless.

"Dad says he's running for governor," I finally say. "He hasn't announced it yet though. He's keeping it on the down low until he hires a campaign manager."

"And that's a problem?" Sam asks.

"*Duh,*" I say. "Get ready for your little Liv's face to appear on the front page of the *Los Angeles Times* when the announcement happens. It won't be as easy as his other elections. He's not going to be the incumbent this time, which means *a lot* more media coverage. TV appearances. Articles. That kind of thing."

"That actually sounds pretty exciting," Antonia says.

"Mason's coming home next weekend too," I add. "I'm not looking forward to that either. We've had our share of problems."

"That's not a *big* problem," Antonia says. "That's just family."

"I guess you're right," I say, but I don't really agree in my heart. Not when family is my biggest problem next to a certain boy named Zach. Just thinking about him motivates me to keep restricting and purging until I reach my goal weight.

I have to talk to him again.

And I have to look good when I do.

eight

"So, Sam told me something interesting," Antonia says, pulling her messenger bag up over her shoulder.

Even though I want to know the gossip about Sam, I'm having a hard time listening right now. I can't concentrate. I'm so *hungry*. I was starving when I woke up this morning, but I stuck to my morning grapefruit and tea. It's working at least.

"Wait. What?" I ask.

"He joined debate club. Forensics or whatever. Why do they call it that? I thought that was supposed to be related to some kind of *CSI* crap."

"He did?" I wonder why he didn't tell me. I suddenly feel a little hurt—like maybe Sam is getting back at us for going to the party without him. "When did he say that?"

Students are spilling out into the hallway. Eastlake Prep, home of the "most talented student body" in the Los Angeles area. The pressure to be successful, to set yourself apart from everyone else, is ridiculously high. How else are you going to feel, when most of your classmates are actors on cable television and world-class athletes?

I glance around the hall. I'm desperate to see Zach again. I start to feel butterflies just thinking about him—his dark hair, his defined jawline—but then I get queasy.

Antonia slams her locker shut. "When we were walking out to our cars after we studied... I mean, after we drank in your bedroom."

"That was like..." I start counting in my head "...a week ago."

"I didn't think you were going to think it was *that* big of a deal." She puts a hand on my shoulder. "Don't get so jealous. He just said he forgot to tell us."

"Him? Likely not," I say. "He's been acting weird lately. Did you see how jealous he got when you started talking about what happened at the boat party with Jackson?"

"He's definitely not the same guy." Antonia curls up her arm like she's lifting a weight. "Did you see those biceps? Those surf camp babes must have been all over him."

"That's not what I meant," I say, dragging her toward class, though I have noticed that Sam has begun to fill out the last few months. "Let's talk about something else."

"Wait a second," Antonia says. "*Zach Park* might have a thing for you, but secretly you *actually* have a thing for Sam, don't you? Since when? *All along?*"

"Don't be stupid," I say. Antonia has teased me about having a crush on Sam ever since I told her about the one time we kissed on the bench last year. "I mean Sam's a great guy, but I know him too well. There's no mystery there."

I think there was maybe a chance for us once, but after I cried on his shoulder after Ollie dumped me, I felt too awkward to let myself think about Sam that way. My feelings about our friendship were confusing. It felt natural to share the details about my relationships with him, but Sam would get hurt and never say anything. I couldn't figure out where I stood with him. In some ways, I guess I'm still trying to solve that problem.

As Antonia and I enter the building, Jackson passes by with

one of his friends. He doesn't stop to talk, but as he walks by us he says, "Looking good, Liv."

I roll my eyes at Antonia, hoping that I don't look completely awkward. After the way he acted at the boat party, I feel like I'd better steer clear of him for a while. I definitely don't want Zach's best friend to think I'm into him. So I pretend not to hear Jackson, but Antonia notices him slapping his friend's arm and laughing after they pass.

"What was *that* about?" Antonia asks.

I shrug. "Guys being guys, I guess."

"Terrible excuse," Antonia says. "What a creeper."

"Yeah," I sigh. "Sam has never liked him. Maybe he has something there."

"I have a theory," she says. "About Sam."

"Yeah?"

"I can't think of any reason he'd ever join speech and debate unless it's for a..."

"...girl," we say at the same time.

"Sam doesn't do extracurricular stuff," Antonia says. "He's too busy studying or surfing."

The greasy feeling in my stomach is getting worse. I want to ditch class, curl up under my blankets at home and fall asleep with my Frida painting watching over me.

"I'm guessing you want me to ask you more about your theory," I say.

I can't *not* ask. If I try to change the subject again, Antonia will really think something's up with me and Sam, and Antonia is the worst about prying things out of me.

"Well," Antonia says, "just by chance I saw him talking to Nina Jaggia outside the cafeteria on Tuesday." She leads us past the school's chapel and toward the off-white arches at the entrance of the classroom building. We're on our way to US history.

"So?" I ask.

"So, Nina's on the speech and debate team."

"And?"

"Well you weren't there. You didn't see their body language."

My pulse starts to speed up. It's not entirely because of Sam, even though I am kind of hurt he hasn't said anything to me. We're about to cross paths with the school's trio of most popular girls, including Cristina. Felicity and a girl named Amy Hernandez, a former Disney Channel dancer, are walking on either side of Cristina. This is about to be trouble.

I haven't talked to Cristina beyond seeing her in the bathroom at the yacht party, but you can't go to Eastlake and not know who she is. Her parents work for an Italian car company bringing in imports, and let me tell you they have millions, and even sponsor two Formula One cars and a portion of the privatized space industry—some kind of experimental engine called the X-Change.

And Cristina is *really* smart. Her robotics team won some major student competition last year, and all this was before she started dating Zach and snagged that major modeling campaign. She may have been following him around on the yacht, but I'm sure that was a one-night thing, because any guy would be following *her* around.

With her signature long red hair, Felicity completes the trio with her contacts in the art world. Her father works as a major collector for an international luxury goods conglomerate. They know *everyone*. If anyone is always going where I want to be, it's Felicity. Only she doesn't want to be an artist herself. She just wants the limelight.

Antonia hates them.

"Don't look now, but here comes the Hydra," Antonia says under her breath as we stop walking. They're literally blocking our way through the archway into the building.

"Hi, ladies," Felicity says.

"Be careful what you call them," Amy says. The way Amy talks makes you wonder if she's trying to be sarcastic or if she actually hates you.

"Hi," I say, trying not to take offense.

"I heard you and Zach had quite the conversation on the yacht," Cristina says. "He told me you were like a little puppy dog, following him around when I wasn't in the room. That must have been annoying."

I'm trying to like Cristina, but she's not giving me much of a reason to—especially the way *she* was actually hanging all over him at the party even though, according to Zach, they had already broken up by then.

"I was talking to him about the show," I say, trying to add to her jealousy since she obviously thinks she still has some kind of ownership over Zach. "I've seen every episode of *Sisters & Mothers*. It's so *addicting...*"

Cristina suddenly cringes, looking at me strangely when I use that word, which I actually didn't plan to say. Now I know she's just as afraid of my revealing her secret about snorting up in the bathroom as I am of her revealing mine.

"You watch that show?" Amy laughs. "It's terrible. Zach is way better than that role. Everyone knows that he's going to be a big star someday."

"I watch all kinds of shows," I say, sensing Antonia's blood boiling. I'm hoping she doesn't go for Amy's throat.

I pinch her discreetly so that she won't say anything.

She lets out a little squeak.

"What's that?" Amy says to Antonia. "I didn't hear you."

I pinch Antonia again. Harder.

"I didn't say anything," she says, squirming. "But we have to go study the Lake of Lerna." That's the lake where the Hydra lives. It's also the entrance to the underworld.

"Lake of Lerna," Amy repeats stupidly. "Sounds fascinating."

"Should I ask what's in that lake? Maybe we should test you," says Felicity.

Antonia pops her gum. "Water serpents," she enunciates slowly.

"So?" Felicity says.

Antonia goes for the subtle punch line even though I'm pinching her. "So, their heads grow back when they're chopped off."

"That's gross." Felicity doesn't get the mocking humor. She turns to me. "I heard you're into art." How does she know this about me? Did Zach talk to her about our conversation on the boat? Why would she bring that up in front of Cristina?

"I'm thinking about going to art school after graduation."

"That's cool," Felicity says, but she's not really listening. "You must have heard about the opening of LeFeber's new show in Laguna Beach?"

I squint at her in disbelief. She obviously wants to show off.

"Wasn't he supposed to be at that party in Marina del Rey last week?" I ask, not wanting to get my hopes up again even though I still can't get the thought of meeting LeFeber out of my head. It's too bad that my only shot is probably going to be through Felicity, especially since she's Cristina's best friend.

"How am I supposed to know? Something came up, I guess," she says like it's no big deal. "His show is exclusive and it's totally impossible to get on the list."

"I saw the preview of one of his new pieces in *ArtNews*," I say. "He's one of my favorite living artists."

I try to talk about how LeFeber tries to make his installations participatory—he doesn't want people to just *look* at his art; he wants his audience to explore and interact with the installations—but Felicity interrupts me.

"Does he?" Felicity says. "Maybe we can bring you back an autograph. I'll try to remember when my parents and I are having dinner with him before the show."

Is she trying to make me jealous? Does she want me to beg for an invitation? Not going to happen. I really want to go, but I don't want to owe her or Cristina anything.

"Exciting," Cristina says, turning to me. "How's your stomach?"

My muscles begin to tighten as anger rushes through my body. I want to say *How's your nose?* But I hold my tongue. I get her point. She wants me to stay away from her man, and also to not do anything to threaten her.

So I just say, "Fine. It's fine," as Cristina and her friends walk away from us.

Antonia snickers in my ear. "The Hydra doesn't even know I was making fun of their multiple snake heads."

"Yeah." That's about all I can manage. I want to go to this LeFeber show. I have to find a way to get in, and Antonia probably isn't going to be able to help this time. These girls have no idea how much his work means to me. LeFeber's a brand name to them. When I look at his art, I get this feeling that he knows some deep secret about me though we've never met. It kills me to be so close and that I have to basically go through my crush's ex—who obviously hates me—to meet him.

Antonia is disturbed by my response. "Why didn't you stand up for yourself? Do you want to be friends with those snake heads? Don't tell me it's because of LeFeber."

"I don't know. It's nothing," I say, opening the door to the building. It's getting close to the end of the passing period and the hallway is almost empty. My stomach churns. I shouldn't have eaten so much this morning. The fat is making me feel sick. My energy is crashing from all the sugar in the iced coffee. The uncomfortable fullness nags at my mind. I feel like purging everything from my body to feel normal, but I fight it off.

"Doesn't seem like nothing," she says.

"Just drop it," I say. "It's not worth fighting over."

"I need you to do something for me," Antonia says, changing the subject. "It's a date. You'd just have to come with me."

"Um, no," I say, not wanting to be a third wheel.

"Don't say no yet—you haven't even heard me out. It's not a big deal."

My stomach is in knots from the conversation with Felicity and seeing Jackson, but Antonia is my friend. She helped me get invited to the yacht party. I owe her a big one.

"Okay, what?" I ask.

"Don't act so hurt. Geez…"

"I'm sorry," I say. "My mind is just on other things."

She smiles. "There's one catch though."

"See? I knew something was up."

"I'm going out with a girl," Antonia says. "Heather. Obviously."

A boy from our class hurries down the hallway to the room, nodding at us as he passes. Antonia pulls me toward the wall and begins to whisper. "Look, I want to go out with Heather. Remember I told you about her? The girl from the track team?"

"Don't get me wrong, Antonia. I'm totally cool with you going out with a girl. But I still don't want to be your third wheel. It'll be so awkward."

"I want to make her feel more comfortable."

"If she doesn't want to go on a solo date, why can't we just have a kick back or something? We could hang out at my house. Or yours."

"It's not the same. We need to go *out* together. I want her to feel accepted. She hasn't told anyone she's gay. I just think she's going to feel more comfortable going out as like a group of friends. It'll lessen the pressure."

"I still don't see how my going makes sense," I say. "I don't want to get in the way of your romance."

"Well…" Antonia hesitates. "There's something else. My cousin Mika is coming into town that weekend and my parents said I had to take her out to do something, but that happens to be the night I agreed to go with Heather. I can't get around it."

"So…" I cross my arms, waiting to hear the rest of Antonia's story. I knew there was going to be more to her story. She always withholds information.

"She's a little weird. Chatty. And I don't want her to totally take over the date. I need someone to entertain her," she says, looking up at me with pleading eyes.

The bell rings. I don't want to be late for class.

"When's the date?" I ask.

"End of next week," Antonia says. "Plenty of time to think about it…"

"All right," I say.

"All right?" She seems shocked I've already made up my mind.

"If it's all about making your date feel accepted, then I guess that's a good thing."

"Exactly." Antonia grabs my shoulder. "What could be wrong with that? I know of an all-ages place we can chill. Lots of people. Bands. Just hang out."

I guess it's also a good way to avoid Mason and the rest of my family for at least part of the weekend. Mika can't be that bad. I'll just have to make small talk.

"Yeah," I say. "Sounds like a blast."

nine

"A dysfunctional family is any family with more than one person in it."

—MARY KARR

I woke up this morning feeling like crap.

I purged again last night.

Mom made lasagna last night, and I couldn't help myself. I stuffed down two huge pieces. I *can't* gain any more weight, and I'm sick of purging. It feels terrible. My throat's sore. My back hurts from hurling. My face is puffy. I've started developing a sore on one of my knuckles from my teeth scraping against my hand when I stuff my fingers down my throat to make myself vomit.

It's such a stupid cycle.

I have to take my punishment now before everyone wakes up. The rest of the day is going to be super busy. Dad's calling a family meeting about the campaign, Royce and Mason are down here to visit and I have that date with Antonia and Heather tonight.

The house is completely quiet as I walk into my bathroom and shed my pajamas. I pull on my running shorts and shoes. After getting dressed, I go downstairs and put two frozen waffles in the toaster. While they're cooking, I take a kitchen knife and cut an apple into tiny, thin slices. I eat half then leave the rest out on a plate. When the waffles are finished, I pull them out of the toaster and bite off a piece from each.

I chew until the waffle becomes mushy in my mouth, then spit the food into the sink. I tear a few pieces off and put them on the plate with the apples, then dump syrup all over them. The rest of the waffle goes down the garbage disposal. I make sure to leave the plate out. Mom will tell me I'm being a slob, but she won't ask me about breakfast.

I leave for my run, heading up the road for the canyon. The rosy pink dawn is beginning to burn off the night. I start off slowly, stretching my legs, then hit my stride, running faster and faster, until my calves begin to burn. With each step, I feel the blood circulating through my body. Other joggers begin to come out. Young mothers push strollers up hills, which motivates me to run even harder until I finally reach the canyon and take a break. Sweat drips down my chest and back and I have to use my shirt to wipe off my forehead. The sun's all the way up in the sky now. I jog the trails around the canyon for another hour until I'm so exhausted that I have to walk back to the house.

When I finally get home, Royce is splayed out on the couch, head back, snoring like some kind of ugly swamp monster. He's in his senior year at Stanford. The article he had published in the *New York Times*, which was about the effects of climate change on rural America, helped him decide that he wants to work as a reporter for an international Associated Press bureau after graduation. He's way too busy to be hanging out here. Royce is one of the most even-keeled people I know. It's unsettling to see him so off balance. Things with Jas must really be going wrong.

"What are you doing here?" I ask, waking him up. "You're snoring."

Royce blinks for about twenty seconds. He has that just-woken-up-red-eye look.

Is he even awake? He used to think I was funny when I woke him up like this. I guess that was already a long time ago. We haven't been living in the same house for four years. "Sunshine?" I say. "Come in, Captain Sunshine."

"I'm awake," he says, as if I'm the current problem in his life. "Why do you still call me that?"

I gave him that nickname back when we were both in elementary school. Royce has always been a heavy sleeper and Mom used to send me—the annoying little sister—into his room to wake him up for school every morning.

"Because you are," I say, standing over him. "Why are you here? I thought your classes and job were taking up all your time."

"Dad's campaign. I just got in this morning."

"How could I forget?" I say sarcastically. Royce probably knew about the campaign before I did. Mason only recently cleaned his act up after drinking so much and getting into trouble when he was my age, but Royce has always been the golden boy. "Is today the day we're supposed to sit around the living room while he lays out his grand plans about how we're going to tour every city in California and dine with all the important people in state politics? Oh, and how we're to only talk about winning if we're interviewed, but don't get interviewed unless his campaign manager is there with us?" I swing my fist like I'm so excited. "Or how we're all supposed to be strong as a family, and if we have any differences with each other to air them out now, or to at least promise to bury them during the campaign? Something like that?"

"Why don't you want to help Dad?" Royce asks. "He said you were acting super weird about the whole thing."

"How am I supposed to act?" I ask. "I really want to know."

To be honest, I can't say I've been trying that hard. I don't want to be consumed by his campaign. It's not what I want to do with my life—I didn't sign up for this.

"Just…not weird," Royce says.

"Well, that's me," I say. "I'm weird."

Out of us three kids, I've always been the black sheep. Although my parents respect artists, they don't think *I* should be an artist. Whenever I mention wanting to go to art school, they change the subject. That's another reason I want to talk to LeFeber. His parents didn't accept him as an artist. They didn't even really accept him as a person. What kept him going? Did he stand up to his family? Did they ever believe in him?

Royce and Mason find the campaign trail exciting. It sounds like hell to me. Arguing about politics? Meeting with strangers to win their vote? No thanks.

"I know." He rubs his eyes. He looks like he hasn't slept well in at least a week. Maybe longer. "But you don't have to act like this is the worst thing you'll ever have to do in life. There are a lot worse things that could be happening."

I hear some kind of subtext in what he's saying, like he wants to tell me something but won't. "What do you mean?" I ask.

Royce turns away as if I've struck a nerve. "Nothing. It just means things could be worse so you should stop thinking about yourself and think about what Dad's doing to help our family. It's not going to be *that* different from any other campaign he's run."

"Isn't being a congressman enough? Haven't our entire lives been given to his campaigns? To the Blakely family *image*?" Royce sits up on the couch. I can tell I've finally gotten his attention. "It's my junior year. Even though he probably won't announce until the end of this calendar year, you know he'll be planning for months ahead of the campaign. Then there will be the actual campaigning, which will go until November of next year. If he wins, then that means half of senior year in Sacramento. I just want to figure out who I am on my own for once."

"Politics matter. Or at least *policies* do. Take Jasmine—"

Royce interrupts himself before he can finish his sentence. It's like even saying Jasmine's name is physically painful for him. I've never seen him this way. They get feisty with one another, but always seem to make up. This must be worse. Something big.

"What were all those texts about a couple weeks ago?"

"Nothing. I shouldn't have sent them to you," he says.

"Do you need to talk?" I ask Royce. "Did Jasmine come down with you?"

He shakes his head.

"Where is she?" I ask. "Still at school?"

Royce swipes his hand over his bedhead. "I don't know."

I'm worried for him. He honestly looks like he's on the brink of falling apart. He's probably stressed about graduation, finding a job and now the campaign on top of figuring out his problems with Jas. I want to comfort him, but I don't know what to say.

Leaning on the arm of the couch, Royce opens his mouth, then changes his mind before he finally speaks. "We're trying to figure out what's next."

"You mean like marriage?" I say.

Royce shakes his head. "No. Like careers. I want to start reporting for an international bureau. She's planning to apply to medical schools. That's *seven* more years of studying and residencies. Who knows what else."

"That's a long time," I say, trying to be understanding of him even though I want to ask why that's such a big problem for their relationship.

He slowly gets up from the couch. "Want breakfast? I'll make something."

"I already ate," I say, feeling nauseous at even the thought of eating food. "I'm not hungry."

I usually don't have to worry about Royce catching on to my eating habits. He's oblivious about that sort of thing.

"Come on," he says. "Talk to me in the kitchen. I'm starving."

I lean on the kitchen counter while Royce pulls enough food from the fridge to feed a small family. It's disgusting how much food he can eat and still stay so thin. It's like we don't even come from the same gene pool. I eat one burrito and gain two pounds.

Royce turns on a burner. He cracks eggs onto the pan. They sizzle and hiss from the heat. Then he starts mixing pancake batter. It smells so good. I want to eat some, but I have to stop overeating. It's the only way I'm going to get down to my goal weight.

"How's Eastlake?" Royce asks. "I miss that place."

"You would," I say, staring at the pancakes bubbling on the stove. The smell of the batter makes my stomach turn. "Everyone liked you."

Royce laughs. "I don't think you really remember right…"

"Whatever. Everyone likes you, Royce."

"Believe me, I wasn't that popular. I just had a small group of close friends before I met Jasmine…" I can hear sadness and longing for a simpler time in his voice.

I suddenly feel bad for Royce. His life is probably so intertwined with hers that he wouldn't know what to do if they ever broke up. "Want to go to the de los Santoses' house?" I ask, trying to cheer him up. "I'll go with you. I haven't seen Jas's family in forever."

Royce shrugs. "It's not really where I should be right now."

Now I'm really worried. Did they break up already?

"You go visit them," he says. "I need to stay here and be a part of *this* family."

"I thought Jasmine was your family. *Our* family, actually."

I don't mean to push him, but I want to understand the problem.

"Don't be like this, Liv. I told you—if you want to go visit

91

them, go right ahead. I'm going to finish my breakfast, then help Dad when he gets home."

"I'm sorry," I say, touching Royce's shoulder. "You know me. I like to fix problems."

He attempts a half smile. "It isn't your problem to fix, Liv."

"I just want to help, but I guess I don't really know how."

"It's okay." Royce pinches his nose between his index finger and thumb. "You better go take a shower. You kind of smell."

I'm about to head upstairs when Dad walks in with Mason and a bald-headed guy with thick black glasses I don't recognize. He looks at me like I'm a dirty dish towel.

"Hi, honey," Dad says to me. "This is Rich Nguyen."

"I'd shake your hand, but…" I hold up my palms. "I'm kind of sweaty. Just went for a run."

"That's *okay*," Rich says, assessing everything about me. I can tell already that Rich is going to be a control freak. "Tell me something about yourself."

His question takes me off guard. I was expecting a simple greeting, not a job interview. "I love Frida Kahlo," I say. "She's one of my favorite artists."

Rich scrunches his eyes. "That's the one with the unibrow, right?"

I'm appalled. I don't even know how to respond. I want to tell Rich how Frida had to overcome so many obstacles to be able to paint. How polio left her crippled as a child. How she was riding a bus one day that was hit by a streetcar, sending an iron rail through her pelvis. How she learned to paint while her spinal column was shattered. I consider telling Rich how way ahead of her time Frida was and how much pain she had to go through to even be able to paint, but he won't care. That's not why we're talking.

"Well. I'd like to meet with you to put together what I like to call an 'image promotion plan.' Your brothers will need to put one together too, but yours will be the most important.

Teenage girls present the most difficult challenges to navigate for political elections. On the family front, that is."

I've just met this guy and he's already calling me a *difficult challenge*? I look to Dad for support. Maybe an explanation? Or a smile? Nothing. "Could you explain what an image promotion plan actually is?" I ask. I have a guess, but I don't think this is going to go anywhere good for me. I've been around PR people who have helped my parents before. I generally don't fit into their image of what a politician's daughter should be.

Rich shrugs his shoulders and straightens out the sleeves of his perfectly pressed lavender shirt. "Let me put it this way. Think of any major modern charismatic leader or well-known person. JFK. LeBron James. Angelina Jolie. Pope Francis. Oprah. Bono. They have to construct a public persona. Then they have to *promote* that image."

"Isn't that what Dad has to do? What does this have to do with me?"

All of a sudden, Rich gets really excited. "Oh no! Of course you have to worry about your image. It's good you're a girl to begin with. Daughters of politicians are always preferred to sons by voters. Except that can be a double-edged sword because being placed on the podium means that you can fall farther. Higher expectations."

"I'm sorry," I interrupt. "It's just that I don't plan to be that involved. Right, Dad?"

Dad slowly sips his coffee. My heart sinks.

When I was younger, Dad could bring me out for photo opportunities, but the press generally didn't care too much about children. There wasn't enough of a story there. Now I'm a teenager? That's huge fodder for the news. All bets are off.

"We didn't really need to bother with this stuff for you when I ran for Congress because you were so young, but your brothers have had to put together an image plan. It's really not so bad. You just have to think of yourself as a character."

"A character?" I'm nearly shaking. "I'm a real person, Dad, I'm not—"

I don't want to turn into a pawn in a political chess game.

"Come on, Liv. You know that part of being a political family means you're in the public eye. We're not trying to control your private life. We've just invited Rich to help us craft a plan for you."

"So then what's this gonna involve?" I ask. He'll obviously want me to keep a low profile. Forget hanging out with Zach. Why does this have to happen right now?

Finally his turn to speak, Rich gets all excited again and sets his binder on the table. He opens the papers so I can flip through them. "First are the values. What are three abstract qualities you want to represent? For example, Barack Obama, I'd say, attempted to embody a mix of sunny optimism and cautious reserve. That's our starting point anyway. We'll figure out the nitty-gritty of what colors to wear for TV appearances and other things of that nature later on when the campaign is announced."

Everything Rich is saying makes me think of Ollie Barrios. Dress this way. Look that way. Hang around with these people. Be my little Barbie Doll all the time.

I look to Mason for backup. He shrugs.

"You've really thought all this out," I say to Dad and Rich. "I should go, I need a shower."

"Honeybee," Dad says, stabbing into one of Royce's pancakes. "The boys and I are going to start working on the campaign with Rich. You should stick around."

"I have plans," I lie. "Royce can't wait though."

Royce emerges from his haze. "Sorry. Been a long night."

"Aren't they all?" Dad says. "I'm telling you, getting this campaign in order has cut my sleep in half. You don't have to go," Dad says to me. "You have a say in this too."

"Sorry, Congressman Blakely," I say. "Duty calls."

"What duty is that?" he asks. "There are some family items we really need to run over."

Items. Run over. Like our conversation is a *press release.*

"I already figured those out with Royce. Just ask him. Look, if I don't get to a shower ASAP, we're going to have a problem, as you can probably smell..." I say, leaving the room as Mason shrugs at Dad.

Forget spending my entire Saturday working on the campaign with the boys and being told what to do by Rich Nguyen. I'm going to the de los Santos house stealth style. Maybe Danilo will know what's going on with Royce and Jasmine.

After I shower and dress, I sneak back downstairs. Dad and the others are debating something in his office as I walk into the kitchen. I pull up my phone and order an Uber. It's going to be an expensive ride all the way out to Chatsworth and Mom's probably going to kill me when she notices the charge on the credit card, but I don't care. I need to get out, talk to someone who isn't part of the mess that's my life right now. I need to talk to Danny. He's someone I can talk deep with too—art and dreams and all the other things people seem so afraid of revealing about themselves. That used to be Sam. If he really joined the debate team to pursue a girl, I figure I better keep my distance. Not to mention that I have feelings for Zach. Maybe we have to be less close.

"Honeybee?" Dad shouts. "Come here. I want to talk to you about something."

I head into Dad's study. "I only have a few minutes. Sam's picking me up."

"I really want you to take this image thing seriously," Dad says. "You do understand that my career rides on this election? That this is my job."

"Yes, Dad. I understand. It's cool." He's right. Complaining isn't going to stop him from running. And fighting with him is only going to make him think I need more babysitting from Rich. I glance at him. He doesn't exactly look that excited to be working with me either. "I'll start working on the image plan or whatever."

"Thank you, Liv. I think you'll learn a lot from this campaign as long as you're willing to be open-minded."

I walk by the fruit bowl and grab another apple to take with me on the way to Danny's house. Then I check my phone. My ride's almost here.

As I'm walking out the door, I see Mom pulling into the driveway, which makes me nervous. She's going to ask too many questions. I just want to get away from here for a little while and soak up some time to myself before the campaign really gets started.

She parks her car and steps out, her hair and makeup perfect. "You were up early this morning," she says.

"I ran to Franklin Canyon," I say, not offering much information. I'm hoping I can get her to go inside before the car shows up. There's no way she'll take me all the way out to Chatsworth without wanting to stay and chat with Jasmine's parents.

I'd rather hang out with the de los Santos family myself. When Jas and Royce started dating, Jas became part of our family, but—even better—I got to become part of hers. They're easy to be around. They're not constantly focused on politics like my family and always ask about my art when I come over. I really don't want to lose them.

"That's a long way. I hope you took a snack," she says, opening her back seat and pulling out a box of books. "You need fuel to run those kinds of distances."

"I ate before I ran." Exercise and restricting my food is essential to meeting my goal of a hundred pounds. I want to meet that goal for myself, but I want to look good for Zach too. He's around tiny actresses all the time. I have to look my best.

Mom starts walking toward the front door, carrying her box.

"Just be careful not to overdo things. You tend to push yourself too hard."

"I'll be careful," I say, checking my phone again. It says that the driver's about a mile away. "Dad's inside talking to Rich and the boys about campaign stuff."

Mom exhales a deep breath. "So you finally met Rich? I trust your father with these kinds of choices, but this one's a little intense for my taste."

I nod. "Yeah. He also thinks Frida Kahlo is the 'one with the unibrow.'"

"*Cretin.*" Mom laughs.

I'm lifting my arm up to push a stray hair back behind my ear when Mom grabs my hand. "What happened, Liv? These sores look awful."

I pull my hand away from her fast. My heart is racing. She probably won't figure the real reason about the sore right away, but she's the kind of person who will look up information on WebMD for hours until she figures out all possible causes of a symptom. It would only be a matter of time before she confronted me on my secret.

"I was working on the throwing wheel at school this week and the clay was really rough," I lie. I'm not even in ceramics. "It cut up my hand a little."

"What have I told you about putting Neosporin on wounds? You have to do that or the sore will turn into a scar. You have such pretty hands, Liv."

"I know," I say. "I just forgot."

"Do you need a ride somewhere? I just need to set down this box. We're collecting donations for elementary school libraries…"

"Sam's picking me up," I lie again, silently apologizing to Sam in my head for using him as an excuse to get away from my family. Thinking about him reminds me of Antonia's comment about how much Sam has physically changed this summer.

It won't be long until he gets a serious girlfriend and whatever feelings were growing between us last year when we kissed on the bench at the marina will be completely gone.

"I've always loved that boy."

"I know you have," I say hesitantly.

"I just wish you and he could—"

"Mom, please. Not right now."

Thinking about Sam like a potential boyfriend hurts my head. I have feelings for Zach. Sam obviously likes another girl. We're too much like siblings to date.

She opens the front door. "Well," she says, sounding disappointed, "be back by 5 p.m. tonight. We're finally going to have a proper family dinner."

ten

"Life shrinks or expands in proportion to one's courage."

—ANAIS NIN

I'm standing at the front door of the de los Santos family home when Jas's youngest brother, Isko, answers in tapered black sweatpants and a track jacket. He's got the whole athleisure look going on with his outfit. He's also wearing eyeliner. It looks hot. His dark eyebrows look way better than mine, like he just had them threaded.

"Isko!" I say, hugging him, automatically feeling more at ease here than at home. "I just texted your brother."

"He told me you were coming," he says. "You look radiant. Are you seeing someone?"

"Seeing someone?" I hesitate.

Does Isko know something I don't? I don't know how to answer the question. I've had a crush on Zach forever, who finally seems to be interested and available. Maybe.

"You know, like, *romantically*? I have this theory that people in love have this glow around them."

He's barely in high school, but Isko seems so grown up now. He's so self-confident. "I *am* radiant," I tease. "But no, not seeing anyone. Have my eyes on a few."

"Story of my life." He laughs.

We both enter the house, and Danny comes running up. He's wearing jeans splattered with paint spots, a wrinkly black shirt and striped socks. Danny and Jasmine are both much less fashion conscious than their younger brother.

"Get away from my girl," he says to his brother.

"*Your* girl?" Isko says. "She's her own girl."

"Got that right," I say, walking over to Danny to give him a hug. "I haven't seen you in six months. How are you both so much taller when I haven't grown an inch?"

Isko whistles. "I'll say. Look how tiny you are…"

His words feel both like a jolt of affirmation—finally someone's starting to recognize my hard work—but I also feel ashamed. He has no idea what I've been doing to lose the weight. It isn't pretty. It's not the kind of weight loss you can brag about.

"It never stops," Danny says. "Isko just keeps getting skinnier, taller and funnier looking."

"Speak for yourself," Isko says. "You might be a senior now, but you look like you're in second grade with that baby face."

"As you can see," Danny says to me. "Isko is just as annoying as ever."

"Only to *you*," he says. "I have to go. I'm going to the movies with Simon. Or something like that." He winks. "I'll catch you both later."

"He's so grown up," I say to Danny as Isko runs out the door. His confidence inspires me. He really knows how to live with… What did Ms. Day say that French term was? *Joie de vivre?* I'm almost jealous of the constant joy he seems to find in living.

"I know, he's really discovering himself."

"How are your parents taking it?" I ask.

"It's driving them a little crazy to be honest. Jas never gave them trouble. The only thing I do that annoys them is spend most of my time locked up in my room, drawing. He's always been a handful, but now he's really coming out of his shell."

"That's great," I say. "I wish I felt that carefree in front of *my* parents."

"They're just going to have to get used to him being the life of the party."

I hear a cough from the kitchen and peek through the doorway to see Lola Cherry sitting at the kitchen table with a crossword puzzle in front of her.

"Not as long as I'm alive he's not," she says.

"Lola!" I say, walking into the kitchen. I'm so excited to see her. Though Lola Cherry isn't Danny's *real* grandmother, she pretty much counts—which means she's my grandmother too. I love her. She's so feisty. She doesn't take crap from anyone.

"Hi, darling," she says. "Good to see you, little baby."

I give her a hug and a kiss on the cheek.

"You look beautiful," I say.

"I know."

"God, Lola," Danny says. "Are you running for Miss USA or something?"

"I'd win," she says, setting down her crossword puzzle. "And then *I'd* be the life of the party. You should see me in a bikini."

"Oh, Lola," I say. "I missed you."

"Good for you," Lola says.

"This is what I love about you guys." I laugh. "Always fun. Always make me feel so…welcome."

The tension I've been carrying in my shoulders this entire school year begins to loosen. The stress from all the drama—especially due to the campaign—begins to wash away. I feel accepted here. I don't have to be anything more than I already am.

I know every family has their problems, but I've always felt safe around the de los Santos family. They can *argue* with each other and actually work things out. Not like mine. We can fight until we're blue in the face and not get anything done.

"Look who Danny dragged in through the door," Pilar says, entering the kitchen. "Are you hungry?"

That's always her first question. I don't know how Jasmine stayed so thin living with her mother. It must have been all the cheer and dance practices. Jas probably has better willpower than I do too.

Pilar opens the fridge. It's jam-packed with food, and she has to rearrange some bottles and boxes to see around everything. "I have leftover *lumpia*. I'll heat some up."

"Thanks," I say. "I can't though. I'm on a diet."

If I start eating Pilar's cooking, I don't think I'll ever stop.

"That's what Jasmine always used to say when she was your age," Pilar mumbles into the refrigerator. "Why a diet? You get smaller every time I see you."

"You didn't tell me we had *lumpia*," Danny complains.

"Maybe you should look in the fridge once in a while," Pilar says. She turns her attention to me. "Are you sure I can't make you something? I can cut up some pineapple or mango. It's healthy."

It feels rude to keep refusing her, but I have to save my calories. There's no way I'm getting out of dinner with my family tonight unless I fake sick, which I can't do since I'm supposed to meet up with Antonia for our double-date later tonight.

"I can't ruin my dinner," I explain. "Royce and Mason are home for the weekend and Mom's cooking."

"I can understand *that*," Pilar says. She walks around the counter and gives me a hug. "You should come more often. It's so good to see you. What brought you over?"

"She missed me," Lola says, winking.

"Lola, let the girl talk," Pilar says.

I hug Lola and say, "Dad's running for governor. He's working on the campaign tonight, and to be honest I really don't want to be in the spotlight. I was talking to Royce and thought of you guys, so I texted Danny and came over." I look around the room for Jas's dad. He's nowhere to be found. "Where's Mr. de los Santos?"

"He went up to Stanford," Danny says. "Father-daughter talk."

My stomach drops a little. It seems like a big deal for him to go all the way up there just to talk. Maybe Royce and Jas's relationship problems really are that serious.

"Oh boy," I say. "Sounds scary."

I don't get why Royce wouldn't wait for Jas to go through medical school before he takes an international job at a news bureau. He could just work in the United States.

If I were in her shoes, I would be anxious too. She's graduating this year and has to figure out what she wants to do next. She already has to fight bureaucracy to even stay in the country *and* Dad's campaign will affect her too. She's been through *so much*—immigration hearings, political drama with my family, scholarship applications, what seems like the longest path toward being able to apply for citizenship—just to get where she is now.

"I don't think so," Pilar says. "They do that now and then."

It's weird that Pilar isn't mentioning Royce. Usually it's "Jasmine and Royce this" and "Jasmine and Royce that." Are they officially breaking up? My anxiety starts to rise again. I don't know what I would do without being able to go to Jas for advice. Or losing the de los Santos family. Even more, Royce would be in worse shape than me.

"When my dad tries to talk to me one-on-one," I say, trying to lighten the mood, "I want to hide under the table." It's actually true. He can be a little intimidating. I guess he has to be that way at work. He has to show his strength, his conviction of character.

"Enough about your father," Lola says. "What are *you* doing?"

"Not a whole lot. Just trying to stay on top of school," I say, even though I'm thinking about how I really haven't gotten anything of substance done for the gallery show. "I'm also putting together a portfolio to apply to a gallery show for young artists."

There's a chance I may not even be accepted, but I figure telling them about the show might motivate me to get more work done. I need to be better about pursuing my goals. It's frustrating to feel like I'm working so slowly. I need to be more disciplined.

"That's awesome," Danny says, putting his arm around my shoulder. "I've got a few drawings to show you too. You ready?"

Danny was actually one of the people who inspired me to start drawing. When Jas and Royce first started dating, Danny and I were in middle school. Royce would bring me over with him, and Danny would show me whatever doodle he was working on. He even gave me this book that explained all the basics of how to sketch shapes and shade drawings to make them three-dimensional.

His sketches were fantastic even when he was young. I wanted to be as good as Danny so I started sketching all the time too. Our styles now are pretty different though.

"I'm taking a figure drawing class downtown right now," Danny says. "I don't know why they don't do that at my school. It's such a basic skill you have to learn."

I follow him to his room.

"I mean, there's the whole posing nude thing too..."

Danny laughs. "Yeah. I guess. But they're just bodies..."

"Tell that to the guys in *my* art class," I say. "They totally lose it when the teacher so much as shows us a *photograph* of a classical statue."

"I would practice on Isko..." he continues. "But he can't sit down for more than two minutes at a time, and Lola Cherry won't stop repeating the story about the time she was the most beautiful girl who ever won the Miss Rice Festival Pageant in her village."

I laugh. "I wouldn't want to use my family as models either."

At least I get to do some figure drawing at school. Ms. Day shows us techniques and makes us practice drawing each other all the time. She says it's good for artists to know what their models are going through when they sit for a sketch or painting.

"These are from the figure drawing class," Danny says, having me sit at his desk, which is covered in paints and charcoal. I sort through the figure drawing pen-and-inks and a few Conté crayon drawings too. Even though his subjects are stationary, the way he draws makes them seem like they're moving and breathing on the page.

"These are beautiful," I say. "These lines. They're so confident. Your use of positive and negative space… I mean, the way your subjects are positioned…" I'm in awe. "Honestly, I'm kind of jealous. It's better than what I can do, that's for sure."

"I want to go to Otis College of Art and Design next year."

"You'll totally get in," I say.

"I'll be lucky to," he says. "Applications are due by the end of the month. Honestly, I don't know how I'll pay for it. We have green cards now, so I qualify for some aid, but I don't want to be a burden on Mom and Dad."

I feel guilty. I hate that my parents could afford to send all three of us to nice schools while the de los Santos family struggles to make ends meet. Sometimes I wonder whether that ever bothers Jas or affects her relationship with Royce, but she doesn't say anything.

"You'll get in." I set his drawing down. "You will."

"I'd have to get a scholarship—like Jas—so my application has to be killer." Danny's serious now, like he's confiding in me. "I was thinking, though, about maybe doing something really different there."

"Like what?" I say, excited to hear about it. His work is that good.

"Toy design," he says. "It seems crazy fun. They have a whole program for it. I have so many ideas for action figures.

It's like they're always pouring out of my head. And I love sculpting. And 3-D modeling. I don't know, I think I'd be really good at it. The same way you'll be so good at whatever you want to do."

"I'm supposed to submit a proposal of the concept for the show plus one finished painting and sketches for the rest in late spring. It's due in May for a summer show."

"That would be so dope," Danny says, jumping up from the bed. His hands move around a bunch when he gets excited. "You have to go for it. What's your concept?"

"I'm not exactly sure, but I've been looking at a bunch of different stuff to get ideas. I know how I want the visual style to look, but I don't know what I want to *say*, you know?" I remember how Ms. Day told me I needed to find my voice, but I don't know how I'm going to develop my voice when I can't figure out what I have in my heart that's worth spilling all over the canvas.

"You'll figure it out," Danny reassures me. "It's only fall. There's still plenty of time."

"I've already fallen behind though," I say, thinking about all the things I have to juggle. "There are so many classes I have to study for. And SATs. Visiting colleges. I just forget to even think about my art sometimes. I see what you're doing, and it just makes all my dreams come rushing back. I need to come up with better concepts."

"Why don't you come to the figure drawing class with me? Just for some extra practice. You're welcome to join anytime," Danny says. "Hey. That just gave me an idea."

"Yeah?"

"Can I model an action figure after you for my application?"

"Me?"

"It would be so rad," Danny says.

Has he actually seen what I look like? I'm in no shape to be an action figure. I start laughing, thinking of the absurdity of seeing myself as a tiny plastic superhero. "It would be a failure if you modeled an action figure after me. It wouldn't fly or repel bullets. It would be slow and fat and wear too much lip gloss."

"I think that sounds cool," he says. "Superheroes are boring anyway. Too perfect. Flaws are what make a person interesting."

"I must be the most interesting girl in the world then." Turning through the pages of Danny's portfolio, I think about how there are so many things I want to fix about myself. *My grades. My family. My anxiety. My body.*

"I feel the same way. Like there are so many more things I'm bad at than good. I love drawing and painting, but sometimes I feel trapped, like it's the *only* thing I do well."

I look up from Danny's drawings at him. He's being sincere.

"Anyway," he continues. "If Isko were here he'd tell me to stop being so hard on myself."

"Wise kid," I say, wishing I didn't beat myself up so much sometimes. It's difficult being your own worst critic, but I have to be critical because my expectations for myself are so high. I just feel so mediocre all the time. It's depressing.

"I envy him. He lives his life the way he wants without worrying about what other people think. I'm not that way. Neither is Jasmine. I don't know where he gets it from..." He pauses for a moment, then begins to speak.

"Lola Cherry," Danny and I say at the same time.

"Do your parents know?" I ask.

"That he's gay?" Danny sits down on his bed and rests his elbows on his knees. "They know. I think they're still coming to terms with it. They love him. I think they just worry about how he might be treated here. The Philippines is actually more accepting of gay people than the United States in some ways. It's hard anywhere though."

"What about Jasmine?" I ask.

"Isko told her first, actually. She and I are just happy that he's happy. He's already going to have to face enough criticism from other people. He doesn't need any from us."

"It's cool that you guys are so supportive. I don't know what my dad would do if I was a lesbian." I hope that going with Antonia on her date with Heather tonight really will make her feel more comfortable, but I'm not looking forward to having to make small talk with Mika the whole night. I'm just not good at coming up with things to say.

"Really? You think he'd flip?"

"I mean, I think he'd love me no matter what, but a gay daughter wouldn't really match up with his campaign values."

That's one of the main reasons I don't like talking to him about politics. Dad can be pretty open-minded, but I don't understand how he can still hold some of his beliefs when some of the people—like the de los Santos family—his party's policies affect are so wonderful. There are all these questions that sit at the back of my mind, nagging me, whenever Dad talks about his campaign. What happened if Jas and her family were kicked out of the country? Are politics more important than the people you love?

"I guess not," Danny says. "But if Jas and Royce get married someday, then your dad's going to have a gay Filipino immigrant son-in-law. Think about that!"

I laugh. That wouldn't bother Dad. He *loves* Isko.

"I may not be happy Dad's running for governor, but I have to give him a little credit. He's changed a lot these last five years. Especially after what happened with your family's immigration status. I think getting to know Jas and all you guys, then realizing that you could be deported at any time, really shook him. I know Royce argued with him about softening a lot of his policies during that time. He's a lot more moderate now."

"How's Royce doing?" Danny asks.

Crap. It's not just Royce acting weird. There's obviously

something big going on between them. I wonder what Jas has told Danny. She seems pretty private.

"He's acting kind of weird, I guess. How's Jas? The only times I've texted her she seemed pretty busy with studying and stuff."

"Jas hasn't really been around much. Mom complains when she calls because she hasn't come down from Stanford to visit in months."

"Something's going on with her and Royce," I say. "Don't tell your parents. Royce would kill me."

"I figured. She hasn't mentioned him in a few weeks."

"Do you know what they're fighting about?" I ask.

Danny shakes his head. "I was going to ask you," he says.

"She hasn't said anything to me either, but Royce said something about her wanting to apply to medical school while he wants to get an international job. I don't know where. I guess she wants to stay in the States."

"That makes sense," Danny says. "Leaving the country would get kind of complicated for us based on our immigration status. We're not totally in the clear yet."

"I guess every couple has their problems," I say, reflecting on how Royce and Jas breaking up would probably be as bad as my parents getting a divorce. It would really feel like losing half of my family. "But they've always been so solid."

"If Jasmine could handle standing up to your dad and dealing with Mason being a jerk before he went to rehab, they'll be able to work anything out."

"I guess you're right," I say. "None of our business anyway."

"I did overhear one thing," Danny says. "Lola and Mom were talking about how Jas called crying, saying how much she loves Royce, but that the stress of figuring out what they're going to do after they graduate is overwhelming to her."

"That would be overwhelming for anyone. Even someone like Jas," I say. She's pretty much the most hardworking, loving and motivated person I know. I can only imagine how she felt when Royce announced that the spotlight was going to be on our family again. I have no doubts that the media would bring her into the campaign at some point. It's a lot of pressure. "But at least she's going after what she wants. That's inspiring."

"Yeah. That's something I've always admired about her." He smiles mischievously. "But please don't tell her that. We have a sibling rivalry to maintain."

"You know what?" I say, filled with a rush of inspiration.

"What?" he asks.

"If Jas is committing to med school and you're pursuing your art, then there's no excuse for me not to commit myself to painting."

"Let's make a promise then," he says, putting his arm around me. "We'll meet once a week to share our work with each other—it will encourage us to keep going. And also it'll be cool to hang out or whatever."

"All right," I said, feeling excited for the first time about my life since my conversation with Zach at the party. "You got it."

eleven

"A life spent making mistakes is not only more honorable,

but more useful than a life spent doing nothing."

—GEORGE BERNARD SHAW

"Thank you for taking time out of your schedules to be here tonight," Dad says, standing in the middle of the room before dinner, talking to us like we're his staffers. "It's only October, but it's time to get this campaign running!"

Mom and I are sitting on the couch next to each other. Mason's lounging in an armchair while Royce sits on the floor, leaning against the couch, stretching his legs out.

I can't remember the last time all five of us were in the same room together. It's something I'm not used to. With Dad living in DC half the time for the past eight years and Mom working as a lawyer up until I started high school, I don't think we've had a family dinner other than for a political event, birthday, or holiday in at least a year.

"You all know why I've gathered you together," Dad says. "I've hired a campaign manager and started to gather a publicity team. We'll officially announce in a few months, but there's so much to do before then."

"He's about to marry us to his campaign," I mutter under my breath.

"Glad you can join us, Liv," Dad says. "Everything all right?"

"Just perfect, Congressman Daddy."

My mother shoots a sideways glance meant to put me in line. Mom and I have a closer relationship than I do with Dad. Though the boys definitely had their own problems, I think he knew what to do with Royce and Mason. He knew how to talk to them. Everything I do or say seems to disappoint him. I used to be his perfect little girl, but somewhere down the line we stopped being able to find much in common.

"Good," he says, rubbing his hands together. "I wanted you all together to tell you that we're going to win this election. My opponents just don't carry the same kind of clout our family does. So, be proud of that. We've all worked hard to make it that way. Every poll has us up by twelve points over our nearest competitor. There's definitely a buzz about the upcoming announcement. California's a tough state to take, but I think the platform I've developed with my staff will give us a winning edge."

Royce perks up, sitting up on the floor. He loves this stuff. "What's the platform? Different from when you ran for Congress?"

"Since the country's recovering from an economic slump, I've chosen to focus on promoting commerce through common sense legislation. Let's bring the high-speed rail to increase business opportunities in an economically and environmentally friendly way. We need to use our state's great resources to build a budget surplus," Dad says. "Only then can California expand social programs. Our economy has to be robust first."

"It's good to tap into the economy issue," Mason says. "From working in Silicon Valley, I can tell you that California needs to do whatever's possible to keep the tech industry based here. It's the fastest growing industry in the state and not going away."

"What about immigration?" Royce asks.

I'm sure that's a big question on Royce's mind, especially

since Jas isn't a full citizen yet. The de los Santos family managed to get lucky and secure temporary green cards, but they're still not guaranteed citizenship.

"Immigrants are obviously a major part of our state's economic and cultural fabric," Dad says. "We need common sense reform in that area too. We need to reward those who contribute their hardworking values to our state. Let's help them to get on their feet so all of us can work together for a better California."

Dad's already completely in campaign mode. His speech sounds like a well-oiled machine. It's not that I disagree with most of his politics. It's that I don't think I have the energy to get up in front of strangers and pretend to be a person I'm not.

"Only bridge building through back doors for now," Dad drones on. "Setting up how we're going to steamroll this thing. When we do win the election, we're moving to Sacramento. With you boys out of the house, it makes sense to downsize. If I win, then Liv will already be well into college by the time my first term is up."

Mason nods, his arms folded. "Sounds good," he says. "Anything you need."

Royce shrugs and nods. I can tell he really doesn't care right now, though he supports Dad. It doesn't matter as much to them. They're adults.

I'm the hostage. Dad doesn't lose elections. He's great at campaigning. Unfortunately. Not even the thought of living in the governor's mansion for the last half of my senior year makes me happy about the campaign.

"I don't know about you all, but I love the state capital," Mom says, like she's a real estate agent trying to sell us an ugly house. "I love the architecture, the neighborhood, the people. There's a lot for me to do. A great private school for your senior year, Liv. We could even move up early, depending on how polls are looking."

That's the last thing I want to hear. Mason and Royce aren't too concerned because they're already out of the house and have their own lives. They're both living in the Bay Area—Royce is going to graduate and will probably have a grown-up job by that point, while Mason's working for a Silicon Valley venture capital firm as a junior associate. But uprooting me isn't fair. I won't know *anyone* in Sacramento.

"I don't see why you're doing it," I say. "You're supposed to move up from Congress to the presidency, not down to governor." It's the opposite of what I really think—I'd hate to be in the kind of media cross fire of a presidential election—but I thought Dad would feel defensive about going back to state politics after having been in Washington for so long. It *is* an unusual political move. "I'm not just trying to be a jerk. You already know all the journalists and talk show hosts are going to ask that question."

"Oh, Liv—" Dad sighs "—don't belittle a governorship." I can tell he's about to launch into a history lesson, upset that I challenged him. "The state of California is one of the greatest in the union. Its economy is the largest in the entire country. Besides, *many* governors have not only run for president but have become president." He starts counting on his fingers. "Thomas Jefferson, James Monroe. Both Roosevelts. Clinton and Bush. And let's not forget Ronald Reagan was governor of California."

"Like what, a hundred years ago?" I say. "He adopted some of the worst mental health policies in generations. And pretended AIDS didn't exist until way too late."

"Liv," Mom says, warning me, but I can't help myself.

"Don't even get me started on Nancy and how she was using an *astrologer* to help influence her decisions," I add to my argument.

I may not *like* politics, but I know a lot of history. When you're the daughter of a politician, you have to stick *some* things in your back pocket to rile up your parents.

Mason snickers. Royce looks like he's on another planet. He's probably still thinking about Jasmine. Dad just crosses his arms, waiting for me to finish.

"I could deal with living in DC," I say, shaking my head. At least Washington is more metropolitan than Sacramento. "It's close to New York."

"I really do think you should consider other places to go to college," Dad says. "Just to keep an open mind. What about Georgetown, my alma mater? Those were some of the best years of my life. Or your mother's? Smith is a wonderful school."

Mom sits up straight. "All kinds of women from across the political spectrum got their start there," she adds to the pep talk. "Barbara Bush. Gloria Steinem. Sylvia Plath. Yolanda King. That's Martin Luther King's daughter."

"I appreciate the advice, but I'm not like the rest of you. I don't need to go to a traditional college to do what I want. I *know* I want to make art my career."

"That's a tough career path," Dad says. "Almost nobody makes it. What will you have to fall back on?"

"I don't know yet," I say.

"Exactly," Dad says, thinking he's won this argument.

This is exactly why I hope to talk to LeFeber. How did he answer these questions? His career didn't take off until he was middle-aged. Did people tell him they never thought he was going to make it? How was he able to believe in his dream for that long?

"Sorry, Mom," I say, changing the subject back to the election. "Sacramento might be a cool town and awesome if you're working your way up through the state assembly, but how much better is it for the family to keep its LA image? You really want to lose that in gloomy, rainy NorCal?" I turn back to Dad. "You might think you're ahead in the polls now, but we won't be a cool LA family anymore. We'll have a dusty image. Good old boys and that kind of thing. You're making a huge political mistake."

I'm trying my best, but the truth is I am so done with this meeting. But I know I can't get up and leave. Dad's going to say his piece. Maybe Mom too. Royce and Mason probably won't talk. They'll be mentioned in the news some and get trotted out for big nights—major campaign highlights—but they'll be able to be more detached.

Daughters of politicians always get more media attention than their sons. People love to gossip about the girls—Malia and Sasha Obama, Christina and Katherine Schwarzenegger, Georgina Bloomberg. Anything one of us does while our parents are in office—and sometimes even for the rest of our lives—will be up for major media and public scrutiny.

"That's a good argument," Dad says. "I hear you. I recognize how these decisions might be hard for you, but Mom and I already made our decision. And I want to make this *very* clear. I don't want any of you to do something that puts you in the news other than for campaign coverage. That *especially* means you, Liv. You're still a minor."

I can see it now. My junior year is going to become all about the campaign. Fund-raisers at the house. Appearances at events. Interviews on news channels. Looking put together all the time. Staying out of trouble. A well-timed father-daughter lunch at a public place. Spending summer canvassing for him. Watching the polls. Making calls.

The election will happen at the beginning of senior year. If he wins, I would have to move to Sacramento by January, effectively cutting off the rest of my time at Eastlake to do anything that's not related to the gubernatorial race.

"Clearly you don't think I'm part of this family," I say, feeling the anger bubble up my throat. "Otherwise you would have asked me what I thought about your decision to run before you made it. Don't let me get in your way."

"Olivia." Dad says my name like he can't believe what I just said, like I should just agree with everything that comes out of his mouth. "That's completely out of line."

"Both of you need to calm down," Mom says, standing up from the couch. "Come to the kitchen with me, Liv. I need your help finishing up dinner."

The last thing I want to do is talk things out with Mom, but I don't have any choice. It's either that, or being stuck here alone with the campaign dream team.

As I follow Mom out of the living room into the kitchen, I hear Mason suck up to Dad. "I can't take a lot of time off from work, but I can definitely help out with donors."

"At least someone in this family actually wants to help," Dad grumbles. "I don't know what's wrong with Liv. Has she always been this way?"

"Something has to be going on," Royce says. "Probably something at school."

It would be nice for them to actually talk with me about my feelings instead of talking about me like I can't hear them. Is that too much to ask?

Mom puts me straight to work once we're in the kitchen. She asks me to wash a bowl full of baby spinach, then start cutting the carrots and radishes for the side salad.

I take the knife from the knife block and begin slicing the radishes. I fantasize about slipping as I cut one of them and plunging the knife through my finger just to get out of this miserable dinner.

"I know you're feeling frustrated," Mom says, pulling the beef Wellington out of the oven. The smell of the steak's juices with the pastry puff is starting to make me sick to my stomach.

"It's not my fault Dad doesn't listen," I say.

Mom sighs. "It's not always *not* your fault either. You have to learn how to meet him halfway. He's trying to set an *example* for you."

"You mean by being gone for most of my childhood? Or for dragging me to a completely new city for my senior year of high school? What an example…"

Mom stops paying attention to the food and looks at me. I'm starting to get on her nerves. "I understand why you're upset, but you're making this into too big of a deal. We aren't expecting you to do that much related to the campaign. Just a little more than you have in the past. We need you to be aware of how what you do affects our family."

"I've always been aware of that," I say, setting down the knife. "Can I go to my room?"

Maybe I'm overreacting, but my emotions feel out of control. I can't tell whether that's from the bingeing and purging or from all the pent-up anger I can't let go of, or what's going on. It's all swirling around my head and I just want to go to sleep.

"No." Mom shakes her head. "Stay. We're finally all together."

"Suit yourself," I say, dumping the radishes and carrots into the salad.

I know my broken relationship with Dad is partially my fault. I haven't been the best daughter. I want to live up to my family's expectations, but at the same time I don't want the same things that they want for me. It's an impossible situation.

Mom calls Dad and the boys into the dining room as I finish setting the table. Mason and Royce do their best to chat with Mom as if my blowup from before never happened, but Dad and I don't make eye contact. I know I should apologize for how I reacted, but my feelings are the same. I just want a chance at a normal teenage life.

"This is amazing," Mason says, devouring a massive bite of the beef Wellington. "I can't remember the last time I ate something cooked at home."

"You don't cook for yourself?" Mom asks.

Mason shakes his head. "Too busy at work."

"Like you know how to cook anyway," Royce says.

"Better than you," Mason shoots back.

"What are you focusing on at work, honey?" Mom asks, delicately wiping her face with a napkin. "You said something about doing research on a new start-up?"

"My firm is thinking about funding a company that's building technology to scan a bunch of different sources for information about potential job candidates. Social media. The internet. Different universities and companies. The idea is that eventually, in certain industries, businesses will stop wasting time with wasteful recruitment costs and general advertising of jobs and be able to go straight to the source—the top candidates."

I take a look down at my plate. I've separated each type of food so nothing is touching. I don't want the beef Wellington to contaminate my salad. My stomach is grumbling, but I'm too emotional to eat. I can't let my body win.

"That's interesting and all, mister big Silicon Valley hotshot," Royce says, "but let's get back to the real conversation. I bet you don't know how to cook *pancit*."

I push a tiny white potato back and forth across my plate, concentrating on its path from meat to salad back to the other potatoes. It's taking all the energy I have to sit here. My shoulders ache from tension. I really would rather be alone.

"I see," Mason says, cutting another piece of beef. "Jasmine must have made you a regular Filipino chef."

"I guess so..." Royce trails off.

"You should cook that for us sometime," Mom says, turning on the cheer, happy her two golden boys are finally home. "How's the job search coming? I'd love to know..."

"Stop!" Dad shouts all of a sudden. He slams a fist down on the table, which startles everyone. Mom's eyes widen with surprise, but she doesn't say anything. "You're nearly seventeen years old. I shouldn't have to tell you to stop playing with your food."

Everyone goes silent. I look down at my lap, feeling tears welling up in my eyes. There's nothing I can say that will make him happy. I'll never be the perfect daughter. I'll never live up to their expectations. Why should I even try?

"Why don't you eat? Your mother went to the trouble of making this incredible meal and you can't even pretend to care," he says.

Mom turns to him. "It's really all right..."

Dad sets his fork down. "It's not all right, Debra. She's been completely ungrateful. After all we do for her—give her a beautiful home, send her to a world-class school, provide her with anything she could possibly need—and all she does is sit there and pretend that none of us are here? I won't stand for it." He turns his attention to me. "Eat."

"I've lost my appetite," I say, pushing my chair back. I can barely look at Mom because of the tears welling up in my eyes. "May I be excused now?"

She barely has time to nod before I'm out of my chair, dumping my uneaten food into the trash can. I practically run up the stairs to my room.

I go to my bathroom and open the medicine cabinet, finding my package of straight razors. The blades are clean and sharp and I want so badly to slice open my skin. To feel anything other than what I'm feeling right now.

I'm about to take one of the blades out of the package when I hear my bedroom door click open. Stuffing the blades into my pocket, I shut and lock the bathroom door.

"Thanks for the privacy," I say, sitting on the toilet.

"I know you're upset with us," Mom says through the door, "but your father and I really did think about you when we were discussing whether to campaign or not. Trust me."

I flush the toilet and wash my hands. "Why do you want to move to Sacramento?" I ask, opening the door. I'm starting to feel guilty for ruining her dinner. I really have been awful to them. My diet makes me so irritable, but when I eat, that hateful voice in my head gets louder and louder. "It sounds like retirement," I say.

"Your father still has a lot of work he wants to accomplish, and both of us are getting older. We're tired of flying back and forth across the country."

When Dad was first elected to Congress, Mom argued for us to stay in LA. She wanted to keep working as a lawyer for a while and didn't want to uproot all three of us kids. That means I pretty much see Dad only on the weekends and during his recess periods, but he's always working or meeting with someone even when he's home.

"I wish you'd thought of that before my junior year..."

"It's not the ideal time. I know. There might be a way for you to graduate early." Mom moves out of the doorway. "But I don't know where you're going to be next year—you could end up at Stanford like Royce... I'd really like to be in the same state as my children. You know how much I love you."

I start to feel a pounding at the front of my forehead. Graduating early? I can barely handle all the classes I'm taking right now. "Can we not start this right now?" I walk by her and sit down on my bed. "I love you too, Mom. But you know I'm different from Royce and Mason. I don't need to go where they went. I don't...fit in. I've been trying to find my own way... but... I don't know. I have a headache."

"We all love you. I don't know why you don't think you fit in. Each one of us is different. You can have your own dreams and still be a part of the family, Liv. We want you to be happy. Come back down. Eat some dinner. You'll feel better."

Do they think this campaign is going to make me happy?

Why can't Dad find a job in the private sector or something? Hasn't he been a politician for long enough?

"I'll eat later. I need to be alone right now."

I keep thinking that, no matter how much I try to fight Dad about this campaign, I'm still going to have to make all these appearances with him and pretend to be his perfect, perpetually perky daughter. Everything about me—from the monochromatic suits and American-flag pins to the smile plastered across my face—will be phony.

"I want to talk to you about something else," she says, sitting next to me. "Just us girls."

"What's there to talk about?" I ask.

I really wish she would leave. Every minute she spends up here talking to me is another minute Dad will be fuming about my being selfish and keeping her from dinner.

"I don't know. Your life. You're probably worried about a lot right now. The campaign is a lot to throw at you. That, and you've been distant lately. You seem tired all the time."

"Sorry," I say. It's an automatic response meant to push her away. I tend to clam up when anyone asks about my feelings. Almost like I don't want to admit that I have any at all. Normal people can talk about what's bugging them or why they're angry. Not me. My thoughts loop through my head, overwhelming me. *It's all your fault. You're a terrible person.* It's just hard to not ever live up to your own expectations, to see your flaws so clearly. "I'll try harder," I say, and I do mean it.

I don't want to feel like this all the time. I don't want to disappoint my parents or act pissed off at people who love me.

"I'm not asking you to try harder," Mom says.

I twirl a strand of hair with my finger. It's a nervous habit.

"What are you asking then?"

She's sitting there, thinking. I can see it on her face. She doesn't know what to say. She's dealt with my brothers, but she doesn't know how to crack me.

Fortress me. She can't do it.

"I just want you to feel like you're a part of this family," she says, reaching up to tuck a loose strand of hair behind my ear. "And that you can talk to me."

"Okay," I say, knowing there's no way I'll ever talk to her about my problems, especially about the terrible thoughts I have about food or my body. She's my mother. She could never understand why I hate myself so much. I barely understand it myself.

How can I be so messed up when I've been given every opportunity? Loving family. Good education. Wealth. My life checks all the boxes. What's wrong with me? Why can't I be grateful?

I'm about to totally shut down when Mom changes the subject. "How are your drawings going?" she asks. "Anything I can do to help with your portfolio?"

This makes me feel even worse. I wish I'd never told her about the gallery show. I probably won't even be able to apply. I haven't gotten anywhere with my sketches. I hate everything I've done so far. I keep trying to find inspiration in other work, but nothing's clicking. I don't have a coherent concept. Or a plan for the one painting I have to submit.

That's another question I'm desperate to ask LeFeber. What do you do when you're blocked? How do you find the motivation to paint when you can barely get out of bed? I don't want my mom's help. I just want to be left alone.

"No," I say, suddenly remembering that I have to go on that date tonight.

I forgot to ask Mom earlier if she could take me. I'm not in the mood to go out at all right now and this definitely isn't the best time to ask her for a ride, but I can't just ditch Antonia. "But I'm supposed to hang out with Antonia and her cousin in Silver Lake tonight. We're going to watch a concert. Can I get a ride?"

"We really need to teach you how to drive." Mom sighs, standing up from the bed. "Sure. I'll take you. But you'll have to find a ride home."

twelve

When I finally show up to the Silver Lake Lounge, I see Antonia sitting with her girl and an older girl who I assume must be Mika, hunkered at a round table far from the stage.

Though she and Heather are sitting close to each other, her date seems apprehensive about the whole thing. The multicolored lights revolve around the room, bathing her in color as she keeps looking over her shoulder for anyone she might know to walk in and find her on a date with Antonia.

I don't want to be here after the disaster that was our family dinner. I thought about canceling. Then I thought about how I'd hate to have a friend who was always such a flake. I try to remind myself to have fun. It's just like any other night of hanging out with Antonia. *This is about Antonia*, I tell myself, *and making her girlfriend feel comfortable. You talk to people you don't know all the time. No reason to be nervous.*

Antonia sees me and jumps up from the table. "Hey, girl!" she says, grabbing my hands. "This is Heather. It feels like I've been talking you up to her for months."

Heather has the most amazing red hair that she wears in natural afro-tight curls. Her eyes are honey brown and her arms and legs are lean and muscular like a runner's. I can see why Antonia is attracted to her. They look like they would make a great couple.

I shake Heather's hand, imagining Antonia holding hers. Any girl would be lucky to go on a date with Antonia. I really hope this works out for them.

"Hey, Liv," Heather says softly. "Antonia talks about you all the time."

My nervousness begins to melt away. This isn't going to be so bad.

"What does she say? That I'm a total head case?"

Heather laughs. "Not at all. She says you're loyal, the best girl to have in your corner. And she's always talking about your art. I'd love to see it sometime."

Antonia turns to the girl with them. "This is my cousin. Mika."

"I'm Olivia," I say, holding out my hand. "Nice to meet you."

I pull out my politician's daughter tricks. Smile nicely. Speak as little as possible. It's easy to give a good impression when you let the other person do all the talking.

Older than us by probably a couple of years, Mika seems more confident than Heather. She has black hair with dark pastel lowlights and is wearing skintight black leather pants and a white blouse that shows a lacy black bralette underneath. Fashionable. Intense.

Through her circular, John Lennon–esque glasses, Mika gives me the up-and-down, cracks a smirk, brushes the hair hanging in front of her right eye and shakes my hand. "Antonia says you're an artist?" She pulls out a chair for me. "Are you a serious artist, or is it a side thing?"

I'm not sure how to answer the question. In my heart, I know that creating is the only thing that makes me feel halfway decent about myself, but I'm so blocked that saying I'm an artist makes me feel like a fraud. I'm only sixteen. How can I actually *call myself* an artist? I haven't really achieved anything yet.

"I'm working on putting together a show," I say, hoping that telling people will inspire me to work on my paintings more.

"I've always found painters to be sexy," Mika says.

"Thanks," I say, feeling awkward. I don't think she's hitting on me, but I'm not sure of her intention. Does she just say that kind of thing? "Me too, I guess."

She's focused on me, scrutinizing everything from my eyebrows to the stack of rings on my fingers, staring at me so intently with her intense dark brown eyes that she makes me nervous to sit across from her. I glance at Antonia. She turns to Heather and they start talking. This is good, I think. Heather's comfortable for now. Mission accomplished. I can't just leave though, or do what I really want, which is to find something to drink. With the music playing and the people talking and the chatter going on in my brain, my nerve endings feel raw and frayed. I could use an anesthetic.

"The show's not until the summer," I say to Mika, not wanting to explain the whole process. "But I'm behind on my work with school and everything."

"You want to know what I do?" she says, not really asking me.

"Should I guess?"

Mika leans in closer. "Yeah. Guess."

I don't want to play guessing games. I'm glad I could be here for Antonia, but my stomach still feels sour after fighting with Dad at home. I'd rather be at home in bed.

"Do you work somewhere?" I ask.

"I write poetry," she says.

"Oh, a poet," I say, stumbling for words. "What kind?"

It's a dumb question, but I don't know what to ask.

"The kind that splices life," she says. "That's what a poet does, you know."

"Oh?"

"I splice from one part of my life into another, overlapping emotions and circumstances to give them greater meaning. I extract bits of soul. I write them in my journals. I read them to whoever will listen. I perform. I love. I wither. I grow."

I may be an artist, but Mika is beyond my realm of understanding. She leans back. Her eyes meet mine. She's doing that staring thing again.

"Antonia said that you're from out of town," I say. "Where are you from?"

"I'm not *from* anywhere per se. Poets must be nomads. Getting attached to one place is bad for the soul." Mika twists a ring around her finger. "I've been camping near a vortex in Sedona, Arizona. It's sort of near the Grand Canyon."

"A vortex?" I ask. Antonia *did* say that Mika was into these sorts of things. I figure I should be nice and ask her about her interests. "What's that?"

"It's a natural site where spiritual energy converges into a giant vortex," Mika says. She makes a sweeping motion with her hand like it's a tornado. Antonia gives her a sideways glance, then goes back to talking to Heather. "They're magical places where trees exhibit this swirling and twisting of the trunks. The energy moves in a big spiral that helps with spiritual transformation. I've been working through some issues there. Wanna see some pictures?"

"Sure," I say. I mean, why not? I might as well learn all I can about whatever Mika's talking about right now.

"Stupid WiFi," she says. "I only have one bar." She keeps trying to refresh her app, but when that doesn't work she starts talking to me again. "Antonia didn't tell me you had such a powerful aura."

"Thanks," I say. "You're over twenty-one. Right?"

Mika nods.

"Could you get me a drink?" I ask. "I'll pay."

Antonia hasn't said one word to me since I first arrived. I'm not trying to be critical of her spiritual beliefs, but Mika is pretty intense. If I have to deal with her all night, I figure I might as well get drunk.

"Yeah," Mika says. "Sure. What do you want?"

Score.

"A double Jack and Coke," I say. If anyone's snooping on us, I can tell Dad that the drinks were just soda. "Actually. Would you mind bringing two doubles? That way you don't have to go to the bar again for me. Do you mind?"

I dig my wallet out of my purse and give her some cash.

"Intense," Mika says. "Let's do this."

Across the table, Antonia and Heather are deep in conversation. Antonia's reaching over and lightly pulling at one of Heather's curls. It's really cute, but then I start getting paranoid about whether someone will recognize us. We may be at an all-ages venue—and I sort of have an excuse about the drinking—but Dad's not going to like me being seen with Antonia about to practically make out with a girl from our school.

That's his problem. Not mine.

Mika returns with the drinks and sets them on the table. "I took a couple shots at the bar already," she says. "Hope you don't mind!"

I grab one of the doubles and start slurping down the liquid. It burns in my belly, then warms my whole body.

"So…" I figure I better talk to Mika. "How do you find inspiration for your poetry? Like when you're blocked?" Maybe *she'll* have some answers.

"Oh there's a lot that you can do. I really like to inhabit my body when I feel a creative blockage."

"What do you mean?" I ask.

"It's like having a sickness. You have to diagnose where the

129

blockage is coming from. So I meditate, you know, get really quiet so my body can talk to me."

Her words are unexpected, but there actually seems to be some wisdom in what Mika's saying. I polish off the first double fast, then start on my second. It feels good to finally loosen up a little.

"What I would say *usually* happens," Mika says, taking off her round glasses, "is that your Svadhisthana is somehow blocked. That creative energy can't flow through."

"My svadhistanawhat?" I blurt.

"It's your second chakra. It's between your pubic bone and your navel. It's the main site on your body for creativity and sexuality. Those two aspects of your life are *very* much linked together," Mika says, leaning into my personal space.

"Oh." I take another gulp of my Jack and Coke. "I see."

"It's part of our nature to create. We're also sexual beings. I have to be in a relaxed mental state to create, like with sex. You don't want to be all anxious, otherwise nothing will work."

"I'm anxious all the time," I say awkwardly. The drinks are loosening me up. I can't believe I'm talking to a random weirdo about my problems, but what she's saying makes sense.

"Here. I want to show you something." Mika stands up from the table. "Come on. Stand up. Yeah. Seriously." I slam down the rest of my second drink. I need to be way more buzzed to deal with all this chakra talk, but I stand next to Mika anyway.

"So I want you to use your hand to close your right nostril. Then I want you to inhale and exhale through the left nostril for about eight to ten breaths."

I look around. People at the other tables are totally staring at me, but I go along with Mika's suggestion. Maybe whatever she's talking about will actually help me to unlock my creativity. Why not?

"Good," Mika says. "Now I want you to do this."

She inhales, pushes her knees together, puts her hands on

her hips and starts making these huge circles with her pelvis while exhaling.

Is she crazy? That's where I draw the line.

I may be drunk, but I'm *not* doing that in public.

I look over at Antonia for help. She's running her hand along Heather's neck. Their legs are hooked around each other's under the table. Heather looks pretty comfortable to me.

"I'm going to run to the ladies' room," I say.

I lean over and whisper in Antonia's ear to meet me at the bathroom in a couple of minutes, then I'm up and hurrying away from the table, trying to regain some control of my senses. My head is spinning from the drinks and I'm nearly tripping over my feet as I walk to the bathroom. Now I have to act happy about hanging out when I'm not.

When I get to the bathroom, I check myself out in the mirror. I'm really unhappy with my outfit. Everything—my fat knees, my underarm flab, the loose skin around my stomach from losing weight—disgusts me. My body is a map of all my past sins.

I wish I could wash everything clean. Start over. The fact that I haven't started working much on my sketching or paintings nags at me again, like I've just been watching my dreams wither and die and I'm doing nothing to help them grow. And I'm pretty sure it has nothing to do with my second chakra.

I'm smoothing down my frizzy hair when Antonia saunters in like she's having the time of her life.

"Antonia…"

"What?"

"I know she's your cousin, but…"

"Spit it out," Antonia says.

"I'm not against talking about spiritual energy or chakras or whatever, but Mika's weird. Really weird."

"I warned you." She looks up at the mirror and fixes a piece

131

of stray hair. "Talking to her can't be that bad. She's chatty. She does all the work for you."

"I know the purpose of tonight is to make Heather feel comfortable and that you're on a date and everything, but could you just join the conversation for a few minutes? Save my sanity?"

"Chill. You're doing awesome and Mika really likes you."

"Too much. Did you see her trying to help me unblock my chakra?"

"What?" Antonia laughs. "That seems like her."

"What am I supposed to do now?"

"Just sit across from her. Talk to her for a little bit longer. Please? It's working. Heather is loosening up. She's starting to see that being out with a girl is not such a big deal."

"Okay," I say. "But only this once. And only for you."

Antonia winks at me. "That's my girl. Now try to have a good time, you deserve it. Relax a little."

She checks her makeup in the mirror on her way out of the bathroom, then disappears into the lounge's darkness. Even though I said I would stay, I start thinking about how I can get out of the situation anyway. Why did I get tangled up in this mess?

I'll just go out there and see what's up. I hear a band starting anyway, so at least I won't have to talk to Mika for too long. Tonight's opener is International Criminals. There's a small crowd gathered around the band. As I try to move through, I see that Heather and Antonia are talking again. Mika's nose is in her phone.

Then I spot Zach and Jackson in front of the stage.

Zach looks like he just stepped off the set of *Sisters & Mothers*. Everything about him is perfect. That head of dark hair, those cheeks tapering into a strong jawline around his pouty mouth. And I look like a lumpy sack of potatoes. I try to duck behind a tall guy next to me so they won't see me, but Jackson spots me and summons me over to them.

I'm really not trying to ditch Antonia, but I can't ignore him.

"What are you doing here?" Jackson asks. "Haven't seen you around much lately…" He smiles like the thing on the boat never happened and hugs me, lingering a little longer than normal. I really don't want Zach to get the wrong impression, so I pull back as soon as I can.

"Hey, Liv," Zach says. "What's up?"

I glance at him, taking in his sinewy arms that I wish were touching me. I want to say something, but I hesitate for too long. He turns his attention to the stage.

All right. He's watching the music.

He's not even acknowledging my presence at this point. What about those looks at the party? Did I imagine the chemistry? I don't get why he's acting so hot and cold. Maybe he was just trying to be nice on the boat. Or maybe he had had too much to drink and felt like I was far enough outside his world that he could confide in me.

Zach keeps watching the band play, but doesn't talk to either of us. After the song ends, Zach tells Jackson he has a phone call and excuses himself from the dance floor.

"It's my agent," Zach says. "Text me later."

I sigh under my breath. I've blown the one big opportunity I've had to talk to him outside of school. I thought I was obvious about how I felt about him, but I guess girls probably have crushes on him all the time. Maybe he just isn't interested in dating me.

Jackson turns to me. "Have you been drinking?"

I smile mischievously. "What if I have?"

Jackson's far from the perfect guy, but I don't want to hang out with Mika or be the third wheel with Antonia and Heather. Flirting a little can't hurt.

"Then you should definitely share some."

"It's all gone," I say. "But I can try to flirt with a guy to get you some."

Jackson laughs. "No. That's okay. I have some in my car. Do you wanna go out there with me?"

"To your *car*?" I ask.

"It's just so loud in here," he says. "Let's talk."

My head is dizzy from the alcohol. I don't want to give Jackson the wrong impression, but I figure maybe I can get on his good side. Or find out more about Zach. They're best friends after all. I think about texting Antonia to let her know I'm going outside with Jackson, but decide not to. I won't be gone long. She's been super into Heather all night and probably won't be checking her phone much anyway.

"Yeah. Let's go," I say. "I just can't be gone too long. I came with some friends."

In his car, Jackson turns on an R&B album and pulls out a flask. He offers the liquor to me, but I already feel pretty buzzed so I shake my head.

"Suit yourself. More for me," he says, chugging from the flask. He doesn't say anything else, so I start asking him about himself. The only thing I really know about him, other than that his father sells yachts, is that he's on a club soccer team, so I start there.

"Are you going to play soccer after you graduate?" I ask.

"Yeah," he says. "That's the idea."

"I don't know anything about soccer."

God. I'm such an idiot.

"That's okay," Jackson says. "That's not what I wanted to talk to you about anyway." He turns in his seat and squeezes my bicep with his fingers. What's he doing? Trying to test how jiggly my underarms are? I try to pull away, but he pinches my arm even harder. "You look so good, Liv. I wish I'd seen you more at the party."

"Thanks," I say, feeling both flattered and uncomfortable. Jackson leans over slowly and kisses me.

I panic. Have I already ruined my chances with Zach? I

definitely should not be kissing Jackson, but based on how Zach barely spoke to me earlier tonight maybe I didn't have a chance with Zach in the first place. At least Jackson isn't sending mixed signals. My head's spinning from the alcohol and, though I know this isn't the best idea, I decide to kiss Jackson back. It feels good to be wanted. I'm not the best kisser, or maybe I am and I'm just underconfident, or maybe it's the way Jackson seems to be pushing at me, like he's trying too hard. I can go with this, and I do—it's just making out—and I'm not entirely turned off even though Jackson goes way too fast. Talk about zero to sixty.

I pull back for a moment to get some air. It's sticky and hot inside his car. "You're a good kisser," he says. "You must get a lot of practice."

How am I supposed to respond to that?

"Not really," I stammer, thinking I should kiss him again just so he'll stop talking. He's definitely not as charming of a conversationalist as Zach.

"Then let's get you some more."

He kisses me again, but then Jackson takes it too far. His hands start moving around my body, and I can't keep up with them. He tries to grope my breasts over the fabric of my dress, but when I push his hand down he takes that as an invitation to try to lift up the skirt.

"No," I say, squirming away from him. I want to shove him off me, but I'm worried he'll tell everyone at school I'm a tease or, worse, a prude. Jackson completely ignores me. He's moved his hand away from my legs, but now he's awkwardly trying to slide his hand between the seat and me to grope my butt. "No," I repeat again.

I'm totally uncomfortable.

I wish I were back inside the lounge.

Why did I ditch Antonia? Will she even be there when I get back?

I've ruined everything.

"It's kind of hot in here," I say. "You must be burning up too. Maybe we should get some fresh air." He keeps pressing himself into me, running his tongue along my neck like he didn't hear me. It feels like I'm suffocating. I start to take a deep breath, but I feel like I can't draw any air into my lungs. I need to get away from him.

"I have to go. I better find my friends," I nearly shout.

"But we just got in here," he says.

"We've been in your car for a while." I start to open the door. "Won't Zach wonder where you went?"

"Not at all," he says. "He's probably still on the phone."

He reaches for me again, grabs my arm, then my knee.

"I'm serious," I say. "My friends will be looking for me."

He finally gets the point. Jackson pulls away.

I feel relieved, but at the same time I don't want to make him angry.

To soften the situation, I ask, "What are you doing tomorrow?"

"I don't know," he says. "You should go now."

And just like that he wants me out of his car. He's disgusted by me. By my rejection of him. It's clear that since he's not getting his way, I'm not welcome. I can't tell if I'm angrier at him for being so awful or at myself for coming out here with him.

Talk about a disaster. I feel a weight on my heart, a pressure as if my chest is pushing in on itself. *You're so stupid, Liv. You thought because you've lost weight a guy would be interested in you? No one actually cares. You're lucky Jackson gave such a fatty the time of day. Zach's not going to even look at you. You're just sloppy seconds now.*

I head back to the venue. Antonia, Heather and Mika aren't at the table. Did they leave? Did she see me go outside with Jackson? Does Antonia think I ditched her? I check my phone, but I don't see any messages. Maybe they're on the back patio or out in front of the lounge. I think about going to find them, but I feel a heaving in my stomach that I can't ignore.

I run back to the bathroom, this time to puke. A whirling ball of negative energy is spinning throughout my body. My nerves are on fire. I can't stop rehashing the thoughts spiraling through my brain. *Your family doesn't like you. You're a crappy friend. Boys will never really want you. They'll all be like Ollie. And Jackson. Your stomach is a slab of fat. You're a prude. You can't even let them touch you because you're so afraid...*

I lock the stall and hold myself over the bowl. It's the only thing I can think to do to feel better. Nothing comes out. There's nothing in my stomach. Just this noise of the beat of the music outside the bathroom pounding into me, into the rhythms of my life, into the chaos of my heart, taking control. I start to feel my body shake, to lose control.

The squeezing is tighter around my chest, like everything is constricting into a narrow tube, like I'm being compressed from every angle.

I turn and sit on the floor. I stare at the door in front of me, at the gray-green paint, at its dullness, at how my life is turning into that door, how I'm turning solid, into an object, something for someone to get through, something covered with a splatter of drab paint. I take a small flat razor from my purse and lift up my dress.

I've done this a few times before, only when things get really bad, when I get so upset this is the only way I can hush the whirling inside my head. I feel sick. I can still feel his hands on me, creeping up my thighs, stroking my neck, grabbing my butt.

I make a cut inside my thigh. As soon as the blood pools on my skin—warm and wet—a sense of relief washes over me, like my heart is pumping blood again. The pain makes me present. It makes me feel real. Everything starts to come into focus again.

I'm Olivia Blakely. I'm in control.

I breathe in. I exhale. I breathe in.

I'm still here. I exist.

Then I stop up the blood with tissue paper.

Guilt washes over me. The tears well up. I don't have that same pressure around my heart. I feel a different kind of pain. The kind that means I'm letting everyone down.

I leave the bathroom and the venue without knowing where I'm going or how I'm going to get there. I can't bear to look for Antonia. She'll be so pissed that I ditched her, and I don't need another fight. I check my phone for texts from her. Nothing.

Before I know it I'm on a park bench drinking from a bottle of cheap whiskey that some college guys bought for me at the liquor store across the street. It's pathetic, but that's what the guys brought me. I'm not complaining.

The streets are dark except for the glow of streetlights. I take a swig from the bottle. Then another and another until I've slammed a quarter of the liquid. Instead of drowning out the thoughts—*fear fear fear fat fat fat worthless*—the whiskey only amplifies them until I can't take it anymore. I need to talk to someone. I need Sam.

You're drinking alone in a park. Pathetic.

All of a sudden there's a loud banging noise. Realizing this probably isn't the safest place for a drunk teenage girl to be sitting by herself, I scan the park. I think there's someone digging through a trash can, but I can't tell. It's too dark.

If my parents ever found out I was here my life would be over.

I pull my phone out of my purse, balancing the whiskey bottle between my legs, and make the call.

"Liv?" Sam asks. His voice is crackly and hoarse, almost like he's either been sleeping or hasn't spoken to anyone for hours. "What's up?"

"How are you?" I ask.

It's lame, but I don't know what else to say or how to start the conversation.

"*Where* are you?" Sam asks. I notice a hint of exasperation in his voice, but mostly he just sounds worried. I feel bad. I didn't want to make him worry about me.

"Enjoying the night air," I say, trying to keep him from realizing that I'm an emotional mess right now. I just want to talk to him so I can calm down a little.

"You sound weird," Sam says. "Are you okay?"

Trying not to slur, I tell him about Mika and how everything was so weird, but I leave out the Jackson part. I'm vague about my location. I could be anywhere.

"That is weird," he says. "Did you drink?"

I ignore him. I don't want to answer that question.

"You're so sweet," I say. "So sweet to me. I want to put my head on your shoulder and just fall asleep."

"You didn't answer me." He pauses and I can hear a girl asking him a question in the background. He tells her he'll be there in a minute. "Do you need a ride?"

It takes a moment to sink in, feeling a tinge of jealousy that I immediately try to tamp down. *Sam's on a date.*

"Liv. Seriously. Are you okay?" He sounds upset. "I'll come get you."

Here I am. Being the damsel in distress yet again. No wonder Sam thinks he has to be so protective. He should have never picked up the phone. I don't deserve him as a friend.

"No," I say. "I was just thinking about you. Look, I gotta go."

I hang up on him. I don't want Sam to see me like this. I can still smell Jackson on me. I feel so stupid. There's no way I'm telling him anything more about tonight. I can't even figure out what to feel about what happened in the car. Did I lead Jackson on? Was I assaulted? Was he trying to ignore me? Or did he really not hear me at first?

I suck up my pride and text Mason. He's the only other person I can think to contact to give me a ride home.

I for sure can't call Royce. He wasn't perfect in high school, but he was an angel compared to Mason. He'd probably badger me to tell him what's going on.

Mason's a screwup. Like me. He may act different now, but he's still afraid of himself. Still afraid of how horrible of a person he can be. I can tell. I may talk about how much I don't get along with Mason, but we're not all that different from each other.

LIV: Need a favor. Srsly.

MASON: What?

LIV: Pick me up? Plz?

MASON: U ok?

LIV: Just need a ride.

MASON: Where r u?

LIV: Silver Lake. Txt u the addy.

MASON: For real?

LIV: Plz mason?

MASON: Ya. I'll be there.

By the time Mason shows up, I've polished off half the whiskey bottle. I can't even look at my phone because the screen looks so blurry and makes me dizzy. I'm slouching on the bench, looking at the three missed calls from Sam, obsessing over how I've let him down yet again, royally messed up both my chances with Zach *and* ditched Antonia when this night—her first night out, *out*—was so important to her.

Mason parks his Lincoln Navigator and comes out to the bench.

"Come on," he says, helping me up. "Get in the car."

I stand up and leave the half-empty whiskey bottle on the

sidewalk. Barely able to walk straight, I look down at my feet so I don't trip. My toes and ankles are swollen and purple. I finally lift myself up into the passenger seat, sitting as still as I can to try to get rid of the spinning that's starting to take over my brain.

"You need to get your act together," he says.

"Coming from the guy who was drunk for half of high school and most of college," I say, pressing my head against the window. "I was there."

"I don't need any reminders." Mason hands me a bottle of water. He's prepared. "It was hard to get clean but I did it. You need to think about what you want out of life. I don't mind picking you up when you need me, but you're better than this…"

I feel disgusting. I just want to take a shower and wash off all the grossness from this night—the vomit in my hair, the blood on my thigh, the feeling of Jackson all over me. I so don't need this lecture right now. Not from Mason.

"Well, apparently I'm not," I slur as I try to twist open the bottle cap. "Whatever. I don't need a lecture from someone who turned into literally *the* biggest jerk every time he drank."

"That's not true," Mason says. "And you know it."

"You're such a hypocrite." I slam my head back against the headrest and close my eyes, trying to get rid of the spinning. "Going to rehab doesn't mean you get to pretend it didn't happen. You were awful to me when we were kids. Even when you *weren't* drinking."

"I'm not trying to fight with you."

"You sound just like Dad." I take a sip from the bottle. The cool water slips down my throat. "You probably don't even remember some of the things you said to me." Evidently I *am* trying to fight.

He focuses on the road, as if he's too afraid to look at me.

I've never talked to him about those years. My feelings are

hitting the surface so hard and fast that I'm barely aware of what I'm saying as I lay into him. "Let me remind you." The way the words come out sounds so vicious that I wonder how long I've been holding on to all this anger. "It's a Saturday night. I'm having a sleepover at home with my three best girlfriends. We're making ice-cream sundaes in the kitchen."

I close my eyes again. I can smell the fudge being poured over French vanilla ice cream. The frosty feeling of the spoon against my tongue sends chills down my neck. The memory's so vivid I feel like I could reach out and touch the younger version of myself.

I miss that girl. I want to go back in time to tell her that she should never grow up. Things are only going to get more messed up. She would never listen to me though.

"Enter you. Drunk. You saunter into the kitchen, and all of my friends can only pay attention to you, the cute older brother, while I'm trying to hide how totally embarrassed I am. Does this sound familiar?

"You then walk over, lift up my shirt and pinch my stomach—in front of my friends—and tell me that no guy will ever want to date me if I keep eating like a... What were the words you used? Oh yeah. You said no one would ever love an *obese porker* like me. I was *twelve* years old."

"I'm sorry," he says, almost whispering.

It's not enough.

Mason doesn't speak for the rest of the way home and I'm grateful for that, grateful for the chill in the night, grateful for the dark and the quiet hum of the car engine.

Grateful. For now.

thirteen

Turning off the shower, I step out on the bath mat and wrap a towel around me. As I twist out the excess water from my hair into the sink, I face myself in the mirror.

I look like hell.

The mirror tells me all I need to know about last night. Red eyes. Puffy cheeks like a chipmunk. Swollen glands. After Mason went to bed, I raided our cabinets. I grabbed whatever food I could find that didn't need to be cooked. Chips. Pretzels. Trail mix. Cashews. Rice cakes. Bagels. Royce's old leftover pork rinds. Disgusting? Huh?

I can't stop thinking about how horrible I feel about bingeing on all that food. It didn't even taste as good as it used to. Nothing does. Nothing has a taste anymore.

I hate chewing. I hate swallowing. I hate puking.

It's all so repetitive and boring.

Last night, after what happened with Jackson, I kept thinking that maybe I shouldn't have lost weight. If that's what happens to skinny girls, I thought in my drunken stupor, I'd rather eat myself to death. It's stupid logic. I know. Bulimia logic. It's not like I want to go untouched forever. I just wish Jackson hadn't been such a creep. Is he always like that? Does Zach know? If he does, I can't imagine them being friends. It seems so out of character for Zach. I know I don't know everything about him, but he wouldn't think that was cool. My head spins from all the questions. I don't think I've purged all the alcohol yet. Nausea sits in the pit of my stomach, gnawing at me. I should probably try to eat some food to settle my stomach, but my throat stings from vomiting when I woke up this morning. I was so tired last night that I fell asleep without purging first.

Putting on my bathrobe, I walk downstairs to grab some water. I'm on the landing when I hear a knock at the door. I'm really not in the mood and I'm not dressed. I look around to see if someone will get the door first, but no one else seems to be in the house.

The person knocks again. This time a little louder and more insistently. I think about ignoring them and going back upstairs, but they keep knocking.

Knock. Knock. Knock.

I answer the door. It's Antonia.

She steps past me into the house without giving me a chance to invite her inside. "Why didn't you answer my texts? I've sent you like ten already this morning."

"Sorry," I say. "I didn't see them. My phone's dead. I forgot to plug it in."

"I saw you leave with Jackson." Antonia gives me the same up-and-down look that Mika gave to me, only Antonia adds a sneer like she's been practicing it all day just to use it on me. She's not happy. *Clearly.* "I can't believe you ditched us for him."

"I didn't ditch you," I say. "And you didn't text me."

I hate when Antonia gets mad at me. It always becomes this huge dramatic fight that consumes my entire life. *Everything* is my fault. She's going to tell me what a selfish friend I am. Which I already know. I wish I could go to bed and fall asleep for a hundred years like a fairy-tale princess frozen in time. Forget last night happened.

"You ruined everything," she says.

"Did I miss something? You guys barely acknowledged me the whole time. Then you left."

"After *you* went outside with Jackson and completely disappeared. You not only ruined everything, but you didn't have the...whatever...to even call me and tell me. I'm lucky I happened to see you walk outside with him."

"You could have come looking for me," I say, trying to come up with a lame excuse. "I wasn't gone that long."

"You put me in the worst position! I had to lie to Heather about where you went. She was worried about you and wanted to call your parents. And we had to listen to Mika talk all night. She ended up being the third wheel, which—let me tell you—was more awkward for us than it probably was for her."

I know she's expecting a big fat apology, but after what she just said I am not in the mood to let that happen. "You could have told her the truth," I say. Now I'm pointing at her. "Thanks for sticking me with Miss Mika the Chakra Clearing Queen, who was creepier than any horror movie I've seen in the last ten years."

"I didn't *drag* you there, Liv. You didn't look like you were having *that* bad of a time. Were you? How many drinks did you have? Three? Four? More than that?"

I know I should just tell her what happened with Jackson, but I can't make myself do it. I open my mouth to respond, but my throat tightens like I'm about to cry.

"Now you're so worried about what I drink or not?" I say, barely getting out the words. "You obviously didn't care what happened to me last night."

Antonia's jaw drops. "Why should I care? You're the one who decided to jump ship to hang out with Jackson. He's such a sleaze. I thought you had a crush on Zach."

I want to tell her about Jackson—about how he groped me until I practically had to push him off—but I can't get the words out. It'll just confirm how stupid I am.

"Plus," Antonia continues, "you can't just expect Heather to deal with everything all at once. *I'm* still trying to sort out my feelings about coming out. And I can't believe my best friend's not there to support me."

"Of course I support you," I say.

It breaks my heart that Antonia doesn't think I support her. This has nothing to do with Antonia wanting to date Heather.

"Please, Liv. You've barely asked me about it." Antonia isn't one to back down from a fight. "You've been so self-centered. Everything's about you and your problems."

Antonia storms off to her car, leaving me standing there. I fold my arms over each other, hugging them tight to my chest. I feel completely alone.

Just then Dad and Rich pull up the driveway. I must look ridiculous, standing in the open doorway sopping wet and wearing only a bathrobe.

"What was that all about?" Dad asks once he's out of the car.

"Nothing," I say, adding, "I'm going back to bed."

"Oh no you're not. We have something to talk to you about."

"What? Does Rich have to be here?"

"As a matter of fact, yes, he does. It's about your part in the campaign."

"Can't I put some clothes on first? This is embarrassing."

Dad nods. "You come right back down."

What I want to do is cry, but I know once I start, I won't be able to stop for a while. And I've got to go face whatever Dad wants to talk to me about that's so urgent.

Once I'm upstairs, I pull on a shirt and sweatpants. Then I pick up all the wrappers from last night and hide them in the garbage can under my sink.

Dad and Rich are talking at the dining room table when

I enter. Rich goes completely quiet, like a ghost just walked into the room.

"Take a seat," Dad says. "We need to discuss your behavior."

Did Mason rat me out to Mom and Dad last night?

"What are you talking about?" I ask.

"Perhaps you need a little photographic reminder?" Rich pushes a tablet across the table at me. "That was published on Radar Online at 4 a.m. this morning."

Looking at the tablet, I see a headline splashed across the screen. BUSTED! UNDERAGE OLIVIA BLAKELY CAUGHT PARTYING IN SILVER LAKE.

The headline is followed by a picture of me downing a drink next to Mika doing her pelvic circles followed by another of me flirting and dancing with Jackson.

The photographs are all dim and grainy. Probably from a cell phone.

"I think I've seen enough," I say.

"You should read the entire article," Rich says. "It's rather enlightening."

The bright screen makes the pounding in my head even worse, but I look back down at the tablet and start reading anyway. I'm not getting out of this one.

Olivia Blakely, teenage daughter of high-profile Republican Congressman Colin Blakely, was caught Saturday night partying with friends at Silver Lake Lounge. Though her father is a famously staid and reserved politician, Olivia seems like she has a little more fun! There's no way for us to know what Ms. Blakely was chugging, but she did seem to get pretty cozy with two as-of-yet unidentified guests at the lounge— a woman and a man, one of whom she later joined in a car. Blakely's bender leaves more questions than answers. Are they friends? Lovers? Is the Speaker of the House's daugh-

ter just being a teenager? Or is she a wild child? Leave your comments below.

"Don't look at the comments," Rich says, stealing back the tablet.

"Why not?" I ask. "I've already seen the worst."

Rich chuckles. "No you haven't—just leave the comments to me."

"I'm not even going to ask you what happened last night, but I thought you had a better head on your shoulders, Olivia." Dad takes off his glasses and wipes his eyes. "You look like a total party girl. Is that what you want to do with your life? Repeat Mason's mistakes? That's not the Liv I know. Or is it? You tell me."

I hold back the wet, hot tears welling up in my eyes. I want to tell him I'm not a complete screwup, but I'm humiliated. These pictures aren't what he thinks they are.

"If you have nothing to say for yourself, then you may as well go," Dad says, frowning. "I hope you enjoyed your night. You're grounded for a month. At least."

I storm past him, through the living room, down the hall and up to my bedroom. I sit on my bed, brushing my hand over the scabbed-up scar forming on my inner thigh. This is so *stupid.* I'm sick of all these arguments, especially with Antonia. I don't want to fight with her. We barely just started hanging out after she was gone all summer.

Why couldn't I explain to Dad what happened last night? Why couldn't I tell Antonia, *my freaking best friend*, about Jackson trying to basically maul me?

Why is life filled with so many secrets?

I walk over to the drawings I've been doing for the portfolio. They stare at me with their shaky lines and erase marks, mocking me. I rip them all apart, crumpling and throwing them on the floor. Nothing I do will ever be good enough for anyone.

Especially me.

fourteen

"The real test of friendship is: Can you literally do nothing with the other person? Can you enjoy those moments of life that are utterly simple?"

—EUGENE KENNEDY

Sam's on his way to pick me up.

I'm finally not grounded. It's been almost a month since I fought with Antonia. It's only a few weeks away from Thanksgiving and the air is beginning to cool down.

We're going to *our* place. Marina del Rey.

We usually sit on a bench and watch the harbor. We always joke about escaping on a boat together and living far away. We sit. We watch the boats. We imagine how our futures might turn out. Then we go back to our lives.

Antonia's still mad at me. We haven't spoken since our fight. Maybe Sam and Antonia are hanging out together, but I don't ask. Antonia seems to mostly hang out with Heather and her friends. Sam's been wrapped up in speech and debate. He's probably been going out with Nina—the girl I'm almost certain he was with when I called him the night of the Jackson disaster—but I don't really know because Sam and I have barely talked outside of school this last month. And my life has basically been school or campaign events. Dad wouldn't let me go anywhere on my own for the whole month.

Now I have a pretty strict curfew.

Music blaring over the car stereo, Sam rolls up to the house. He's energetic, smiling, singing along with the music. His blond hair lifts in the breeze and I suddenly catch myself wanting to run my fingers through it. I haven't seen him in this good of a mood in forever. I don't know what, but something's definitely changed about him.

"Hey, Liv," Sam says. "Buckle up."

Maybe a little distance was a good thing for our friendship. Maybe Sam and I were too close to allow each other to change and grow. I like the mystery.

"Thanks for helping me deal with this whole thing," I say sheepishly. I explained the disaster to Sam the day after. Except I left out the part about going to Jackson's car. I'm sure Sam saw the article too. The whole school looks at me like I'm a wild party girl now, which is kind of weird, since I've pretty much always been a loner.

I've only talked to Zach a few times at school. We exchanged numbers and text occasionally, but both of us are pretty busy. I guess there's still some hope though.

"I got your back," Sam says like it's no big deal. "You know that."

I feel terrible. Sam's such a good person. I still don't understand why he would want to be friends with a girl who's a total mess.

"Didn't you have a debate competition last night?" I ask, watching the scenery flash past the window.

"Yeah. I won second place," Sam says. "I think I'm getting really good, actually. Last night's topic was national security and digital privacy—some of the stuff I heard made me think twice about posting selfies. Apparently the NSA uses them as mug shots."

"Well, mine would just be a bunch of duckfaces," I say,

making Sam laugh. "By the way, how's...uh... Nina? That's her name, right?"

"How do you know about Nina?" Sam asks.

"Oh. Antonia told me you were talking to her a while ago."

"We hung out after the debate actually. Played mini golf at that place shaped like a castle."

"That's awesome. I'm terrible. I have literally zero aim."

"I always thought I was decent, but she actually kicked my butt. She got a hole-in-one by putting the ball up a fiberglass dragon's mouth."

"That sounds fun," I say absentmindedly, trying to gauge how I feel.

It's weird to hear Sam talking about a girl. Am I jealous? Or am I just afraid that I might lose him as a friend? That *too* much distance will come between us?

I pause just long enough to make my question sound casual. "Are you guys dating then?"

Sam shakes his head. "We're just talking, I guess."

"So are you into her?" I know I shouldn't interfere, but I can't help myself. "Because you shouldn't lead her on."

"Jesus, Liv," Sam says, turning into the parking lot at the marina. "Since when have you been interested in my love life?"

"I'm not trying to interrogate you or anything. I just want to catch up."

"If I decide to date someone, I want to make sure I really like that person. That's all."

Sam and I find our bench along a strip of green and watch the boats in the harbor.

We listen to the way the water laps across the boat hulls, the way the waves trickle along the edges of pylons and rocks. I can tell what Sam's thinking. He's dreaming our dream again. We're on a sailboat heading out to sea. The ocean is quiet. The wind is catching the sails. The horizon calls us with its long blue arm, saying, *come gently this way.* Sam scoots closer to me. My knee is nearly touching his.

"What are you thinking?" he asks.

"I'm just thinking about our boat," I say, though I'm really thinking about so many other things too, like what I want my future to be. Where will I go to college? If I go to art school, will I keep studying painting or will I specialize in something else?

"Someday I'll buy my own," Sam says.

"What should our boat's name be?" I ask.

He laughs. "Not the *Antonia.*"

"Hey," I say. "That's mean."

"*You* want to ride on that boat?" he says. "That would be one crazy ride."

"Okay, fine then," I say. "How about the *Jasmine.*" I blurt the name out without even thinking. I don't know. I've just always looked up to her.

"Yeah, I kind of like that," he says. "That's our boat then. The *Jasmine.* Just don't tell her or Royce. She'd probably think that's pretty weird."

"Scout's honor," I say. I squeeze his hand and hold on. We've always done this. Held hands. But only here. Only on this bench at this marina. We don't say anything about it—almost like it's a secret even to ourselves. It just sort of happens.

"By the way, you and Antonia really need to hash things out. This whole fight seems pretty ridiculous."

"Have you talked to her about it?"

Sam shakes his head. "Nah. I figure that would be breaking the *girl code* or something."

I turn to face him. "What do you mean by *girl code*?"

"Whoa there. Easy, tiger," he says, holding up his hands. "I'm not being sexist. I just mean that whatever happened was between you two. Not me."

"You're right. I do need to talk to her. Do you think she's moved on?"

"I don't think so. I haven't talked to her about whatever you guys were fighting over. We don't really hang out with you. I think she probably wants you to be the first one to say something. You know Antonia. She's just stubborn as hell."

"Thanks, Sam." I lean over and put my head on his shoulder. "Talking to you always makes me feel better. Well, most of the time."

"What are you doing tonight?" he asks. "I thought just you and I could..."

My phone rings just as I'm about to answer him.

No one ever calls me. Except for my parents.

"I better get it," I say. "Might be my mom."

She's been texting me all morning telling me I need to be more supportive of Dad and that she wants to talk to me. I text her back and everything, but she keeps saying she needs time with me. I take the phone out of my purse.

It's not Mom or Dad.

It's Zach.

"I'll just be a minute," I say, standing up and walking toward the water's edge.

Boats are slowly docking and undocking. Sailboats glide by while rowers bend back and forth, pulling their oars through the water. I can even spot a group of women doing paddleboard yoga across the water near Marina beach.

"Liv," Zach says. "Do you have a second?"

"Yeah, sure," I say. "What's up?"

"I wanted to talk more at the yacht party, I'm sorry we didn't get to. Things were kind of crazy with Cristina."

I don't understand why he hasn't mentioned any of this stuff until now. What took him so long?

"Yeah, they were," I say, remembering my exchange with her in the bathroom.

"We'd broken up already, like I told you, but we were fighting again. It just wasn't… Anyway, I wanted to talk to you at Silver Lake too, but… I mean, I had a lot on my mind. We ended things a while ago, but I had to make sure that she understood that I didn't want to get back together. I wanted to do things right. So if you want to go out soon…"

Get real. Zach Park is asking *me* out on a date?

I'm so stunned that I don't answer right away, but then the silence starts getting awkward so I blurt out a hurried "I do."

Sam's sitting over on the bench waiting for me. I haven't answered his question about tonight. Will Nina care? Does she know Sam and I have kissed before? He's tilting his head to the side, wanting to know who I'm talking to on the phone.

"Can we talk about this later?" I ask, then pause and bite my lip. I look over at the harbor, at all the uncertainty floating out there. What will Sam think?

"Oh sure," he says. The poor guy sounds confused.

"I'm glad you called. I really am," I say, then hang up.

Christ. The guy I've had a crush on for two years has *just* asked me out and now I'm trying to rush him off the phone. This is definitely *not* how I imagined this moment.

Returning to the bench, I'm really trying not to look excited even though I want to burst. I don't want Sam to feel rejected. And I don't want things to get weird between us.

"Who was that?" Sam asks.

"Zach," I say. "He asked me out."

"Oh," Sam says, fiddling with the button on his cargo shorts. "When?"

"I don't know. He didn't say."

Is he upset that Zach and I are going to go on a date? I can't tell whether he cares or not.

Sam looks up at me. "Do you still want to hang out tonight? We could catch a movie or something."

"Of course!" I say, trying to reassure him. Just because Zach asked me on a date doesn't mean I can't hang out with Sam. I hope he doesn't think I'm replacing him.

"Right," Sam says. There's an awkward silence between us. I can't help but wonder whether Sam was actually trying to ask me out on a date when Zach called. "How does six o'clock sound?"

fifteen

"Among my stillness was a pounding heart."

—SHANNON A. THOMPSON

I'm sitting next to Mom on the couch, watching a house hunting show, when she turns to me with this concerned look on her face. "How are you doing, Liv?"

It's been a few hours since I got back from the marina with Sam and I can't stop thinking about Zach. I keep wondering when I should call him back. I don't want to seem too eager or desperate.

"I'm okay," I say, staring at the couple on the screen demoing a wall. It's amazing how they're all so good-looking and never seem to get dirty even though they're doing construction. "School's all right. Antonia and I still aren't really talking."

"You never told me what happened." Mom turns down the volume. "You know you can talk to me, honey. I feel like you've been kind of distant since this summer."

I don't look at her. Her words make me feel guilty for not being a good daughter. For swinging between being depressed at home all the time or getting into trouble.

"It was a stupid fight," I say, not explaining further. "Junior year's kind of the worst. I feel like I'm failing everything."

"Your grades are decent," she says, confused. "We're not

getting any calls home about anything. I think you need to be a little less hard on yourself."

"Less hard on myself? Since when?" Now I'm the confused one. I've been expected to be perfect for as long as I can remember.

"I'm worried about you, Liv. You go to bed so late it's hard to wake you up in the morning." It's true. I haven't really been sleeping well. Anxiety—over doing well in school, over getting my portfolio together, over my body—keeps me up late. I usually don't fall asleep until well after midnight. And I'm always hungry.

"You and Dad expect me to get good grades, so that's what I have to do," I say, trying to place all the blame on school even though I know part of the problem is that I'm not eating normally. "I have four AP classes. Of course I'm tired."

"I just want to make sure you're taking care of yourself. I never see you take a lunch to school," Mom continues without skipping a beat. "Don't wait all day to eat. You need to eat to be able to concentrate to do well. I want you to be healthy."

My phone buzzes. I look down and smile.

It's Zach.

"Sorry, Mom," I say, excusing myself from the room. "I have to take this. It'll be just a minute."

"Guess where I am?" Zach asks.

I love hearing his voice. It's deep and musical.

"I don't know," I say. "At home?"

"Try again," he says.

My heart skips a beat. He must be on his way to see me. It's easy enough to figure out where I live without having to ask anyone, because of Dad's job.

"Figure it out yet?"

"I think so," I say, smiling. "Are you here already?"

"I'm waiting outside in my car. I wanted to surprise you."

I'm totally not dressed up to go anywhere, but I don't care.

I just want to see him. I tell Zach I'll be outside in a couple minutes after I grab a couple things.

"What's wrong?" Mom asks when I return to the living room.

"Just boy stuff."

"I hope it's good news," she says.

"The best," I say. "I gotta go. Is that okay?"

"Where are you going? Remember your curfew."

"I know. I'll be home on time. I'm not sure where we're going. He said he wanted to surprise me, but I'm sure I won't be out for that long. Just a date."

"I didn't know you were dating someone," Mom says. She gets a questioning look on her face. "You don't have to ask permission, but I'd at least like to know his name."

I'm holding the knob at the front door, anxious to get out of the house. "Zach Park," I say. "Can I go now? He's waiting outside."

Her eyebrows go up. "The one from *Sisters & Mothers*?"

She watches the show too.

I nod and smile. *Come on, Mom.*

"Well," she says, near speechless. "He's quite a..."

"Yeah," I say. "He *is*."

I start turning the knob.

She nods at the front door. "All right. Just make sure you're not back too late."

I slip out of the house, glad there's no send-off with Dad and Mom and annoying older brothers, though I know Mom will want to meet Zach sooner than later.

Sitting in the driver's side of his black Audi, he's everything I dreamed of. His gorgeous dark eyes examine me as I walk down the driveway toward him. He's wearing a denim coat over a white T-shirt, and I'm practically melting before I get in the car.

He's unexpectedly quiet when I sit down. It's almost like he's nervous, which comes as a huge surprise to me. How could a guy who's used to so much attention be nervous when *I'm* around?

Zach starts the car. "You look amazing," he says, looking over at me. "Like always."

"Yeah right." Then I realize how ungrateful I sound. "Thanks. You do too."

I'm blushing like I've never been complimented before.

He gives me a little smile, then pulls out of the driveway past the neighbors who are starting to put up Christmas lights. The holiday's still almost a month away.

"Where are we going?" I ask.

"Not telling... It's supposed to be a surprise."

He drives down to Hollywood and parks next to someplace I can't even see the name of because we're going in the back. I can't even tell what kind of business it is. A restaurant? A theater? A venue?

Zach takes me through the unlocked back door. A woman greets him. She's older than us, yet she speaks to him formally.

"Mr. Park. I hope you're doing well. Are you ready?"

"Ready for what?" I ask.

"Sure, Genevieve," Zach says. "Hope you don't mind I brought a friend. This is Liv Blakely."

"Congressman Blakely's daughter?" she asks. "It's a pleasure to meet you."

I shake her hand and smile pleasantly. Did Zach tell her who I am? I'm pretty used to people knowing me, but I'm sure I don't get recognized nearly as much as he does.

"Right this way," Genevieve says, heading into a hall.

I give Zach a look and he just chuckles and shrugs, pretending not to know where we're going. I start to figure it out when I see a red light on outside a door. We pass by and come to another where the red light is off. Genevieve opens the door and in we go.

There's a guy inside I don't recognize. He's thin, has dreads and a nose piercing, and all kinds of the coolest rings and necklaces you've ever seen.

"What's up, Zach?" the guy says. They bump fists.

"DJ Whuz," Zach says. "Haven't seen you in a while."

"That's 'cause you never come on the show. What's up? No love for the Whuz?"

"I love you," Zach says. "I guess my agent had the real stars to promote."

"Zach, man. You're the real deal. Up-and-comer. Who's this lovely lady with you? She gonna be on the air too?"

"Oh no, I'm just watching," I say. "I don't know how to do these things."

I recognize DJ Whuz from KLAB Radio. He runs a music segment, does interviews with all kinds of musicians and hot actors. He calls listeners who phone in his Lab Rats. He was one of the DJs at Coachella the last few years.

"Come on. I don't bite," DJ Whuz says, holding up his hands to show his innocence. "We just gonna talk about what my buddy Zach's up to. It'll be great. No one can see you. We don't even have to use your real name. Who you wanna be?"

I look at Zach, totally embarrassed. Half the time, I feel like I'm floundering whenever I'm talking to Zach alone. How am I going to hold a decent conversation knowing that there are hundreds—maybe thousands—of people listening?

"Up to you," he says. "I think you'd be great."

"I won't know what to say. What would I talk about?"

"You just do what you're doing now, angel," DJ Whuz says. He winks at me, then makes a signal at his producer outside the glass window. "All right. Headphones on."

He points to a pair of headphones for me to grab and slips some on himself. So does Zach. When I put the headphones on, I immediately hear the radio. Some commercial is playing. There's a microphone in front of me, and I'm terrified to even breathe next to it. I've been to a couple of radio stations with Dad. Boring talk radio. But I was never allowed in the studio. I always had to sit out in the lobby.

Now I'm in a room with Zach Park, thousands of invisible listeners and basically the coolest-looking DJ radio show host you could ever meet. The commercial wraps and I suddenly hear intro music dancing around my ears. DJ Whuz comes to life. He really does. He's animated, dancing, moving his hands all over the place, laughing, so into it that I'm trying not to laugh out loud.

"KLAB experimenting on you... DJ Whuz in the house! All you Lab Rats listen in. We'll play some music a little later on but in the first half hour we have a guest from the ratings-leading show *Sisters & Mothers*, just like I promised, probably the coolest heartthrob from the show...my own heart is leaping wildly right now like some kind of maniac, because right here, right now, feeling it with me, with you, is up-and-coming star... did I say *star*? I did. Welcome to the show, Zach Park. Yeah!"

Zach laughs, because he just had the coolest intro ever and obviously knows it. "Thanks, Whuz. Always love to be on your show. Everything about it is current, the music, the guests, and you're always helping out everyone, like when there's a charity event, you seem to be the one rallying the troops."

"That's because I *am* the troops. I'm DJ Whuz, everyone, in case you forgot who I am, and I'm here with Zach Park. You play Gina's hilarious acoustic-guitar-toting, serenading boyfriend Beau on the show. Seriously, what's that like?"

"It's fun really. I mean, I'm not on every episode, but my character is pretty important as one of the stable love interests. And he does a lot. He gets caught up in weird situations, and occasionally he sings, which means I get to sing, and I think that's kind of the best part for me."

"I think it's the best part for a lot of people," DJ Whuz says.

"With your voice, man? You should think about making a record."

"We'll see," Zach says, like he wants to tease the listeners, but I'm really wondering if he's going to make an album too. That would be so amazing. To be honest, Zach is probably an even better singer than he is an actor.

DJ Whuz spins around and turns his attention to me. "I see you brought with you a guest. A lovely creature. Is she a singer? Can she even *speak*?"

"I can speak," I say.

"Oh she does! She does! Tell everyone your name. Sing it!"

"Liv. Liv Blakely."

"Ay, yeah!" DJ Whuz screams. "Oh wait, I know who *you* are. No hiding now, congressman's daughter. Tell your old man to come on the show. We'll talk politics and get up all in America's grill. But hold on, let me get back to Zach baby, because there's a reason you're on the show and it's to talk about a charity appearance cast members from your show are doing to help out cancer-stricken mothers. Those of you Lab Rats who've been listening awhile know we take time out on KLAB to help the community raise money when the need arises and let me tell you there's always a need..."

I can't believe that Zach took me on a public appearance. We're moving so fast, but no one has ever done something so romantic for me. He's handsome. Hilarious. Easygoing. Well-liked by everyone. How can I *not* fall for him?

After the show on our way home, Zach and I are talking so much that I don't even realize there's a voice mail from Sam waiting on my phone until I get up to my room. A *voice mail*? Weird. No one leaves voice mails unless there's something wrong. I press Play and cradle the phone next to my ear, wondering what it is. Sam's voice comes over the speaker. I wince. Crap. I *completely* forgot that I told him I would come over tonight.

He sounds a little bit flat, but there's emotion bubbling underneath, like he's trying not to sound upset. "I heard you on the radio with Zach," he says. "I should have known you weren't going to show up tonight. This is twice you've ditched me for him. I love you, but I refuse to be a pushover. You can't just call me every time you need someone to rescue you, and then ignore me. Hope you and Zach had a great radio show. Please don't call me back until you're ready to tell me what's going on with you."

sixteen

"I watched him with wonder like the stars watch the moon,

falling in love with every crescent, dark side, and dream."

—PIPER PAYNE

I think I'm falling for Zach. Hard.

We've been on a few dates now. He even took me to watch a taping of one of his shows at the studio and introduced me to the rest of the cast.

Going out with Zach is my only break from school and the campaign, especially since I've ruined my relationships with Antonia and Sam. Zach's chosen most of the places so far, but tonight I'm taking him out—or at least I'm telling him where to go since Mom and Dad have still been too busy to teach me how to drive.

I haven't called Sam. It's probably for the best.

Do friendships between men and women always end in hurt feelings? Maybe there's a certain age you get to when you can't be best friends with a guy anymore. Maybe those expectations have been there below the surface for a long time. I need to focus on myself anyway. After our date last week, I couldn't stop thinking about how Zach has the confidence to pursue his dreams outside of school without letting the rest of his life hold him back. Why can't I do the same?

When Zach knocks on the front door, I feel my stomach cramp. Or are those butterflies? Either way, Mom and Dad aren't home. Early December means that the fund-raising process is gearing up before Dad announces his campaign in January. They know I'm going out with Zach in general, but they don't know we're going out tonight. Dad still doesn't want me going out at night. I have to make sure I'm back before they get home.

"Look at you," Zach says, grabbing my fingers and guiding me through a twirl. It feels silly, but also so romantic I could melt. "You look fantastic."

I blush.

"Have you always been this smooth?" I ask him, practically laughing. "Or did you have to practice?"

"You ready?" He puts his arm around my waist and squeezes. I tense up for a moment, but I try to relax. I'm not used to people touching me. The air outside is chilly and being wrapped in his arms spreads warmth throughout my whole body.

"Where are we going?" Zach asks.

"It's *still* a surprise," I say. "Let's go. I'll give you directions."

Zach and I jump into his car. I look at the map on my phone while giving him directions. I end up taking him the long way just because I want to spend more time alone with him. I want to savor every moment. I want to memorize the lines on his hands as he grips the steering wheel and the sound of his laughter.

Traffic's busy on Wilshire as Zach navigates through Beverly Hills past the chic shops and the palm trees in the center divider wrapped in tiny glowing lights for the Christmas season. He keeps trying to trick me into telling him where we're going, but I just tell him to keep driving. After what seems like forever, I direct Zach around a corner into LACMA's underground parking garage. He starts laughing.

"Of course you would take me to a museum," he says, pinching my neck. "It's kind of funny, but I've never been here. I'm always too busy."

"This is one of my favorite places in the city. It's kind of touristy," I admit, "but I think you're really going to like it."

We head for the museum, holding hands without talking. It feels so comfortable to even be silent next to him. There's a family with a few small kids walking from the parking garage to the museum, but the area isn't as busy as I expected, which makes the moment even more romantic because we're practically alone.

"Is the museum closed?" Zach asks.

"Not this part," I say. "I can't believe you haven't guessed already."

"I'm not as artsy as you," he says.

"It's a *landmark*. It's already been here for years."

We walk around the concrete building of the museum to find a large installation of around two hundred restored antique cast-iron lamps. The lamps are painted white and are lined up in rows that ascend in height from the outside to the center. The bulbs glow with a pure white light that seems almost heavenly in the dark Los Angeles night.

"It's even more beautiful than the last time I came," I say, gazing up at Zach. I love this place. The atmosphere takes you back to another century. "What do you think?"

"It's amazing," Zach says, pulling me close to him. "It's so simple, but so striking."

"It's sad to think that all of these beautiful street lamps could have gone to waste," I say, putting my arms around his neck. "I'm glad the artist saved them."

"Me too," Zach says, pulling away. "Let's see what this thing looks like from the inside." He grabs my hand and starts pulling me toward the center of the installation.

We navigate around the rows of lights separately, nearly bumping into each other then slipping away. I keep my eyes trained on Zach so I don't lose him. It's almost like walking through a labyrinth of light. Zach fakes like he's hiding from me. When I reach out to grab him, he dodges my arm then somehow spins around and ends up behind me.

"Got you," he says, pulling me into him.

"Not for long," I say. I turn around and look up at him.

I can't believe I'm staring into his eyes. The green eyes I always thought I'd be trying to catch glances of for the rest of my high school career. I feel like I'm in a movie.

"What can I do to make you stay?"

Dad's campaign surges into my thoughts. If he wins, I would have to leave Zach. That's the last thing I want to do right now.

He entwines his fingers with mine.

"That's not something you have to worry about," I say, laughing his question off. "I'm not even really that sure why you like me."

"How do I love thee?" Zach asks sarcastically. "Shall I count the ways?"

"No. Definitely not," I say, trying to pull away from him. "I probably sound like I'm trying to fish for compliments."

He holds my hand tighter.

"Sorry. It was a bad joke, but there are honestly a ton of things that I like about you, Liv. It sounds like a ridiculous thing to say, but you're a deep person. You think about things on another kind of level that other people barely ever do."

"What do you mean?" I ask.

"I don't mean to bring her up, but take Cristina for example. All she ever talked about was how great she and her friends were. Or what kind of kombucha is the best for hangovers. Stuff like that. I don't think I've ever talked to her about an actual book. She doesn't even read *Vogue*. She just looks at the pictures."

"So you guys are really over then?" I ask.

"I'm not seeing anyone besides you," Zach says. "And I don't plan to." Does he mean that he wants to be *exclusive*? That he wants to be an official couple?

Couple is such a weird word. Two people who are closely associated, who are of the same sort. I start thinking. Are we of the same sort?

I hope so. I've needed someone to love for so long.

seventeen

"A man must dream a long time in order to act with grandeur,

and dreaming is nursed in darkness."

—JEAN GENET

I'm working on some sketches in my room, trying to figure out what I want to submit for my portfolio for the gallery show, but my mind keeps drifting to Zach. He's charming, sweet, a talented actor. He pushes me to work on my art. He actually wants to be seen with me. For the first time in what feels like my whole life, I finally feel visible.

After destroying all the sketches I had done, I have to start over. I still need to do new sketches and one full painting. The application date for the portfolio isn't until May, but like Ms. Day said, I have to push myself. I have to find my voice somehow.

What do I want to say?

I pick up my pencil and look at my drawing. It's of a blue heron, my favorite bird, taking flight. There's something I've always loved about them. The pale translucent blue of their feathers. The graceful curve of their neck. The slash of black across the crest of their heads like the marking of a graceful warrior. It's said that the heron symbolizes the ability to move between worlds. They keep one foot on land and one foot submerged underwater. They hunt at twilight—the time that is neither night nor day.

I'm thinking about how I'm constantly living between two worlds—the one my family wants for me and the one I want for myself—when there's a knock at my bedroom door. I close my notebook.

"It's open," I say, watching the door crack open slowly.

"Hey there, Honeybee," Dad says.

He's been in Washington since the disaster that was our last family conference. I probably overreacted when Dad talked to us about the campaign, but I didn't want him and Mom to not consider my preferences before they decided to throw our entire family into a high-profile election for the next year.

Dad walks over and sits down on the edge of my bed. He rubs both of his eyes with his palms. "How are you, Liv? We haven't talked in a while."

I'm still not happy about the way Dad shouted at me at the dinner table, but I'm willing to make peace with him. It's not like I'm going to change his mind about running for the governorship now.

"I'm okay. My art classes are going well. English and history are pretty good, but math and chemistry are hard." I sigh. "Which isn't surprising."

Dad runs a hand through his salt-and-pepper hair. He looks tired.

"Can't fault you there. You come by it honestly. Your mother was a better mathematician than I was in school, but neither of us was an Einstein. Sam's pretty good at all that stuff though. Isn't he? You should ask him for help."

I wonder whether to tell Dad about us.

"Yeah." I shrug. "We haven't been talking that much lately."

"I see." Dad raises an eyebrow.

He's seen Sam and I on the rocks before, but we've never gone without talking this long. Except I don't want to explain all that to Dad. I don't want to tell him what a terrible friend I've been or that I can't seem to be straight with Sam about my feelings for Zach.

"But what's going on with you?" Dad asks. "Anything new?"

I think about my dates with Zach. The radio station. His TV taping. LACMA. All the late-night phone calls and texts. I'm sure Mom told him about us. Is that what he's here to fish out information about? I call his bluff. "What did Mom say?"

"Just that you've been going on dates with a boy from your school. What's his name again? Zach..."

"Park," I finish his sentence. "You don't have to worry about him, Dad. He's a gentleman."

"I'm sure he's a fine boy," Dad says. "I'm not concerned about his behavior. Your mother and I have taught you how to handle yourself. I *am* concerned that he's an actor."

"Why?" I say in disbelief. "Do you not think that's a worthy career?"

Dad looks uncomfortable. "It has nothing to do with the worthiness of his career. There's going to be a lot of media attention on you, Honeybee, with the campaign and all..."

I know where this is going. Dad isn't used to me wanting to date, especially after what happened with Ollie my freshman year. He's going to have to adapt.

"You're not worried about that, or you wouldn't be running for governor," I say. "You just don't want me to cause a scandal. You don't want me to do something in the public eye that you can't control."

"It has nothing to do with my *controlling* you. In fact, I'd say that perhaps your mother and I have let you make *too many* of your own decisions."

"Whatever," I say, trying not to counter him with something worse. It's not like he's actually been *around* for most of high school to even make decisions for me.

"You don't understand," Dad says. "Yes. The campaign will

mean that the media will pay more attention to you than normal. *But* dating an actor will make that worse. You're not just going to be the congressman's daughter anymore, Liv. You'll be the congressman's daughter *who's dating an up-and-coming actor.* There are all sorts of things the media will start rumors about when you're linked to a guy. You have to be aware of that. Honestly, I thought you would have taken this differently, with your anxieties about the media attention from the campaign in the first place."

"I'll take my chances," I say, getting up from the bed.

Now that I have a shot at a relationship with Zach, I'm not going to let anything get in my way. Suddenly, I remember the painting of the woman on the swing, kicking off her shoe to her lover, that Ms. Day showed us in class. Why should I let Dad's campaign squash out my *joie de vivre*? What's wrong with a little romance?

"I don't want you going out with him," Dad says.

Is he kidding? Now he wants to control my love life too?

"I'm not trying to piss you off, Dad. This is the first time I've really felt comfortable with a guy I'm seeing. I can't help that he's an actor. I actually think you would like him. He's funny. He's smart. He's way better at talking to people than I am."

"I'm sure he's a stand-up guy," Dad says. "But I don't want you going out with him alone at night. No dates. It'll attract too much public attention. We're announcing the campaign in a few weeks..."

"That's completely unfair, Dad." I feel sick to my stomach. He's stalling. If it weren't for the election, Dad wouldn't care about Zach. This is totally about him. "This wouldn't be a problem if we were a normal family."

"But we're not a normal family, Liv. We never have been. When are you going to accept that and move on? You're a Blakely. Them's the breaks, kid."

"Why can't you just let me have a life?" I plead. "Zach's

the first guy I've liked in a long time. And he likes me back. I promise I won't do anything to reflect poorly on the campaign."

"I don't think you're seeing my point, Olivia. This isn't a good time. And, to be honest, I think you should be focusing on yourself right now. You need to stay healthy. You're under a lot of pressure at school. You'll thank me when you get into a good university next year."

What's with everyone worrying about my health all the time? They used to praise me for getting skinny. Now they beat around the bush. A fleeting thought flashes across my mind. *Just tell him. Tell him that you puke between classes. Tell him that you hide a cup in the shower so you can vomit at night without anyone hearing you. Tell him that you hate your life and Zach is the only thing that's making it any better.*

"Yeah. Thanks a lot," I say.

I could still probably see Zach outside of school sometimes, but we would have to sneak around and Dad would find out eventually. Then I'd never see Zach again. Tears start to well up in my eyes. I don't want to go back to feeling invisible.

"Look. You can talk to him or whatever you kids call that these days, but I'm not going to let you put yourself out there to get crucified by the media again. You can see him at school. Maybe even hang out with a group of friends. We'll see."

What group of friends? Both Antonia and Sam aren't talking to me. Does Dad have any idea how isolating this will be? It'll be just like this summer. I won't have anyone except for the computer screen. I don't say anything. He's already made up his mind.

"This is for you, Liv. You're my baby girl. You always will be." Dad squeezes me so tight I can barely breathe. It hurts and I don't want him to touch me. Fear surges through my body. I don't want him to know how much weight I've lost so far this year. I'm already down twelve pounds. I have sixteen more to go for my goal weight. I'm not stopping now.

"Stop," I say, almost too harshly. "I'm not a kid anymore."

"No," he says, letting go. Dad stands up from my bed and walks to the door. "You're certainly not."

My stomach is in knots. I don't know what to do except to call Zach. I tell him I need to talk to him and to pick me up down the street from my house in half an hour.

I pull on some running shorts and a warm hoodie, thinking about how I'm going to get out of the house without having to answer many questions. After a few minutes, I quietly walk down the stairs, but I run into Mom walking to her bedroom.

"I'm going for a run," I say, nearly choking on my words.

Mom can hear the upset in my voice.

"It's pretty dark, honey," she says. "Can't you wait until the morning? It's not really safe to run this late."

I want to ask her whether she knows what Dad said to me about Zach, but I figure they've already worked it out between them. It's their bad cop, good cop act.

"I need to clear my head," I say, walking past her. "It'll be quick. Only a mile or two. Half hour tops. I'm taking my phone and staying in the neighborhood."

"Okay," Mom says. She hesitates like she's going to apologize or ask a question, but I'm already halfway to the front door. She calls out after me, "Be safe!"

I slowly start jogging into the night, trotting down our front yard, then along the sidewalk that leads along the golf course by our house. How am I going to break this to Zach? There's already so little time I can hang out with him one-on-one because of his work schedule. I don't know how we'll spend time together. If we can't go out on real dates or be alone together then will he still want to see me? Will he lose interest?

I've jogged two blocks away from our house to the meeting

place when I see Zach's Audi pull up behind me and stop in the street. He rolls down the window.

"Hey, Liv. Are we going for a run?"

He sounds confused. Poor guy. Why do I have to have such a complicated family? I bet Cristina's father didn't care whether she hung out with Zach alone or not.

"Hey," I say. "Can we go somewhere to talk?"

We could stay in the car, but I don't want anyone to see us. My neighbors have been living here for decades and are about as nosy as you can get.

He smiles at me, which somehow makes me feel even worse. "Sure. What's up?"

"It needs to be somewhere kind of close," I say. "I can't be gone more than half an hour. I told my parents I was going on a run."

"Is everything okay?" Zach asks.

"Sort of," I say, looking around. "I'll explain in the car. We just need to go somewhere private. Like really private."

"Okay…" He cocks his head to the side, thinking. "I know somewhere. Morgan lives in this small gated community near here. I know the code to get in."

"That sounds great," I say. My jaw is tight with anxiety. "I really appreciate this, Zach. Seriously."

"I missed you this week." We haven't seen each other since Zach left to film on location last week. "It's tiring to only be around Hollywood people. When I'm with you, I feel like none of that stuff matters. I'm so sick of feeling like I'm acting all the time."

He takes a strand of my hair that's fallen by my face and pushes it around my ear.

God. Why does he have to be so perfect?

It makes having to talk about this so much worse.

Zach drives us to Morgan's gated community and parks the

car at a small park that's lush with foliage. I feel nauseated. His car feels stuffy. I need to breathe.

"Do you mind?" I say, gesturing to the park. "I need some air."

Zach and I get out of the car and start walking. We stop under a big gum tree with wispy red flowers and greenish gray leaves, and Zach takes my hands.

"Something's not right," he says. "You're acting weird. What's wrong?"

My stomach is in knots and my heart's beating so fast. I really don't want to tell him, but I know I have to. "My dad doesn't want me to see you. *Date* you."

Zach looks taken by surprise. "What? Why?"

I'm sure no girl has ever rejected him before.

"He doesn't like that you're a celebrity. He says that our relationship will be too high profile. It's bad for the campaign. They're going to announce in early January."

"That's ridiculous. Can't you talk him out of it?"

I shake my head, tears welling up in my eyes.

"I tried. He said we could still talk and hang out at school, but that he didn't want me to be seen with you unless we were with a group of friends. That's the best I could get from him." Now I start really crying. "I'm sorry, Zach. I ruined everything."

It's dangerous to be sneaking out now. I can't keep this up. Dad will find out. If I start going on night runs all the time, Mom will catch on sooner than later.

"It's not your fault," Zach says. "It's not like my career doesn't make things worse too. If I wasn't an actor... I'm sorry, Liv."

"You can't apologize for doing what you love," I say. "That's why this is so stupid. It has nothing to do with *us*. It's about appearances. Or whatever."

Zach kisses the top of my head.

"Try not to worry, Liv," he says, pulling my head to his

chest. "We'll figure a way out. Let's just be low-key for a while. Give him some time. He might soften up."

"What does low-key mean?" I ask.

I'm worried Zach will want to date other girls. I wouldn't blame him. What guy wants a girlfriend he can't physically be seen with or talk to privately?

"We'll see each other at school. I'll keep calling and texting. Maybe I can come over to your house. I'll even wear a disguise." His joke makes me laugh a little through my tears.

"Great," I say. "So my parents can chaperone? I don't think so."

Part of me doesn't want my parents to meet him. It seems like they take over whatever they touch. I don't want to give them more control over my relationship.

"If I meet him, do you think he might change his mind?" Zach asks.

"Maybe," I say. "I don't know."

"I'm not going anywhere, Liv." Zach uses his hand to wipe some of the tears from my cheeks. "Try not to worry."

eighteen

"I had learned early to assume something dark and lethal hidden at the heart of anything I loved. When I couldn't find it, I responded, bewildered and wary, in the only way I knew how: by planting it there myself."

—TANA FRENCH

Know how many minutes there are in a school day? I do. 380. Five seven-minute passing periods between classes. A thirty-five-minute lunch. The other three hundred and ten minutes are class time. Zach and I don't have any classes together.

It's like being in a long-distance relationship. When Zach actually is at school instead of acting, I might be able to squeeze in an hour with him. We try to find private places to talk, but there's always someone—usually one of Zach's friends—interrupting us. Now that I can't see him as much, I worry that Zach will lose interest.

It's hard to get out of bed. Some days I barely have the energy to shower. Then there's the paranoia that Zach's cheating on me with his castmates or other girls he meets at networking events. How long can our relationship—if *that's* what you call our arrangement—possibly last? I can tell he's losing interest, and I've gained three pounds, which makes me feel even more like hell.

I've practically flushed my grades down the toilet along with everything else. Including art. There's no progress on the portfolio. Everything I draw looks ugly. I know I'm disappointing Ms. Day. This was *supposed* to be *my year*, but I can't seem to care anymore. It's as if, at the same time that my life started turning into the fairy tale of my dreams, I was also cursed with this massive depression weighing down on my back.

If I'm being honest with myself, I haven't quite been the same since Antonia and Sam stopped talking to me. Yeah, I have Zach. Technically.

I get lonely at night so I've been spending a lot of time on the pro-mia websites for other girls—and the occasional guy—like me. I used to only check on them every once in a while, but now I read and comment on them every day. I've made a few friends, but I don't know their real names. My username is Friducha. That's what Diego Rivera nicknamed Frida when they got married.

It's a place to talk to people who are as messed up as you are. We don't judge each other. The girls on the threads are actually pretty supportive. At least they understand my emotions. Our conversations are about tips and tricks or holding each other accountable for making our goal weight, or sharing bingeing and purging stories, but most of the time I just find myself talking to them about how I feel about life.

LanaLoo: So I fasted for six days straight and had to binge but then I wasn't able to purge. I tried for like three hours. The more I tried the worse I got. I panicked and swallowed a bunch of pills because apparently I'd rather die than gain weight. I'd legit rather die than not be able to purge. The only thing I remember the first day at the hospital was the IV and having the worst stomach pain. They transferred me to the psych ward for three days. I can't even eat without wanting to die. This is going to kill me.

LilMisfit: I binged and I couldn't purge like you. Tried for hours. So at first I

started crying, then I smashed my room up then ended up hysterically crying.

again in line at the grocery store. Love you xo.

XxXSkinnyXxX: Whenever I can't purge i almost always have the thought that maybe I can just OD so the doctors will make me vomit anyway. I'm so sorry you're going through this.

Friducha: I have the same problem with not being able to purge sometimes. I used to be able to purge all or almost all of what I've eaten. But now I can only purge about twenty percent so I cut myself to keep from bingeing, but then I think maybe I should just cut deeper so I won't have to deal with fighting off the urge to binge anymore.

LanaLoo: Thanks for your support x. I've never felt this alienated. Honestly I feel.

like I was mostly disconnected from my emotions throughout the whole hospital thing and it really only hit me today. I was bingeing at a restaurant on my own and as dramatic as it sounds I could see my reflection in the window and that's when I realized how I'm the biggest loser ever. Never thought my life was fun but the whole puking daily thing isn't even that bad…it's just accepting that's what your existence has come down to that isn't so easy.

I'm still scrolling through the thread, thinking about how only the most screwed-up people are there for each other, when Mason barges through my door.

"Don't you knock?" I say, slamming my laptop shut. "Or is that not your style?"

I've been dealing with Mason visiting from Silicon Valley almost every weekend to help with the campaign. Mom and Dad want Royce to focus on schoolwork because this is his senior year, so he hasn't been coming down as much. Just my luck.

"It's Friday night. Don't you have any friends?" Mason asks.

"Not really," I say, feeling lonely.

I think being with Zach lessened the pain of being distant with both Antonia and Sam for a while, but I can't tell Zach everything, like my past with Sam or the kinds of things I would share with Antonia since she's—or *was*—my best girlfriend.

"I thought you had a boyfriend. That actor guy."

"That actor guy works most weekends," I say. "And Daddy Dearest has banned me from dating him or 'appearing' with him. Don't you have something better to do?"

"Whoa, Liv. Can you not take a joke?"

"What was supposed to be so funny?" I shrug.

"Do you want me to leave you alone?"

"That would be preferable."

He considers this for a second.

"I'm going to ignore that request," he says, plopping down on my bed. "You don't have any booze? Do you?"

Mason has been sober for at least a couple of years.

He's just fishing for information.

"No," I lie. "You don't have to try to trick me. You can just ask."

"Look, I know we don't have the best relationship, but whenever I come home you're all locked up in your room. It's not healthy."

"Who's to say what's healthy?" I argue.

"You're a teenager. You should be out having fun."

"Yeah. Dad makes that really easy."

The truth is that I'm not sure I would even *want* to go out. Any social interaction feels exhausting.

Mason ignores my comment and walks over to a sketchpad that's sitting on my desk. He starts flipping through the papers. I'd normally hide them, but I'm so unmotivated I don't even care right now.

"These are pretty good," he says. "Are you going to use them for your portfolio?"

"How do you know about that?" I ask.

"Mom told me you've been working on something."

"Not really," I say.

Mason tosses the sketchpad back on the desk. "If you really don't have any plans, wanna get dinner with me?"

"I'm not that hungry."

"You don't have to eat," Mason says. "Just come keep me company."

What else am I going to do? Mason's right. I might as well get out of the house. Maybe then he'll stop bugging me and I can spend the rest of the night in my room.

Mason takes us to a Mexican restaurant down the street that's pretty popular. Waiting for a table, I stand next to a wall of Polaroids of customers who've completed the "Big Cali Burrito Challenge" over the years. It's a six-pound burrito filled with beans, potatoes, cheese, salsa and meat. I may be thinner than most of the people in the pictures, but I've expanded my stomach so far that it could handle that burrito, no problem.

A waitress seats us and asks for our order.

"I'll take three fish tacos and a Coke," Mason says. "Liv? You eating?"

He has no idea how complicated that question is for some-one like me. If I don't eat, then I'll look like I'm an anorexic because I'm skinny. If I do eat, I'll either gain weight or have to purge, which I've been terrible at lately. It just won't come out.

"Liv?" Mason asks again.

The waitress is staring at me, tapping her notebook with her pen.

I have to make a quick decision.

"What's that burrito called?" I ask, pointing to the wall of photographs.

She raises an eyebrow. "The Big Cali? Sure you want to try, hon? It's huge."

"Do you care, Mason?" I ask.

I don't know why I'm doing this. I guess I want to make him uncomfortable. I just feel like punishing him for making me come out to this restaurant with him.

He shakes his head, but he tries to talk me out of it. "You sure, Liv? I thought you said you weren't really hungry. When did you start doing eating challenges?"

"If I can't finish, I'll take the rest home," I explain.

The waitress starts to turn away. "I can come back…"

"No. That's fine," Mason says. "We'll take it."

We're silent a moment when Mason tries to strike up a conversation to ease the awkwardness of the situation. "So things are pretty rough at home?"

"It's whatever."

"I think you should talk to Dad about all this. If his rules are really affecting you that much, then you should tell him."

"Don't you think I already tried?"

"Forbidding you to see Zach kind of seems over the top. Even for Dad," Mason says.

"It's Rich. Dad listens to anything he tells him."

The waitress returns with Mason's tacos and soda. She has to go back to get my burrito, which is sitting on the plate like some kind of limp fat dead thing. It doesn't even look good to me right now, but my brain tells me I have to eat it. I have to punish myself.

"What's going on with Sam?" Mason asks, sipping his drink.

I stab at the burrito with my fork and knife.

"I don't know," I say. "I think he's dating a girl on the debate team."

"I thought you guys were really close."

I take a bite of the burrito. It's cheesy and greasy and easily slips down my throat.

"We were too close, I guess," I say. "I think he liked me."

"Oh," Mason says, biting into his taco. He starts talking about a girl he used to be friends with from high school. Something about how he had a big crush on her, but could never tell her because they were too close. Honestly, I'm not really listening.

For the rest of the meal, Mason and I chat about the campaign, but I'm not really paying attention. I get about three quarters through the burrito when I feel too bloated to fit anything else in my stomach. But I keep going. I hate myself. I hate food.

It takes all my effort to eat. I take one bite after another as Mason talks, shoveling the food down my throat. I chew and chew, mashing the food smaller so I can fit more into my stomach. I should have never led Sam on. I shouldn't have gone with him to the beach or the bench or held hands with him. I took advantage of our friendship just because I wanted to feel like someone was attracted to me. I didn't want to admit that I was emotionally using Sam for a long time, but I realize now that's what I was doing. I depended on him to ease my insecurities about myself. What a bad friend.

"You done?" Mason asks.

I nod. I feel disgusting.

The waitress stops by the table with the check. While Mason's pulling out his wallet to leave cash, an older Mexican man with a gray mustache approaches us.

"I heard you completed the Big Cali Burrito Challenge!"

Everyone around us dining at the other tables look over. In their eyes are expressions of surprise and disgust. They must think I'm a total joke.

The owner puts his hand on my shoulder. "Let's take a picture of you for the wall!"

"No," I say. "I really don't want to have my picture taken."

"But you finished the burrito! You're so skinny too."

He starts to pull me out of my seat.

I feel so ashamed. I can't have my picture taken. I'm so fat right now. And I don't want this showing up in the newspaper or on TV. I can see the headlines now. OLIVIA BLAKELY GOES ON ANOTHER BENDER, DESTROYS SIX-POUND BURRITO.

"No. Please. I don't want a picture," I plead.

Tears are welling up in my eyes.

I feel so ashamed of myself. How could I binge in public?

Mason looks panicked. He doesn't know what to do.

"Mason? Please? Can we go now?"

"I didn't mean to offend," the owner says, putting his hands up.

I stand up and push the chair out.

"It's okay. I don't feel well."

Mason leaves the cash on the table and apologizes to the owner as I run out of the restaurant. I barely make it out to the parking lot before I bend over in the grass and heave. I don't need to stick my finger down my throat this time. Like the binge, I don't have any control over this. It's coming out no matter what I do.

nineteen

"The loneliest moment in someone's life is when they are watching

their whole world fall apart, and all they can do is stare blankly."

—F. SCOTT FITZGERALD

Finals are over. It's the last day of school before winter break.

I'm happy to finally end this semester. Antonia and Sam have moved on with their own lives. I see her walking with Heather in the halls. Even though they don't hold hands in public, I'm sure they're still dating. And I hear Sam's name announced over the speaker practically every other week because he's been winning all these debate tournaments. I want to be a trifecta again, but I don't really know what to say to them.

Too much time has passed. It's too late.

Zach and I are still talking, but he's already left on vacation with his parents. They're taking him skiing for the break. We've finally come up with a plan to get my dad to let me go out with him. Zach and his father are going to come to a big fund-raising gala that Mom and Dad are hosting at the house after the New Year. Then I'll give a speech to Rich about how Zach and I seen together as a couple could provide positive press for the campaign. He's got a squeaky clean image.

I've just gotten out of my AP art history final and I'm returning some textbooks at the library when Sam walks by me.

My heart skips a beat until I see that he's with Nina, a petite Indian girl wearing a trendy purple cable-knit sweater over dark gray leggings. They're both laughing about something. They look so happy.

"Hey, Sam," I say hesitantly. "How are you?"

I didn't want to admit it to myself, but I really miss him. It's not like I haven't wanted to talk to him for all this time. I just didn't know what to say. I feel like I totally failed him. That maybe not being part of his life is the best gift I could give.

"Hi, Liv," he says, lacing his fingers through Nina's. "What's going on?"

Nina looks me up and down like I'm a spider that needs squashing.

I mean nothing to her. Sam has probably told her how awful of a friend I am.

This was a terrible idea. I never should have said anything.

"Are you okay?" Sam asks. "You look like you're not feeling well."

I can't say anything. I think I'm having a panic attack. I literally have no voice. My skin begins to buzz with anxiety. Darkness wraps around me like vines twisting and contorting out of control, threatening to take over my whole body. I don't deserve to be alive.

I rush out of the library, hoping Mom's waiting in the parking lot to take me home. All I want to do is crawl into my bed and stay under the blankets for forever.

I can feel someone walking close behind me so I speed up. I don't feel like talking to anyone. Then I feel a tug on my shoulder, stopping me in the middle of the path.

"It's been way too long," Jackson says, leaning over me.

"Yeah," I say, feeling nauseous. "I guess so."

His closeness reminds me of the night in his car. My stomach cramps a little when I think of how his fingers ran all over my body. Why did I ever agree to go with him?

He's the absolute *last* person I want to talk to right now.

"I hear you and Zach are getting pretty serious."

I don't really know how to respond. What's he getting at?

"Do you need something, Jackson?"

"Do I have to need something to talk to you?" He zips up his leather jacket so that the collar covers his neck. "Zach's my best friend. If you're not serious, don't lead him on."

I'm almost positive he hasn't told Zach about that night in his car, but I can't be sure.

"You have nothing to worry about. I'd say I'm pretty into Zach," I say, turning away from him, but he grabs my hand. "My mom is picking me up. I'm going to be late."

I'm at a frequency I can't control. There's *nothing* I can control. Antonia and Sam both hate my guts. Finals grades will be posted next week, and I know I didn't do well. My family's demands are getting crazy. But my worst fear, the one that gnaws at me, is that Zach will find out about me making out with his best friend because I'm a stupid girl who can't deal with not getting enough attention. My stomach muscles are cramping up, and I feel this emptiness deep down within my body that tells me I need to get out of here *right now*.

"Didn't feel that way when you were making out with me in my car," Jackson says. "You seemed pretty into it."

"I have to go," I say, wrestling my arm away from him. "Merry Christmas."

When Mom picks me up, I'm in such a terrible mood that I barely talk to her. I'm supposed to go with her and Dad to a holiday party for her literacy organization tonight, but I pretend to be sick so I can stay at home.

Even though Zach's still interested in me, I feel like nothing I do will make the loneliness and emptiness go away. It feels like I'm drowning while everyone around me is still breathing. They're happy and having fun, and no matter how hard I try I can't make myself feel anything except numbness or shame.

I wait until they leave for the party before I go downstairs and tear through the cabinets. I grab a jar of peanut butter, a huge container of leftover chicken alfredo, a half-eaten bag of chips and three brownies from a pan sitting on the stove and take them all up to my bedroom. I eat as fast as I can, shoveling the food into my mouth so fast that I can barely breathe between bites. The faster I swallow, the more my throat hurts.

Each bite makes me want to puke, but I can't stop. I don't deserve to be talking to Zach. I don't deserve to have friends. This is what I deserve.

part two

Pain, pleasure and death are no more than a process for existence.

The revolutionary struggle in this process is a doorway open

to intelligence.

—FRIDA KAHLO

twenty

"Cries for help are frequently inaudible."

—TOM ROBBINS

It's New Year's Eve.

I don't know what I weigh. I just know I'm bloated. My insides stretch against my skin. I can't bear to look at the scale. The entire Christmas break has been one massive binge of baked goods one right after the other. Tonight I'm starting over. I open the cabinet under my sink and find the box of laxatives I've stuffed away to hide from Mom.

I unscrew the bottle and scatter five of the tiny blue pills on my palm, hoping that this will be a new beginning. A way to start over. I put them up to my mouth and swallow them with a cup of water. They easily slide down my throat. *No more emotional eating. No more letting your feelings control you. You are a new you.* The laxatives should take about twelve hours, leaving me enough time to feel empty as I go to bed. That's how I want to wake up tomorrow. Empty for the beginning of the New Year.

Then I'll only eat like a normal person. And I won't purge.

I can't figure out what to do about Jackson. Is he going to tell Zach about the night at the lounge? It's been months and I thought he would've said something already. I don't know what Jackson wants from me other than the ability to make me squirm.

Do I tell Zach what's going on myself and risk him getting angry and ruining our plans? I haven't been texting him much anyway since his parents have taken him to a chateau somewhere up in the Swiss Alps with barely any reception for the holidays.

The only people I've talked to the last two weeks are my parents, my brothers and Jas. I saw her once at the beginning of break at the mall, but Royce was with us and I could tell that things weren't normal with them. They're usually holding hands and making inside jokes. Instead, Royce was sullen and Jas was polite but distant. She asked about my art and I talked to her about classes, but the conversation was strained.

I hope they're able to work things out.

I don't want to lose the only sister I've ever had.

At least I'm finally drawing again. It's the only thing that helps me cope with my anxiety. I pick up my drawing pad, sit cross-legged on the bed and start working on my most recent piece of a girl. She's nude and ropes are wrapped around her tiny wrists, pulling her arms up above her head toward the sky. The girl is a skeleton covered by skin. Her concave chest pushes in toward where her heart should be beating, but the girl is dead on the ground, her arms and legs contorted around her. There is a second girl—another version of the dead girl—crouching on a cliff, staring down at her body. Her spine ripples under her skin. Her hip bones jut out and her long spindly fingers are splayed against the ground as she watches the corpse, her dead self, her body crumpled and spent, watching the live girl with her black eyes, silently beckoning her to jump.

This is my self-portrait. One girl is me. The other is my shadow self. Except I can't tell which one I am right now. My floor is covered with pencils, paper and charcoal. I have an art book open to a print of one of Frida's self-portraits called *The*

Two Fridas for inspiration. The two Fridas, sitting next to each other, are holding hands. Except the old Frida—the one who's wearing a stiff-necked bridal dress—has cut one of her arteries with a pair of scissors. The blood spills out onto the white fabric. The old Frida is killing herself, but she's also running one of her arteries to her double—the liberated Frida wearing bright clothes—pumping her with blood, giving life to a new version of herself. She's dying and transforming at the same time.

I'm shading the contours of the shadow girl's body when I hear a knock on my bedroom door. "Liv," Mom says. "I need your help with a few things."

She opens the door.

I slam my notebook shut. "I'm working…"

"If I didn't really need the help, I wouldn't have asked." Mom stays at the doorway. She knows how much I hate when someone looks at my work before I'm finished. "Just help me take down the Christmas tree? Dad and I are meeting with friends tomorrow. We won't have time. I won't bother you for the rest of the night. Promise."

"So I can skip game night tonight?" We normally play board games or cards on New Year's Eve until the ball drops on television, but I don't actually know what the plans are because no one seems to be at the house right now except for us two.

"Why would you want to skip game night?" Mom asks.

"I'm just not in a very game-y mood," I explain.

What I really want is to go to sleep early. If I stay up much longer, I'll start obsessing over how much of a loser I've been the whole break.

She thinks this over and says, "I don't think either of your brothers are going to be around tonight anyway. But there's a Meg Ryan marathon on you could watch with me."

"Gonna have to pass on that one." I stand up from my bed and tiptoe through the pathway around my art supplies. "I'll start putting away the ornaments."

Mom and I tackle the tree together. I'm in the middle of pulling the angel off the top when she suggests that we listen to a Christmas album.

"In case you haven't noticed, Mom, Christmas was over like almost a week ago."

"So?"

"Haven't you had enough?"

"You can never have enough Christmas music," she says, smiling. Without waiting for me to start complaining, Mom puts a record on the record player.

A woman's voice smoothly sings over some groovy retro-sounding bells while a few backup singers *oooh* and *ahhh* behind her. A wistful sax solo follows the first verse.

"What are you *playing*? It's so *vintage*," I say, laughing at her.

"Oh god," she says, "I've done a horrible job raising you." She passes the vinyl sleeve to me. It's called *Christmas Portrait*. On the front of the album there's an elf helping Santa Claus paint a portrait of a couple with the most '70s hairdos ever.

"It's the Carpenters. *Please* don't tell me I've failed to expose you to Karen Carpenter."

"Karen *who*?" I ask.

"Carpenter." She fake-slaps my arm with the back of her hand. "She just happens to be one of the greatest singers from my childhood." She sings along with the record. *"The logs on the fire fill me with desire…"*

I'm about to slap Mom's arm with the cover when Royce walks in with this look on his face that's the same as when his dog, Champ, died. Like he's on the verge of throwing up.

"Jasmine and I broke up," he says, hanging his head. "Or we're on a break, I guess. Whatever that means."

"Baby…" Mom immediately drops what she's doing and goes over to him. She hugs him tight. "What happened? What's going on?"

"I'm sorry, Mom," he says. "I really loved her."

I don't know what to say, so I just walk over to them and squeeze Royce's shoulder. The pain of it hits me in the stomach like I've just lost someone too. I can't believe this is happening. Jas was family. She was his everything.

"I still really love her," Royce says.

"What's the problem then?" Mom asks, stroking Royce's hair like he's a boy again.

Royce pulls away from her. "We've been fighting all semester. Jas wants to apply to med schools. I want to get a bureau job overseas."

"Can't you report here?" I offer. "Or maybe Jas could go to school in the country where you get a job."

"That's sweet," Royce says. He's not making fun or being condescending. It's genuine. "But we have no idea where Jas will get in or where she'll get a scholarship. We don't know where I'll be offered a job. Everything is so uncertain."

"Why do you have to break up though?" I ask. "If you still love each other?"

"I don't want to talk about it right now," he says. "I tried though. I really tried."

"I know how much you care for her," Mom says. "But sometimes people are just ready to move on, whether we want them to or not."

"Thanks, Mom." Royce's breath is sharp, like he's trying to keep himself from crying. "I just don't know what to do. I thought I'd be asking her to marry me at the end of college, not breaking up."

I hug Royce. "I love her too," I say.

It's true. How can you stop loving someone who means so much? I had always assumed that she would just be my sister someday. That I'd be a bridesmaid in their wedding. Should I call Jas? Does she need someone to talk to? Would she want to talk to me right now? I can't call her. Not yet anyway. That wouldn't be fair to Royce.

We end up abandoning the Christmas tree. Pine needles are scattered all over the floor. Half of the tree is bare while mismatched ornaments weigh down the other half.

Mom convinces Royce to let her cook him dinner, but I tell her that my stomach's upset and that I'm going to go to my room. She doesn't argue with me.

It's Royce she's concerned about tonight.

As I walk up the stairs, I think about Royce and Jasmine's relationship. They were more in love than my parents. It's not like they didn't have problems, but they always seemed to be able to work through them. Why would anyone want to throw that away?

If Royce and Jas can't make it, I don't know how Zach and I will, especially since I barely have any time to spend with him. I'm lucky he still seems to be interested at school, but I have to figure out a way to convince Dad to let me officially date him.

Then it hits me. I'm not really worried about Dad. I'm worried about love in general. Shakespeare may seem cliché, but I love how he seems to be able to capture these big, crashing truths about love. I guess I did learn something in English freshman year when our class read *Romeo & Juliet*. Maybe Jas and Royce really are meant for each other, but because of family, they're torn apart, doomed. Or, like me and Zach, family politics and fame are getting in the way like stupid sword fights under stage lights.

How can I fall in love when there seems to be so much in the way? Maybe I'm just being stupid, but love sure seems hopeless when you can't ever be alone together.

twenty-one

"What strange creatures brothers are!"

—JANE AUSTEN

Dad's announcing his campaign to run for governor at our house today. Election Day is ten months away, which isn't much time for campaigns. Mom and I are running around making last-minute preparations while Dad works on his speech.

I'm nervous because Zach's going to be here.

Mom and Dad are finally going to meet him.

"Everything needs to be perfect," Mom says, pointing to the west end of the family room. "Can you fit a few more chairs over there?"

I'm rearranging furniture in our family room to fit lots of people. There's a section where people can sit in front of a podium where I'm sure Dad's going to give his latest rally-the-troops speech about needing their donations in order to transform California into the modern American state it needs to be. No more dragging our feet on high-speed rail. More development for corporations that stay in California. I've heard Dad talk about them so much over the past couple of weeks, I've memorized all the key talking points.

Mom anxiously checks her phone. "I can't believe the caterers are so late!" She's on the verge of tears and I don't know why. Under Mom's cool surface, I can't help but think she's barely holding it together. So I suck it up and push my own problems to the side to help her keep things together as much as possible.

"It's okay, Mom. I'll tell them to go around the back and set up once they get there. You have to go mingle."

"You're a dear, Liv," Mom says, hugging me. "I'm really proud that you've started to embrace your role in the campaign."

"I wouldn't go *that* far," I say, straightening the last of the chairs. "But this is too much for you to do by yourself."

"Can you greet the guests? Show them where to come in?"

I nod and take my place outside the front door as Mom disappears to go find Dad. People start streaming into the house. I smile and shake their hands. Introduce myself. Lots of parents from my school who already support Dad. Many elected state officials. Assemblywomen and men. A couple of district attorneys. Lots of lawyers. Businessmen.

It's nearing time for the event to officially begin when Zach and his father walk up the entryway. I realize that this will be the first time our parents actually meet each other in person, which is weird. Zach hops up the steps and kisses me on the cheek.

"Liv," he says. "You look great."

I hate the Rich-picked outfit I'm wearing—a sober dark gray structured dress with no personality at all—but I smile at him anyway. When I look into his green eyes, all of the stress of preparing for the gala begins to melt away. Zach somehow manages to make me forget myself. Being with him is like an out-of-body experience. My problems seem trivial when he's around.

"Hi, Mr. Park. I'm Liv," I say, extending my hand. Zach's father is dressed formally in a charcoal gray suit and blue tie. I can see where Zach got his thick black hair and flawless skin. Mr. Park must be around Dad's age, but he looks ten years younger.

He takes my hand. "Zach talks a lot about you. I don't know why he hasn't brought you over," he says, glancing at his son. Zach looks at me sheepishly, like he's been caught doing something wrong. "Though I'm sure you have a busy schedule with your father's campaign. Anyway. Come by the house when you have time."

"Thanks, Mr. Park. It's a pleasure to meet you..." I'm only halfway done with my sentence when Mr. Park sees someone inside the house and calls out to them. He makes a beeline through the hallway, leaving Zach and me alone on the front steps.

"Thanks for coming," I say.

I try to kiss him, but he pulls back.

"Not here," Zach says. "It'll end up as news."

At first, I hate his response. Why should we have to be so careful all the time? Why *can't* we end up on the news together? Does he not want to be seen with me?

"You're being paranoid," I say.

"I'm just being careful. I'm watching out for you. There's a news van parked right over there," he says, nodding at a couple of cameramen hooking up their equipment. "Do you really want to be known as the politician's daughter who makes out with a TV actor on the front doorstep?" Zach must sense how confused I am by his response, because he takes my hand and pulls me into the house.

"But I'm—"

"*I* know you're not *only* a politician's daughter and I'm not *only* a TV actor," he says, touching my neck. "*You're* Liv and I'm Zach. But that's how the world sees us, especially since we're both so high profile right now. They'll spin a story just for ratings."

Even though I'm annoyed by not being able to kiss him

when I want to, I know he's right. The public pressure is only going to get more intense now that we're dating and Dad is about to be officially in the governor's race. Zach gives me a little squeeze on the neck, then releases me. "I have to go find Dad. He wants to introduce me to some people."

Zach heads for the other side of the family room, where Mr. Park is talking to a small group of people I don't recognize. While I mingle with more guests, Zach and I smile at each other from across the room, but I understand what's happening here. Zach is in son mode. He accompanies his dad around the room. They help each other. It makes his dad look cool to have such an aspiring actor son who already has success. It makes Zach appear responsible and family-oriented to be mingling in this way.

I'm half listening to a judge tell a story about a defamation lawsuit some has-been celebrity filed against a plastic surgeon for telling a gossip magazine she had work done when Mom interrupts the conversation and asks me to come help carry food trays from the kitchen. Mom has always liked to put us to work. My brothers are supposed to be here to help out, but I haven't seen them yet. Of course.

After several rounds of food pass through the crowd, Rich finally announces that Dad will be making his speech. I'm really bored. Zach hasn't spoken to me at all since he arrived, and I've had to stand next to Rich the whole time. Dad's on his way to the podium and some of the guests are taking seats when I spot an empty drink tray that's about to topple. I grab it. This is a perfect excuse to make a quick getaway to the kitchen.

Dad's already cracking jokes at the front of the room. I tune him out, set the tray on top of other empty ones in the kitchen, smile at the caterers and exit a side door that goes to the backyard. The yard lights are on, though I can still see some stars. The breeze feels good as I hear laughter from inside. I guess they like Dad's corny jokes.

Then I hear a voice from behind me.

"I thought you'd come out here," Mason says.

He surprises me so much that I jump a little, nearly twisting my ankle from the heel of my stilettos getting stuck in one of the patio's cracks.

"You know the escape route," I say.

I haven't seen him all night. He's sitting in one of the patio chairs, peeling an orange and drinking from a bottle of water. It's funny—Mason probably hasn't had a drink since he went to rehab during college, but he's the one who gave me my first beer when I was in middle school. I still remember how that beer seemed to represent a secret we shared that not even Royce could understand. A secret about needing to numb pain, about drowning out our need to be successful, our need to be loved.

"Kitchen. Side door. Patio. Same as always. Dad telling his jokes yet?"

"Something like that," I say.

Mason keeps peeling his orange. "Anyone else out here?"

"Not that I know of."

"Good, then we can talk."

"Not you too," I say, sitting down on a chair next to him. I flex my foot. I can already feel my ankle swelling. I should have worn the grandma pumps Rich picked out to go with my outfit.

"Why?" Mason asks. "Who else was trying to talk to you?"

"Mom is always trying to talk to me. About my *feelings*."

Mason sets his peel to the side and offers me a segment of his orange. I shake my head.

"Can you blame her though?" Mason asks.

"Yes."

"She's just trying to get through to you."

"Right," I say, kicking off my shoes. I wish this whole gala were already over. I've got at least another hour or two before all of the guests finally leave the house.

"Well?" Mason asks. "Did she get through?"

"No," I say.

"So much for talking."

I can hear Dad's voice booming from inside the house. The crowd cheers at his speech. Honestly, I wish I were standing next to Rich right now, which is saying a lot.

Mason leans toward me. "You have to get help though."

I look down at my ankle. "Don't we all?"

"Sure. But your condition..."

"I don't have a condition. I drink a little. So what?"

"Don't push me away," Mason says. "You know you need help."

I stare at my brother. I wouldn't let Mom break in. I won't let him either.

"Come on, Liv. I'm serious."

"Do I really have to tell you this again? I'm not *you*, Mason. I don't drink to oblivion."

"It's not only about how much you drink, Liv. It's *why* you drink."

"I drink why anyone else does," I say. "It's social."

Mason crosses his arms. "So you're telling me you've never had something to drink when you were alone? Or when you were angry or sad?"

"It's when I'm having fun with friends, like anyone else. I mean Jesus Christ, give me a break."

"You didn't seem like you were exactly happy or having fun when I picked you up the other night."

"That was different," I say. "It wasn't my fault."

I rub my ankle. It's already swelling up.

"It's not just about the drinking," Mason says.

"You're barely ever here—you don't even know that much about me anymore."

"You're really going to make me say it?" Mason asks. His tone isn't angry like I expected. He just sounds sad. "I didn't tell Mom or Dad because I wanted to give you the chance to bring it up yourself, but now I wish I'd said something sooner."

I don't say anything.

"Fine," he says. "Bulimia."

I've thought that word a million times. I've read it all over the internet. Yet somehow hearing the word from someone *else* and directed toward me feels like a bomb has just been dropped on my life. I panic. How does Mason know? He's barely around.

I can't let him tell Mom and Dad. They'll make everything into *such a big deal*. I don't want them to treat me like I'm sick or crazy or like I can't handle life on my own.

"Actually, I'm healthy," I explain. "And you have no business saying anything to me about my weight, though I guess I shouldn't be surprised."

"What is that supposed to mean?"

"You've always seemed to be so concerned about how I look."

"I've apologized to you about that more than once—please don't hold that over me forever."

"I'm done talking," I say. "I'm supposed to clear dishes after the speech." I try to get up, but my ankle hurts too much so I sit down again.

"You think you're not obvious, but I can tell more than anyone exactly *because* I'm here the least. Every time I come back home, you look more skeletal. You never eat with us unless Mom forces you. You use exercise as an excuse to get out of things you don't want to do. No one ever says anything to you because you're so sensitive and you start attacking them."

"You don't understand—having weird eating habits is just part of being a girl. It's not a big deal."

"It isn't? When I was your age, I tried to hide too. But I wasn't hiding as well as I thought. I wish someone had just, you know, been there for me."

I feel bad that Mason is trying to help me, but I really don't want to have this conversation with him. "I just have a lot of anxiety," I say, at least sharing part of the truth. "I get nervous. I feel better when I don't eat very much."

"You're playing with your life," Mason says. "You're already thin. You don't need to diet. It's dangerous."

I stand up from my chair, forgetting the pain from twisting my ankle. "I'm not *playing* with anything. What do you care about what I do with my body anyway?"

"Will you stop it? Just stop. You sound ridiculous. I'm not Mom. We're not in therapy. I'm not Dad, and thank God for that, because you know he would freak out if he knew. You have a problem. You're going to admit it. And you're going to get some help for it."

This is the worst my stomach has ever felt. I want to get sick right here. Right now. I want to cut too. I want to cut and bleed and vomit and disappear into my room. I hate this. I hate what he's doing to me. I want to tell him everything, but I can't—I have to keep going. I don't have a choice. I don't have control over that anymore.

The pain wants out. It comes up, heavy and heaving. It falls out of my mouth in a sudden sob—something I don't expect.

"You can't do this," I say. "You don't understand."

"Can't do what? Get you to admit your problem?"

"Not here. Not tonight. Please."

"Just say it," he says.

"Please, you can't say anything," I beg. "I'll take care of it."

"How?" Mason asks.

"I'll eat more. I'll put on weight." I start wondering if I'm telling the truth or not. I can't tell whether I actually *like* bulimia or *hate* what it's doing to me. I don't even know who I would be without the purging or cutting, or any of it.

"That's not enough," he says.

"I'll get help. Just don't tell Mom and Dad."

"And keep this secret?"

"Just a little longer. Please."

Applause sounds from the house. Dad's speech must be over.

"This isn't the right place," I say, hoping my brother will see how horrible and embarrassing telling our parents would be right now. "It's not the right time."

Mason looks at me like I'm hiding something. He pauses a moment, then picks up his orange, shaking his head. "Fine. But you have to tell them soon. Or I will."

"I promise," I say as guests begin walking out from the house into the backyard. I quickly wipe the wetness from my cheeks and start putting my shoes on.

When I stand up, Mason gives me an awkward hug. I really don't want to be touched at the moment. "We all just want you to be happy," he says.

"I know," I say, pulling away. I spot Mom and Dad walking out the back door with Zach and his father. Rich is trailing close behind them, holding a clipboard close to his chest.

"Good to see you finally arrived," Dad says to Mason. They hug, patting each other on the back. Mason and Dad used to have a tough relationship.

He wasn't exactly the best example as a big brother either.

"You look a little pale," Mom says. "Are you okay?"

Zach and Mr. Park stare at me, trying to assess what's wrong.

"I'm fine. I just rolled my ankle on the bricks." I look down at my feet and realize that my ankle has swelled so much that I can barely tell where my ankle begins and my calf ends.

Rich shakes his head. "Where are the pumps I had set out for you?"

"Not now, Rich," Mom says, glaring at him. "I'll get you an ice pack."

Zach steps next to me and puts my arm over his shoulder. "Don't worry about it, Mrs. Blakely. You and Mr. Blakely are busy. I'll get her an ice pack. I'm a great nurse."

Mason rolls his eyes. Like he's ever been *half* as gentlemanly as Zach.

"Looks like you raised your son right," Dad says to Mr. Park.

Zach and I are barely two steps away before our parents have launched into a discussion about some big real estate development plan for West Hills.

"Thanks, Zach," I say, barely able to hobble through the kitchen. "I feel so clumsy."

Guests are staring at us and I can't tell if it's because of my pathetic wounded-animal limp or because they recognize Zach from his show.

Zach tries to take more of my weight on him, but I don't want to crush him and I can feel myself resisting. It makes our walk even more awkward and I nearly knock him over. "Stop trying to keep your weight off me," he says. "You're tiny. I can handle it."

I'm about to argue with him to just let me plop down on a chair right in the middle of everything when Zach quickly bends down and scoops me up in his arms.

"What are you doing?" I ask.

Normally I'd protest at someone picking me up, especially a boy, but I'm so exhausted from fighting with Mason I'm not even mad. Just stunned.

"Taking you upstairs. You need to rest, and we're never going to make it up the stairs with you fighting me like that," he says, laughing. "Have you always been so stubborn?"

"It's my most endearing quality." I lean against him, pressing my head against his shoulder. His freshly washed hair smells like fresh peppermint, which causes my muscles to relax. I'm trying not to worry how heavy I must be in his arms and just enjoy being held by him despite the pain throbbing around my ankle.

Zach carries me up the stairs to my bedroom while trying to explain to the guests that I've twisted my ankle. They all sigh at me and compliment him on his chivalry.

He sets me down on the armchair in the corner of my room.

I lean back against the chair and pull my ankle up over my knee. "Thanks. Sorry you had to do that."

"Stop apologizing," Zach says. "Put your ankle up. I'll get the ice."

I laugh at Zach being such a demanding nurse. "Yes. Sir."

While Zach's downstairs, I hobble over to my bed and put my leg up on a pile of pillows. I try slowly inhaling and counting my breaths to reduce the pain.

Zach comes back into my room and says, "Don't forget that I'm your nurse. You have to do what I say."

I laugh. "All right, Dr. Nurse."

"Hey. That was pretty funny for a gimp," Zach says. He lifts my leg and puts the ice pack underneath my ankle. The temperature makes me inhale sharply.

"That's *cold*."

"It's ice," Zach says.

He hasn't taken his hand from my leg. In fact, Zach begins rubbing my leg up and down. It feels so good, but I can't get over the fact that he's touching my *cankle*.

"Your skin's so soft..."

"Thanks," I say. "I moisturize."

He laughs. "Feisty."

"That's one word you could use to describe me."

"That's what I like about you, Liv. You're not afraid to be funny. Or to show who you really are."

Does Zach *really* know who I am? Does *anyone*?

"That helps." I look down at his hand, which is now rubbing my foot. I make a mental note to get a pedicure soon. "I hope I don't need crutches."

"Probably not. The swelling already looks like it's going down." He pulls the ice pack off my ankle. "You should take this off for a few minutes."

Zach sets the ice pack on the carpet, then walks to the other side of the bed. He sits next to me as I keep my foot propped up. "Liv? Can I say something?"

"Yeah," I say, not knowing how to respond. Is Zach going to break up with me? Is he going to tell me he's back together with Cristina? Or that he's too busy to date?

"I've been thinking about this for a few days, and I was going to wait to tell you somewhere else, but..." Zach leans over and brushes my hair behind my ear. "I think I'm really falling for you."

twenty-two

I'm standing between Mom and Rich outside Dad's office. He's wrapped up in an exclusive interview with KTLA, verbally performing this high-wire act where he both praises and bashes the other candidates in the race for governor.

It's the usual spiel. Pete Zhang may have made $100 million via online marketing, but that doesn't transfer to balancing state budget woes. Julianne Summerlin was raised in a small town in the Central Valley, then became mayor of Stanislaus, but so what? That doesn't compare with being a congressman and especially the Speaker of the House during a time of terror and war. He goes on and on about his qualifications while I'm standing, smiling at the other journalists interviewing Mom.

Only I feel the smile wanting to slip off my face.

So I try to think of happy childhood moments. This is difficult because the cameraman is aiming right in my direction and I know millions of people will not only have access while they're at home, in doctor's offices and in every sports bar in LA, this stuff is going to be online too. And that's what truly horrifies me. My face. *Everywhere.*

It's not like anyone is reading about *my* accomplishments. To them, I'm just one of Dad's pretty accessories, someone to be shown off as a testament to his wonderful parenting skills. I have to think about something else.

I force remembrances of amusement parks and chasing our old cat, Zoe, around when she was a kitten to help me retain my smile. That lasts five seconds. Maybe ten. The negativity creeps back in.

Rich is standing next to me, making sure everything goes as planned. His cologne smells awful. It's so strong I want to gag, but I can't because of the cameras.

"You're *wilting*," Rich whispers under his breath.

"I'm *trying*," I say through my teeth.

"Imitate your mother," he says, gesturing to her as she effortlessly charms the journalist who's interviewing her. "Learn from her. She's perfection."

"Why do I have to be here? No one's looking at me."

"No complaining at public events." Rich waves his hand like he's batting my comment away. "You'll seem ungrateful. And don't wear that color next time," he says, looking me up and down. "Yellow does not work for you. Try blue."

Why do I have to deal with public appearances when Royce and Mason never have to? I'm still in high school. I don't need a control freak politician wrangler micromanaging my life. I need to be at home studying, drawing, thinking about Zach.

Dad decided this would be a good time for me to help with the campaign. What did he call it? A "low-stress opportunity" to show off the Blakely family to the public.

I don't have to say or do anything. Just show up, look nice, or at least try to, because the polls say that having a beautiful family somehow makes a candidate trustworthy. Even though I won't be interviewed, videos or photos of me will show up everywhere. That means I have to trust hundreds of strangers, these people who are hungry for drama, to make me look good. This is why I have to appear cheerful. This is why I, *apparently*, should not wear yellow.

I can't trust them. Any of them.

Any of these media people might be a spin doctor just waiting to pounce on the headline, Olivia Blakely Seen Making Faces at Congressman's Campaign Interview. Or something worse like, Daughter Hates Father, Her Face Says It All.

Did I mention this kind of stuff shows up in *Politico*, *Buzzfeed* and the *New York Times all* the time? President's Daughter Gives Dad the Side-Eye During Annual White House Turkey Pardon. Politician's Daughter Twerks on Stage at Coachella. I think every daughter of every politician in America goes through these feelings.

Maybe some are more confident than others. Maybe some don't care. But we all think about it. How we're just there to represent that our parents *are just like* the people who vote for them. Instead of *Stars—Just Like Us!* it's a game of *Politicians—Just Like Us!* I can imagine the campaign ad now: Dad pointing at me, saying, "Look! I have a daughter and I didn't screw her up *too* bad. Vote for me!"

Let's start with the article on *SFGate.com* when I went with Dad and Mom to Golden Gate Park for the Bay Area Brain Tumor Walk last week after the campaign announcement. I won't even get into how boring the article was, or the video, and how the wind was blowing my hair everywhere as I was standing behind Dad giving his speech at the podium.

You can just sit there and watch it from the comfort of your own smartphone and see me constantly wrestle with pushing my hair out of my face while trying to look like I don't actually care about what my hair is doing. You can even slo-mo it if you want to. Their site has that feature. Stupid, isn't it? I hope nobody notices it but me.

Anyway, there's a comment section and people say the most

idiotic things about Dad, about politics, about their know-it-all whatever, about space aliens, about how Dad secretly has twice as much campaign funds as he says he does. It goes on.

But what I scroll for are all the words about me. The ones I obsess over because no matter how much I try to ignore them, I can't. All I can think about lately is how much some creepy trolls—*SFWilliam79* and *49erfan4life5000*—comment on every article about how they love the way I touch my hair, and how *they* want to touch my hair, or how other commenters say how I look like a fake girl with no feelings.

Then there's the GIF someone made of me last week wrestling with my hair like I'm a modern-day Cousin It moshing around at a heavy metal concert.

It went *viral*.

Sure. It was funny. But it was *me*.

One showed me trying to deal with the wind flipping my hair around in slow motion, except I'm surrounded by dragons. Then there's the one with unicorns frolicking around me. It showed up with captions like SLAY and WHEN YOU JUST CAN'T.

And of course all the endless cruel tweets:

What's wrong with her hair? Bride of FRANKENSTEIN. #livblakelyhair.

Blakelys are all fakes. #livblakelyhair.

She's the worst. Rich people suck. WHTVR. #livblakelyhair.

100% FREAK. I HATE HER HAIR. RAT'S NEST. #livblakelyhair.

She's out of control too. #livblakelyhair.

His politics, her hair, one giant mess. #livblakelyhair.

Now I'm basically the poster girl for BHD—Bad Hair Day. So, yeah, I'm done with these interviews. I'm done with Rich. I'm done with this entire campaign.

"I have to go," I quietly say to Rich. "I need some water."

"Fine," he says.

When I'm at an event, I can't do *anything* without getting Rich's permission first. I'll get an earful otherwise. I walk over to the office kitchen and grab a bottle of water.

I pour the water down my throat and hope the twirling, whirling weirdness in my stomach disappears. I wish I could disappear. I feel like I'm the little wooden manikin I use as a model. Position me any way you like. Then sketch whatever you want on my face. Probably a smile. You know the one. The one that other girls look at and say, *Fake.*

After a few minutes, Rich pops his head into the kitchen. "Let's have a talk," Rich says. He gestures to me to sit down in one of the folding chairs next to us.

Sit. Stay. Roll over.

"I know you're young and this is probably hard to understand," he says with a look of mock concern on his face. He pulls up a chair next to me.

I want to smack him for acting like I'm a stupid child, but I fake interest because I'm *trying* not to be terrible to Dad. Fighting Rich is pointless. Dad will back him up.

"There are repercussions to this campaign. Not just political. They're personal too. I know this is a sensitive subject, but I'm worried about your appearance."

"I saw the GIFs," I say. "Did Mom put you up to this?"

"It's more than the GIFs, Liv. Frankly, I don't think you have a strong perception of how you appear to the public."

"You think I can't handle it? If you think I can't handle it, then quit putting me behind Dad during his speeches."

"Social media is only going to get more cruel," Rich says.

"Even people you know in person will say things. I'm just trying to prepare you—"

"What about my appearance is damaging the campaign now? Am I not wearing the right color lipstick? Will cutting my hair a certain way boost the polls a couple of points?"

Rich sighs. "Your mother doesn't want me to show you this, but I think you ought to see. You ought to know what's being said about you. It came out today."

He pulls out his phone and taps a few times. Then he hands the phone to me. It's an article on the front page of *TMZ* that reads, OLIVIA BLAKELY: IS THIS PROOF SHE'S SUFFERING FROM BULIMIA?

This is not happening right now. I scroll down to read the article.

Olivia Blakely is battling a secret eating disorder—as the stick-thin teen compulsively forces herself to throw up after every meal! She is the daughter of Representative Colin Blakely, who's currently running a tight gubernatorial race against Pete Zhang and Julianne Summerlin. Rumors of Blakely's possible eating disorder circulated earlier this year from when she was caught binge drinking with friends at Silver Lake Lounge. Though Blakely has kept a low profile since the incident, the public remains fascinated with the House Speaker's daughter. TMZ has obtained photographs from Eastlake Prep's yearbook showing Blakely's startling descent into bulimia.

Then the article shows my yearbook photo from the eighth grade—when I was still chubby—compared to my junior year photo. The captions claim that my current yearbook photo shows telltale signs of bulimia. Puffy cheeks. Red eyes. Yellowing skin.

I shove the phone back at Rich.

"The second one is obviously Photoshopped," I say. "These tabloids are trash. I'm sure they trolled their commenters' theories for a completely fake story then bribed some stupid kid who works on the yearbook staff to give them a copy..."

"I agree," Rich surprisingly says. "These types of publications will do anything to turn you into a story. But they have to start with some semblance of truth."

"What are you saying?" I snap back.

"*Shhhh*. You're getting too loud," Rich says, watching Mom and Dad gab with the radio host. "I'm in no position to diagnose that sort of thing. That's a family matter." He slips his phone back into his pocket. "Remember that image promotion plan we talked about? We need our own story to counter their story."

There are so many questions swirling in my mind. What are Mom and Dad going to say about this article? They've told me they've been concerned about my health, but they meant normal things like sleeping or taking lunch to school. Am I being too obvious? Will they take the article seriously? Or dismiss it as tabloid trash?

I've been eating in front of them so that they won't think I'm restricting, and I'm careful to not let them hear me purge. This is the last thing I need to deal with right now.

I'm so upset I can barely think straight, but I can't miss the opportunity to run my plan about Zach with Rich. Maybe I can get him to help me.

"What were you thinking?" I ask. "Did you have something in mind?"

"We need to show that you're a normal teenager. That you go to school, eat lunch with friends, go shopping with your mother. That kind of thing..."

"I thought Dad was all about keeping me out of the spotlight," I say.

Rich squints his eyes. He knows what I'm doing.

"I stand by our decision to keep a low profile for you after that first catastrophe. But I've asked him to reconsider. I think you need to project a healthy image."

I want to laugh.

Rich doesn't want me to *actually* be healthy.

Then I think for a second. Maybe I do want to be healthy. Maybe I can get better.

"I'll go with your plan," I say, lowering my voice. "On one condition."

Rich leans in to listen.

"Get Dad to let me go out with Zach Park."

twenty-three

"I feel like there's this impossible standard I'm never going to live up to," I complain at Zach. He's rifling through his backpack, looking for his history textbook. Zach may be able to remember his lines, but he's super forgetful of everything else.

"I'm taking a ton of APs," I continue as I watch Zach struggle. "*That* work never stops. Then I have campaign events during the week *and* most weekends. Did I tell you about what Rich was saying to me yesterday?"

Zach zips up his backpack. He's finally found his book.

"He gave me a lecture about how people are *cruel* on the internet. *Okay*, Captain Obvious. I'm in *high school*. Like I don't know how nasty things can get online. I've seen all the comments." I almost mention the article about the eating disorder, but then I stop short. I don't want to bring that up with Zach. Now that I finally have a shot at *actually physically going out* with him, I don't want to bring up the big stuff.

"What did he want you to do?" Zach asks.

"He told me not to look. At *anything*. Mom said the same thing. They think it's too much pressure. I don't get why they can't just let me make that decision on my own," I say. "How could they expect me not to look?"

"That would be ridiculous," Zach agrees. "It's a lie if people say they never Google themselves. I used to all the time."

"But then you stopped?"

"I couldn't handle it anymore. All of the conflicting opinions. That stuff's toxic if you read it without being in the proper frame of mind."

"What's that?" I ask.

"To laugh at everything no matter what. People, even when they're being mean, are generally trying to be funny. It's just that most people aren't funny, you know? And you *have* to understand that the people making fun of you are only making fun of an image…a character. It's not really you."

I take Zach's arm as both of us walk down the hallway.

"They don't know the real me," he explains. "People who get to know the real me aren't going to just sit around laughing drawing mustaches over my face. People who get to know me actually want to have a conversation of some kind. So, all that stuff on the internet, or even on TV…it's all a lie. It's just as unreal as the public image of you they think they're making fun of."

"You're right," I say. "It's just the pressure to fit this image of what everyone thinks I should be according to who my parents are."

Talking with Zach makes me feel a little better but doesn't take away this whirling ball of anxiety that constantly lives in the pit of my stomach. Even though I'm feeling a little better than I did at Christmas, I can't seem to make that feeling go away. It's something I think maybe I'll have to deal with forever.

Zach and I say goodbye, separating from each other to go to our classes, which are at different sides of the building. I'm walking down the hallway, thinking about Zach's comments, when Felicity walks up to me. It's rare for her to be alone.

"Hey, Liv. *Love* your outfit," she says.

That's a huge compliment coming from her, but I'm skeptical. She's easily the most fashionable girl at Eastlake—even more so than the girls who do work as models. Since I've been hanging out with Zach, Felicity has warmed up to me at school. She and I actually talk during English sometimes. She's still best friends with Cristina though.

"Thanks," I say, trying not to raise an eyebrow.

Did Zach put her up to this?

"Remember when I told you about that gallery show a while back?"

"Oh yeah." I try not to act excited, though my heart is already a wild monster in my chest anticipating what she's about to say.

"Yeah, the one with LeFeber," she says. "They changed the date. It's next weekend now. The first Friday of February. Dad put you on the list. We can hang out. Synchronicity, right?"

I give her an awkward hug. "Thank you," I say and squeal. I can't contain my excitement. I'm in. I'm really *in*.

Felicity pulls away, chomping her gum. "You're so cute."

"Should I bring Zach?" I ask.

Honestly, I would go without him just to *see* LeFeber's work, let alone actually meet him. But I'm still hoping Rich will talk to Dad today to get me the go-ahead.

"Cristina will probably be there, but I think she's finally over him. She's seeing some new guy. I hear he's foreign."

As soon as Felicity walks out of earshot, I spot Sam and Antonia walking together, only about twenty feet away from me. I can't decide whether I want to hide or say something to them. It turns out I don't have to do either because—rather than avoiding me—Antonia heads straight for me, leaving Sam trailing a few feet behind her.

"Felicity? *Really?*" Antonia says. "You used to hate girls like her. Now you're one of them."

I'm stunned. She's caught me completely off guard. Sam just stares at me. He doesn't say anything. He must think I'm totally crazy after I ran out on him and Nina at the library. I wouldn't blame him. Nothing I've done around him makes any sense.

Before I think of something to say, Antonia speaks up again. "I hear that when you cut off one of the Hydra's heads, another one grows back. I forget. Is that right, Liv?"

My heart breaks. It hurts how much I miss them. I miss our conversations. I miss the way they used to know what I was thinking before I said anything.

I can't keep this up. It'll destroy me.

I miss *us*.

twenty-four

"Here then at long last is my darkness. No cry of light, no glimmer,

not even the faintest shard of hope to break free across the hold."

—MARK Z. DANIELEWSKI

I'm desperately trying to get my head above water with my grades. It's only about a month into the second semester, but I feel like a permanent fog has settled over my brain.

I'm sitting in the back of pre-calc, trying to work out some complicated trigonometry problem, when my teacher calls me up to the front of the class and hands me a pink slip of paper. I'm being called out to speak to my counselor, Mrs. Cline, about my senior year schedule. At least I get out of class for a few minutes.

"I know you're busy with your academics," she says, looking at my schedule on her computer as I sit down. She rattles off my classes. "Almost all AP or Honors. That's impressive."

"I guess," I say. "It's not like I'm at the top of my classes."

Doing well in school is just expected in my family no matter how hard you have to work. It's status quo. Nothing special.

"Most students tend to expect senior year to be their hardest," Mrs. Cline says. She's wearing her bleached blond hair in a stiff hairstyle piled on top of her head. "But after working at this school for twenty years, I can tell you that junior year is certainly the most stressful time for most students. You've got your first year of AP classes, SATs to prepare for, researching colleges you may want to attend..."

Just listening to her talk about all the things that I should be thinking about when I spend most of my time focusing on other things is stressing me out.

"And—in your special case—your father running for governor. How are you handling things?" she asks as she pulls up my grades. "I see that you're doing well in most of your classes. Chemistry is lower than normal, but nothing that can't be salvaged."

"I'm working on it," I explain.

"That's good to hear. And the campaign?"

I shrug. "It's the campaign."

"I hope your father wins his election," she says. "At the same time, I'd hate to see you leave us early. Would your parents consider making plans to let you stay?"

I look out the window at the campus. Despite all my problems with Antonia and Sam this year, I feel like I was finally getting comfortable here. I don't want to leave. I don't know what to say to her, so I just smile weakly.

"Well... We've got to build your schedule for next year anyway. Have you thought about what you might want to study in college? That might help you decide."

"I don't know," I say. "My parents want me to go to one of their schools."

Mrs. Cline peers at me over her glasses. "Is that what *you* want?"

Do I tell her what I actually want to do? Or what my parents want me to tell her? Is planning for senior year even worth having this conversation if I might have to leave halfway through school? I might as well tell her the truth. It won't matter anyway.

"I want to study painting."

"You're a very talented artist." She nods.

"It's one of the only things that makes me happy."

It's true. Despite constantly feeling like I'm struggling with my work, I feel like I could be a great painter one day. It's the one thing that helps me settle my mind. I can forget about my body when I'm making art. I can put my pain on the canvas.

"That could be a good direction for you," she says. "But I'd like to see you put it to critical use in your education. You might consider going to a traditional university and taking art and design classes. It would give you more options."

"Honestly, I don't even know if I want to go to college right now..." I say. My voice trails off as I try to think about the future. It's a big black hole.

"Is everything okay?" Mrs. Cline asks.

"Oh sure," I lie, which causes my stomach to knot up.

"It's normal to get jitters about college," she says, giving me a reassuring smile. "Have you talked to your parents about studying art?"

"They want me to keep my options open. I think they're afraid of what a struggle it is to be an artist. They don't think being a painter is practical. Or important."

Mrs. Cline leans forward in her chair like she's excited that she might actually get to discuss something other than class schedules or graduation requirements.

"Have you asked yourself why you want to be a painter?"

That's something I thought LeFeber might ask, not Mrs. Cline, the high school counselor.

"It's what I like to do with my free time," I say. "But I haven't been getting much work done lately. I've been too busy this year. I feel...stuck."

I think about painting.

I love how painters are able to observe their surroundings and combine them and transform them in new ways. I love the colors of the paint and the textures of the brushstrokes. I love how when I work deeply for hours on end I can just forget my thoughts and exist as I paint. I love how painting helps channel emotions and remakes them into something beautiful.

"I've heard this many times," Mrs. Cline says. "It sounds like a motivation problem. There has to be an underlying motivation for why you want to pursue this path. The reason I bring it up is that motivation connects the part of your brain that *feels* with the parts responsible for *action*. Once you identify motive, then you can start taking the action required to achieve success."

Her words sound like psychobabble at first, but I know she's right. If I could only figure out what I want to say with my art, maybe I could get over this slump of not being able to finish anything. Sure, I've been drawing and painting, but that's not the same.

It's not what's going to get me into the show at that gallery.

"Some people don't discover their motivation for many years. But you're young and smart, and I bet you can figure it out. Is it developing the skill, the technique? Is it simply a love for art? Maybe it's the creativity required. Or, is there something even deeper?"

"Like what?" I say.

"I don't know. You tell me," she says.

Frida was injured in an accident that severely limited her mobility, but she didn't condemn herself to never walking again or to hiding her injury. She decorated her shoes. Embroidered them with gorgeous, brightly colored flowers. She laced her boots with ribbon and tied bells to them.

Everyone knew she was coming. She didn't hide under her clothes.

I'll never be as brave as her, but maybe I can try to do the same. Maybe I can use art to make something beautiful out of broken things.

"Thanks, Mrs. Cline. You've given me a lot to think about,"

I say, standing up from my chair and heading toward her office door.

Mrs. Cline is right. I have to figure out more of my life, or I'm just going to be lost until I'm forty or fifty years old. I need to discover my motivation. I don't want to be some guy's trophy or the daughter of a famous politician my whole life. I want *my* name to mean something. I want to make the world more beautiful.

I hope I get to talk to LeFeber at his show.

As I head out of the office, I'm feeling more determined than ever to finish my portfolio when I run smack into Antonia. She almost knocks me into the wall. Apart from her sniping at me in passing, we haven't spoken since she came to the house totally pissed off at me, and I'm totally paralyzed about what she's going to say this time. Antonia can hold a grudge.

"What are you doing here?" Antonia asks, blocking the doorway.

"I have to get to class. I'm going to be late."

"I didn't know you cared so much about school."

"What's that supposed to mean?" I ask defensively.

Anger surges up my throat. Why does she care about anything I do? She practically pretends like I don't exist at school except for when she's telling me off.

"It seems like you're more interested in your social life… I mean, look at you," she says, crossing her arms and looking me up and down. "You're a Cinderella story. Dating Zach Park. Great job. You're in with the popular crowd. None of them even knew you existed until you started dating him. You must be *really* proud of yourself, Liv."

Is she jealous? My life definitely isn't worth being jealous over, but I don't try to explain. I know how Antonia and I both get when we're angry. There's no use.

I try to move past her again, but she doesn't budge. She's

227

going to make me listen to her. I have no choice. "Stop, Antonia. I don't need to hear—"

"The shy, awkward artist daughter of a famous politician who's never fit in with her perfect family somehow gets herself a celebrity boyfriend, then dumps her best friend so she can climb the social ranks by sucking up to the people she used to complain about when they wouldn't give her the time of day."

"You know that's not what happened," I say, trying to defend myself. "You were the one who pushed me away. I wish I'd never gone! I didn't even want to be there."

"I didn't leave you. You left *me*," Antonia says. "Now you have the famous boyfriend. You want to hang out with his glamorous friends. I get it."

"That's not how it is," I try to explain.

"You could've explained what happened when I came over to your house, but then you blamed me for leaving the lounge and going home without telling you."

I'm breathing hard. I'm shaky. My skin feels clammy. I need to eat something for my blood sugar, but I don't want to gain any weight. It's the one thing I can control.

"It was a bad night..." I want to tell her what happened in the car with Jackson, but I don't want anyone in the office to overhear us. "I have an explanation."

"You don't need to explain," she says, cutting me off. "Your actions have been speaking pretty loudly. I see how easily I'm replaced. I've seen you fawning over Felicity and that dumb art show. It's been your plan the whole time. To get in with Zach and his crowd. Congratulations. You've done it. You're such a fake. Everything about you is fake."

"In case you haven't noticed, I haven't been living it up," I snap. "That was never my plan. *You're* the one who stopped talking to me. You've been ignoring me."

"Fake," she says, elbowing her way around me. "You and your fake friends."

Everything I do or say comes out wrong. Everything about me is wrong. My emotions are wound around the knot in my stomach like rubber bands. I can't take this right now. I finally have one moment where I start feeling that this year might not be a total disaster, then the next I'm attacking my best friend. Maybe our relationship isn't salvageable. Maybe I waited too long. I close my eyes and imagine my insides rotting and decaying, turning black and crumbling. I'm becoming the skeleton girl from my portrait. Nothing left except an empty rib cage.

A secretary looks up as tears start to run down my cheeks, so I leave the office as fast as I can and text Mom to come pick me up from school because I'm feeling sick.

When Mom drops me off at home and leaves for a meeting, I go straight to the kitchen and grab the food with the most fat and sugar I can find. Peanut butter, raw cookie dough from the fridge, candy bars my parents bought from a school fundraiser, anything and everything I can get my hands on that my parents won't really miss.

I eat until I'm so full I want to die.

This body needs to be punished.

It makes me feel sick. I'm shaking and cold. And now I'm feeling guilty for letting my emotions control my eating. I lean over my toilet and wait for the weight to magically lift from my stomach and disappear, but nothing comes out.

I poke my finger down my throat, gag and heave.

The food begins to come up. It comes up over and over again. The act of vomiting is so forceful that my entire body heaves and shakes. Tears form at the edges of my eyes. The smell of bile cuts through the bathroom, stinging my nostrils. I just want everything out.

I want to be empty. I want to start over.

I heave again, gagging on my own bile, but nothing comes up this time except for painful memories. Those don't purge.

They just swirl around in my head while my stomach burns from the knot still on fire in me.

I slam the lid closed and try to catch my breath.

I feel disgusting. I *am* disgusting.

I grab the straight razor wrapped in the bottom of my makeup bag. Nothing else can work as well to get the anger out. I'm angry with myself for being a terrible friend. Angry at Antonia. Angry at my parents for creating this big gray storm cloud over my junior year. Angry at my body for its disobedience. I need this fog of anger to lift.

The blade gleams in the fluorescent light like a silver fish that wants to leap onto my skin and swim along the surface of my thigh.

I scrunch up my skirt over my waist and pull the skin tight between my index finger and thumb. Then I push the blade down through my skin and slowly pull across my thigh. I watch the pain drip. Dark red blood slowly pools around the blade then slides down my pale leg, dripping down the toilet onto the white tile floor.

And then I snap out of it. I'm back. I'm me again. In control.

There's blood everywhere. *On me.* On the floor, all over the toilet seat.

It drips and drips.

I'm terrified. I've never cut myself like this.

I grab piles of toilet paper and press against the wound. Images of Jackson pushing me against his car seat and trying to reach up my skirt flood my mind. His hand touches my inner thigh, lingers and brushes against my underwear, his body so heavy on top of mine that I can barely find the air to breathe.

I lean back and try to think about Zach. I need to see him— he'll make me feel better—but I suddenly feel like I might cut our relationship so deep that it'll bleed out like a fatal wound.

twenty-five

"A person learns how to love himself through the simple acts of loving

and being loved by someone else."

—HARUKI MURAKAMI

I can't take it anymore. I've lost Antonia. I can't lose Sam too. He's my oldest friend.

It's the silence I hate. We've been through deaths of family members together. We've been through graduations. Through arguments and road trips and summers you couldn't find one of us without the other.

I figured I would start with Sam. He's easier to talk to than Antonia after a fight. Less stubborn. I sent him a text to meet me at the harbor. Everything is blue. The sky. The water. The reflections on boats. Nothing feels right without Sam in my life.

When Sam walks up to the bench, I stand up and hug him. He's quiet at first and his hug feels stiff, but when I apologize he starts to loosen up.

"Please, Sam. Please. You have to forgive me."

Sam deserves better. I acted like such a loser. An apology doesn't seem like enough to make up for how I acted. I was confused about our relationship, but I was also jealous that I wasn't the only girl in his life, so I led him on then blew him off.

I never tried to make things better.

I start crying. It's embarrassing, but I can't stop.

He's standing there, wearing his sunglasses, trying to hide his face. He probably doesn't want me to see how little he cares about me now. This is probably hopeless.

"My behavior has been so awful." I wipe my nose on my sleeve. "You deserve better, and I want to do better. I miss our friendship. I miss you. Please forgive me."

I fight the tears. I feel my face redden, and I try not to care who might be watching. "I know I haven't earned your forgiveness, but please don't give up on me like Antonia did. I can't imagine my life without you in it. I don't want to lose your friendship."

He doesn't respond. I'm probably scaring him.

"I'm lonelier than I've ever felt in my entire life," I confess. "I can't sleep. I can't focus."

"What about Zach?" Sam asks.

Wiping the tears with the palm of my hand, I tell Sam the truth. "I really like Zach, but I can't talk to him like I talk to you. He doesn't know me the same way."

"Maybe you should have thought about that before you held my hand last time," Sam says.

"I know," I whisper. "I'm sorry. I seem to disappoint everyone I love. My parents. Antonia. You. It really makes me hate myself."

"Jesus," Sam says. "I didn't know you felt this bad."

Sam lets out a sigh and finally really holds me, and I crumple into his arms, listening to his heartbeat. It's the comforting kind of hug I've needed for so long. The kind that says things *are* different.

After a moment, I sit up on the bench and look at him. My eyes are puffy and my vision is blurred from crying, but I can tell that Sam's face has softened.

"Of course I did," I say. "But I didn't know how to say sorry. I was wrapped up with Zach and the campaign. And when Antonia stopped talking to me, I kind of shut down. It's not an excuse for how awful I was, but I care about you. I've always cared about you."

"Liv," he says. "We'll always be friends. I'm sorry I've been silent for a while. I guess I needed some space. Some time to just step away and stop running after you."

He's right.

"I guess what it comes down to," he says, "is you can't pretend like I'm everything to you and then treat me like I'm someone you can just blow off. I won't put up with that anymore. Not to punish you. Just because I can't take it. It's not cool."

"I'm sorry," I say again, sniffling.

"Also..." Sam says.

"What?" I ask.

I'm ready to plead even more if I have to. I guess friends have to do this sometimes. I'm ready.

"You're going to fail science if you don't start working harder. I saw your grade. It's pretty awful. You've totally tanked the first quarter."

And that's all it takes. We both start laughing.

He shakes his head and gazes out at the water.

"Will you help me? Please?"

I don't want him to think I'm taking advantage of him. I just need his help. He's right anyway. I need to get back on track with school. Zach and the election can't be the only things I focus on. I need to concentrate on making my own dreams happen too.

He throws an arm around me. "Duh. Haven't I always?"

We laugh again. Talking with Sam is so easy. I want to tell him everything. About my depression. About the cutting. About how there are days I can't go to sleep at night without puking up whatever I ate for dinner.

"I do a lot on my own," I say instead.

I can't tell him. He'd think I was disgusting.

"Of course you do. I don't mean that," he says. "You've helped me a lot in classes too. It's what friends do. Oh hey, look!" He points.

And then Sam laughs even harder, because he spots a crab boat sputtering past that has a fish painted on its hull smoking a cigar and holding a rifle. It's named *The Codfather*. I laugh too. At the same time, I cling on to his arm, thinking about more than fixing my relationship with him. He's there for me, and that's a revelation, because everything had been feeling so broken. But not everything is fixed, or perfect. My nerves well up, disguising themselves as laughter. As I feel Sam's warmth and sudden acceptance, I'm excited about seeing LeFeber's art. Because, if art reveals anything, it's how much love matters in the world.

twenty-six

"If you ask me what I came to do in this world, I, an artist, will answer you:

I am here to live out loud."

—EMILE ZOLA

The LeFeber show is at a private Laguna Beach art gallery set against a hill less than a mile from the water's edge. The lot is already filled with cars and people greeting each other as Zach pulls in and parks. Everyone's dressed to the nines in suits, dresses, shoes, handbags and chic eyewear. The women are fashionable in that edgy, artsy way.

It's the first time Dad has let me go to an event with Zach.

I want to look good next to him.

Cristina and Felicity are going to be here.

My stomach grumbles. I've been fasting for four days.

I reached my goal. *Finally.* When I stepped on the scale this morning, I thought I was going to scream. 100 pounds. Double zeros. Put together they almost look like the sign for infinity. It took me a little longer than I thought, but Zach telling me he was falling for me at the campaign announcement was just the motivation I needed. Every meal I skipped, every calorie I worked off. Every day I netted under zero calories.

It was all worth it.

I'm totally nervous to meet LeFeber. I have so many questions. *How did you find your voice? When did people start to notice your work? Why is making art so hard? And why do I avoid my paintings when not working on them makes me feel like I'm dying?*

It's a long shot, I know. I'm a nobody. He'll probably be too busy to speak to me. Then there's the fact that I don't actually know what he looks like that well—LeFeber is famously protective of his image and doesn't let anyone photograph him.

"You're kind of quiet tonight," Zach says, turning off the ignition. "I thought you were going to be more excited. You've been talking about this thing all week."

After running into Antonia in the office, I threw all my focus into this show. It's the only thing I have to look forward to right now. I want to forget everything that ever happened between us. I don't want to care about her anymore.

"Sorry," I say. "It's sort of overwhelming."

"I don't know why you get so worried." Zach places his hand on my knee. "Don't think about all these people. Just enjoy the show. You're here for you. Not anyone else."

"Thanks, Zach," I say, trying to smile. "Going to a LeFeber show is supposed to be like walking into a different planet. He creates another world that you get to be a part of for this tiny bit of time. It's a dream come true. Maybe it's *only* a dream."

"It's hard for me to tell what's going on with you," he says, taking my hand. "Liv Blakely. Mystery woman."

"I don't mean to shut you out." I give him a quick worried kiss. Zach is pretty much the only thing I have going for me at this point. "It's not you. I just live in my head a lot. And I didn't think you'd care about all this stuff."

"I do care. I'm just not into the art industry as much as you are. Felicity never made it sound so intriguing. Don't get me wrong, I like Felicity. But you're so different. You create. She just shows up. I've seen your drawings—they're good. She knows these people because her parents work in the industry. You actually have talent. A lot of people come just to be seen."

"Is that what you do?" I say, trying to tease him, but the comment comes out half-wrong. "That's not what I meant…"

"Every actor does," Zach says. "It's part of being a celebrity. You socialize. You attend events. And you meet people who will help your career. Hopefully."

"Whatever," I say, watching people stream into the gallery, hoping to get a look at LeFeber. "I'm not really concerned about who's here. I'm glad to finally be part of something I can just enjoy for myself. I hate going to my dad's campaign events. I don't get to wear what I want. I don't get to say what I want. I'm just a prop."

"You don't think I feel the same way?"

I don't think Zach really understands. *Everyone* loves him.

"Honestly, I'm not here tonight for the art," Zach says.

"That makes me feel worse," I say.

He takes my hand and kisses my palm. "I'm here for *you*."

Who *is* this guy? Where does he get these lines?

"You're sweet." I give him a big hug and kiss. "This is the best date ever." I'm so impatient I can't linger in the car any longer. My whole face scrunches. "Can we go in now? I think I see Felicity going into the gallery."

He laughs. "Of course. Anything with you."

The building is white, single story, and has a sloping glass paneled roof that's so clean and clear you can see stars out of the windows.

When Zach and I enter, the gallery staff tells us that—per LeFeber's request—the audience must stay in a waiting room until the installation officially opens. He's also specified that each guest must pair up with another guest and enter the installation together. It's meant to be experienced in pairs. Each pair will be let in a few minutes after the other to allow for a more complete experience. I'm already so excited to see the installation, but it's even more special because Zach and I will get to experience the installation together in the way LeFeber intended.

There are Hollywood actors, influencers, all types of fashionable people waiting with us. Some of us are underage but sneaking champagne from the catering trays. No one seems to care. We haven't entered the installation yet, but the atmosphere is so ethereal—buzzing with energy and excitement—that I feel like I'm already on another planet.

Felicity grabs a champagne. It's her second already.

"I needed a drink," she says. "These things are so stressful."

"Your parents don't care that you're drinking in public?"

If I want to date Zach, I can't get caught drinking in public again. I told Dad I was only drinking soda last time, but I'm not so sure he believed me.

Felicity laughs. "Don't be silly, Liv. You're in my world now. Things are different here. We're part of something important, you can feel it in the air, and the only way to take it in sometimes is with some of this in your blood."

I think about Felicity's statement. They *don't* live by the normal rules. They don't have to constantly watch what they're doing so their parents can win votes. They don't have to pretend to be who they're not. They don't have to be happy and smiling all the time and try to get good grades and never ever mess up. I should be able to enjoy myself, forget about all my problems for once. I'll be careful.

When the cocktail waitress walks by again, I grab a glass of champagne for myself and make sure I bunch up close to Zach and Felicity so that no one can get a picture of me drinking. Most of these people probably don't recognize me anyway.

I take a gulp. The champagne is dry and bubbly and fizzes down my throat. After I finish the first, I crouch behind Zach and down another as fast as I can, careful not to be seen. Then I hand Zach the glass to put on one of the stands placed around the room.

I probably look silly—no, I *know* I *definitely* look ridiculous—but desperate times call for desperate measures.

I'm downing my third, observing the room and wondering whether LeFeber has shown up yet, when Felicity suggests that we go to an all-ages club to dance.

"This is taking forever to get started," Felicity says. "I just wanna skip to the after-party."

"And miss the installation?" I say. "I hear it's gonna be... I mean, I hear that no one's even seen it yet. Like, no one."

"That's just buzz," Felicity says. "LeFeber creates these wild metaphors and I don't know what they do other than get his name spread around like wildfire. And not letting the press take his picture? That's a publicity stunt too."

"I don't know," I say, countering her. "Maybe he actually wants people to pay attention to his art more than his personal life. And why shouldn't art be sensational? It should be something you experience with your entire body. It should be like something you usually only experience in your dreams."

Felicity gives me a smile. "You're really up on this stuff. You should intern for one of the big art blogs. I can introduce you to some writers."

I grin. "That's sweet of you, but I'm not really a writer."

"She can draw though," Zach says.

"Can you?" asks Felicity. "I didn't know. You better learn how to market yourself or you won't get anywhere. Tell your congressman daddy that you need money to get started. It's not cheap to live as an artist—you should ask for a million."

I choke on the champagne. "A million? I should go to school first. Learn the craftsmanship. Get a job at a gallery or as a graphic designer for a while."

Felicity's smile is losing some of its warmth. "I guess you don't want to be a true artist. You want to work for someone else." She shakes her head. "You just want to be *in* the industry. Let me tell you something... You can go work for peanuts for someone, or you can make a splash. You choose. I'm friends with those who *splash*. Those are the people I want to fill my life with. I'll be seen with LeFeber because he's made a name for himself. Doesn't matter whether or not I think his work is trivial. Plenty of people think his work is marvelous. Be seen, Liv. *Splash*. Don't work for someone else."

I look at Zach for support.

"She has a point," he says quickly. "That's why I love my Felicity. Go big!"

"My Zachy," Felicity says, kissing his cheek.

I don't know whether to puke or laugh. She's being so pretentious, but maybe she has a point about stepping out on your own. What happened to thinking about art as a way to understand or express your humanity instead of as a way to measure how much you're a show-off? Then again, I could learn something from Felicity. It's not like I'm going to get anywhere by hiding in my room all the time. This is where I want to be—about to see one of the world's most cutting-edge artists—and I'm on cloud nine, or eleven, or maybe a hundred and eleven.

The champagne is making my head spin a little. I'm scanning the foyer, trying to scope out whether they're going to open the doors to the show or whether someone has recognized LeFeber yet, when Cristina squeezes through the crowd. Someone I don't recognize right away follows her. He seems familiar, but I can't quite place him. He has a wide forehead, angular jaw and aquamarine eyes. He's immaculate. He's beauty incarnate. This guy is objectively more handsome than Zach, which is kind of a rare situation for him to be in.

I can sense Zach tensing around Cristina and her new fling, but he hides it as well as he can. Cristina exchanges glances with him before she and Felicity share hugs and cheek kisses. "You look delicious," Felicity says. "That *dress*."

"I missed you lovely ladies." Cristina glances at me with the slightest of smiles. At least she's trying to be polite. "I was in Germany for a little while…"

"Who is this with you?" Felicity asks.

"That's what I'm trying to tell you." She pulls the young man to her side. He gazes into the distance like he's bored with us already. "This is Andi von Allmen."

Andi nods. Before he can speak, Cristina starts yammering on about him. "Andi's from Germany. Earlier this year he modeled the underwear line for Nils Broms. You know that luxury men's brand? Anyway, Andi's going to be the next big thing stateside. I met him when I was doing the campaign for Calvin Klein this summer."

"I recognize you," I interrupt enthusiastically, admiring his amazing cheekbones. They look like they've been chiseled from marble by an Italian sculptor. "You had MADE IN GERMANY painted across your chest and stomach. Right?"

Andi laughs. "That's me," he says in a thick accent. "I'm surprised you know."

Zach teases me. "I guess Liv keeps up with underwear campaigns."

"I'm sure she does," Cristina groans.

"Lighten up, Cristina," Zach says.

"It's fine," I say. I'm not looking to get in a fight. Not tonight. I just want to enjoy the art and forget about the rest. I notice a gallery employee beginning to gather people by the entrance to the installation. "It looks like the show's about to open."

Cristina turns away from me. "See you all. Come on, Andi. There's a photographer over there who I want to make sure sees us together."

As soon as they leave Zach mutters, "Flavor of the week."

I polish off the rest of the glass of champagne. Did Cristina come over here to make him jealous? Does Zach still have feelings for her? How deep do those feelings go?

The curators are opening the doors to the show, letting in pairs of people at a time.

Felicity excuses herself while Zach and I wait at the back of the line for our turn to enter the installation. Everything feels awkward after that conversation, so I try to break the ice.

"What do you think LeFeber looks like?" I ask.

Zach ignores me. He keeps his eyes trained on his phone.

"I've seen some old pictures of him. He had red hair," I say.

"Why do I care?" Zach snaps. "What does the color of his hair matter?"

"I was just trying to make conversation," I murmur, pulling back from him. What's wrong with him? Just a few minutes ago, Zach was telling me that he only came to the show to be with me. I feel like the night has taken a drastic turn. The champagne sloshes in my empty stomach. I suddenly don't want to be anywhere near Zach.

"Where's the bathroom?" Zach asks.

"On the left." I point across the room. "What's wrong with you?"

"It's complicated," he says. "Cristina and I have a long history. I'm not used to seeing her with other guys." He heads for the bathroom.

I try not to feel burned by his reaction. I won't let his *complicated feelings* ruin my night. Tonight's supposed to be about the show. About finding my voice. Not about us.

A waitress comes by with another flute of champagne, which I cradle between my fingers as I watch the bubbles fizz and swirl. I'm too buzzed to really care whether someone sees me now. The line moves quickly. Zach's still in the bathroom—or wherever else, I don't actually know—when I get to the front. I'm pissed.

Who am I going to pair up with?

The curators are getting ready to let the next pair into the installation when a middle-aged man walks up next to me.

"Sorry to bother you," he says. His voice is soft-spoken. "But I noticed you were alone. Would you be opposed to my joining you?"

He's got sharp features, almost like a bird's, and slightly sunken eyes ringed with paper-thin skin. He's wearing a jacket with wings painted on the back, and his hair is dyed a silvery blue—almost like he exists in a fairy tale or a dream.

I glance back and finally spot Zach behind us, talking to some guy. Neither of them are paying attention to the show at all. Zach quickly hands something to the other guest as if he's doing his Hollywood schmoozing, but I can't see what he gave him.

Forget Zach. He lost his chance.

"No," I say, smiling. "That would be nice."

The gallery staff opens the door for us. I feel goose bumps prickling up across my forearms. It feels like I've been anticipating this moment my whole life.

We walk into a dark room. Music plays over the chatter of the people inside the installation. It's got a heavy beat that's slow and rhythmic. Keyboards drift with odd cosmic sounds. Ethereal. Trancelike. A foggy mist covers the floor, enveloping the guests as they slowly pass through the installation.

An undulating sea of lights illuminate the ceiling, creating a dreamy, spacey atmosphere. The man stands close to me, surveying the lights. I close my eyes and try to center myself. The ground shifts a little under my feet and I feel like I'm floating on air.

After a moment, I open my eyes to take in the installation. Hundreds of clear glass bells float in the air. They're hanging by tiny translucent threads, but they appear to float on their own because of the dimness of the room. A bell chimes and sets off a domino effect, making the other hundreds of bells floating in the air appear to chime without anyone touching them.

"What started the chiming?" I ask.

"Don't you think that's the point?" The man smiles. "To make you ask that question? Who knows why certain things in our lives do or do not happen? There's no causality. Only the hand of God. Or—if you do not like that term—something great and invisible."

Is that what I feel when I'm painting? Is that what I've been trying to access when I make art?

"It looks like there's something to see over there," I say, pointing to a small group of people standing approximately twenty feet across the room.

The man gestures for me to go ahead.

I whisper as we walk. "Do you know this artist?"

"LeFeber? I am fairly well acquainted with his work."

As I reach the group, I gasp in shock. It's a person—or a wax doll, I guess, but so lifelike—crumpled on the ground. Except the figure has giant feathered wings growing out of its back. Bending down, I examine the fallen angel's face. Its expression is mysteriously serene, like the angel is keeping a secret that I'll never learn.

"Do you think angels have secrets?" I ask.

"Perhaps," he says. "Maybe they keep them for us."

"I don't think anyone would want to know my secrets. Even angels."

"Excuse me, but I think I overheard you speaking earlier about this artist in the foyer." The man looks down at the fallen angel again. "You seemed to have insight about his work. What do you think about this installation?"

I pause to think for a moment.

"It's hard to say what an artist's intention might be. Art is so personal," I say. "At first, I assumed that figure was a fallen angel, but now that I look longer I wonder whether that's meant to be a human with wings. You mentioned God. It could be about divinity. But I think maybe this—" I point to the figure "—is actually about being human."

Suddenly, a staff member approaches us. "Mr. LeFeber," he says in hushed tones, "one of our board members would like to meet you."

I'm totally shocked.

"*You're* LeFeber?" I ask.

"I prefer Geoff. It's more personal, don't you think? My dear," he says, "what is your name? You were experiencing the art with the greatest amount of passion."

"I—I'm Liv," I can barely manage to say. I hate how overwhelmed I get. I'm that girl who just can't seem to find her chill. "I've been waiting all my life for this."

How stupid.

He lets out a polite laugh. "Oh have you?"

"I'm not kidding," I say.

"It's a shame that my presence has altered that experience," he says.

The staff member looks impatient, but I can't lose my shot.

"I know you have to go, sir," I say, "but I really want to ask you a question."

From across the room, I see Felicity's gaze trained on me as I'm talking to LeFeber. She looks like she can't believe that he's giving me the time of day.

"How did you know you were an artist?" I stammer.

"If you're asking that question, then you're an artist," LeFeber says. "Don't deny it. I saw your eyes taking apart my installation, reconfiguring it in your mind, piece by piece. I'd like you to finish your thoughts, Liv. Tell me. What did you see in my work?"

I try to think. My head feels fuzzy from the alcohol.

"The way the angel looks so realistic makes me think of the duality of the human condition," I say, realizing I never get to talk this way to anyone except for Ms. Day. "It's divine yet also deeply broken. That's why he's crumpled on the floor."

"The angel-man you see here is sick. Infected with his life.

Broken, falling. Just because you're an angel doesn't mean you're not broken. We all must find our way to peace and health. We must find our way back to our divine nature. We must transform ourselves."

"Why did you choose that theme?" I ask.

"We're all sick, dear. We're all sick. All these people you see here," he says, gesturing to the people milling around the room. "They are numb. They are trying to *feel* something. I don't care if they like my work or not. My goal is to help them wake up, to *stir* them. As I said, I love your passion. I worship it. You are the lone cherub," he says.

I'm in disbelief that he could see something in me. "I know you get asked this all the time," I say, "but I really want to know what inspires you."

He pauses and hums to himself. "I *do* get asked this so much. How do I not sound like a robot? Usually, I say love inspires me, or beauty, or sadness, or hope. So many things I can pull from the air just floating there. *You inspire me.* This is true too, or I wouldn't be here talking with you. The answer you seek, however, goes much deeper. I am often secretly inspired by those early days when I borrowed money to rent a studio in New York. It was a chaotic time. I was full of dreams! In those days, I drew something from myself that often seems lost now. You see, down inside of you is a purity. A gemstone of inspiration. It comes from within, forged from this unexplainable burning desire. You must keep it pure. You do understand this. Purity is everything. Protect it. Mine is housed, guarded within memories. When you do this, you can gaze into the world. What do you see? You see poverty. You see war. You see hate. You see all these terrible things, and they burn in you because you want to help the world. You want your work to speak to the world. You want to save the world. Yet, after all, you are only an artist. You don't create war machines. You don't create political agenda. You create the aesthetics of the world that covers over everything, another form of meninges, a membrane of life and beauty pulsating over the sad brain of the world. Yes. That is *us*. And while the pain of the world is inspiring, it all must eventually pass through the original purity within you in the first place. That gemstone. The one you must keep pure. The one that harbors the seed of all your inspiration."

LeFeber touches my chin. "With that, I must go," he says. His gray eyes are deep and soulful. "Tomorrow I will share my fallen angel with more of the world. And you must share what you have to give, my angel of the hills…look at you…so beautiful…good night…"

twenty-seven

"You must have chaos within you to give birth to a dancing star."

—FRIEDRICH NIETZSCHE

It's early Saturday and Dad is knocking on my bedroom door.

My champagne hangover pounds brain against skull.

"Olivia? Are you awake?"

"Yeah," I say, looking at the time on my phone.

"Olivia..."

"Dad," I grunt. "I hear you. I need a shower."

I try to sit up. My head spins. I just want to sleep, but know I won't be able to even if I have the time. There's a bottle of water next to the bed. I drink most of it.

The shower is hot and washes away the grime from the night before. As it pours over me, my mind goes wild with a collage of visions. Along with the effects of the champagne, the imagery from the night before blossoms through my head. Lights. Bells. Fiber optics. The fallen angel. Wings. LeFeber, talking to me about his art as if I were his confidant. I'm so mesmerized, thinking of the fallen angel with wings that looked like they were made of thousands of real bird feathers, breathing life into the form.

I pull on sweatpants and a shirt, then walk downstairs to

Dad's study, where Rich is pacing back and forth with his eyes trained on me.

"Please sit," Dad says.

"Out late last night?" Rich asks.

"I was at an art show," I say without going into further detail.

"I know," Rich says. He crosses his hands together. "That's why we're here."

"Dad gave me permission," I say, looking up at him for support.

His face is like stone.

"What's going on?" I ask.

Rich walks over to Dad's computer and pulls up a YouTube video, then presses Play. It's a clip from *Extra*. The woman hosting the show sits at a table in front of a screen. Flashing on the screen with her is a picture of Zach and I talking inside his car outside the art gallery.

"Zach Park," the host says, "actor from the hit series *Sisters & Mothers*, was spotted getting cozy with political royalty, Olivia Blakely, the daughter of Representative and California gubernatorial candidate Colin Blakely. They were attending a gallery opening for Geoff LeFeber, the New York artist well-known for his large installations."

The screen flashes a short video of Zach and I walking into the gallery together, holding hands. Then the host reappears on the screen. I let out a deep breath of air. At least they didn't get a photo of me drinking all that champagne inside the venue.

"Another attendee was Park's ex, Cristina Rossi, a model for Calvin Klein. The two have been one of Hollywood's favorite couples. Until now. Is Olivia Blakely a true-love wrecker? Or will Cristina and Zach get back together? Only time—and *Extra!*—will tell."

I'm speechless. This is horrible. I'm the complete opposite of a *true-love wrecker*. They had already broken up before I started dating Zach. Not that I'm exactly happy with him right now.

Even though I found him after LeFeber left, Zach kept acting irritated to be there. I needled him to tell me what was wrong, but he wouldn't say why.

"This isn't something we can't get out ahead of," Rich says, moving on. He runs his hand over his bald head like he's trying to remember whether he still has hair. "But I want to talk about what people you should or shouldn't be seen with and what you should or shouldn't be doing. No more flashy events from now on."

I lean in the chair. "You can't be serious."

Dad finally looks up from his phone and speaks. "If you're going to be dating a celebrity, then you have to know how to handle these kinds of situations."

Rich opens a file that was lying in front of him.

He pulls out a photo of Zach.

"What, are you in the CIA now?" I say.

"I keep files so I can be better organized. This is a highly intense campaign. Order helps you to stay focused on the important things."

"Rich has a lot of experience," Dad says. "This is good training for you. If you want to be an artist, you're going to have to learn how to deal with PR too."

Rich continues in his monotone voice. "This wasn't exactly your fault, of course, but you have to be more careful with your boyfriend. With your father's permission, I've drawn up a plan about how you two could best be seen in public, perhaps stage a few photo opportunities, maybe even an interview. Impromptu of course. We don't want it to look planned. Forget the true-love wrecker stuff. People will forget the Calvin Klein model fast enough. This could work in your father's favor. Bring in a younger voting base. Update his image a little."

"This seems a bit overboard," I say.

"I don't want to make you miserable, Liv," Dad says, leaning back in his chair. "This boy obviously makes you happy. But I need you to be more conscientious."

Rich looks at me and puts Zach's photo back in the file. "You were at a show last night for Geoff LeFeber. He's quite the controversial artist."

Even though I feel like hell right now, I try to put up a fight. "Controversial? That's what people who want to control art call it."

Ignoring me, Rich pushes up his glasses. "I'm a little concerned about you going to art shows. It's too flashy. The focus should be on your father. Museums are fine. But not gallery openings."

"But I'm pursuing art," I say. "How am I supposed to become an artist if I can't even—"

"Yes. I know you have an interest in that. Perhaps we can delay that announcement. Could you maybe have an interest in being a business major for the next few months? There are conferences we could have you attend. You could be seen with some important corporate presidents. Major American products appeal to many constituents."

I push back my chair a little too hard, causing the legs to scrape against the floor. "You want me to fake an interest in business because voters like certain *products*?"

"Yes. Of course," Rich says. He seems to barely even register that I'm upset. Is this what business as usual is for him? "It's been proven through research."

I can't handle this discussion anymore. My head is pounding. I want to throw up the rest of the champagne sloshing at the bottom of my stomach.

"This is psycho. You know that, right?" I turn my attention to Dad as I walk out the door. "I said I would help the campaign, but I won't be, like, some *puppet*."

I run into Mom in the front room. She's working on a finance spreadsheet for her literacy organization. "Liv," she says distractedly. "Morning, sweetie."

"Mom. Rich is insane."

"Can we talk about that later?" She looks down at her watch. "I have therapy in fifteen minutes. You're coming, right?"

"No. But Rich should. He needs a huge dose. Maybe a sedative too."

She ignores my jab at Dad's campaign manager. "I thought you said you were going with me. I asked you on Thursday. You can support me by getting some extra counseling. We're dealing with so much campaign stress already. This is a normal thing. We took Royce and Mason to a children's therapist the first time Dad ran for Congress. You can talk about these campaign manager concerns too. It's only an hour."

"Are you serious, Mom?"

"One hour."

I hear Rich coming down the hall, looking for me again.

"Okay, let's go," I say, ducking out of the room. "Meet you in the car."

twenty-eight

"A painter should begin every canvas with a wash of black, because all
things in nature are dark except where exposed by the light."

—LEONARDO DA VINCI

An assistant takes us into the therapist's office. There are big
abstract paintings on the walls, and the floor lamp is dimmed
to make the room seem cozy. Dr. Lisa M. Larson's name is on
the door. Seems harmless enough.

Mom and I each take a chair.

"Dr. Larson will be with you in a moment," the assistant says.
She closes the door behind us.

"Thanks for coming, Liv," Mom says. "I feel like none of us
have been doing enough for ourselves lately. I think this will
be good for both of us."

A woman enters the room wearing white pants and a black
top. A gold necklace hangs loose below her collar. She has au-
burn hair and seems barely older than Jasmine.

Royce probably needs this counseling more than I do.

"Good to see you, Debra," the therapist says.

"Hi, Lisa." Mom nods at me. "My daughter, Olivia."

"Nice to meet you," Dr. Larson says. "Your mom has told
me about you and your brothers and this campaign. It must be
a lot of pressure."

"Yep," I say. "Mostly the media attention."

"Tell me about some of it," Dr. Larson says. "Does it stress you out too?"

"You could say that." I don't want to get personal with this therapist, so I keep things simple. "I'm sure my mom will tell you about it if she hasn't already."

"She's told me a lot, but mostly we talk about her role in the campaign. When she mentioned her concern about how the campaign is affecting you, I suggested that she ask if you would like to come in as well."

"I'm here to support Mom," I say. "She has way more responsibilities than me. I don't think I really need to be here…"

This is starting to make me uncomfortable. Why did I agree to come?

"This is for you too," Mom says, patting my knee.

"I'm going to ask you to let her speak, Debra."

Dr. Larson smiles. It's smug. Friendly. Cold. Warm. I can't tell. She's got more masks on than a Bourbon Street parade. Mom pretends to zip her lips shut.

"How's your personal life?" Dr. Larson asks.

"It's fine. You know, high school stuff."

She demurely crosses one leg over the other. "Such as?"

She's not going to give up with these short answers. I have to give her a little information to get her off my back. At least then I can control the conversation.

"Classes. Studying for midterms. Getting ready for college. Friends," I say, knowing that I barely have enough friends to mention. "I'm dating someone."

"How do you feel about that?" Dr. Larson asks.

"I like him. He likes me. But he's on a TV show and I have the campaign, so sometimes that makes things hard. Nothing major though," I say.

I don't want to talk about my love life with a stranger. Especially in front of Mom. There are some things a girl should be able to keep to herself.

"My own relationships usually affect everything I do," Dr. Larson says. "I sometimes have to remind myself that how I relate to others in my personal life affects how I relate to those in my professional world."

Why does she want to know so much about my feelings? I thought this was supposed to be about Mom. Or Mom and Dad. Why isn't *he* here?

"This is all new for me, so I haven't really thought about it much."

"It's sometimes hard to do that when relationships just begin," Dr. Larson says. "They're affected by our pasts, by our family life, by any stresses we previously had. Everything gets placed within that new relationship too. Do you feel any of those pressures already affecting recent changes to your life?"

I'm not really sure how to answer the question. I have no idea what she's getting at—does she really want me to talk about my relationship with Zach? Is that what Mom wanted me to come here for?

Dr. Larson doesn't wait for my answer anyway.

"Have you noticed any changes in your habits?" she asks, staring me down. "You may have found your appetite has decreased? Perhaps you don't enjoy certain foods like you once did before?"

Suddenly, I'm aware.

This is an *ambush*.

This isn't about supporting Mom. This isn't even about the campaign's ridiculousness or Rich's awful controlling of me. This is about *me*, digging into my past, my secrets, my relationships, all the things I keep to myself that my parents desperately want to know about. It's about what I eat, what I don't eat, how much I eat or not. Mom's using Dr. Larson to do her dirty work. She suspects something, but doesn't want to ask me herself.

I stare down Dr. Larson. She's not going to get in.

Not in a million years.

I take her down another road. I can talk political crap all day to this woman.

"This campaign is so-o-o stressful," I say. "I really feel like I'm under attack." I look at Mom. "Is it okay if I say that? We can be honest here, right?"

"Of course," Mom says. "Everything we discuss here is private."

"It's just a lot to put on someone in high school. I mean, Rich has drawn up a plan for the image my boyfriend and I need to cultivate as a couple. He wants me to *lie* about my major? I can't go lying for the family for the sake of some twisted reality."

"Perhaps your father could tell Rich to ease up," Dr. Larson says. "As a young adult, Liv needs to be able to make decisions for herself." She turns her attention to Mom. "And you have to be able to trust her, Debra."

Mom stares at her lap, not saying anything.

"Do you not trust me?" I ask.

"Should I?" Mom says. "You're a teenager. God knows I wasn't a perfect angel when I was your age—and I've tried to give you freedom—but I'm concerned about you. When you're home, you shut yourself in your room. You're angry and tired all the time. And, frankly, I'm worried about your drinking. I found an empty vodka bottle in your room."

"But I..."

Mom holds up her hand. "I'm not here to argue with you. I want to have an open conversation with you, Liv."

I focus on the abstract painting above the desk. It's a black ink blob on a pink-and-yellow background. This conversation isn't going anywhere good, but I'd rather talk to Mom about drinking than my eating habits. I would be on lockdown if she knew how bad my bingeing and purging have gotten this year.

"Fine," I say. "So I drink sometimes. Big deal."

"What do you think about that, Debra?" Dr. Larson asks.

Turning toward me on the couch, Mom looks seriously concerned. "It's normal for teenagers to experiment. I know that... Your father and I both went to some parties when we were young. But times are changing. There's a lot more out there than beer. And the drinking leads to other things too. I guess with Mason's history..."

"I'm *definitely* not Mason."

Mom nods. "You're your own person. Of course. I still worry about you. Mason was the kind of kid who wore everything on his sleeve. We *knew* he was having trouble. He acted out. You don't talk to us. You just shut yourself up in your room."

"It's not my fault that—"

Dr. Larson puts up her hand. "No one's blaming you. We have to try to avoid becoming defensive in order to communicate with each other. Your mother is simply voicing her feelings and observations."

I'm sick of this conversation. No one cared about my *feelings* before. Why do I have to talk about them now? Why do I need a complete stranger telling me how I should speak?

"Fine," I say. "I'm trying to juggle a lot and I get tired. Sometimes I just want to be alone when I'm at home. It helps me recharge."

It's true. After being at school all day, I'm tired and I want to be by myself.

It's easier to be alone.

"That's a valid point," Dr. Larson says. "It's more important for some of us to have alone time than others. But it can also be a sign of depression or a variety of mental health problems."

I know I get depressed, but I don't need to have that shoved in my face like I'm something that needs to be fixed.

"I'm not *crazy*," I say. "Plenty of artists spend lots of time alone. And I shouldn't be punished for apparently being the only introvert in this family."

"This isn't punishment," Mom says, raising her voice. "Something obviously is going on with you. I'm trying to give you a safe opportunity to tell us about it."

"I came here to support *you*. Remember?"

"Let's try to keep this conversation productive," Dr. Larson says. "It's possible to share our emotions without becoming *emotional*."

She seems like a nice person, but I wish she would shut up. I don't need therapy. I don't need her telling me how to express my emotions. I don't need any of this.

"If you have a problem with me drinking sometimes, I'll stop," I say, looking at Mom. "But you could have saved your therapy time by talking to me by yourself."

"I would appreciate that," Mom says. "I don't want to be controlling, but I'd rather you be careful."

"All right, Mom. I get it. I'll take care of myself. Can we start talking about what we were supposed to be here for? I'm done talking about me."

"I think Olivia's suggestion is a good one," Dr. Larson says, completely unfazed by my shutting her out. "We can follow up on her self-care at another time."

She probably doesn't think I know what she's doing. Mentioning self-care? I know she's dropping hints. I know that next time she's going to go there.

"You told me you were worried that you're overextending yourself," Dr. Larson says to Mom. "Are there any tasks you can delegate to another person on the campaign?"

We leave the session thirty minutes later with Mom telling me she's made more progress than ever. "I'm glad you finally decided to open up, sweetheart. I know you're a private person, but you can't keep things in forever. It's unhealthy."

"I'm glad you feel that way," I say, getting into her car.

I'm furious as she tells me how she hadn't realized that she was manifesting some of Dad's fears as her own. I start tuning her out as she says, "I need to do more for myself. I need to remember that the campaign isn't the only thing in my life."

"Great, Mom," I say.

Yeah, I think. *Quit trying to ambush me with your therapist.*

"Will you go with me again?" Mom asks as she drives out of the parking lot.

"What?" I can't believe she would even ask.

How out of touch is she with how uncomfortable I am?

"To the therapist," she says. "Will you keep coming with me? I'd really like you to. It would be good for both of us."

"Maybe," I say, barely listening. "I'm not really sure…"

My headache is back. My stomach is acting weird. I'm dizzy with vertigo. I feel weak and cold and like all of my emotions are starting to shut down.

I don't want anything to do with a therapist again.

Never, I tell myself.

Never.

twenty-nine

"Let us be grateful to people who make us happy, they are the

charming gardeners who make our souls blossom."

—MARCEL PROUST

I'm sitting on the couch, working on an English essay about whether the penny should be retired or not. After the conversation with the therapist, I agreed to Mom's request that I spend less time locked up in my room so I'm spending more time in what she calls "shared family spaces." Anything to keep her off my back.

I have to maintain my goal weight. I can't let her get in the way.

I'm practically falling asleep from boredom when Sam texts me a string of worried-face emojis, with eyebrows pulled up toward the top of their little yellow heads and massive frowns.

SAM: Help? 😩 😩 😩

He follows that with suit and tie emojis. I light up as I look at his texts. He needs me. He needs a woman to help him make a decision. I can be her. I'm just happy Sam and I are back to normal again. We may not have our trifecta back, but at least I can prove that I can be a good friend.

LIV: Sure, I'll help you pick out a suit and tie.

Sam picks me up fifteen minutes later and we're off shopping for his upcoming debate championship. We go to the suit shop Dad goes to. I admit Dad can dress pretty hip when it comes to wearing suits, though I'd never tell him. His head would get too big.

The clothing racks are endless.

Everything I pick out causes Sam to crinkle his face.

"I'm sorry I haven't been to any of your debates," I say.

He's been practicing nonstop, spending most of his time out of class in preparation. I know most of the debates are out of town, but there've been a few I could have made if it weren't for helping out Dad's campaign.

Sam shrugs. "It's not like I go running to hear Mr. Blakely give a speech."

"You could at least show up to watch me stand there playing with my hair."

He laughs. "I'd be too tempted to make memes."

"Hey!" I lightly punch his arm.

I love Sam's sense of humor. He's the only person I know who can tease me and make me laugh at the same time. He never lets me off the hook.

Sam pretends to be hurt. "You true-love wrecker!"

We both laugh even though I know it's true. This is my generation. What we do to each other walks the fine line between bullying and ultimate sarcasm.

"Some of it's funny," I say honestly as I pore through a rack. "But I really hate it. Why should *I* have to make so many sacrifices for *his* career?"

I tell him how controlling Rich Nguyen has been.

"Can't you just say that to your dad? He seems reasonable."

"Believe me, I've tried. But then he starts spouting about my place of honor in the family and our calling to serve this *great nation*. I think he uses what he says to me in his speeches at the House of Representatives. Or maybe it's the other way around."

"I guess I'd call him out," Sam says.

"It's not that easy."

I hold up a navy suit with a double-breasted jacket.

Sam cringes. "What do you think I'm going to be doing in this suit? Smoking pipes and discussing the advantages of investing in stocks versus bonds?"

I put the suit back on the rack.

"You know what I really missed about you?" I say.

Sam raises his eyebrows goofily.

"Your stupid sense of humor."

"I think the word you're really looking for is...refined. Yes." He imitates holding a pipe up to his lips.

"We can't let our lives interfere with our friendship." I pull out a weird pinstripe suit with oversized collars. I immediately return it to the rack.

"So... I didn't just call you to come help me pick out a suit. I mean, your choices *are* pretty atrocious. For being a politician's daughter, your *taste*..." Sam teases.

I give him a death glare. "What?"

"Oh...you know what, it's nothing," he says.

"No. You were about to say something. Spit it out."

"I guess I have a confession to make."

"Whaaat?" I draw out the word like it's stuck in my throat.

"Nina and I are dating."

By the look of her face that one time in the library, Nina probably hates me, but I try to act excited anyway. "That's great," I say, trying not to choke on my words. I really am happy for him. Mostly. Sam deserves all kinds of happiness and all that.

It's just that... I don't know how I truly feel. My feelings for Sam have always been complicated. On a certain bench in Marina del Rey, he's always been my boyfriend. Or *practically* my boyfriend. Our sphere just never expanded from there into the real world.

"And Zach," Sam says. "He's not such a bad guy. If he makes you happy, I can't argue with that."

"Yeah," I say, holding up another suit. "He's been good for me."

I'm strangely glad that Sam has warmed up to Zach. He'd hardly said a word about him before. In fact, these may be his first words about me dating him.

Sam makes that face again.

That means no.

"We have a lot to look forward to, don't we?" I ask.

Am I reaching by saying this? We do, right? I'm praying inwardly even though there's this awful thing staring me in the face called GOVERNOR BLAKELY.

Sam rests his elbows on a rack. "Yeah," he says. "I think. Senior year is supposed to be the best year of your life."

Now I'm thinking about everything I'll have to leave behind.

I suddenly change the subject. "Do you still hang out with Antonia?" I ask.

I wonder why that came out. I guess she's still on my mind.

Just when I think Sam is going to slip into lecture mode, he only offers a few words. "We talk sometimes. Maybe you should try and fix things with her."

"Yeah...like that's easy to do..."

Sam sighs. He probably hears the same words from her. "I really think she's just waiting for you to make things right. She *wants* to be friends again. I can tell. That's why she blew up at you. She can't handle it either. Don't be as stubborn as she is."

"Oh look!" I grab a slim, cobalt blue suit off the rack that I'm not even sure I like. I hold up the hanger. Sam's eyes go wide. Both his thumbs go up as he grins.

Mission accomplished. *Finally.*

thirty

When Sam drops me off, I find Royce's car parked in the driveway.

Why is my brother here? Dad said he wasn't coming back for a week or two. In fact, now that I think of it, I heard Royce say the same thing—that he'd be in school.

It hits me. *Mason told him.* I suddenly want to melt into the cracks in the driveway, turn into a tree so I can hide in plain sight or, better yet, poof into a cloud so I can be an untouchable mist melting over the ocean.

If Mason told him, then Royce would come straight down here to talk to Mom and Dad. He would never be able to keep quiet. He's not like that—he has to get all his emotions out *right now.* Maybe that's why he and Jasmine aren't working out. You can't tell your significant other *everything.* Some things you have to keep to yourself.

Why can't I be eighteen already?

Why can't I have an apartment of my own?

I just want to leave. But I can't.

I unlatch the gate, make my way around the back of the house. If I can just slip into the house without him noticing, maybe I can buy some time to figure out what I want to tell them. I don't want to walk right into some kind of intervention meeting.

The back doors are locked.

They're *never* locked.

Royce knows. He's trying to trap me. He knows all my tricks and probably locked my bedroom window too. Without even checking, I take a few deep breaths and go around to the front door. I take off my shoes and slip in as quietly as I can. Mom and Dad don't seem to be home. That's a good sign. Maybe Royce wants to talk to me alone.

No Royce in the foyer.

No Royce in the hall.

No Royce in my bedroom.

I look everywhere in my room. It's empty. If he were in my bedroom, I'd kill him anyway. As soon as I slump onto my bed my door flies open. It's Royce.

"There you are."

I jump. My stomach drops.

There's something in his eyes.

He knows. He knows. He *knows*.

"You scared the hell out of me," I say, panicking. I want to jump out the window. "Can't you knock? Do I show up to your apartment and just walk in?"

Royce can see I'm furious. He softens. It's not what I expect. His eyes change too. I'm confused.

"I just want to talk to you about Jas," he says.

My heart slows. My panic quickly subsides. "Jesus, Royce."

"I know. I'm sorry. I've been on edge for a long time. It's this breakup." He doesn't step into the room yet. "Can I come in?"

"Yes," I say, my tone still angry. "Close the door, idiot."

He's like a sad little boy as he looks around like he's never seen my room before. "Haven't been in here in a while." He makes his way to my couch. "You still have this?"

"Yeah. So what?"

He shrugs and thumbs through a book on my couch, then sets it aside. "Liv, I really don't know what to do. I still love Jas. And I know—I *know*—she loves me..."

Now I feel bad. Royce doesn't want to get me in trouble. He just wants to talk about his own problems. What can I say to comfort him?

My mouth opens, but words are hard to get out. It's like I can't articulate anything. "So...what are you gonna do?"

He thinks hard. His wheels really spin. "I don't know. Everything was going great. We were making all these plans. Plans for after graduation. Travel plans. Possibly getting engaged... She just...she's like you, so independent."

"And that's a bad thing?"

He backpedals. "I don't mean it like that. I really don't. I just mean..."

"Aren't *you* independent? What's wrong with people being independent? I don't buy this whole 'she's independent' thing as the reason you broke up. I don't think she would leave you because she wanted to just be on her own."

He pauses a moment, then says, "I think she's scared to admit that one of us might have to sacrifice our dream for the other. I guess maybe I am a little too."

I'm shocked that he would tell me any of this. I'm no relationship fixer. I can barely face my own problems. I don't know how to fix myself any more than Royce knows how to repair his relationship. All I know is, they seemed perfect for each other. They really did.

"When I saw you and Zach at the fund-raiser," he says, "it reminded me of when Jasmine and I first started dating. We were in high school too."

"Why does that matter?" I ask. "You've been together a long time. You and Jas have been through a lot more than Zach and me. That must mean something."

"I'm trying to get in touch with what made things work for me and Jasmine. Maybe you know something."

"I don't know anything," I say. "I haven't talked to her lately." Maybe that came out too harsh. I actually do miss Jas. I want to talk to her. But I'm also kind of mad at her. It feels like she broke up with our entire family. Like, now that she's not with Royce, maybe I won't mean anything to her either.

"I don't mean like that," he says. "I just want to ask about this thing with Zach. Maybe it will help me understand what Jasmine and I were all about. When you first start dating, is it really just this comfortable honeymoon?"

Nothing about our relationship has been a comfortable honeymoon. At first I thought dating Zach might be slightly glamorous, but the fact that his job and my family put us in the public eye makes everything more difficult.

"How am I supposed to know that? We're still getting to know each other. And I have all this…" I stop for a second, thinking of how messed up I've been for practically this whole year. "Stress. How's that a honeymoon?"

He nods. "Yeah…that must be hard. I mean, so like, what do you see in Zach? Why do you like him?"

I'm already uncomfortable with these questions. Why did I agree to talk to Royce? What do I say? That Zach's attractive? Talented? Charming? That he's a success? All those things?

"I need someone to love," I say.

"Does he love you?" Royce asks. He seems so lost.

"He said he does. I don't know—it's what people say."

Royce shakes his head. None of this is helping.

Things have been sort of strained between us since Zach started acting weird at the LeFeber show a couple of weeks ago. I don't know where we stand right now.

"Look, I can only say this. Maybe you need to let Jasmine know that people do sometimes make each other better. I know it sounds cheesy, but you have to ask yourself, 'Do I make Jasmine a better person?' You said that she was afraid that one of you might need to make a sacrifice for the other. Maybe she's afraid of having to give up everything she worked so hard for? If you really love her, maybe you have to consider giving up something for her."

"But…"

"Look, Royce, I love you, but don't ask me any more relationship questions. It's too weird." He seems to get it and hugs me before he leaves the room.

It's not a big hug. It tells me that I haven't said enough. But how can I answer Royce's questions when I can't answer my own? He's got me thinking what Zach means to me, and that's enough to make me nervous, because, like him, I don't know.

thirty-one

Zach and I are walking on the sprawling grass between tombstones at Hollywood Forever Cemetery. It's movie night and already there are hundreds of people camped on blankets waiting for the sun to slip from dusk to darkness. A large screen has been erected in the middle of the cemetery. Music is playing and people are enjoying picnics.

We spread our blanket and cuddle up in the cool breeze, staring at all the palm trees lining the horizon and tombstone silhouettes guarding us with their ghosts.

There's an introduction fifteen minutes later, followed by commercials, then the feature movie: *Casablanca*. I was hoping we would catch an old Brat Pack film like *Sixteen Candles*, but I'm just happy to be out and not thinking about everything for once.

"Have you seen this one?" I ask.

"A long time ago," Zach says. "I don't really remember it."

"It has beautiful shadows," I say. "I've never seen more perfect lighting."

His eyes scan the audience. "Is that right?" he says, half listening as he shifts away from me to the other side of the blanket.

"What are you looking at?" I sit up. "Is that Cristina?" I ask, pretty sure I've spotted her sitting twenty feet away. I doubt that this is a coincidence. Is she following us? Did Zach tell her we were going to be here? Are they closer than I thought?

"Are you guys still talking?" I ask.

"Don't be jealous." Zach starts to get up. "We need to leave."

"Are you serious?" I say, trying to pull him back down. "What's going on?"

"We need to go." He's already up.

I let out a confused sigh and stand. He doesn't even fold the blanket, just bunches the fabric together and hurries off without waiting for me. I apologize to other people on blankets as I step between them to catch up to Zach.

"Hey, is that...?" a woman starts to say to me.

"Yes," I assure her. "That's him."

"Stardom," the woman says. "Always hard to find privacy."

I hurry after Zach. By the time I catch up, he's halfway to the car.

"Zach. *Zach*," I say. "Can't you wait? It's not like she's going to follow us all the way out here."

He slows down. "Yeah. Sorry," he says.

I take the blanket from him and fold the fabric.

"Maybe she really just came to see the movie," I say tentatively, hoping Zach might offer up some information. He seems testy and I don't want to push him too hard.

Zach runs his hands through his hair. "Are you done?" he says.

"Okay," I say. We're off again.

I start to worry. There's obviously something I don't know.

We're sitting in his Audi a few minutes later. He leaves the movie viewing area and drives deeper into the cemetery. "Where you going?" I ask. "What's going on?"

"Just getting away from everything," he says.

"We can go somewhere else. Want to go to Mount Hollywood and park somewhere?"

Being surrounded by all these ghosts makes my skin crawl. I've never liked cemeteries. Whenever I walk on the grass, I feel like old bones are crunching beneath my feet.

"That's all right. I like it here," he says, pulling over. "It's so hard to just *get away* from people. I'm sick of being recognized all the time. Let's just sit here."

I look at the white mausoleum next to the car shining under the moonlight. "Here? In the car?"

"Yeah. I don't want to walk around. Is that all right?" He brushes some hair out of my eyes.

"I guess. It's just… I was having a good time."

"Come on, Liv." He smiles. He still has a hand on my shoulder. "There are other good times to be had. Am I right?"

Am I right? I don't even feel like looking him in the eye.

Now he puts a gentle hand on my face. "Am I right?"

"Yeah," I say.

"That's my girl," he says and kisses me. "Are you my girl?"

"Yes," I say between kisses. I'm still wondering what's going on. Is he trying to distract me from what just happened back there? Or am I acting like a jealous girlfriend?

As we kiss, I don't lose myself in him like I usually do. I keep seeing Cristina in my mind. Why was he freaking out? He didn't at the gallery. Though he did look at her weird, now that I remember. Is he seeing her again? Is she following him around, trying to mark her territory? Am I falling for the oldest trick in the book? A man's charm?

I pull away. "I need to go home."

His touch on my skin makes me feel sick. Something must be going on with him and Cristina. Maybe they never really broke up all the way. Why would she follow him otherwise? He must have given her some hope to hold on to. Was Zach lying at the boat party when he said the breakup was hard on Cristina? Is he the one who can't let go?

"Wait.. What?" he says. "We just got here."

"No, I'm serious. I need to go home."

It serves me right, thinking a guy like Zach might actually like me. He probably asked me—the weird artsy girl—out to make Cristina jealous. I can't believe I didn't see this coming. She's always been a better match for him, even though I'm as skinny as I've ever been.

Zach looks at me like I'm crazy. "I'm not going home."

"I'm not joking. I'm getting sick."

It's not an excuse. I am starting to feel intense nausea.

"You're really going to give me the cold shoulder?"

"Will you just quit being a selfish jerk?" It suddenly feels too warm inside the car. I feel like I'm suffocating. "Please. I want to go home."

"*Me?* You're such a tease. Why'd you even let me kiss you? I don't like this hot and cold act. Here, let me help you." He reaches over and opens my door.

This isn't the Zach I know. It's like some other guy has taken over.

He's acting just like Ollie. And Jackson.

"What are you doing?" I ask.

"You want to go. So go."

"I'm not getting out in the middle of a dark *cemetery*."

"Get out or I will throw you out."

"Who *are* you?" I start to tear up, but I don't want to cry. I get out.

"Stupid tease."

I slam the car door, basically crying, not saying anything else as he speeds farther into the cemetery. I watch his taillights— they're like ghoulish red eyes hovering in the night.

He's gone.

He's really gone.

I let out a breath, feeling the excruciating pit in my stomach churn. I didn't want him to touch me, but now what I want more than anything in the world is to reverse time back to before we started fighting. When I try to imagine a guy wanting me ever again, I can't—and I don't mean that dramatically. I never used to be like this. Hope was such an easy thing to have. Now I honestly can't bear the idea of having to go through letting someone touch me only to have him realize he never really wanted me at all.

I start walking toward the distant movie screen, trying to dry up my tears. All I see is the glow against the night and trees. I call Sam. He doesn't answer. He must be at his debate tournament. I let out another breath, sobbing into my palms.

"This is not happening," I say, crying all over again.

I scroll through my parents' numbers. Not calling them.

Mason. Not calling.

Royce. Not calling.

Jasmine. Not calling.

Antonia. *Calling…*

She doesn't answer right away. When she does, she stays silent.

"Antonia?" I say.

She's still silent. I hear her breath.

"Antonia," I say. "Antonia? I'm sorry."

Finally…

"Yeah?" she says.

This time I'm trying to be quiet, though the painful sobs are racking my chest. I feel like cutting right here in the cemetery, blood running black into night.

"Are you all right?" she asks. "Are you crying?"

"No… Yes… I need a ride. Please help me? I think something bad was about to happen with Zach. Or did happen. I don't know what happened."

"What did he do to you?" Antonia sounds like she wants to kill him.

"I'm alone now. I'm scared."

"I'm coming. Where are you?"

I tell her how to find me. We decide on a place to meet, and I hang up. I didn't tell her I feel shadows all around, invisible hands all over my body, touching me.

I start running. I won't tell her I'm about to scream. I won't tell her I fall on the ground, that I feel completely violated, or that I drag myself behind a tombstone and shove fingers down my throat and cry and grunt and try to puke, but there's nothing there. I'm empty. I'm so completely and utterly empty.

I'm an abyss. I'm a void. I'm a cage of bones filled with dark matter threatening to crush me from the inside.

I slip a razor blade out of my purse. I haven't cut myself in a while, but I've started carrying a package of them everywhere now. I can't let myself go anywhere without them. Even running my finger over them makes me feel better for a moment, until I realize what I'm doing and hate myself all over again for not being normal no matter how hard I try. I'm a total mess.

In the pitch black of night, listening to the faint whispers of *Casablanca* playing across the cemetery, I pull the razor across my left thigh three times.

Slice. Slice. Slice.

Blood drips then slides down my legs, dampening the grass. The cuts are deep, but they're not deep enough. I wish I could flay myself open. Let the darkness out.

I don't think I want to die, but I can't live with all this pain.

thirty-two

"And when at last you find someone to whom you feel you can pour out your soul, you stop in shock at the words you utter—they are so rusty, so ugly, so meaningless and feeble from being kept in the small cramped dark inside you so long."

—SYLVIA PLATH

I hear Antonia's voice faintly at first. My mind is frozen. I don't know why I wasn't strong. I don't know why I snapped. I sit up. *Over here*, I try to say. *Over here.*

Then I see her flashlight. She's found me next to the tombstone a few feet away from the access road running next to the cemetery where I said I'd be. The light bounces through the dark like a will-o'-the-wisp. I feel arms around me. They help me up.

There's a buzzing in my head trying to take over.

"You have to go to the hospital," Antonia says.

"No…" I groan. "I'm okay. I've done this before."

"Here," she says, taking off her sweatshirt and pushing the fabric up against my legs. "Use this to stop the bleeding. If it doesn't stop, I'm making you go…"

"Fine," I whisper.

She holds me for a while, then after a minute or five or ten, I'm sitting in her car.

"I'm bulimic," I say. I can't hold back the secrets anymore. "It's taking over my life. I can't control my anxiety. I can't control the feeling that everything about me is rotten..."

Antonia doesn't say anything. She just listens and drives.

"I cut myself too. I cut and bleed, and when I do I feel pain drift onto a cloud. But now I have scars. I cut those too...when throwing up doesn't work."

"This is scary," Antonia says. "I don't know how to help."

"You can't take me to the hospital," I say. "I'm not ready."

"You have to take care of yourself," Antonia says. "You're precious. You're loved. This is your life. Do you understand how serious those cuts are?"

Her voice is softer than when she was on the phone. She sounds like she cares. I start to feel secure. "I'm sorry," I say. "I didn't mean to cut that deep..."

A sleepiness consumes me as she continues talking. "We can't pretend to be people we're not," she says. "I'm sorry I hurt you. All of that was dumb. It was too much pressure for everyone. I was being selfish."

"I'm being more selfish than anyone," I say. "It's horrible. I can't do anything. Even when something starts going right, this urge to sabotage myself takes over. I can't even feel joy for long. It keeps turning into this thing. This horrible selfish knot that has to come out."

"We need to make up," Antonia says. "We need to just be cool with each other again."

"I want that," I say.

I really do. No one gets me like Antonia does. Except for Sam. I start to panic. I can't let him see me like this—I can't let him see this side of me, all the pain and darkness.

"You're going to get through this. As for that little dirtbag

277

Zach? You're better off never talking to him again. You need to delete his number."

It feels good to tell her about my problems.

"I don't know why he got so weird," I say, not telling her about Cristina. It's just too much right now anyway. "Please don't tell my family," I add.

"I won't," she says, keeping her eyes on the road. "Not right now. Just feel safe."

"Please don't tell Sam either."

Of all the people I know, I don't want him to find out.

I want to keep some shred of innocence.

"Is the bleeding stopping?" Antonia asks. "I can't make these promises unless you're going to be okay. I don't want to lose my best friend."

I pull the fabric up and lift up my skirt a little. "Yeah. It's not as deep as I thought. It was just a lot of blood. Sorry I ruined your sweatshirt."

Antonia squeezes my knee. "Promise me you're never going to do that again. I know what's inside of you, Liv Blakely. You're not empty. You have a lot left to give the world. You can't leave us yet. It's not your time."

thirty-three

I haven't heard from Zach since he left me at the cemetery. I
dreaded being at school today, but he's probably filming and
won't be here.

I'm walking to my chemistry class to get help from my
teacher during lunch—which has the double benefit of boost-
ing my grades and distracting me from eating—when I get a
stream of texts from Antonia. She's been checking in on me a
couple times a day since the cemetery.

ANTONIA: If I see him can I punch him in the mouth?
ANTONIA: How about I tell him off the way my Mama does?
ANTONIA: TOTAL tirade. Hope you're feeling better xoxo

That was my worst breakdown yet. It was embarrassing,
but I've felt better since sharing my problems with Antonia. I
haven't purged or cut. I'm still sticking to my rules to keep the
pain and anxiety under control.

It makes me hate myself, but I think about Zach all the time.

It's a problem. I need to be strong. Antonia wants me to ignore him. And I will for now. But I want to see what he has to say. I'm angry at him yet I don't want that conversation to be our last.

The weather's finally starting to heat up and I want to wear shorts, but I can't because of the cuts. I really screwed up. Forget wearing miniskirts or bikinis this summer. Forget swimsuits altogether.

Who knows whether I'll be able to get rid of the scars?

I'm almost to class when Felicity rounds the corner and makes a beeline toward me. She's pale and holding back tears. I still don't feel close enough to her to ask what's going on, but she waves me over. Immediately, I think of Zach.

Is he hurt or something?

I may be pissed, but I still have feelings for him.

"What's wrong?" I say. I can barely talk again.

"He's gone," Felicity cries.

Something feels ripped from me. Breath, lungs, throat, stomach.

Everything seems to spin around me.

"It's so sad," Felicity whispers through tears. "I've been looking for you. I thought, 'How could she know? She wouldn't know yet. I have to tell her.' And I didn't have your number or know where you live, or I'd have gone directly to your house."

I gulp air. I can't cry. I can't think. I have to think. I have to.

"Who?" I groan.

It sounds like I'm not even human anymore.

"LeFeber," Felicity says, her voice cracking. "I'm so sorry."

I'm waiting to feel relieved that Zach's not hurt, but I feel like a vise is grabbing on to and twisting my stomach. LeFeber can't be dead. All I can think of is having spoken with him, how he was inspired by both the brokenness and divinity of man. Was he hinting at something? Was he hurting too?

"How did he die?" I ask.

Felicity says, "His agent said he'd been sick a long time but refused to tell anyone."

"That's so horrible," I say, wondering why he didn't want to tell anyone about his pain. Maybe LeFeber couldn't tell anyone he was dying for the same reason I can't tell anyone about my sickness. You don't want people to look at you like you're broken.

"I just thought you should know," Felicity says, pulling away to leave for class. "Since you love his work so much."

When someone like LeFeber dies, someone who created so much beauty and love, the world feels so much dimmer, like a bright star in the night sky has been extinguished never to return. What if he had passed away without ever making his art? What if he never turned his pain into beauty? I need to take LeFeber's life as an inspiration. I need to be more motivated to work on my art. What legacy will I leave behind?

I'm heading toward class when I hear a familiar voice.

"Liv. Hey, Liv." It's Sam.

"Sam. Hey." I try to smile.

He puts an arm around me and squeezes. "Guess what? We won the tournament. I think the suit really helped! It's regional championships next, and guess what else?"

Sam's beaming with genuine happiness. How can I possibly tell him about LeFeber? Or Zach? Or everything that's wrong with me? I need to let him be happy.

"What's the big surprise?" I ask.

"I'm going to Costa Rica for part of the summer. I got another counseling job at a surf camp. The town's between the beach *and* the rainforest. It's going to be killer."

My first thought is that I should be excited for Sam—and I am—but I also know how unhealthy I got over this summer because I didn't see him or Antonia much. I spent half this year without them. I don't think I could survive a few more months right now.

"That's amazing," I say. "Really...really cool."

I feel so stupid about my fight with Zach. I wish I could tell Sam, but he'll act like Antonia about wanting to confront him. Probably worse.

"Maybe you could convince your parents to let you come visit me..." Sam keeps talking, but I can't pay attention. It's too late. Sam will be gone all summer. Zach's never going to talk to me again. And now LeFeber's dead. Why is everything I touch cursed?

I can't even keep my body from screaming at me.

Eat eat eat eat eat eat eat eat.

It takes all my energy to refocus on what Sam's saying.

Then I get a text from my mom.

I glance at it, then at Sam. "It's my mom. I better go..."

"No problem," he says. "Glad I ran into you. I'm so stoked."

He's already down the hall when I realize I don't want him to leave.

"Yeah," I say, wishing I could be as happy as him. "Me too."

I look at the text and already hate what I'm seeing.

MOM: Coming to Dr. Larson's this weekend?

MOM: I'm going to pencil you in. Ok?

MOM: Miss you xoxox

She's assuming I'll want to go to please her. That's one of Mom's tricks. To make you seem like you're such a wonderful person that *of course* you wouldn't mind helping her. I don't have the energy to write her back. There's no way I'm going again.

LeFeber. Gone. Dead. This hurts.

I'm devastated by everything. My fight with Zach, Dad's campaign, Mason planning to tell our parents about my drinking and my eating disorder, Royce and Jasmine's breakup, LeFeber's death. Mom obviously suspects something. She wouldn't be asking me to go to a therapist otherwise. I have to be even more careful now.

My secret is starting to split apart. It's getting harder and harder to hide. When I close my eyes, this blackness starts to wrap around my organs, gripping them, twisting, contorting, eating through their fatty flesh until they begin to shut down, one by one.

I'll never be enough. I'll never be able to do enough.

I'm not like LeFeber. I'm no visionary.

I'm not an angel. Even a sick one.

I feel like cutting again. Right here. Right in the open.

And I want Zach back. Right now.

thirty-four

"I don't know what came over me," Zach says.

We're outside the school sitting in his car. After I found out from Felicity that LeFeber died, I sent him a text asking him to talk. I'm listening, but just sitting next to him makes me feel uncertain and queasy. Should I really get back together with him?

My gaze follows his fingers, not his eyes.

Maybe I was wrong to reach out.

"Anyway," he says, hitting the auto lock and starting the car, "I just wanted to apologize for my behavior. I've never done anything like that to anyone before. I was frustrated and should never have left you... How did you get home?"

His hands run along the curve of the steering wheel as if he doesn't know what to do with them. I'm trying not to think about whether his excuse is lame or not. I was out of it at the cemetery. I know I had some kind of breakdown. I don't want to have another one.

"One of my friends picked me up," I say.

"Who?" Zach asks.

Why does *he* care? He's the one who left me there. I stare at him until he realizes I'm not going to respond. I'm not going into the details about what happened after he left.

"It's all right," he says. "So, are we cool?"

I've got too much on my mind to fight with him. He apologized. I take this into account. Most guys don't say they're sorry for anything.

It wasn't like Zach physically hurt me. He wasn't trying to run over me with his car. He stopped when I told him to. Maybe he just let his emotions get the better of him.

I've been there before. I'd be a hypocrite not to forgive him.

Zach's trying not to fidget. I want us to be good again.

I want to be the golden couple.

"We're cool," I say.

"Awesome," he says, taking my hand. "I missed you. I really did."

I'm glad we're back together, but I have so many questions for him. Why was he being so distant and weird at the cemetery? Why was he acting that way at LeFeber's installation? What's his reason for being so hot and cold? I still don't understand.

"Do you want to go to a movie or something?" he asks. "Wait, I have an even better idea. How about a drive up to the observatory?" His suggestion sounds pretty good, but then he adds, "We can get some food afterward. Let's do that."

The last thing I want to think about is eating food in public. Every meal has become something to fear. Every trip to the bathroom something to lie about. It's exhausting coming up with excuses about why I'm not hungry or I have a sore throat or a stomachache. It takes all my energy to walk around at school. I'm so tired.

I wish I could sleep forever.

"What about taking me home?" I ask.

"You don't want to go home, do you?"

Without waiting for an answer, he takes off, holding my hand as I wonder if I have any feeling in my fingers. My nails are painted dark purple to hide their newly blue tint. I'm wearing a ponytail to keep any clumps of hair from falling out.

My body is finally being obedient. Shedding off excess.

I don't have anything to say, so I just smile even though I'm not really sure if I'm happy. I shouldn't be feeling so numb, so lifeless. This is Zach Park's hand I'm holding. I should be happy, overjoyed, beside myself that he wants to give me another chance. Everyone will be jealous all over again. All the girls wanting him will want to be me.

The drive is beautiful. And terrifying. Zach is a speed demon. He takes every curve like a Formula One race, every straightaway as if his life, our lives, depend on getting to the next curve. I pull my hand away to hang on for dear life. One second I love the speed, the next it feels like we're about to sail off into the clouds. My stomach can't decide what it wants to do.

Behind us is a gray-blue haze of suburbia, the snakelike back of the freeway, houses blending into hills. And then the hills themselves take over everything. It feels so open up here, like I can finally get my arms around the world.

Zach slips the car into a lot and parks. We sit in silence for a moment, then he leans across the seat and wraps his arm around my shoulders. Only, I don't really feel like being held. I know we just made up. But I don't feel romantic. He feels strange. Not the same Zach as before. Like LeFeber telling me he's sick, going to die.

We can hear cars whiz past. There's a breeze and rattling leaves. He wants to kiss me, and we do, but only for a little while. I already can't breathe.

I pull away and say, "Can you believe all this?" I try to laugh, but it comes out weird, just like what I said. I try again. "I mean, what was this like when there was nothing? Only trees and grasslands and these hills. No cars. No jets in the sky. Just all of this and people. Natives, explorers. Settlers. And all the sounds that came with it."

Zach pulls away a little. "What are you talking about?" He tries to laugh. His laugh is as strange and distant as mine. He kisses me again. I let him. My neck feels numb under his lips. His hands on my arms feel like a trap. They slip down my sides.

I pull back. "I'm just trying to see things with different eyes," I say. I think of LeFeber and how curious he seemed about the world. I think of that pure part of myself I'm still trying to define. Something that will guide me through all of the chaos.

"So am I," Zach says, hungry for me. "Come back here. You're so beautiful."

I'm feeling more and more uncomfortable with his advances. His hands rub my legs, my face, my shoulders, my breasts, only I don't feel hands. I feel the bogeyman coming in through the night. My skin is a cold layer of needles. Everything is ice. Whatever warmth that's usually there has frozen solid. I don't even want to move.

"I'm just not comfortable," I say. To add to the strangeness, no matter what he just said about me being beautiful, I feel ugly and fat. I don't want *anyone* to touch me. It's like I have no emotion left.

"All right," he says, taking his hands off me. "What would make you comfortable?"

"Nothing will." I realize this sounds harsh, but I can't help shivering. Is it Zach? Is it the anxiety? Or the hunger?

"Something has to," he says. "Everyone has to have that one thing to make them comfortable. Think about the one thing that makes you feel good every time."

"What do you mean?" I ask. "Like when you buy something on sale that you didn't know was on sale? Or when the clothes you put on are still hot from the dryer?"

Zach laughs. "Not exactly." He leans over and pulls out a small plastic bag filled with white powder from the glove compartment. He puts some of the powder on a little piece of glass he pulled from the center console and snorts it. I'm shocked. I had no idea Zach was a user. I remember Cristina doing drugs in the bathroom at the boat party. She saw me purge. I saw her snort. We both carry each other's secrets. Only now I know Zach and Cristina were probably using together. No wonder she was searching for him at the cemetery.

Maybe he's her supplier. Zach knows a lot of people, after all.

"Here," he says, putting some more on the glass. I don't know what to say. I've known people who have done drugs, but I don't do them. "You'll feel a thousand times better. Serious."

He's really determined, and I don't know what to think. He's still clearing his nose, sniffing and blinking. I can tell he's craving more. It's not like I don't want to forget my problems for a while. I'd *love* for the pressure to melt away for a few hours.

"It'll make you forget all your problems," he says.

"There are a lot of those," I say. "Everywhere in my life."

"I know," he says. "It's too much to handle. I'm saying I understand. This stuff helps you focus. I do it before show tapings."

"Every time?" I ask.

Everything I thought I knew about Zach is starting to seem like a lie.

"Pretty much," Zach says, hovering his hand over the glass to hide it from view. The sun is beginning to go down, but it's still light out. "Gives me energy."

"Don't you have enough energy?" I ask.

"Not really. I probably couldn't do it without this. Here. I want you to just try a little bit. You'll thank me."

"I'm sure I will. That's why people do that. Because it's addictive. Because it makes them feel in control."

Maybe I'm being hypocritical. Maybe I'm worse than Zach.

"See, you get it," Zach says.

I think about Sam's older brother, James.

How Sam found his body. How James died alone.

I shake my head at Zach. "I can't," I say.

"Suit yourself," he says. He snorts the little that's on the glass and leans back. "I'm surprised you don't want any. Most girls like you use something to help them…"

"What do you mean, girls like me?" I ask.

"We've been dating for a while now and I've only actually seen you eat a meal a very small handful of times. Not to mention that whenever you *do* eat, you end up in the bathroom less than an hour later. I'm in the industry, I can spot it a mile away. I could tell you were that kind of girl even before I asked you out. I just didn't say anything because you seemed like you'd be embarrassed."

That kind of girl?

I sink into my seat. How could I be so stupid?

Zach turns to me and tugs my ponytail a little. "Go a little farther with me at least. We've been dating for a while now. Don't you think I deserve it?"

My mind's spinning. He just snorted something twice in front of me. I know I have problems, but I don't push my disorders on anyone.

"No," I say. "I told you. I'm not feeling it."

"That's the problem," he says. "You won't loosen up. Come on. Try some of what I have, or just cut loose and *live* a little. Don't be the politician's daughter all the time. Do something you're not supposed to do. Try. You'll get into it."

"Why do you think it's that easy?" I say. "I don't have an internal switch like guys do. I can't just shut off my feelings."

"I don't get you." Zach turns away. "We just made up."

"That doesn't mean you can order me around."

"So? Other people like it too." He puts away his baggie in the glove compartment. It's finally starting to get dark and people are parking next to us.

"I'm not going to do drugs with you," I say, trying to keep

the thought of Sam finding James dead at bay. I've done a lot of messed-up things, but I don't want to go down this path.

"I don't understand," Zach continues. "You've already hooked up with my best friend. Am I not good enough for you?"

"*What?*"

I stare at him in disbelief. Is he really bringing that up now?

"Yeah. You and Jackson. He told me all about it. You had sex *in his car.*"

"I did *not.* We kissed. And that was before you were interested!"

"Who do you think I'm going to believe? Girls like you are loose with anyone who gives you attention. Can't ever make up your mind."

"Girls like *me*?" I sneer.

"Cristina made the same excuses," Zach says. "I thought because you weren't as hot I wouldn't have this problem with you."

My head is spinning. How long has he known? Did Jackson tell him, or did he figure it out? Why the lies? Jackson was bragging about stuff that didn't even happen. How can Zach use that as an excuse to get me to have sex with him, or whatever it is he wants? This isn't the guy I thought I saw on *Sisters & Mothers.* This isn't the guy who took me to meet DJ Whuz, or who came to my house to support my dad, or who told me he thought he might be falling for me. I don't know who this is.

"You're not who I thought you were," I say and get out of the car. Before I close the door, I whip around to face him. "We're done."

After I close the door he rolls down the window. "Liv. Come on. This is stupid. Come back. I'm not going to leave you out here again."

The *chivalry.*

"No, really. You can go," I say, texting Antonia to see if she can pick me up again. "We're done."

I really have to get this driver's license thing figured out with my parents. I can't be the damsel in distress like this all the time. It's ridiculous.

"Fine," Zach says and peels out.

"Whatever, asshole," I say as he speeds off.

thirty-five

"Our wounds are often the openings into the best

and most beautiful part of us."

—DAVID RICHO

Danny and I have plans to meet after school. It's been a few weeks since Zach and I broke up and I've been focusing on my portfolio, which is due in about a month—right before school gets out for the year. I finally have work to share, and I want him to know that I really do miss him and feel guilty for not getting in touch.

He's family. Royce and Jasmine's breakup doesn't really change that.

We meet in an open art space downtown where he comes to paint on the weekends. He's got a grant to use this space, so he's lucky not to have to pay for it. There are many artists here. Easels, drawing pads, couches. Live models dressed in skintight clothes are posing on two different stages.

"How's everyone?" I ask, hugging Danny. I pull back and look at his face. He looks so much older than when we first met each other. It feels like forever ago.

"We're all good," he says. "Mom and Dad are struggling a little bit with Isko being gay. But, I'm telling you, everyone *loves* that kid. Even Lola."

"He'll be trouble in about a year," I say. "He's a wild one."

"Seriously." Danny rolls out a chair for me to sit at his work-table. "But what's going on with you?"

I show him my portfolio. It's filled with sketches and photographs of my paintings. He takes out some of my latest colored-pencil sketches of birds. I've been experimenting with mixing ink and watercolor to better capture the movement and texture of the wings. I want my drawings and paintings to look like they're almost their own moving organisms made up of motion and light.

"Wow, Liv. Look at these. They're *really* good."

I breathe a sigh of relief.

I'm so happy he likes them. Danny is a terrible liar. If he hated my work, I would be able to tell. "I don't think it's my best," I say. "I'm making myself work hard though. I'm trying to be as creative as I can. Trying to be unafraid. Trying to find myself in my art."

"I think you've really figured out something with these," Danny says.

He holds up various pieces and gawks at them all.

"You're pretending to be excited," I say.

I'm kind of embarrassed. Art teachers have always praised my creativity, but I've never quite gotten this reaction about my work. It must be getting better.

"Liv," he says. "No I'm not. It's like you don't even have to go to college."

"I don't know about that… I'm just trying to come up with something I can share with the world."

"And you will," he says.

Danny's own work is complex, brave, colorful, bold, sexy and alive. He shows me page after page of lovely art: drawings, watercolors, oil portraits, pen and inks, acrylics, even blends of textures on canvas. He was just working on charcoals of the models, and each one feels so vibrant. The strokes are confi-

293

MELISSA DE LA CRUZ

dent and bold, and the bigger pieces feel like something that could hang in an art gallery or museum.

"Every line you create is inspiration for me," I say. "The way you capture the models is beautiful."

"I love being able to talk about this stuff with you," Danilo says. "Seriously."

I return his kindness with another hug. "I don't mean to change the subject," I say, "but has Jasmine told you anything about her and Royce?"

"I haven't heard lately," he says. "She seems to be constantly studying and hasn't visited home much. She keeps things close to the chest—I think she doesn't want to bother us with her problems. I hope they get back together."

"Me too." I start gathering my work back into my portfolio. "I wish they would just realize they're the perfect couple so I can get my sister back. I miss her."

"Believe me," he says. "I'd like to have my sister back too. Who knows? I can never tell what she's going through. She doesn't confide in me."

Jasmine and I are the only girls in our families. We formed a special bond when she and Royce started getting serious. Even though they're away at college, she has been there for me whenever she could. Now everything's weird.

"I don't know," I say. "I think I can understand. It's hard sometimes to be able to say everything that's on your mind. Even when you need to."

I think about what's hidden deep inside me. The things I can't seem to express to anyone. The gemstone that LeFeber mentioned. I need to grow that place within myself, for his memory, for me, for my future. The more I think about what he told me, the more I realize I'm in a special place at a special time because of what I heard from him and saw at that show. I need to make use of this knowledge, this special bond we shared for such a short time. Frida used her pain. LeFeber used his sickness.

They embraced their suffering.

Did they ever figure out the balance between suffering and beauty?

They say Frida died from an overdose. It might have been deliberate. She had been taking painkillers and drinking. Yet her last painting was a still life of ripe, juicy watermelons with the engraving VIVA LA VIDA. *Live the life*.

Did she want to die? Or was she leaving a message for the rest of us? Did LeFeber need his sickness to help him create? Was his pain inseparable from his identity?

Sometimes I think I'll never get better. Sometimes I don't want to. Sometimes I want to destroy myself. Sometimes I want to die. Then there are moments when I feel that tiny, nearly imperceptible pulse beating through my chest.

Viva la vida. Viva la vida.

Live the life.

And I think maybe I still can.

thirty-six

"None of us know how to fix ourselves, at least not entirely, not well enough."

—CATHERINE LACEY

Mom picks me up from my meeting with Danny to have dinner with Dad.

I'm eating a Caprese salad, but every bite's a chore. As I cut slices of tomato and mozzarella, I listen to Dad talk about the campaign. He barely pauses to take a breath.

"We're ahead in the polls," Dad says. "Still a long way to go though."

This is his way of making small talk.

"Oh yeah?" I say. "Were you not leading?"

He cuts into his steak. Mom's been trying to get him to eat healthier lately—lean meats like chicken and seafood—but Dad loves red meat. "We slipped a few weeks ago."

"But we were still in the lead," Mom says, spotting someone from the corner of her eye. She turns to me. "Liv, isn't that the boy you've been dating? Zach?"

I see Zach crossing the restaurant. My skin crawls.

What a terrible coincidence.

I still haven't told my parents about the breakup.

He's got none other than Cristina Rossi on his arm. He sees

me and starts heading our way. *Please don't.* I nearly drop my fork. I down some water.

"Yeah. We're not seeing each other anymore," I say. "Don't say anything weird."

"Weird?" Mom says. "Why would I do that?"

Zach stops at the table and looks at me. "Liv, Mr. and Mrs. Blakely. Just thought I'd say hello. My dad is very excited that you're ahead in the race for governor."

"Please tell your father I appreciate his vote of confidence and his continued support," Dad says. "We're in an uphill battle and could use him on the front lines."

"He's there for you, sir. If you'll excuse me, we have a reservation. Don't want to lose our table."

"Good seeing you, young man," Dad says, trying to stay polite. He's obviously confused about why my boyfriend is on a date with another girl.

"Great to see you too, Mr. Blakely. Mrs. Blakely." Zach keeps his focus on my father. He doesn't bother giving me a glance, but Cristina does. She can't help herself.

In fact, she stops in her tracks and says, "I hope you're not still making yourself throw up all over the place like you did at the boat party. You should really take better care of yourself. You look pretty skeletal." She glances at both of my parents. "Just thought someone should tell you."

Before I can process what just happened, Cristina turns around and catches up with Zach. Mom and Dad put down their drinks.

Mom stares at me. Dad looks down at the tablecloth.

I can't think. I can't say anything.

They're devastated. It's obvious.

"I have to go," I say, getting up, making my way through tables to the restroom.

Did Zach know Cristina was going to say that? Had she been

waiting for the perfect moment to expose me? Did she want to humiliate me all along?

I don't even go in a stall. I have vertigo right there at the sink. I can hardly breathe. I can't even fathom what just happened. I want to be away from everyone. I don't want anyone to look at me. I'm disgusting.

Mom comes into the bathroom. All I can do is turn away, horrified.

"Liv," Mom says. She's concerned, but I can tell she's trying to hide the disappointment in her tone. "It's true. Isn't it?"

I head toward a stall.

"Liv." Mom puts a hand on my shoulder. She's gentle. I could pull away, but I don't—I feel ready to give in to her. "I already knew. I didn't tell your father. I should have never let you keep going on like this… I thought you were turning around."

"You tried to trick me," I say, pulling away because I'm too sick to stop myself. I feel the food come up and lurch toward the toilet. I heave and then heave again. Mom is in the stall, holding back my hair. She closes the door.

"Mason told me," she says. "He didn't want me to say anything yet. That's why I wanted you to come to the therapist. Honey, I'm so sorry. You know how much I love you. I just want to help."

Mason *promised* he wouldn't say anything. If Mom already knew, why did he want me to tell them myself? Why did I think I could avoid everything by avoiding him?

Mom and Dad aren't going to let this go now.

I'm so embarrassed I just want to die.

"Everyone has known this whole time," I mutter.

I can barely talk. I heave again.

I feel betrayed by her. By Mason, Zach, Cristina.

By everyone.

part three

I am not sick. I am broken. But I am happy to be alive
as long as I can paint.

—FRIDA KAHLO

thirty-seven

"Of all the liars in the world, sometimes the worst are our own fears."

—RUDYARD KIPLING

Dad's livid. *Really* livid.

"Then that article with your yearbook photo was true? I dismissed it for regular tabloid trash. Why would you do this to yourself? I can't believe you didn't tell me."

I want to crawl into a hole and die.

We're in the living room. He's pacing. Is this what he does on Capitol Hill? Pacing back and forth, screaming at his interns before he goes on Fox News and speaks with a talking head, then does the same thing before going on CNN, and again with whoever is filming a video for *Politico*?

Mom sits on a chair across from me.

Fine. Don't sit by me. I must be *contagious*.

I'll take up the whole couch. What do I care?

"I just want to know why this was kept from me," Dad says. He runs his hands through his salt-and-pepper hair. He looks old all of a sudden. I notice the wrinkles around his eyes. The firmness of his neck has begun to go soft around his collar. "Especially when I have a campaign to run," he continues. "What if news gets out that our daughter has a mental illness?"

"It's an eating disorder," Mom says. "Forget the campaign for a minute."

"It's certainly something that has to be addressed and taken care of immediately."

I cross my arms. "God forbid you lose points in the polls."

"Why are you being so awful to us when we want to help you?"

"Because you're talking about me like I'm a political problem that needs to be fixed," I say. "It's not like your campaign hasn't had something to do with this."

Mom turns to him. "I had my suspicions, but I thought maybe it would correct itself. I was trying to help her without stressing you out. It just wasn't enough."

"So you thought you'd just do this yourself?" Dad says, looking at both of us. He shakes his head. "What happened to helping each other get over the hurdles?"

"By getting into each other's business all the time?" I shout. "I hate the way you're so ruthless that you *control* other people to control me. I hate the way you try to solve things that aren't even problems. I hate the way you make me say what you want, dress me how you want, while I'm the one who gets ridiculed. I'd rather die. My problems are *not* your problems."

Dad sits down next to me on the couch and puts his hand on my shoulder. "Liv, I love you. You're my baby. My daughter. I don't understand what's happening to you." He turns to Mom. "Do you?"

"Of course," she says. "She has an eating disorder. It's common for teenage girls." Mom looks at me. Tears are welling up in her eyes. I *hate* making Mom cry. It makes me feel like a failure. "I just didn't think it was this bad. I should have monitored you better. I should have asked you instead of tiptoeing around."

"This isn't about the campaign, Liv. We want to help," Dad

says, turning to Mom. "So where do we take her for treatment? Do we go somewhere right now?"

Mom rubs her temple like she's starting to get a headache. "I don't think tonight is the time to go anywhere. I have some treatment facilities in mind. I'll contact one of them in the morning. She may have to be admitted."

"So you're going to have me locked up?" I start to stand up, but Dad shoots me a look that means *sit down*. "Why can't you talk to me? I'm right here!"

"Stop. We're not going to have you *locked up*," Mom says. "We're going to get you help. You'll probably have to stay somewhere a few days. You'll get therapy. There might be medication. It depends on the severity of what's happening."

"Medication for what?" I ask.

I don't want to be numbed out on pills.

"Depression. Anxiety. I don't know all of what they prescribe and what for. You need professional help, Liv. This has been going on for way too long." Mom gets up, walks over to the couch and hugs me. "It'll be difficult, but we'll be your support."

"This can't get out," Dad says. "You'll stay here tonight. I can't have you running around causing problems. We have to handle this carefully."

"*I'm* running around causing problems? I wasn't the one who walked up to our table. Believe me. I'm not interested in making my problems your problems."

"What was that girl saying about a boat party?" Dad asks.

"It was nothing. A school thing," I say. "It doesn't matter now."

"I don't remember that," Mom says.

Dad agrees. "She didn't look like the kind of girl who does school things."

"Will you both just stop?" I yell. "It's embarrassing enough that you're suddenly controlling my life more than you already have been."

"Liv, do you think we want you to be sick?" Mom says.

How can I answer that? If she knew I had a problem, she should have pushed harder. The other part of me feels like a jerk for lying to her about how badly I've let my eating habits take control of my life. And Dad? He's been so wrapped up in the campaign that I've practically been invisible to him the whole time. Except for when I'm in the press.

"No," I say. "But I don't think you know what's going to make me better." I stand up from the couch. I need to be alone and think. "I need to go upstairs."

"You're not going anywhere. Or you can kiss your future of going to an art school goodbye." His words gut me. How could he hold that over me right now?

"What do I care?" I say, calling his bluff. "You were never going to let me go. That's just a carrot you dangle over my head to get me to do whatever you want."

Dad looks flabbergasted. He starts to open his mouth, but he doesn't end up saying anything. How did our relationship get so broken? How did I get so broken?

I run up the stairs, wiping the tears from my eyes. I'm on lockdown at my own house. I'm desperate here. There's going to be surveillance everywhere from here on out. I'm not going to start gaining weight to please my parents. Not after I worked so hard to reach my goal weight. I just wish I'd been more careful that day on the boat.

I throw myself onto my bed, fantasizing about how Cristina Rossi is going to wake up one day with her fake eyelashes glued shut. If she hasn't told people already, Cristina will. She'll brag. Everyone is going to know my personal problems, and I won't be able to hide. I pull out my phone—they haven't taken that away from me yet—and text Jasmine. Her advice would be good to have now. She's levelheaded. She had everything so together during high school. How did she do it? How did she survive?

LIV: Hi Jas

LIV: I know I haven't talked to you in a while. And now I really need to.

LIV: Just personal stuff. Girl to girl. Nothing about you and Royce.

LIV: I'm just stuck. Really stuck.

House arrest sucks. I feel so isolated. So alone. It makes me feel even worse. I think about calling Sam, but there's no way I want him to know. But then again, maybe he does by now. Maybe by tomorrow, everyone will. Maybe I'll just send out a press release to *Politico* myself. Daughter of Congressman Driven to Purge Over Constant Self-Defeat. Then I can do the talk show circuit and write a book.

That's the formula, right?

Next up, Antonia.

I don't want to text her for some reason. Writing things down makes them feel more permanent. More real. I call Antonia's number, hoping she doesn't think I'm asking her for a ride again. When she picks up the phone, I can hear her mother chatting in the background.

"Hey, Liv. Hold on a sec. Let me go somewhere I can hear you." A moment passes before I hear her voice again. "Sorry. My mom's back from tour."

"Can you talk?" I ask. "I can't leave the house, and I really need someone to talk to right now. I'd invite you here, but my parents won't let anyone come over either."

"You're under house arrest?" She asks the question like she can't believe what she's hearing. My parents *never* ground me. "What's going on? Are you okay?"

"I've been caught," I say.

"What did you do? You better have not snuck out with-out me."

"Purging," I barely whisper. "Mom and Dad. They know. It really, really sucks. Cristina Rossi said something in front of them at dinner."

Antonia scoffs at the mention of Cristina's name. "She's seri-ously America's biggest loser. How could she do that to you?"

I continue with the story. "And Zach was there *with* her, try-ing to act all cool. It was awful. I wanted to crawl into a cave and hibernate for a million years."

"What did your parents do? I bet they freaked."

"Dad was the worst. He's *so* concerned about his campaign. Forget me. I'm pretty much on lockdown. They want to send me *away* to an eating disorder program. They're probably set-ting up therapy appointments right now. It's so bad."

"So you don't have any say in what happens?"

"Since when have I ever? Even if I wanted to die right now, I'd have to ask permission. They don't care about my thoughts. They make the decisions."

"Don't talk like that—I care. And don't make those jokes either. They really aren't funny." I use my sarcasm as a shield, but Antonia sees right through my act.

"I know," I say. "I love you."

"You need to be rescued. Literally. From your family. I can't even imagine how trapped you're feeling. You need to get out of there."

"I wish I could just leave. I wish I could go anywhere."

"It's not like escaping is hard. You just need to climb out a window the way everyone else has been doing since the sev-enth grade."

I'm hesitant, but her idea feels right. Why should I let my parents control every waking second of my life? Freedom is the right move. I can at least get out and go somewhere for one evening. What more could it hurt, right? Besides, I have only this last night of freedom before my family has me locked up somewhere. I tell Antonia that I'll go.

"It better be somewhere fun," I say.

I need to forget all this mess. I need to have a good time.

"You know it."

Antonia promises to text me when she's ready to pick me up.

Just when the hour finally comes to sneak out the window, I get a text from Sam. I sit on the edge of the bed and answer him while Antonia waits for me just down the street.

SAM: Bad news ☹

SAM: Nina doesn't want to go out anymore

LIV: What? Why?

LIV: That sucks. I'm sorry.

SAM: She says she doesn't want to get serious.

SAM: Should I quit the debate team? It's gonna be awkward.

SAM: What do you think?

I think about Sam's situation. I'm in no state to be giving anyone advice, but I don't want to see him give up something he loves doing for someone else. I don't want him to end up like me with Zach. I should have never wasted my time with him.

LIV: Don't quit.

LIV: It's your life.

SAM: ☺

SAM: What are you doing? Want to hang out?

I'd give anything not to be locked up here right now, but I can't explain what's going on. If Mom and Dad make good on their threats and force me to go somewhere for treatment, I'll eventually have to tell him something. But, right now, Sam needs me to be a good friend—a better friend than I've been most of this year. I should focus on him.

LIV: Sick unfortunately ☹

LIV: Might be out of commission for a few days.

SAM: What's wrong? The breakup?

SAM: He's not worth suffering over.

LIV: It's just the flu or something.

LIV: Don't worry. Talk soon xoox

I'm so embarrassed he even knows about the latest disaster that was my breakup with Zach. I didn't give him all the details. Only Antonia knows.

Sam would have wanted to beat him up or tell him off, and that would've caused even more drama. I was hoping to keep my breakup with Zach as low-key as possible, but I guess Cristina couldn't help herself.

Why did he have to just text me? I hate lying to him. But I can't include him in this. I need Sam to think I'm just that girl on a boat sailing with him around the world. I can't ruin our dream. *Sorry, Sam*, I say to myself. *You don't need to see this. You won't. Not unless you're going where I'm going tonight.* I suddenly go rigid with the thought.

I have to risk it. I can't stay in this house one more second.

thirty-eight

"Reality denied comes back to haunt."

—PHILIP K. DICK

Antonia and I are standing outside Club Paradise, checking each other's faces and outfits. We've put on heavier makeup, trying to make ourselves look older even though most of the clubbers seem to be around college age. Every time the door swings open, I can hear the blaring sounds of the electronic synths pumping throughout the club.

We're waiting outside with the crowd, wedged between a bachelorette party and a pair of sleazy guys wearing polo shirts who keep looking over at us.

"What's the name of this lipstick?" I ask.

"Violet Femme," Antonia says. "It looks good. Just don't act all bubbly. Be cool and follow me. We have to wait for Joey to give me the nod."

"Joey?"

"The bouncer."

We hang outside near the door. Antonia lights up a cigarette, which makes it look like we're just smoking. Joey, her 350-pound Samoan wrestler friend, is a fan of her mother's music so he'll do anything for us, she says. All she has to do is bring him a signed 12-inch vinyl of *Mamacita Rica*. He wears a scowl like he's going to literally pick us up and toss us two streets over. I'm feeling so underage I'm starting to squirm like I'm wearing a training bra all over again. No way anyone's going to think I'm twenty-one.

"How come we've never done this before?" I say.

Antonia grins. "Because you're usually Miss I'm-too-good-for-everything, always staying home studying, doing something responsible with your family."

"I guess I can't deny that."

"Try having a mother who's a pop star in her native country. When she's gone, you think I'm going to stay home? Hell no. There's a big world out there and I'm going to go have some fun in it."

We're finally up near the front of the line. Joey checks all the IDs of the girls in the bachelorette party one at a time. It seems to take forever. As the girls stumble into the club, Antonia walks up to Joey and gives him a big hug. He nods at me.

"We still cool, Joey?" Antonia squeezes him.

"You bring that album tomorrow. Signed. You hear?"

Antonia smiles. "Yes, sir."

He gestures at Antonia for us to enter. I squeak out a thank-you as I walk by, barely believing how easy it was for Antonia to get us into the club.

The club is filled with people talking and dancing. Neon lights flash up and down the walls, illuminating Antonia's face with bursts of purple and blue. "Are we going to be able to drink?" I ask, wanting to forget everything by drowning myself in alcohol. Zach. Cristina. My parents. My life. "Will the bartenders card us too?"

"I'm not sure…" Antonia says, glancing around the room. She spots the pair of guys from next to us in line coming our way. "Okay, hold on. Those guys are coming over. Just be quiet and shy, okay? We need drinks. This is the only way we're going to get them. I don't want you blowing our cover."

She turns to the two guys stopping by the table.

"Want a drink?" the taller one says. He's wearing a purple polo shirt and heavy cologne. It's definitely not a good look for him. I let Antonia do the talking.

"Something strong," Antonia says. "It's been a long week."

The other guy leans on the table. "Has it?"

"Of course. Why do you think we're here? Time to wind down or turn up."

"All right." The guy laughs and straightens his collar. "We'll get you something."

Antonia smiles at them as they walk away.

"What was that?" I say.

"The game," Antonia says, quickly reapplying her lipstick.

"The *game*?"

"Don't worry about it, I can get us drinks all night."

When the guys are on their way back, Antonia leans in. "Ignore them," she says.

"Ignore them?"

Antonia nods slowly. "Otherwise we'll be stuck talking to them all night."

"What's wrong with that?" I ask. "I don't want to be a complete user."

The taller guy sets the drinks on the table. There are only two chairs, so he doesn't sit down. I try to talk to him, but the music is too loud to carry a proper conversation. I let him babble on about something related to finance while Antonia makes small talk with the other guy. They both seem to lose interest after they realize we're not here to hook up, and they make an excuse to wander off. The same routine happens with two other sets of guys.

By this time, I'm slurping my third drink and can hardly see straight.

"Honey," Antonia says. "You don't look so good."

"I'm fine," I slur. "We should dance."

Antonia puts her hand on my shoulder. "Did you have dinner?"

I shake my head.

"When was the last time you ate?" she asks.

"I'm not sure," I say.

"You said you were starting to eat again. We've talked about this."

I can tell she sees that look in my eyes that means I haven't been honest.

"Liv, you need to watch yourself. Last one, okay?"

I sip my drink. "I'm all right," I say. I know I'm trying to outrun all my worries and pain. But so what? I'm ahead of the game tonight. It feels good for once not to feel anything. It feels even better not to care. I get so sick of caring.

While Antonia makes small talk with the guys standing by our table, I decide to text Sam. It's a bad idea—I know—but I can't help myself.

LIV: Do you ever feel empty?

LIV: Sometimes I just want to feel nothing.

SAM: I take it you're not feeling any better.

LIV: Are you going to come or not?

LIV: I'm doing something really stupid right now.

LIV: I thought you could share in my waywardness.

I sip my drink, listening to Antonia chat with some other girl sitting at the table next to us and waiting for Sam to respond. He finally does after a few minutes.

SAM: Where are you?

LIV: Club Paradise.

SAM: How did you get in?

LIV: Antonia

SAM: How am I going to get in?
LIV: That's for you to figure out 😊
SAM: Coming... 😕

By the time Sam shows up, I can barely focus. I have no idea how he got into the bar and I've lost count of drinks and managed to eat half of a packet of crackers. The crumbs are all over the counter.

"Hey, baby!" I throw my arms around him and plant a big kiss.

"Sam?" Antonia says. "How'd you find us, hot stuff?"

I'm not fast about prying myself loose.

"You are so drunk," he says. "I don't think I've ever seen you quite this bad."

"Only a little," I say, stupidly grinning at him.

"It wasn't easy getting in here," he says to Antonia, looking over his shoulder. "I had to sneak in through the back and bribe some dude twenty bucks. I promised him I wasn't here to drink."

"That's love right there." Antonia laughs. She has another drink in her hand. How can she drink so much? I can barely keep up with her.

I've lost count and try to push him my drink. "Here, loverboy. I can't handle any more. It's making me. I dunno. Sick?"

"You don't look well," he says to me.

Antonia slaps him on the shoulder. "You know how to make a girl feel better."

"Yeah," I say. "Tell me I'm beautiful right now."

"What?" Sam says. "You're not serious."

"Tell me right now," I demand. Everything about me is dramatic right now. I feel like I'm an actress all of a sudden. They're artists, aren't they? I think so. "Tell me you love everything about me."

313

I can't believe the words that are falling out of my mouth right now, but I can't help myself. I need someone to love me.

"Something's not right," Sam says. "Are you supposed to be here?"

I scoff at his question. "Right. You think my parents know I'm here?"

Antonia starts laughing. "She's on the *run*..."

"I am not running." I laugh and turn to Sam. "But of course I'm supposed to be here." Suddenly I double over with a rush of stomach pain.

"What's wrong?" Sam says. "Hey, Liv. What's going on?"

"Nothing," I moan, starting to see black spots in my peripheral vision. I've been drunk, but I've never felt this bad before. "I get these all the time. Give it a second."

"That's not good," says Sam. "You look kind of pale."

I point in his face. "What did I tell you? You tell me I'm beautiful or you can go home," I slur. I realize I'm trying to push him away, but I can't seem to stop myself.

"That's not funny," Sam says.

"Go home, Sam."

"That's not even funny."

Sam looks hurt, but I can't stop.

"Then tell me I'm beautiful."

"Tell her she's beautiful," says Antonia, nudging him. When my stomach pain soars, I bend over again. Sam tries to touch me, but I knock his hand away.

"Stop touching me," I say. "Everyone wants to touch me. Why? Why do you want to do that? You, Zach, Jackson. Just quit already."

"I'm trying to help," Sam says. "You need to go home."

"Don't touch her," Antonia says, trying to make fun of the situation. Her words are starting to slur a little too. "And she *definitely* doesn't need to go home."

Some jock in a tiny shirt, all muscles from ears to toes,

overhears and steps over. "The lady said to quit touching her. Buzz off."

"I wasn't touching her," Sam says. He holds up his hands.

"That's not what the lady said." The jock's neck muscles are wider than Sam. He eyes Sam closer. "Why you in here anyway? You look like you're twelve years old."

Sam looks at me pleadingly. "I'm just trying to take her home."

"I can tell. Not gonna happen. Get lost, kid."

I get in between them. "Hey, hero," I say to the jock. "It's all right. He's my friend. He's not so bad once you get to know him."

The guy takes a look at Sam. "All right. But if I hear anything else from him I'm kicking him out the door." He turns to Sam. "Don't piss off the ladies."

"My hero," I say, patting the jock on the back as he walks away. "You hear that, Sam? No funny business or else!" I laugh, but Sam looks more agitated by the minute.

He's not even asking us for a drink.

"I heard," Sam says.

Antonia is already talking to another guy, ignoring the both of us. This time when my stomach racks me, I can't take it. "I gotta go throw up," I say. "I'm starting to get the spins. Get me to the bathroom." I can barely walk on my own.

Sam puts my arm over his shoulder and helps me through the crowd. It's a one-stall bathroom, so Sam comes in and holds my hair back as I puke up alcohol. I'm too sick to feel embarrassed. This doesn't feel good like when I purge, emptying out. This feels like my insides are being gripped by an invisible fist and turned inside out.

"You can't drink like this," Sam says. "You'll get alcohol poisoning. It's a real thing."

"You didn't even drink with us," I moan.

Everything is finally out.

"You were already drunk," he says. "Besides, this place isn't for us. We don't belong here."

"Sam," I say, catching my breath. "I'm not *that* drunk."

Sam gives me a wet paper towel to wipe my mouth with. "Yeah. They all say that."

"Okay, maybe I am. I was just having some fun. Seriously though, I'm in here because of my stomach. I don't think it can handle drinking right now."

"I can tell."

"Sam," I say. Something's coming up—not alcohol, but a confession I've been trying to avoid for what seems like forever—and I know I won't be able to keep it down any longer. "I have bulimia. I mostly don't eat, but when I eat too much, I hate myself so much for eating that I have to throw up. It's out of control, but I can't stop."

Sam simply looks at me. It's not a look of hate or judgment or surprise. It's just like he's waiting to see what I have to say next.

"My parents found out. They were keeping me under house arrest. They want to send me away to a treatment facility. I snuck out."

"You're going to be okay," Sam says. "Let's get you home. You need to rest. I didn't know you were this sick."

He helps me up, but I can barely stand I'm so weak. I pull down my skirt, not wanting him to catch a glimpse of the scars on my thighs. He can know about my eating disorder, but he *can't* know about the cutting. He'd never forgive me for hurting myself.

My skin's dry and I'm totally exhausted like I'll never have energy again. Even my heart feels like it's slowing down. "Just take me back to the table," I say. "I don't want to go home."

Sam holds on to my waist. "You can barely stand or walk."

"Just get me some water," I slur.

Summoning up as much motivation as I can, I walk back to

the table with Sam. He sits me down, then goes to find water. Antonia sees me and comes over.

She's smiling. "Want another drink?"

I groan. "Do I look like I can have another drink?"

"I don't know. You tell me. Wait, are you sick?"

"I'm sick," I say.

"I guess I forgot," she says. "I've been drinking a lot."

Sam returns with three glasses of water. "I hope you're enjoying yourselves," he says. "They made fun of me at the bar."

He makes me drink the first glass. It makes my stomach burn.

I take out my phone. "Oh my god," I say.

"What?" say both Sam and Antonia.

I'm terrified all over again. "My parents know I'm gone."

I have multiple missed calls and texts from both of them.

"What are we going to do?" Antonia asks. "I can't drive."

"I can drive," says Sam.

"I can't yet," I say. "I can't go home. Not like this."

"Why not?" Sam asks. The voice of reason. "Where are you going to go?"

"I can't, all right?" I read the texts from Mom. She begs me to come home. She says to please respond so they know I'm safe. Then another text comes in. It's from Dad. He says to text back now or he's calling the police. I hold it up and show Sam and Antonia. "Do you think he's bluffing?" I ask.

"Well, he's not being very nice about it," says Antonia.

"You want to know what I have to say?" I shut off my phone. *"That."*

Antonia takes out her phone. "Oh my god. They're texting me too. I guess this means I'm shutting off mine." She powers down her phone.

"How about you, Sam?" I say.

He looks at his phone. "Ah, man. It's your dad." He reads

the texts. *"'Have you seen Liv?'* What do I do?" he adds. "This is *bad*. I have to respond."

I feel awful. Not just because my stomach is ravaging me or alcohol is swirling in me. I don't know who I am. Am I who I am because I hate food and purge and cut, or are these symptoms of a sick self? What if the real version of me—the happy and healthy Liv—isn't actually dead? Maybe she's deep down somewhere. Maybe I can still find her.

"I gotta get out of here," I say pushing myself to my feet.

Suddenly the world is getting dark.

I'm exhausted, light-headed. Sharp pains stab me in the gut.

Sam and Antonia are holding my arms as they help me from the table.

We're outside somehow. I don't remember getting from the bar to here. They're talking but I don't hear them. *I don't hear anything.* Suddenly, I can't *see* anything either.

I'm floating in a void of pain.

I'm floating, and the darkness takes me from consciousness into the sickest place I've ever known. This time I may never find my way out.

thirty-nine

"The wound is the place where the Light enters you."

—JALALUDDIN RUMI

I wake up feeling like a nightmare has taken hold of my body. There are vibrations beneath my skin. It's cold. Everything's cold. I feel horrible. I crack my eyes open though I'm afraid of what I might see.

A white sheet covers me.

Sunlight pours through the windows.

I'm in a hospital. There's an IV in my wrist.

I try to lift my arm. I feel so weak.

The night comes back in bits and pieces. I snuck out. I drank. I remember Antonia. I remember a Samoan who likes *Mamacita Rica*. Sam was there. I threw my arms around him. Did I kiss him? I don't remember anything afterward.

What will my family think of me now? What will the entire school think? Please, don't let anyone in this room with a camera. I don't want to be seen like this. I just want to go back to being the old invisible, *who's-that-girl* Olivia Blakely.

I'm about to fall asleep again when the door opens. It's Royce and Jasmine. It's almost a relief that they aren't Mom and Dad. I give them a weak smile. They look awful. Like they've been up all night. Royce has bags under his eyes. Jasmine isn't smiling. Are they back together? I hope they're together. I start to doubt it though. I doubt everything.

"Hi, Liv," Jasmine says. She has tears in her eyes.

Why does she have to see me like this?

"You poor, poor thing," she says and takes my hand. "I was so worried. I've never been so worried. My brothers wanted to come, I told them maybe tomorrow. I wanted to see you for myself first, make sure you want more guests. But they said to send their love. Mom and Dad too. Lola Cherry said she'll loan you her cane."

I crack the tiniest smile.

"How are you feeling, Livvy?" Royce asks, sitting down in the chair next to the hospital bed. "You had us really scared. We've been here for hours. Mason is taking it the hardest. He really freaked out. I mean, we all kinda did."

I turn my head away from Royce. "Where is he?"

"The lobby," Royce says. "He didn't want to come in unless you wanted him to. He said you're probably mad at him."

I think about how Mason wanted to help me, how Mom and Dad wanted to help me, but also how they went about everything in the completely wrong way. Then again, when it comes to these kinds of things, maybe there just isn't a right way.

"Who else is here?" I ask.

"Everyone," Royce says. "Mom, Dad, us, Antonia. Sam is here too."

I feel so awful. Not just physically. I'm pretty numb there, and weak. A lot of it right now is embarrassment. I want to wither away.

"I responded to your text last night," Jasmine says. She still has tears in her eyes. "When I didn't hear from you, I called Royce."

She responded to my text?

I look around the room for my phone, but there's nothing here. Not the clothes I was wearing last night. There isn't even a pair of shoes. I couldn't walk out if I wanted to. There's no hiding now. I'm sure she knows everything.

"Are you...?" I start to ask.

Royce doesn't even let the question hang in the air. "We're here because we both care about you."

I wish he would answer the question. I wish they had never broken up. Their relationship was always something I looked up to—something that showed me how love could last despite all the suffering in the world.

"I thought I had control of my life the way you always did," I say to Jasmine. "I thought I could handle everything myself."

The way she dedicated herself so hard to succeeding. Then did.

Jasmine sighs. "No one has control, it's just an illusion. We can only control so much, and we need help for the rest."

I've always looked up to Jasmine, and now I've let her and everyone else down. I can hardly take it.

"Liv," she says. "Sometimes we're strong. Other times we're fragile, and that's okay. We have to accept that. This world is so big and we're all so small that it's easy to feel unwanted or not good enough. But you have to remind yourself that you're always loved no matter what. You're included in your family, my family. You're bright and smart and sassy. You're beautiful on every layer, even your most painful ones. And it really hurts to see you like this. But I can tell you, this is just part of healing."

She kisses me on the head. I wish that and a wave of the hand could take away all of this. I love Jasmine, but I still feel like a failure. Talking to them should make me feel better, but I actually feel worse. All I can think about is having failed my family, myself, school… Everyone will know, and they're all going to think of me as weak, messed up. *That girl.*

I pull my hand away. "I'm tired," I say. "I better rest."

Jasmine rubs my arm and shoulder. "Okay," she says. "I love you. If you need me just call."

"I love you too," Royce says to me. "You know you're the best sister ever, this doesn't change that. I'll be checking back in. Try not to hate Mom and Dad or Mason. We all love you."

I can't say those same words back to him. Not right now. Not with so much pain and embarrassment. "Thanks," I say.

I watch them walk out, watching the door click shut.

I try to sleep, but I can't. Everything feels wrong. I feel like I'm in prison. I'm hooked up to an IV. Every little thing is being monitored. I'm just a statistic now.

Soon the door opens again. It's Mom.

I feel a surge of pain mixed with anger and resentment.

She pours me some water, puts a straw in it. It's a bendy straw. It's silly, but I've always liked those. I recognize right away this is some kind of peace offering.

I accept it, take a sip. I want to apologize, but I don't have any words. Mom is crying. She's obviously been doing that for hours. She stands next to the bed.

"Sit down," I say. "You're making me nervous."

She does and half smiles at me. "I feel guilty that I didn't help you as much as I could have, or in the right ways. We've pushed you too hard. I know you have a complicated relationship, but Dad's very sorry. He's heartbroken. You're his baby girl. He wants to see you whenever you're ready. He doesn't want to stress you in any way."

I sip some more water, considering what I want to say. I don't think I'm ready to forgive them yet.

Mom waits for my response, then sighs disappointedly. "We're going to get you all the help you need."

I put the cup on the tray.

She meets my eyes with hers. "I'm glad you have a friend like Sam in your life."

I'm so embarrassed about last night that I'm sure Sam won't ever talk to me again. Not that I remember what happened after we left the bar. I'm sure that whatever it is can't be good. Not if I ended up in a hospital.

Something occurs to me just then. Is Sam someone I could

have loved, could have built something with instead of going out with Zach? If so, is the chance ruined forever?

I'm about to agree with her when Mason comes into the room. This makes me twice as nervous. I can't tell whether to feel bad for pushing him away or mad at him for lying to me. I guess Mom knew all along, but they hid things from Dad for my sake, which probably made him even more furious. At first, I thought Dad reacted the way he did after the dinner when Cristina outed me because he was embarrassed about what my problems would mean for his campaign, but I realize now that he was angry at himself for not noticing what I guess had been obvious to everyone else for a long time.

And here I thought I was good at hiding things.

"Hey, I don't want to interrupt," he says. "I just wanted to check in before I go home for a while. I need to get some sleep."

He walks up to Mom and hugs her.

She kisses him on the cheek.

He comes up to me too and stands by my bed. "For what it's worth, I'm sorry I let you stick it out alone for so long without getting you help. Even if you didn't want me to, I should have."

He gives me a giant hug.

I don't have much energy to hug back.

"I love you," he says.

It's like his words are the first that finally reach me. They mean more coming from him. He knows what it's like to be thought of as the screwup, the do-nothing.

I understand now.

"I love you too," I say.

I turn onto my side, cry and sleep.

forty

A new doctor visits me in my room the next day.

She has short hair, dark skin and the most luminous eyes. She introduces herself as Dr. Eleanor and wears a white lab coat. As striking and friendly as she looks, I'm uneasy when she enters. Doctors usually mean bad news.

"I'm only going to be your doctor for a little while. You'll mostly be at a treatment center for your bulimia," she says. "Though I may come to visit…" She looks at a clipboard, then makes eye contact with me. "Yesterday you spoke to Dr. Rodriguez about your condition. He asked me if I would come talk to you about the cuts on your legs because I often work with patients who engage in self-harm."

"There's nothing wrong with me," I say.

Did anyone else see my scars? Or do only the doctors know? I feel naked right now. The sheet and my gown don't feel like enough protection. I want to crawl away. I want to be invisible, but I am about to have this conversation whether I want to or not.

"You're five-seven and 98 pounds. Your BMI puts you at

very severely underweight. You already knew that though. You've been purging for months."

"I went out drinking and lost an extra couple of pounds," I say.

I consider the numbers. Ninety-eight pounds. That's all I've wanted for the past year, but I still feel empty and unfulfilled. I'll never be happy no matter how small I get.

"You don't have to lie to me. I'm not here to grill you about your weight or your cuts," she says. "It's not like that. I'm not here to punish you, or make you uncomfortable. And if it makes you feel better, I used to be a cutter."

"You did?" I say, feeling more at ease.

"For many years," Dr. Eleanor says, looking down at her clipboard. "By the look of the notes on your scars, I was a more violent cutter, and for a really long time. I was even a cutter while I was a young doctor. It was horrible at times. I don't know how I didn't lose everything I had."

"Why did you do it?"

Though I know that I probably know the answer, I want to hear it from someone else. I want to know that I'm not crazy. I might be sick, but I'm not crazy.

"Anxiety, depression. Punishment for my failures. You name it. I was looking for answers and sometimes I felt I could only find them through self-destructive behaviors. It's not uncommon. Especially for girls facing a lot of social pressure."

"But how do I stop?" I really want to know this time.

Dr. Eleanor lets out a breath. "Therapy. Lots of it."

I don't like the sound of those words.

She must be able to tell what I'm feeling by my face because she says, "Yeah, I didn't like the idea of that either. Believe me. I resisted for a long time. But you have to understand, people like us are complicated, it takes a lot for us to understand why we do what we do, but we have to get to the bottom of it if we want to get better. You have to care about the hurt you do, and by the looks of you, you care a lot about life, family, your career. I can see career girl all over you. Women like us want to control our own worlds to the point where we control our pain centers."

I consider her points. She's right about wanting to control my pain, to harness it. The problem was that when I got so thin, everyone complimented me, which made me want to purge and starve myself into being skinnier. It's so messed up. The smaller a girl is, the more visible she is to the world. The more she makes herself disappear, the more she matters. It's all a trick.

"Do you feel like you can be open-minded to getting help?" Dr. Eleanor asks.

"I think so," I say.

Why did I believe starving myself was going to make me feel better? In my mind, I can see all the meals I skipped, all the food I vomited up and flushed into the toilet. I was destroying myself from the inside out, thinking that people would love me more, thinking that I would love myself more.

"Look, we girls have to stick together. I'm certain we'll see each other again. And when we do? We'll give each other this look. I don't know how to explain it, but it will mean, yeah, we have secrets, but *we're the strong ones*. We're the ones with scars, and *they're fading*."

"I like that thought," I say, sitting up in my bed a little. I'm cold and pull my sheets up over my shoulders. Maybe I'm not really as alone as I thought.

She pulls her clipboard to her chest like our conversation is almost done. "Me too. I like the sound of your voice. I hear confidence in it. Is it okay if I come see you again?"

"Sure," I say. "It would help to talk to you."

"It's not as good as therapy, but you're a good kid and I'm happy to do what I can to help. Try to see the good in yourself that everyone else already sees in you."

After she leaves, I'm told by a nurse to get myself up and

around by taking a walk out of the room into the hall and back. I've regained a lot of strength and need to test how well I'm able to do with normal activity. Doctor's orders.

I'm slowly passing the nursing station with my IV stand in tow when I run into Antonia. She looks shocked to see me standing up.

"Liv," she says. "What are you doing out of bed?"

I give her a hug but still feel so frail. "I was going for a jog."

She smiles. "Maybe you should hold off on that."

"Want to walk with me?" I ask. "Doctor says I have to make myself useful. I'm slow but able to make my way… I heard you were here all night that first night. Sorry I didn't wake up. I must have scared you pretty bad."

"We rushed you to the hospital pretty fast. Sam drove. Have you seen him?"

"Not yet."

"He'll come. He's pretty upset."

"I can imagine."

"You know, it's really all my fault—"

"No," I say, slowing down. "Walking is tiring me out already. Let's turn around."

"Okay," Antonia says, helping me with the IV stand. "I'm really—"

"Stop it," I say. "It's not your fault. I'm not mad at you. I did this."

"I didn't realize you were as sick as you are. I'm so angry at myself for not noticing. For not paying closer attention. You're my best friend."

"My problems have been going on a long time," I admit. "I was never totally honest with myself about how serious they've been." Antonia's face shows a look of pain, but she lets me continue talking. "I'm only now starting to see how I was destroying myself. I'm still figuring all of this out."

We get to my room and Antonia helps me back into the

bed. I'm starting to get tired of being in the hospital. I want to go home. I want to move on to the rest of my life and leave all this behind.

Antonia sits on the bed next to me. "What's going to happen next?"

"I honestly don't know. I just hope Sam will forgive me." I pause a moment, thinking about how much I want to share. "I think I might have feelings for him. And if I'm being honest with myself, I always have."

forty-one

"If you hear a voice within you say, 'You cannot paint,'

then by all means paint, and that voice will be silenced."

—VINCENT VAN GOGH

I've been in the hospital for a week. I'm sure the tabloids are speculating about my absence or talking about Cristina and Zach getting back together, but I'm not checking them. I can't get better while keeping tabs on what everyone else is saying about me.

Dad has come and gone to my bedside. He's been in Washington, DC, and back twice, not to mention stuck on the campaign trail in the OC as well as in Fresno for thousand-dollar-plate fund-raiser dinners. Mom keeps me updated, and I scroll to see his sound bites in the news. Journalists have asked them about Mom and I not being on the campaign trail with him, but he tells them that Mom is staying home with me while I'm studying hard for upcoming exams. I can tell Dad is stressed about me, though he hides it well. The close-ups reveal the toll of him being a dad and a politician.

I always thought of him as caring about politics more than his family, but I realize that I was wrong. He's always cared about me. He thought I could handle the pressure. I'd always been so strong.

I guess we both live multiple lives. A social worker told me that we all have many roles—some we're better at than others, and some, the dark ones, we have to cope with and keep under control. We have to find balance. I'm barely figuring out my role as a sick person. I don't want to think of myself as sick, but I guess that's the first step to getting better. If I'm going to get better, I have to confront these things.

Dad surprises me today when he comes in. I can already tell that this time he wants to talk. My head's been cloudy. I guess that's because the doctors said some of my organs were failing and so they need time to get motoring again. They all say I'm lucky I'm young, though unlucky to be so ill.

He scratches his head and sits in a chair. "How you feeling today, Honeybee?"

"Same as yesterday," I say. My voice is still weak. "Just want to sleep all the time. They make me take little walks though."

"That's good. Gotta get your strength back. You wore yourself out." He seems tired, beat down by life, but he's smiling for my sake. I'm not commenting in case he's looking for a recap I can't remember, or don't want to remember. I've come to terms with accepting help from my parents, but that doesn't mean I have to tell them everything.

"I hadn't realized how severe your problems were," he says, leaning forward, hands clasped. "And I'm sorry about that. I really am. We're all torn up about what you're going through. We feel guilty. I told Rich that I don't want him talking to you about anything campaign related. He should have no reason to contact you."

I feel my eyes brighten. "You did?" I ask, haunted by memories of Rich sending me emails with links to articles criticizing every single thing about me.

"The only thing I want you to focus on is getting better."

I'm glad Dad stuck up for me. I'd been feeling pretty alone. The way everyone's been visiting has been nice. Except Sam.

He still hasn't come, and that's hard to take because I thought for sure he would visit, text, something. I haven't called or texted him either, so maybe I should. Maybe he's just busy. He did say we would always be friends but if I wronged him again he would go silent. So is that what this is? Silence for my betrayal of his kindness? Silence for hurting him again and again?

I don't deserve him. I definitely don't deserve my family. They've been so sweet and kind and I've just been a zombie to them. It's these emotions. The doctors said I would be on a roller coaster. I didn't expect it. I had control. Or I thought I did. I thought I knew myself so well. I thought I was preventing myself from stepping onto this roller coaster. One minute I'm ravenous. The next I'm hating myself for feeling hunger.

I never thought one night out would be the tipping point. But doctors say it was the perfect storm and my body was in the middle of shutting down. They say a lot of patients with eating disorders don't truly understand how much their bodies are shutting down from starvation. Now I'm just a silhouette in my own mushroom cloud. Trying to escape the burn. Trying to keep some kind of form of who I am through all this.

"Are you going to hire a new campaign manager?" I ask.

"Yeah, but don't worry," he says. "You won't see him. Not anytime soon anyway. You'll be transferred to an outpatient program soon as you're better. I really believe the treatment there will help you grow and be the kind of person who helps other kids with this later on."

"I'll probably start sounding like Jasmine," I say.

I'm only half kidding.

"Not a bad thing. She has a lot of advice and kind words for others."

I do like that. I love her. I wish I hadn't been so rude to her my first day in the hospital, such a zombie, though I can barely focus even now.

"And if you want to be involved with the campaign, it will

have to be your choice," he adds. "Don't worry about it until you're completely better." He slaps his hands on his thighs. "All right. I better go." He comes over and kisses my head.

My eyes tear up. Can I get better?

Is it still possible for me?

"What is it?" he says, looking down at me.

"Nothing."

He lets out a sigh and kisses me again. "You have some other visitors waiting outside, so dry up."

I laugh. "All right, Dad."

"Love you, kid."

When Dad steps out, Royce holds the door. I can't believe he's coming down on the weekends to support me so much when he should be focusing on school too.

"Don't push her around," Dad says jokingly to him.

"I'll try not to," Royce says as he steps in followed by Sam, who has a bunch of stuff in his arms. "Look who I brought," Royce adds.

"Sam!" I say. My breath catches in my lungs. I'm so excited to see him despite the situation. "I'm so embarrassed. I look terrible."

"You're in a hospital," Royce says. "Play the part. You should be coughing and moaning more."

"Yeah," Sam says. "You need to focus on getting better."

Sam hugs me tight, and I think there might be tears in his eyes.

He pulls back, then looks at Royce. "I asked him to let me into your house to grab some things from your room. We figured you would probably be pretty bored." He places a pile of my art pads, pens and pencils on the hospital bed.

"Still want to show at that gallery, don't you?" Sam asks.

I don't know what to say. Dad said to be strong, so I'm trying not to cry. My heart is beating so fast because he's finally here, because he cares. Sam really cares. He always has.

"You gotta keep the dream alive," Royce says.

I turn to my brother. "Are you and…"

"We're talking again," he says. "What's meant to happen will happen. I'm going to get some coffee, be right back. We brought some games too. Maybe we can destroy the world in a game of Risk, or play cards."

When Royce leaves, Sam says, "He's right, you know. You have to pursue your dreams. It makes you who you are. Being an artist is just about the noblest thing anyone can do. You create something from nothing. You can change people's minds. Influence culture."

"I can't believe you came," I say. "And you're right. I promise to get better."

"Antonia said to say she loves you. She's going to visit soon. The hospital doesn't want a lot of people disturbing you."

"I've wasted so much time this year," I say. "I'm going to get better fast. I'm going to do this."

forty-two

"Confront the dark parts of yourself, and work to banish them with

illumination and forgiveness. Your willingness to wrestle with

your demons will cause your angels to sing."

—AUGUST WILSON

I'm doing outpatient therapy now.

We all gather around in a circle with counselors, sharing our struggles. The first few sessions were difficult. The therapist told me it would be tough even showing up. She's right. You feel this kind of embarrassment. You walk in slowly, as if everyone around you suddenly knows you have a problem. And they know *exactly* what it is. Other kids look at you, smile, hide their faces, hug you, kiss you, laugh, cry.

The strangest thing? After a while you sort of lose that complex. You accept everyone because you know what? They accept you. Your problem doesn't become a problem at all around others with similar obstacles. You start to rally around others. All the laughing and crying and hugging you understand. Then, before you know it, you realize the stronger ones help the newer admits, and the newer ones remind the older ones how far they've come and how they need to keep up the power of healing to survive.

We're all survivors. We form a bond like some kind of sisters. I never would have imagined this dark part of my life would be the scar that gives me confidence to succeed, to feel normal in my abnormality.

I'm feeling stronger. The doctors say there's no long-term damage to my organs, but I do have to take it easy. Moderate walks. Healthy eating choices. Hydration. Rest. Therapy. I take some medicines in light doses. I don't want to be on medications for long, but they help me stop slipping into those dark places. They're concerned that the malnutrition can have long-term effects on my mood that lead to severe depression.

I told the doctors I didn't want to take them, but they mentioned that I could be weaned off pretty quickly once I began learning the tools to help myself overcome my impulses to purge or cut. I'm beginning to learn how to do this. How to retain my focus on health. How to redirect my own behaviors. How to breathe. How to talk to the friends I've made. How to realize no one is perfect. How to understand I should not be ashamed. That's the one I really struggle with. Everyone around the treatment center is being so helpful, so loving. These tools they teach me help me to cope with shame, how to overcome it, how to overcome my own grief for losing parts of myself. It all might sound weird and strange, but when you go through something like this, it all becomes real and necessary, and a part of who you'll forever be.

My portfolio has become my new goal. The thing to obsess about and work toward. When I'm not at the outpatient clinic or at doctor's appointments, I've been finalizing drawings and paintings, working on the birds I showed Danny, which are inspired by LeFeber's angels and the fact that his focus was on creating beautiful things instead of his own sickness up until he died. That place inside my heart, that jewel I needed to grow, has been forged in this fire I've been in over the past months. I am my creations.

And the new ones I create, the ones with artistry in mind, will be more symbolic of me than ever. That's what LeFeber was doing. And that's what I'm doing now. I'll protect the gemstone in me. I'll build walls around it. I'll never forget *me*.

Tomorrow, I'm sending off my application, which includes a cover letter, sample drawings, a photograph of one of my paintings and a recommendation letter that I was able to get from Ms. Day. If I'm accepted, I'm supposed to hear back pretty quickly so I can finish the other paintings for the gallery show.

In my letter I wrote:

Dear Board of Directors,

I am a junior at Eastlake Prep High School. This has been a difficult year for me personally, but being a part of your gallery show is part of my dream for the future me. Let me tell you about the 'me' now.

A friend said, "Being an artist is just about the noblest thing anyone can do." It's who I am, who I plan to always be. Another friend recently told me, at his show, "You were experiencing the art with the greatest amount of passion." I told him I'd been waiting all my life to see his work in person. His show was about fallen angels. Sick angels. He said to me, "Every angel you see is fallen. They're sick. Infected with their own lives. Broken, falling. Our divinity is hidden within us. We must nurture that divine nature. We all must find our way to peace and health."

He told me a story after I asked him about what inspired him. He told me, "So many things I can pull from the air just floating there. You inspire me. The answer you seek however goes much deeper. I am often secretly inspired by those early days when I borrowed money to rent a studio in New York. It was a chaotic time. I was full of dreams! I drew something from myself in those days that often seems lost now. You see, down inside of you is a purity. A gemstone of inspira-

tion. It comes from within, forged from this unexplainable burning desire. You must keep it pure. You do understand this. Purity is everything. Protect it. Mine is housed, guarded within memories. When you do this you can gaze into the world. What do you see? You see poverty. You see war. You see hate. You see all these terrible things, and they burn in you because you want to help the world. You want your work to speak to the world. You want to save the world. Yet, after all, you are only a painter. You don't create war machines. You don't create political agenda. You create the aesthetics of the world that covers all, another form of meninges, a membrane of life and beauty pulsating over the sad brain of the world. Yes. That is our work. Our art. And while the pain of the world is inspiring, it all must eventually pass through the original purity within you in the first place. That gemstone. The one you must keep pure. The one that harbors the seeds of all your inspiration."

His name is Geoff LeFeber.

You see, I've discovered that gemstone. I know where it is. It's part of me now. I'm guarding it. And I'm ready. You have my drawings. You have this letter and the letter from Ms. Day, my art teacher. I'm ready to soar.

Sincerely yours,
Olivia Blakely

forty-three

"The unendurable is the beginning of the curve of joy."

—DJUNA BARNES

Royce and Mason are coming down from the Bay Area to visit. They're in the dining room eating dinner when Mom and I arrive back from one of my therapy sessions that I've been doing after I was released from the hospital. Dad is in Hayward giving a speech. He'll be back tomorrow. I miss him.

Mom gives them that why-are-you-eating-without-us look. This is a big test. Eating in front of anyone.

"We were hungry, Mom," Mason says. "And the delivery guy just showed up out of the blue. It was like a gift from heaven. How could we refuse?"

"The moo shu pork is really good today," Royce adds.

"You couldn't wait for us to get home?" Mom asks. "It's like you're in high school again. The amount of food you two used to go through in a week… My god."

"Those were the good old days."

Mom looks at them as she takes a seat. "I know."

Mason passes me the fried rice. "Want some?"

I take a chair too. "Not from the chopsticks you're using."

"I'm not giving you those," he says.

I pour myself a glass of water. "Just put some on a plate for me."

"Sure thing," Mason says, scooping a small portion onto my plate. I have to eat higher calorie meals, but I also have to be careful about how much I eat.

My body is still sensitive to food.

Just then I get an email notification. I click on the app to open the message. "Mom, it's from the gallery," I say, my heart pounding in my chest. I'm nearly shaking with a mixture of excitement and dread. Did they accept or reject my application?

"Give me that," Mason says, grabbing my phone. "I'll see what it says."

"Oh no you don't," I say, trying to get it.

He takes off running, but I'm after him.

"Give it back to her, Mason," Mom says, taking a bite of paper-wrapped chicken. "Now you're acting like you're in second grade."

Mason runs around the table.

"He may be the oldest, but he's obviously still in the second grade," says Royce. "Come on, give it back to her before she cries."

I'm laughing, but too tired to keep after him. "I give up," I say. "Read it."

"I was just joking," he says. "You read it."

"No. You read it, please," I say.

We make eye contact.

I can see how proud he is all of a sudden that I asked.

"All right." He looks at the email. "Hmm," he says, tossing me the phone. "You're in the show. You've got a couple of weeks to get ready."

I catch the phone and start cheering and high-fiving everyone, even Mom. I've never felt so happy about anything, ever.

forty-four

School's finally out. No one contacted me other than Antonia and Sam.

I knew I was a loner before. That's okay. I've learned that most artists are loners of some kind. We spend massive amounts of time in voluntary solitude creating our art. The less we socialize, the more we create. I've heard that the sooner artists realize this, the sooner they can put in the ten thousand hours needed to become great. There's nothing I want more, except the friendships I do have.

The next time Antonia comes over, I show her one of my paintings. It's a portrait of her. It's not done yet, but Antonia sees it and starts making these little squealing sounds.

"I've seen you make some wonderful things. But *this*? Looking at this makes me want to become a singer. What would I be called? Lady Antonia?"

"Maybe just Antonia." I giggle.

"Mamacita rica Antonia." She laughs. "I could be Madam Yeah, or *Girl Divine*."

I can see her having all those names and alter egos. And I can't stop laughing. "For now, do you want to just be my model? I've been sketching from photographs, and I really need you to sit for me to get everything right."

"Of course!" Antonia waltzes in front of the mirror and stares at herself. "Hair up or down?" she asks.

I get up from the bed and walk behind her. "Up," I say. "Your eyes and lips will be everything. I want to capture your personality through your face."

I love being around Antonia. Her energy makes me feel so alive.

She gets serious for a minute. "Why are you painting me?"

"You're important to me," I say. "I really appreciate and love you. I couldn't have gotten better without your help."

Antonia turns away from the painting and looks at me. "I should have never taken you to that bar. I should have known that you needed help."

"Stop feeling guilty. I mean it. I would have messed up anyway. You're such a great friend to me, and I support whatever you do. If you want to sing, I'll always be in the front row."

"I love you to Pluto," Antonia yells. "You're my girl!"

She's so crazy. I just laugh.

She gazes at me mischievously. "Do you want me to sit then?" She points to the couch on the other side of my room. "May I?"

"Of course," I say. "I'm so glad you're going to model for me. The painting is going to be—"

"Me!" Antonia shouts. "So…me!"

I genuinely feel happy. I don't think I realized how messed up my thinking had become about myself until I finally had to start talking to other people about my pain. The darkness is something I'll always have to live with, but that doesn't mean I have to suffer. No matter what happens, I can still choose to see the beauty in life.

forty-five

I'm finally going to be recognized for my own work.

Not because I'm the girlfriend or daughter of someone else. Or for punishing my body to fit society's expectations. This isn't about me being Colin Blakely's daughter or Zach's girl-friend. It isn't about how skinny or good-looking I am.

This is about me, about what comes from my soul.

It's time for the hard part now. Showing my paintings to everyone I know. I don't think I could ask for more beautiful people inside and out to help me. Antonia, Isko and Danny are helping me to do last-minute checks on my paintings.

The theme of my show is *Metamorphosis*.

It's inspired by LeFeber's advice to me—that all of us have to go through a transformation to find peace in our lives. Those words mean something so different to me now. I think of Frida and how she experienced so much pain. The polio that dam-aged her leg, the trolley accident that almost killed her, mis-carriages and the betrayal by her husband—yet she managed to transform that suffering into beauty. She defied her pain. She created something new.

Everything I've gone through in the past few months—the eating disorder and cutting, the breakup with Zach, the fights with Antonia and Sam, the media attention from the campaign, the crappy way I treated myself and others—I have to use that in my art. Pain isn't beauty, but pain can be *transformed* into something beautiful.

That's *my* metamorphosis.

That's what this whole show is about.

We're all running around, checking that the paintings and my artist statements look perfect on the wall, before the gallery opens for the show.

"Lola's going to try to hit me with her cane," Isko complains. "They better keep her *far* away from me. There's no way I'm letting her outshine you."

"I love Lola," Antonia says. "She reminds me of so many people I know."

"That's because you only know cranky old people," Isko says.

Antonia grimaces. "Your brother said you would be trouble today."

"I'm not trouble," Isko says as I check the last painting. "Well, okay, I am." He laughs. "Better me than Danilo or Jasmine though. *Someone* has to be the bad boy of the family."

"Has he always been this way?" Antonia asks.

"Ever since I've known him," Danny says.

I'm so glad Isko agreed to model for me. His free spirit and ability to be himself in front of anyone has always inspired me.

"Little boy better get his act together," Antonia says. "He has a lot of strutting to do in a few minutes. Everyone's going to be comparing the real you to that painting."

"Don't you worry," Isko says. "You'll be following my lead."

"Does he never stop?" Antonia asks.

"That was his way of saying he understands," I say.

"You're lucky I like you," Isko says to Antonia.

Antonia gives it right back. She points to me while smirking at Isko. "You're lucky *she* likes you."

Eva Wynn, the owner of the gallery, peeks her head into the room and taps her watch. "Five minutes until I open the doors. Are you ready?"

Anxiety whirls in the pit of my stomach.

"Yeah, I think so," I say.

"Don't be nervous," Danny says, giving me a hug. "Your paintings are beautiful. You can't worry what other people think of them or about you."

"Thanks, Danny. I don't know what I would have done without your encouragement. I'm so happy you're all here with me."

"We got you," Isko says.

Antonia nods in agreement.

The paintings of them look so amazing.

Even better than I expected.

Then I feel a tap on my shoulder and turn. It's Sam. My heart starts racing but in a good way, a calm way. He's wearing the suit I picked out for him and looks more handsome than ever. I can see he's doing so well in school. I mean, everything is going so well for him. I consider right then asking him to go out with me on a real date. But then I think about what LeFeber said about fallen angels—*we all must find our way to peace and health, even if we're an angel*—and also what my therapist recently told me, that broken people need to love themselves and heal themselves before they can truly love others, that love is the most healing medicine anyone can give to the self.

"I'm glad you're here, Sam," I say and give him a kiss on the cheek.

He smiles and says, "You're going to be great. You're all going to be great." He's so happy he's practically bouncing on his heels as he starts walking away. "I better go back outside.

Everyone's here. I think they need help keeping Lola under control."

"Believe me, they do," Isko says.

I laugh as Sam backs into the doorway, turns and exits.

Just then Eva comes back. "All right. It's showtime."

The announcer then goes through the lineup. I'm going third.

I'm excited for the show, but still not one hundred percent with my energy levels. In some ways, I feel like LeFeber when I saw him. He wasn't totally well either. A sick angel. Of course he was in worse shape than I am now. I can never forget him and what he did to inspire me and help me to learn so much about myself. I guess I thought art was just something that I was good at, but it's so much more than that. Art makes life on earth more meaningful. It's individuality. Self-expression. A way to understand the universe's infinite complexity.

I peek around the corner as Eva opens the doors to the gallery. Everyone's here. Mom, Dad, Sam, my brothers, Jasmine. The entire de los Santos family. Lola too, wearing all red. I recognize some students from AP art history who I would have never expected to come and support me. Ms. Day is here. And even Dr. Eleanor and my therapist in a distant corner with a handful of new friends from the treatment facility. I take a deep breath, concentrating on the music playing under the chatter of the crowd.

"Welcome, everyone, to the Wynn Gallery's New Talent Showcase. This is our inaugural year hosting exhibitions where we not only discover young, new talent but also showcase them and their work. We have another event planned for next weekend at our sister gallery in San Francisco, and the week after in Las Vegas. In total there are twenty-five shows, culminating in the final major event at our New York gallery. We're highlighting three teen artists today whose portfolios beat out dozens of applicants."

I space out for a moment, staring at the murmuring crowd.

"How are you feeling, Liv?" Danny whispers. "You got this?"

Now I know why LeFeber didn't want to be recognized at his shows. It's hard to have people looking at and judging your work in front of you, but I have to own this moment. "I'm so lucky," I say, letting out a breath.

Antonia winks at me.

Eva introduces the two other young artists featured in the show. Each of us has our own room filled with our work. With all the guests, the main room is nearly packed.

"Our next artist, Olivia Blakely, put together five paintings for her collection. Our judges loved what her art teacher had to say about her: 'She's always drawing. She not only understands the human form, Ms. Blakely understands how to plumb the depths of emotion and the necessity of transformation with her fantastic avian-inspired portraits.' Please give a round of applause for Olivia Blakely and *Metamorphosis!*"

I exchange glances with Ms. Day.

She gives me a huge smile and thumbs-up.

I silently mouth, *Thank you.* I'm so lucky to have had people believe in me before I could believe in myself.

Antonia smiles. "Your turn," she says. "Step up there."

I'm terrified. But for the first time in many months, I don't want to throw up. I don't want to cut myself. I just want to be. I just want to exist in the moment, the unbearable moment, because I can finally accept who I am. I can be proud of what I created.

"Ladies and gentlemen," Eva says, gesturing me over to the center of the room, "Olivia Blakely."

Now there's no turning back. No running away. No hurting myself. I'm the creator, the translator of this vision that so many people have helped me to create in one way or another.

I'm not alone. They're here to see what I've done as me, as someone who matters in this world.

I walk to the front of the room. I don't think about where my hands are, what my posture is, or whether or not I'm on the balls of my feet. I don't have to be beautiful or sexy. I just have to walk. People are cheering, and I'm embarrassed, and I stop and put my hands over my mouth. *It's okay*, I tell myself. *It's okay to do this*, and I start walking again. Everywhere are people with dreams, and I think how we all have them.

I make eye contact, wave to my friends, and I blow kisses to Sam, and to my brothers, and Mom and Dad, because I love them so much. In front of the crowd, I listen to the applause and breathe and smile and wipe my eyes and laugh and spin around once, twice, and I can't think of anything better in my life.

The crowd scatters out across the gallery to look at all the different pieces. I try not to pay attention. I'm worried that I could have done so much better had I been focused on pursuing my dreams all year. I could have put way more work into my paintings.

"You're going to be okay," Antonia says. It's like she's reading my mind. "Everyone's going to love you. You went through everything so you could be here, so you could be stronger, so you could create *this*."

She's right. I breathe. She's right. I can get through this.

Mom and Dad walk over and give me hugs.

"Congrats, honey," Mom says. "I'm so proud of you."

"You haven't even seen the paintings yet," I say, pointing to the other room. "They're back there."

While Dad's talking, I spot Royce and Jasmine talking to each other. He does something to make her laugh and puts his arm around her. They seem like they might be getting back together. I hope they don't let all the pressure of their future careers and Jas's immigration status keep them apart. There has to be a way for them to chase their own dreams *together*. I wonder what Jas will think of the painting I modeled after her.

Following Mom and Dad to the back room, I closely observe each of the five paintings. They're large portraits that incorporate magical realism, showing the people who are most important to me in the process of transforming into a bird that represents their unique personalities and life journeys. I tried to make the poses as dynamic as possible to illustrate the energy and movement of the transformation process.

"This is stunning," Dad says, standing in front of the first portrait.

It shows Jas posing with her back on the ground and her knees up in the air, tucked up by her chest and her legs pointing elegantly toward the sky like a dancer. She curves her arm, which becomes the swan's graceful neck, up back over her head, representing true beauty and the power of self-love.

Dad glances down at me. "Your work's impressive, Honeybee. Honestly. I didn't know your paintings were going to be this professional."

I almost pick a fight about how Dad has never supported my art, but I try to focus on the fact that he's complimenting me. The truth is that I probably wouldn't have shown him my work even if he had asked. It's not like LeFeber didn't have to face these kinds of trials either. I'm pretty lucky. His parents never believed in his work.

"Thanks, Dad. Does that mean I can go to art school for college?"

He smiles. "We'll see. There's still a year to figure things out."

Pointing at the second painting, Mom interrupts us. "That's hilarious!"

The portrait shows Isko looking happily surprised as he transforms into a chickadee. His shock of black hair juts out from his head like a fuzzy crown. He looks down at his hand, held up in shock, as it morphs into a wing. This painting's tone is more humorous than the portrait of Jas and shows Isko's cheerfulness and ability to express himself with joy.

Danilo comes up behind us. "You captured him perfectly," he says. "That's so his personality. He's never been afraid to be himself around anyone."

"I would have painted you too," I say. "Maybe I'll add your portrait next."

"That's okay." He puts his arm around me. "You already gave me the idea to make myself into my own action figure. Nerdy Pinoy Art Boy!"

We all move to the next portrait, which is of LeFeber as a nighthawk, twisting his wings in a powerful movement as if to create a tornado, illustrating how his words awakened me to another realm of creativity and self-exploration. Following his is a painting of Antonia wearing a backless, pale blue, floor-length gown made of airy organza. Her back is to us, but she's twisting her neck to look at the viewer knowingly, like she has a secret she can barely keep. Tiny blue feathers edged with gold sprout from her back.

She's my phoenix. My symbol of hope and rebirth.

When I come to the last painting, I start to get emotional. It's my double self-portrait. Each side of the painting shows my profile. One is a black heron. The other is a white heron. The white heron, my light side, throws up her feathered arm, reaching for her dark counterpart, my dark side. The black heron turns away, using its wing to shield itself from the light. They're in a battle, a dance, a struggle for existence. One can't live with or without the other.

I'll never get rid of the voice that tells me I'm not good enough. I wouldn't want to. The depth of the darkness is as important to my story as the triumph of the light.

Feeling two arms wrap around my waist, I spin around, expecting to see Sam messing with me, but I find Jasmine. She squeezes me so tight and with so much love, I cry a little. Jas has been a sister to me for what feels like half of my life. I've missed her and our friendship so much this year.

"Look at you, Liv! You did the thing," Jas says.

"I'm so glad you came! You're probably cramming for finals."

"I wouldn't miss this for the world."

"Are you graduating this semester?"

"Yep," Jas says, crossing her arms. "Then I have to figure out what's next."

"That's scary."

"It'll work out. It's just figuring out all the details."

"Are you still applying to medical schools?" I ask.

"Yeah, but I'm trying to keep my options open. Royce convinced me to apply to some schools in the countries where he's applying for reporting bureau jobs."

"That's great," I say. "I didn't know you guys were back together."

"I'm practicing what Lola Cherry calls 'flexibility.' I've always been good at going for what I want, but sometimes that makes me blind to other parts of my life." She turns her attention to the painting. "This one is my favorite. It's so honest."

I lean my head on her shoulder. "Thanks. Facing myself was the hardest thing I've done."

Suddenly, Eva approaches me with another older woman at her side. She has completely white hair styled in a fashionable pixie cut and she's wearing funky ruby-red glasses and red Lucite bangles around her wrists. "This is Phyllis Simonson," Eva says. "She's part of the faculty at CalArts and served on the selection committee for the show."

"It's a pleasure to meet you, Liv," Phyllis says.

"CalArts is such a great school," I say. "Didn't Tim Burton go there?"

"Many of our students go on to exciting careers in the arts and entertainment industry." Phyllis laughs. "I don't mean to go around sounding like a talking billboard. I was just saying to Eva here that I think your work is astounding. Are you thinking of applying to schools right now?"

Jas crinkles her forehead and silently mouths, *Go for it!*

I want to tell her how much I'd love to go to art school next year, but I know I'm not ready yet. I need some more time to heal and sort my life out.

"I'm only a junior," I say. "But I'm starting to look into schools."

"Well," Phyllis says, "I'd love for you to consider applying for our summer program. I'm more than happy to put in a good word for you."

"That sounds amazing," I gush. "I can definitely do that."

It would be incredible to go to school with other teenagers who want to paint, not just random people at my high school who happen to take art for an elective. Plus, I wouldn't have to go far away, so I could also go to my outpatient meetings and stay at home. Which means Mom and Dad would probably let me go.

"The application is due soon. Don't forget!" Phyllis says before Eva whisks her away to another part of the gallery.

I see food being wheeled in. For some reason my whole family is still hanging around. Usually at least one of them is busy and has to take off before an event is over, but even Dad is still here.

An announcement booms over the chatter of the crowd. It's Royce—he's in the middle of the main room. "Hey, everyone. Many of you know the party hasn't started yet, but if you don't know, then stick around. We're having a dance party in honor of you all, courtesy of my family, especially my dad, Congressman Blakely. So hang out, have some fun, and thank you, Mrs. Wynn, for allowing us to use the space."

After he puts down the microphone, Royce comes over to me and leans in. "What do you think about the surprise?"

"Dad *would* turn this into a campaign event." I laugh.

I'm not even mad. I'm just happy everyone I love is together.

"Oh no," he says. "I just said that as an explanation. There's a more important reason."

"What's that?" I ask.

He looks down at me and puts an arm around my shoulders. "You."

I lean into him. "What do you mean me?"

"Dad wanted to do something special for you, but I couldn't just go up there and embarrass you and say you've been ill. So, we thought we'd be a little sneakier about it. Gotta admit, it's a big party. Everyone's here." He looks across the room to Jasmine.

She sees him and smiles, then waves at me and runs over.

"I'm so proud of you," she says. "You're becoming everything I knew you would, and in such a short time. What do you think the judges are going to say?"

"I don't know," I say. "All the other artists were so impressive. I feel good about everything. Being shown here made me feel like a real artist."

Jasmine leans in. "You *are* a real artist. You always have been."

Just then Isko goes flying past into the arms of all his friends.

"You see that?" Danilo says, sneaking up behind me and giving me a hug. "That kind of popularity will come crashing down as soon as they realize he's just someone's little brother someday."

"Someone's jealous," Jasmine says.

Danilo smiles. "Only a little. I just never knew that many people. I still don't."

"Let me kiss this girl!" says Lola, walking up to me with her cane. I swear she doesn't even need it. She practically dances across the room to give me a hug.

Jasmine's mom and dad wave to me. Mr. de los Santos says, "Lola, don't put your lips on that girl. She doesn't want to wear your lipstick."

"I saw a lot of boys who would wear my lipstick without even kissing me," says Lola.

I start laughing as Lola kisses me, her bright red lipstick smearing across my cheek. "You become a big-time artist and I'll model for you," she says. "I like posing. I might even bring some boyfriends."

"Lola," Danilo says. "Why do you have to always be the center of attention?"

"I'm not!" Lola points with her cane to Isko, who's dancing in the middle of a pack of his friends, everyone bouncing up and down, laughing.

"I don't have a lot of energy," I say, "but that's not stopping me from going over there." I see Sam nearby. He's trying to give me space, but I want to be near him.

I walk over and grab his hand. "Come on, hot stuff."

"Me?" he says. "I don't know how to dance."

"Either dance with me or Lola," I say.

Lola Cherry smiles at Sam.

"Okay, let's go," Sam says. "But don't get mad if I slow dance with her later."

forty-six

I'm driving myself to the marina today. I got my license a week ago.

Mom and Dad bought me a Mini Cooper. It's my favorite color, a light aquamarine blue. It feels good to drive. Now I finally can give my friends rides instead of having to beg to get picked up all the time.

I'm meeting Sam to say goodbye.

He's leaving for Costa Rica to work at the surf camp for the rest of the summer.

In the seat next to me is a letter from CalArts that came in the mail. I haven't opened the envelope yet. I wanted to wait until I was alone to open it.

Parking in the lot at Marina del Rey, I grab the letter and start walking to our bench. The weather is perfectly cool. Seagulls wander around on the sea rocks. Boats slip along the harbor way.

I start thinking about the future. Sam said he's excited to be a senior. He can't wait to get high school over with and go to college to study physics. Antonia wants to pursue singing after school. I told her we would always be friends, always be close, no matter how far across the world our dreams might take us from each other.

Therapy is still a constant. I mean, I'm a lot better, consistently improving. I love the new friends I've made, mostly girls who have faced similar things. It's nice to know I'm not alone. I'm not unique. Everyone struggles with one thing or another.

The campaign is in full swing, but Mom and Dad decided that no matter what happens with the election, I'll stay here for my senior year to keep working on my recovery. Dad's barely leading in the polls. He teases me that it's closer now because I'm literally not standing behind him. I told Dad I was grateful that he was keeping my illness out of the media. At the same time, I know one day I'll want people to know that I struggled and overcame something that so many others are still in the middle of.

Dad even made me put a campaign bumper sticker on the car. VOTE FOR THE FUTURE. VOTE BLAKELY. So embarrassing to have your name plastered on your own car. Whatever. I don't mind. I'm loving my family again—the way I'm supposed to.

Mom's a lot better. I can see her being herself again. She even takes time off from the campaign to work on her own projects. I told her I want to help with her literacy campaign again soon. It's not like my goofy brothers are around enough. Not with Royce applying for jobs and Mason off on an important firm assignment overseas.

Our bench at the marina is empty. I sit down.

I look at the ocean again, watch a few more boats, then turn my attention back to the letter. I turn it over and think how it's just a piece of paper. Just words.

When I tear it open, I'm sort of shocked.

CalArts doesn't want me to attend the summer program.

Why not? I hold my breath. I have to tell myself to breathe.

That's why I'm here. I have to keep myself under control, under the breath of the ocean and sky.

Finally, I turn my eyes back to the letter, read further.

What's this?

They want me to enter their regular program? *Now?*

They want to know if they can help me get my high school diploma early. They said they would help me earn high school credits through summer programs, that if everything worked out, I could enter their visual arts program within a few months.

Their exact words about my paintings:

Your work displays deft skill, maturity of subject and superior quality compared to other students of your age. We are confident that you will benefit from the mentoring and instruction that you would receive through our school and excellent academic programs in addition to exposure to outlets in the industry.

If you decide to decline the offer this year, CalArts still invites you to attend the prestigious California Summer School for the Arts.

The letter goes on to explain details about the registration. My head goes back and I inhale the ocean air. I kind of always thought I would move to New York, but I love Los Angeles too. It's a big part of who I am. I can't stop smiling. I'm happy I proved to myself that I could follow dreams and succeed. For a long time I didn't think I could. I guess that gemstone has been in me longer than I thought.

At the same time, I'm not sure that I'm ready. I still have so much recovering to do, so much to work on to find a healthy balance for my life.

I see Sam walking down the path so I tuck the letter into my purse and wave.

I'm not ready to tell him about the acceptance yet.

I just want today to be about us.

"What are you smiling about?" he asks as he sits down next to me.

"Nothing." I smile. "Just happy to see you."

"Yeah," he says. "Me too. Me too."

I see another boat. It's my turn to dream. "I like that one," I say. "It has a perfect sail. I'm going to pilot it all the way to Hawaii. We can take shifts. Or we can just take our time and rest in the open sea."

"And race dolphins," he says. "Or keep sailing all the way around the world."

We've gotten pretty close this last month. I wouldn't call it dating. I'm enjoying living in the moment with him. We haven't really gotten physical yet—I'm still trying to figure out how to be comfortable in my body—but spending so much time with him is teaching me how to be more emotionally vulnerable, how to trust others with my pain.

"I have a surprise for you," Sam says.

"What?" I nudge him with my shoulder. "Another one?"

He pops up from the bench and grabs my hand. "There's a guy my parents know who has a sailboat docked here," he says. "He told me I could borrow it. What do you say? Want to sail? It'll be like old times."

"I don't think I remember how to do anything!" I say, but he's pulling me behind him as he bounds toward the dock.

We stop at a small wooden sailboat that's about thirty feet long and has yellow and white striped sails. Sam helps me step onto the boat and gives me a few directions to help ready the sails. After a few minutes, Sam turns on the motor and guides the boat out of the dock. We get a little way away from the harbor before the wind begins to pick up.

"Raise the sails!" Sam shouts.

I loosen the tension on the rope until Sam tells me to secure it. The boat runs with the wind. We pick up speed fast, slicing through the blue waves.

"Want to steer?" Sam asks. "It's easy. Remember that the boat turns the opposite direction you move the tiller. If you want to go right, move the tiller to the left."

He steps aside and sits next to me while I steer the boat.

It's exhilarating. The wind blows my hair back. The cool air and sunshine cradle my skin. I don't feel caged or punished by my body. I feel alive in it. I feel perfectly free.

"Where is this going?" Sam asks, and I know he isn't talking about the boat. "What do you want for us? Where is this going?"

"What's wrong with this?" I say. "It's our place. Always has been."

I grab his hand and squeeze while moving the tiller with my other.

Looking out at the sea, I reflect on the past year. I've spent so much time obsessing on my own imperfections that I haven't been able to love the people who have always truly cared for me. I lean my head on Sam's shoulder, thinking about our future. I don't feel completely well yet, but I know I'm getting better. I'm sure that I'll feel capable of romantically loving someone again. I want to date him, but I still need some time.

There's someone I have to learn how to love first.

Me.

★ ★ ★ ★ ★

author's note

This book is dedicated to those who are very dear to me who have suffered in the way Liv Blakely suffered. Thank you for sharing your stories with me. I hope I honored them well. All my gratitude for helping make the manuscript as strong as it could be. All mistakes and flaws in the telling are my own.

A few notes on the art in the novel.

LeFeber's fictional installation near the end was partially inspired by two different modern art pieces:

Sun Yuan and Peng Yu's *Angel*
Laura Belém's *The Temple of a Thousand Bells*

The LACMA installation described in the book is Chris Burden's *Urban Light*, one of my favorite works of art.

The concepts for Liv's paintings were entirely made up, although there is a long history of bird–human hybrids/transformations in art.

acknowledgments

So many thanks to all the wonderful people in my book life (and real life!), especially my genius editor, Natashya Wilson, my agent and consigliere, Richard Abate, and the awesome Rachel Kim at 3Arts and my fabulous publicity and marketing peeps, Bryn Collier, Shara Alexander and Siena Konçsol at Harlequin. Thank you to my family and my family of friends. Love to all my readers.

How many will it take to find The One?
Keep reading for a sneak peek at Melissa de la Cruz's next novel
29 Dates!
Only from Inkyard Press.

prologue:
the 29th date

NAME: Kang Dae-Hyun
INTERESTS: Debate, Environmental Science, Lacrosse
ACCOMPLISHMENTS: Lacrosse Team Captain, Salutatorian

JI-SU: Hey, I'm Ji-Su.

DAE-HYUN: I'm Dae-Hyun.

JI-SU: Korean name! But you're born and raised here?

DAE-HYUN: Yup, and you moved from Seoul not that long ago?

JI-SU: Yeah, my parents decided it would be a good idea for me to become a last-minute exchange student and sent me across the Pacific to San Francisco. And here we are now.

DAE-HYUN: I'm not even going to try to relate. I can't imagine moving to a whole new country.

JI-SU: It hasn't been the easiest. But I've met people along the way who've made it worth it.

DAE-HYUN: This is gonna sound silly, but I actually feel a little nervous right now.

JI-SU: For real? It's like we're just hanging out!

DAE-HYUN: I know, but it's my first *seon*. Even just saying that makes it sound official and formal. And you're making me nervous. I even asked some friends for dating tips.

JI-SU: And what did they tell you?

DAE-HYUN: That kindness is underrated. And common likes and dislikes are key. Heavy emphasis on the common dislikes. So, you've been on a lot of *seons,* both here and in Seoul?

JI-SU: Yeah, but none of them have worked out...clearly. I did meet some cool guys and I'm actually friends with some of them. But there was never really that chemistry with anyone, you know? I love meeting new people, but I'm kind of over *seons*, to be honest.

DAE-HYUN: I bet the right guy could be the end of all *seons* for you. You seem to know what you want.

JI-SU: What do you want? What are you trying to get out of these *seons*?

DAE-HYUN: Actually, I have a girlfriend, which might really screw me up in the long run if I keep sneaking out. I'm only going on these dates to appease my mother. She kinda hates my girlfriend.

JI-SU: Oh, that's too bad. I actually thought this might go somewhere.

DAE-HYUN: Well, it was nice knowing ya, Jees.

JI-SU: Did you just call me Jees? I hate nicknames. Especially when someone you just met assigns you one.

Chapter 1

The big red 79 percent circled at the top of Ji-Su Kim's history exam wasn't what worried her. It wasn't the fact that she had actually studied hard. It wasn't Mrs. Han's look of concern that made her anxious either. No, it was the disappointment on her parents' faces that Ji-Su could so clearly imagine that made her want to crumple up the exam, crawl under her desk and curl into a ball. She didn't want to let them down.

So, this is how you're going to start the school year? Don't you know how important senior year of high school is? How do you plan on getting accepted into a top school here, or any university in America for that matter? Even if you want to move halfway across the world, your grades still have to be strong. Ji-Su could practically hear her parents' endless nagging, their *jansori*.

There it was in bloodred, mocking her. Only 79 percent. A solid C+! Couldn't Mrs. Han have bumped her over by just one point so that she could squeak by with a B-? The number nine was truly the worst. Anything ending in nine for her was the height of unlucky. Close, but no cigar—almost there, but not good enough. She would've felt equally miserable if she'd gotten 59 percent, 69 percent or even 89 percent. *Actually if I got 89 percent, I would be really happy,* Ji-Su thought. *Except that it's just one point shy of getting a 90 percent. And anything in the nineties is close enough to 100 percent, but still not perfect! Ugh.*

Her parents were the type to question even a 100 percent grade by asking why she didn't get 110 percent—wasn't there extra credit?

"Dae-bak!" Min Park exclaimed, smiling as she looked at her exam. "I didn't even study," she bragged.

Ji-Su peered at Min's test. An 86 percent—a solid B. You didn't need perfect scores to become a pop star, which was Min's dream. How could Ji-Su have done worse than a girl whose life was dedicated to selfies and singing classes?

Ji-Su slid her exam into her notebook so that no one could see. If only she could retake the exam, restart the year and redo all of high school.

"Ji-Su, don't tell me you failed the first exam of the year," Min said as she reapplied her lip-gloss.

"I didn't fail," Ji-Su muttered. And technically she hadn't. One could even argue that she'd scored several points *above* passing. This argument, of course, would never fly with her parents.

"Then how did you do? Why won't you say what you got?" Min never did know when to shut up.

"Oh Min, mind your own business," Euni chimed from behind them.

For as long as Ji-Su could remember, Eunice Ho had always had her back. Euni was born seven days before Ji-Su and, aside from that one week, the two girls had always been in each other's lives, growing up on the same street in Apgujeong, taking the same classes at Daewon Foreign Language High School and enduring every extracurricular activity that their parents pushed onto them. Painting, archery, French, ballet—they were privileged to be exposed to an array of arts and cultures, but more often than not, it felt too deliberate, like they were being groomed to replace their parents in society. Like a boot camp for the upper class. Academics came naturally for Euni, but not so much for Ji-Su. Still, every time Ji-Su fell behind, Euni was there to help her catch up. She was also there for her whenever Min got a little too out of hand, which was often.

"This test was actually really hard," Euni said. "I didn't think I would even finish in time." She was lying through her teeth. All three of them knew that she'd gotten the highest score in the class, as she always did. Euni was a great student but a terrible liar, and Ji-Su loved her for it.

Ji-Su thought about the weekend she had wasted sitting at *hagwon* like a prisoner, doing her school homework and then chipping away at all the additional readings and exercises from her *hagwon* tutors. She could've walked around GangNam alongside the Han River and taken photos on her brand new DSLR. But no, this would've disappointed her parents. *If you spent the same amount of time studying as you do with your camera, your class ranking would be much higher.* If Ji-Su knew anything about herself, it was that she was definitely not the academic type.

"Euni, you're lucky I don't actually try," Min said as she checked her reflection in her compact. "You would have serious competition if I ever opened one of these books."

"No one would want you to." Ji-Su pushed the eraser end of her pencil into Min's contoured forehead. "You might grow wrinkles from thinking too much. Then you'd look like Euni and me, and no record label would ever sign you."

Euni laughed and even Min couldn't help cracking a smile. Ji-Su felt better immediately. Wasn't this how you were supposed to spend your time in high school? Enjoying time with your friends, instead of getting caught up in your anxious thoughts about the future?

"Class, settle down." Mrs. Han's booming voice cut through the chatter. "This exam was a tough one, but I don't want you to be discouraged. Senior year is the most important year. I cannot emphasize this enough. College, your career, your future—the beginning of a great new chapter is about to start. Isn't that exciting?"

It was not exciting.

It was absolutely terrifying. Ji-Su looked at her classmates and could imagine everyone's future but hers. As annoying as Min could be, she was talented. Eventually her perfectly symmetrical face, with her expressive eyes and natural pout, would be plastered over every bus and subway stop in Seoul as part of a major ad campaign for her hit album. It was only a matter of time. Euni's perfect grades meant Harvard or Seoul National University for sure. Then there was the rest of them—there were rumors that Mark Lee would follow his brothers' footsteps to Oxford. Sung Choi was a shoo-in for Yonsei, one of the top universities in Seoul, while Soon-Jung Kang had spent the last three summers playing cello at the prestigious Interlochen Arts Program, making strides with his fellow camp members in securing admission to Juilliard. And everyone knew Yo-Han Wan was flunking, but he was from a chaebol family, so a generous donation would get him into Seoul National University and he'd eventually take over the family business.

But Ji-Su? What was next for her?

Her phone buzzed, alerting her to an e-mail from Ms. Mak, the Matchmaker. Aka the *MatSeon* Queen. Ms. Mak came from a family of matchmakers. It could easily be argued that Ms. Mak, her mother and her aunt were collectively responsible for the social infrastructure of Seoul's upper class. Ms. Mak was well into her sixties, but her excellent psychological profiling skills, along with the consistent pulse she had on pop culture and trending topics, made her successful in pairing off couples left and right, for several decades and counting.

Dear Ji-Su,

This is a courtesy reminder of your *seon* with Noah Ko tonight at 7:00 p.m. at the 10 Corso Como Cafe. Noah's one-sheet is attached again for your review. Please confirm receipt of this e-mail. I hope the two of you have a wonderful time.

Warm wishes,

Ms. Mak

Ughhhh. It wasn't bad enough that Ji-Su wasn't getting good grades at school. After several recommendations from her peers, Ji-Su's mother had hired Ms. Mak and had been sending her daughter on *seons* all summer in the hopes that she might at least snatch a promising boyfriend who would turn into a promising fiancé who would then become a promising husband and complete every Korean mother's idea of a picture-perfect life for her daughter.

But summer had come to an end and Ji-Su had not made a love match. Another flop.

If you can't get into a top college, you should at least date someone who can. Her mother's nagging *jansori* was inescapable. Both her parents' voices were like buzzing mosquitos that wouldn't leave her alone. But she had no choice other than to comply. The *MatSeon* Matchmaker was highly selective about which clients she took on and certainly not cheap. With Ji-Su's not-so-promising high school transcript, her parents likely had pulled some strings to get her on the exclusive client list. Ji-Su hadn't asked for any of this; her parents were doing it all for her. And if she did want anything, it was to be a good daughter. To make all their efforts worth it.

"You have another date?" Euni asked. "I thought your mom said the *seons* were just for the summer."

"Yeah, but none of them turned into anything, which was definitely not my mother's plan." Ji-Su opened the e-mail attachment.

NOAH KO. Occupations: Student, founder of start-up, poet. Education: Stanford University (currently taking a gap year to manage unexpected early success of his start-up and also focus on writing).

It was impressive, like the others, and went on and on with a list of his accomplishments. Ji-Su cringed at the thought of whatever overload of information her mother had sent to Ms. Mak so she could put together her profile.

Ji-Su Kim. Average student. Pretty enough (Min's makeup lessons helped). No real accomplishments (she is seventeen—give her a break).

The truth was she was just an ordinary, average teen. She liked all the things many girls her age liked—*Stranger Things*, selfies, slime videos on Insta, romcoms, candy. And disliked the same things everyone disliked—acne, rude people, those ugly clothes emblazoned with 'empowering' statements. (Seriously, who were they kidding with the $800 "*The Future is Female*" T-shirts?)

Cute boys were in the plus column for sure, but so many of the *seon* guys she met were so serious that, even if they were cute, it almost didn't matter. Her father liked to joke that any guy with an expensive car was handsome.

"Are you sure you're just not being picky?" Euni teased. "What happened to the one with the restaurateur parents?"

"Oh, I remember that one. He was cute!" Min said. "If you didn't like him, you should've set him up with me. A nationally beloved songstress and the heir to Korea's top restaurants—we'd be an amazing power couple."

"I don't know, Min. He was kind of full of himself and kept checking out his reflection. But that's something you guys have in common, so maybe it would work out!" Ji-Su laughed.

"What does the guy you're seeing tonight look like?" Euni reached for Ji-Su's phone. "Isn't there a photo that comes with the resume?"

"Wait, the date is tonight?" Min asked. "I got us those tickets to this week's *Music Bank* taping. You guys said you were coming with me!" She rolled her eyes and let out a dramatic, heavy sigh.

Ji-Su and Euni exchanged a guilty glance. They *had* promised. And unlike the poorly attended open mics and overcrowded celebrity meet-and-greets that Min usually dragged her friends to, *Music Bank* was actually an exciting show that Euni and Ji-Su looked forward to. Many of their favorite pop stars would be performing back-to-back. Ji-Su always watched it on TV, but the thought of being at the studio, right there with her favorite artists, filled her with excitement.

"Oh yeah, that's right. Ji-Su, can't you just reschedule?" Euni tapped Ji-Su's phone and enlarged the attached headshot. "Or cancel?" Euni frowned. "He's not that cute anyway."

Ji-Su grabbed her phone back and looked at the picture on the screen. She wished for a reaction—her heart beating faster, a tiny stomach flip, anything. But her body remained static. There was nothing. He wasn't *not* cute. He just looked like every other squeaky-clean, accomplished, coiffed son of a well-off family.

Sorry, Ms. Mak. I need to reschedule. I have *hagwon* until late in the evening today.

Ji-Su hit Send and felt a wave of relief. She had spent the whole summer going on dead-end dates and had wasted last weekend studying for a test she would've never aced. One night of fun couldn't hurt.

When Ji-Su stepped out of the elevator and into her family's apartment, she was relieved to see that all the lights were out. She carefully removed her shoes at the foyer and slid into her house slippers. From the top floor of their apartment in Daechi-dong, Ji-Su could see the rest of the Gangnam neighborhood below her. A stream of traffic lit up the Dongbu Expressway. The red and white lights of buses, trucks and cars ambled alongside the shimmering waters of the Tancheon.

It was way too late to say that she was coming home from *hag-won*. She had texted out a full, elaborate lie five different ways before simply letting her parents know she was seeing a late movie with her friends. That was all it took for them to believe her.

Ji-Su's ears were still ringing from the concert, which only exaggerated the complete silence surrounding her. Every creak of the wooden floor loudly announced her presence. She held her breath, crept into the living room and peeked at the white leather couch to make sure her father hadn't fallen asleep there while waiting for her to come home. She exhaled quietly. He wasn't there, slouched on one side like he was sometimes. As she made her way into the kitchen, she imagined her mother seated at one of the high stools with her arms crossed atop the cold marble island top. *Don't be awake. Please don't be awake.* But there was no night-light left on, and neither parent was waiting for her. *Thank god.*

Ji-Su grabbed a sheet mask from the fridge and scurried to her room. *Finally.* After placing her phone and camera on her nightstand and changing into pajamas, she crawled into her bed and sprawled her limbs out, as if to stretch and rid her body of the entire weight of the day.

Her phone vibrated. It was a text from Min.

Ji!! Did you get home safe?

Usually Euni was the one who checked to make sure everyone safely returned home.

Also don't forget to send me the photos from tonight!

Ji-Su smiled. Of course. Min really just wanted the photos. Ji-Su sat up, ripped open the sheet mask package and then aligned the mask on her face so that she could properly see and breath out of the eye and nose cutouts. The refreshing smell of cucumber and aloe almost immediately put Ji-Su at ease. The mask was nice and cold and would reduce any puffiness in her features, eliminating evidence of how late she'd stayed out. She caught her reflection in the mirror and laughed. Looking like a wide-eyed and extremely innocent killer from *Friday the 13th* was never not hilarious.

She lay down again so that the sheet mask wouldn't slide off her face. Holding her camera directly over her head, Ji-Su scrolled through her photos. Min dancing, Euni laughing. All the shots of Min were perfectly posed, but somehow still looked candid. How many selfies did it take for her to figure out her best angles? Euni, the stay-home-and-watch-a-movie type, looked like she'd had fun, too. And of course there were the shameless selfies. The three of them cheesing hard, having a good time. Why did having a fun night with friends have to feel so illicit? What was the point of killing yourself to have a "happy, successful life"—whatever that meant—if you couldn't relax once in a while?

And who got to define what a "happy and successful" future looked like?

There was no greater failure than being a senior at Daewon High School and not knowing your five-year plan.

Ji-Su's eyelids grew heavy. She took off her sheet mask, pressed the cold cucumber and aloe goo into her skin and fell fast asleep.

When Ji-Su stepped into the kitchen the next morning and found her parents seated at the dining table with stern looks on their faces, every drop of euphoria from the night before evaporated into thin air. Her limbs grew heavy, and making her way to the table felt like dragging a ton of bricks. She was caught. Of course they knew. How could she have thought for a second that she'd get away with it? Ji-Su seated herself at the table and braced for impact.

"I hope the *Music Bank* concert was fun, because that is the last one you will be going to," Mrs. Kim said as she dipped a spoon into her cup and stirred the tea. Straight to the point. As always. Had Ji-Su's parents have her followed? It honestly wouldn't be surprising if they had.

"Min wants to be a silly pop star, so at least it makes sense for her to go." Mrs. Kim turned to her husband, talking to him as if their daughter wasn't sitting right in front of them. "I'm surprised Euni went. Usually she is good about these things. Her mother will not be happy to hear about this."

Ji-Su gritted her teeth. She could take her mother's endless *jansori*, but she couldn't stand it when she dared to talk about her friends.

"Oh, so *now* you're upset?" Mrs. Kim stared at Ji-Su, whose clenched jaw was probably telegraphing "attitude problem" to her mother. "Now that you've been caught ignoring your responsibilities and coming home late, but not when you barely passed your first exam of the school year?" Ji-Su's exam was still in her backpack, which she'd had with her all night. Her mother must have called Mrs. Han.

"Umma, please. I wasn't happy with my score either," Ji-Su protested. She looked down at her folded hands. "But it wasn't that low of a score. I am really trying. I'll do better on the next one. I'm sorry I can't be perfect."

"Perfect?" Her mother sighed. "No one is asking you to be perfect. It would be more than enough for you to score higher than your class average. But apparently even that is too much to ask."

Her father placed a hand on her mother's shoulder as if putting a brake on his wife's anger. Ji-Su's father was the calm, rational one between the two of them. These were the roles they played: Mrs. Kim as the mother with impossibly high standards and a sharp tongue, Mr. Kim as the father whose disappointment was quiet, but just as devastating, and of course Ji-Su as the disappointing daughter.

"And the *seon* that you missed..." Mrs. Kim sighed again. "A lot of time and energy goes into preparing a meeting with these potential boyfriends. When you blow one off, it's disrespectful to Ms. Mak. It's disrespectful to your date. It's disrespectful to us."

Ji-Su's chest tightened, and all of a sudden it felt hard to breathe. Her arms tensed as if they were wrapped up in a straitjacket. Doing well in school, getting into a good college... Ji-Su could understand why her parents put pressure on her with academics. But orchestrating her love life was taking their obsessive parenting to the next level. She wanted to scream, but frustration paralyzed her. She could only muster a few words.

"Umma, I spent the whole summer going to every single *seon*. I only asked to reschedule yesterday's." Ji-Su dared to look at her mother. "What if I don't *want* to meet anyone through some arranged matchmaker?"

"You want a perfect romance to fall into your lap?"

"Isn't that what happened with you and Dad? That's literally the story of how you guys met," Ji-Su shot back.

She was right. Her mother had been walking across campus when she was knocked over by a group of students protesting the bloody outcome of the Gwangju Uprising. The protest was led by none other than Mr. Kim. Ji-Su's mother had just checked out an armful of books on the Medici family for her research on the birth of entrepreneurship in art, and they were strewn about on the ground. By the time Ji-Su's father picked up each one, he'd gathered enough courage to ask her on a date.

But that was a different time. Mrs. Kim was no longer an art-history scholar, and Mr. Kim's protesting days were long behind him.

Mrs. Kim furrowed her brows and placed her hands on her temples. "Finding a partner today holds the same kind of importance as finding a job. Do you think meeting someone who comes from a good family, has a great education and a fantastic job lined up is just as easy as bumping into them on the street?" Mrs. Kim cupped Ji-Su's face in her hands. "Ji-Su-ya, listen to me. Nothing happens if you sit around and wait. Nothing will work until you do. Every decision you make now affects your future. With school, even with the *seons*."

"Ji-Su, we are supporting you in every way we can," Mr. Kim chimed in, making his best diplomatic effort. He was always the olive branch between Ji-Su and her mother. Ji-Su knew in her heart that her parents wanted her to be happy. She knew that her own optimism and faith in the world were things her parents loved about her, but they worried that she would be hurt by what they saw as her naiveté. Still, at the end of the day, both her parents were going to be supportive of whatever she wanted to do with her life…so long as she was first accepted by the best college she could get into. This logic probably had its roots in her mother and father having studied in not-so-lucrative fields—art history and philosophy respectively—but having done so at Seoul Nation University, the top school in South Korea. The reputation of their alma mater had helped them as they'd both made their way to become head data analysts at the Han Group, one of the most reputable conglomerates in the country.

Mr. Kim looked at his daughter with sympathy, as if he too felt the very growing pains he was putting his daughter through. "If your grades aren't improving and you're skipping out on your *seons*—you can see how we might get upset. We're just asking you to try."

"But I am trying!" Ji-Su cried. "I'm doing my best!"

"Exactly," Mrs. Kim snapped. "Your best at Daewon is not good enough, which is why your appa and I are sending you to Lick Wilmerding High School in San Francisco."

Ji-Su stared at her mother in disbelief. Surely she had to be joking. An empty threat to scare her. But her mother's perfectly unwrinkled porcelain face remained stoic.

"San Francisco? *America*? Why?"

Mr. Kim slid a folder across the dining table. The logo on the front showed a roaring tiger perched above the letters *LWHS*, all outlined in gold.

"What is this?" Ji-Su asked, genuinely confused.

"After the start of the semester last March, your father and I looked into applying for you to potentially attend a school in the States," Mrs. Kim explained.

"We know and understand how tough it is to stand out at a competitive school like Daewon." Mr. Kim looked at his daughter with kind, encouraging eyes but didn't help to dilute Ji-Su's confusion. "It isn't too late for you to spend your final year at a somewhat easier but still highly reputable school in the States."

"When we received your midsemester review in May, we went ahead with the application. And it's a good thing we did, given your scores at the end of the term," Mrs. Kim said.

"My scores weren't *that* bad last semester," Ji-Su said. But she quickly saw the bigger picture, the grand scheme her parents had been cooking up.

Her scores truly hadn't been so bad last term. They were barely above her class average, which was an issue. At any other high school in Seoul, her scores would be great, but at Daewon, where only the best were admitted, she was struggling to stand out as a promising college candidate.

This explained the high volume of seons that Mrs. Kim had made Ji-Su attend. Ms. Mak really had been working overtime in setting her up on as many dates as possible during the few weeks of summer break in July and August. Clearly it had been a last-ditch attempt to pair her up with someone before her pending school year abroad.

"Why didn't you tell me any of this?" The thumping in Ji-Su's chest seemed to grow louder. Her head throbbed, as if someone had hit her with a large steel hammer. How could her parents betray her like this?

"Ji-Su, we don't want you to leave Seoul." Mrs. Kim placed

a hand on her daughter's. "We didn't want it so much that we kept holding off in case you might be able to pull yourself up. But I don't think we have much of a choice now, and this is the last window of opportunity to make the transfer to Lick."

Mr. Kim opened the brochure like a salesman would to a potential customer. "Their academic year doesn't start until September. The orientation for international students is happening this week, but you'll arrive just in time for the first day of school, so the change won't feel so abrupt."

"I don't know how this could feel anything but abrupt, Appa." Ji-Su crossed her arms. She felt so dizzy that she could pass out.

Being grounded, no allowance, having her phone taken away—Ji-Su was willing to endure any of those punishments. But being exiled halfway around the world by her own parents was so unnecessarily harsh. Ji-Su placed a hand on the school brochure. It didn't disappear into thin air. This wasn't a bad dream. It was really happening. She tried to keep a straight face, but her eyes started to well up.

"Don't cry," Mrs. Kim said. "Your face will get red and swollen. You don't want to look like a mess walking through the airport."

"*What*?" Ji-Su pulled her hand away. She let the hot tears fall down her face. When exactly was the first day at school at Lick? How soon were her parents going to kick her out of the country?

"Ji-Su-ya, this is painful for us, too." Mrs. Kim sighed. "But your appa and I are doing it for you."

For you. Each time her parents said those two words, Ji-Su's guilt doubled. It weighed on her shoulders and sank to the bottom of her stomach. The burden of expectation was already too much to bear, but now she had to carry it across the ocean to San Francisco. Sisyphus had nothing on Ji-Su. Or was it Prometheus? Ugh. At least with the last-minute continent move, Ji-Su wouldn't have to take the classics exam next week.

Mr. Kim ushered his daughter out of her seat. "I was able to get you on a flight this afternoon, so get your things together."

"Appa, please don't do this," Ji-Su begged. "I'm sorry! I'll do better, I promise. What about my friends? I can't even say goodbye?"

"Ji-Su-ya, calm down. You'll see them at Christmas." Mrs. Kim stood and smoothed the wrinkles from her tweed skirt. "Until then, you can think fondly about all the fun you had with them last night."

Ji-Su dragged herself to her room, each step feeling infinitely heavier than the last. On her desk was the Korean-to-English dictionary she used at school. Like her friends at Daewon, she was fluent in English, so she wasn't worried about being able to communicate at her new school so much as she was upset about leaving everything she knew.

A long slip of paper was tucked inside the book.

ICN to SFO. Her boarding pass.

This was actually happening.

Ji-Su had always wanted to visit sunny California, but not like this.

Look for 29 Dates *by Melissa de la Cruz!*

Copyright © 2019 by Melissa de la Cruz